NATASHA KARIS

The Breaking Of Dawn

To Luke, Danielle and Ellmarie,
I love you, I love you, I love you.

Contents

Remember...

Check out the back of the book for your exclusive offers from the author.

August

It takes two seconds to figure out I'm being attacked. After he tears my hair from its follicles and yanks with a ferocity that lifts me from the ground. As my back hits the concrete with such force it winds me, I still can't comprehend what is happening. Alert, but reeling, the tug makes my brain shift, and it takes too long to get my bearings and figure out it is intentional. Two seconds is a long time. In two seconds, I could get up, kick out, scream or run. I could fight back. Instead, I do nothing.

He looks down at me. It is only then, once I lay eyes on him, that I know, for sure, he will cause me damage. He doesn't say a word. Instead, he lowers until he hovers over me, his face so close I can taste his rotting, death in the mouth, breath. He doesn't give me a chance to speak. There is no more time to move and not one hope for me to run. I've never felt fear like it; an all-consuming, chest restricting, breath catching, heart pounding terror that I am sure I will pass out from. My fear is justified. He confirms it with a full-on fist punch straight to the face, landing dead centre on my left eyeball, covering the socket and nose, too. Splinters of pain crack open on half my face and my head swerves to the side and then lolls like one of those bobbing figurines on a spring. I see him with my eye that will still open, and already I know I can never forget him. I see the willingness to do anything to get what he is looking for. His fist curls in a ball and hangs in the air as if deciding if another punch is needed. I shake my head. It isn't. I won't put up a fight, I never put up a fight. He hits me anyway, and the world turns off.

Birthday

Nine days before.

Every morning came too soon. The alarm and darkness taunted me. Doing as I always did, I swiped the phone screen as fast as I could and settled back down in the bed, safe in the knowledge the snooze button would go off. Allowed three times, it was only on the third buzz I gave in and opened my eyes.

With a groan, I pulled back the duvet. With no more time to dawdle, still half asleep, I let the monotonous routine slide me along as if on a conveyor belt. Every work morning was identical. The shower first, then moisturise. The unhanging of my uniform and pulling it on. The slurp of tea and the gobbling of some shake or product while trying to make myself look somewhat decent. I pulled back my long blonde hair into a ponytail and checked myself in the mirror, catching my grimace.

It wasn't a normal day. It was my birthday and, even though previous birthdays could only be described as disastrous, I still felt the bubbling of excitement. Every birthday morning, each year, I woke hopeful that it would be different, that one would break the trend and every year so far I'd been let down. My friends had started to call the aftermath *the gloom*. It wasn't imagined or exaggerated, over the years my birthday had gained notoriety. Bad things happened. Like, friends or family forgot. Or I woke up sick, or had accidents, some severe enough I'd ended up in hospital twice. Other times, when I avoided physical danger, the possible or promising boyfriends lost interest, or potential loves of my life broke up with me. Or the not so much loves of my life, the momentary, in between, they'll do for now boyfriends, picked a fight or didn't even show up. Whatever it was, it ended the same way it had for every birthday of my adult life, with me crying and alone and, once *the gloom* came, it stayed for days, weeks even, each passing year adding depth to the others.

It wasn't something I brought on; I didn't look for arguments, as in life, I tried to avoid any hassle. I wasn't worried or upset about getting older either, even though this was a big birthday, I was more a go with the flow girl.

The gloom was like a cloud of bad luck, that gathered and grew in the days and weeks beforehand, gaining in substance and power, building importance and gathering slight dread until it filled and concentrated like a sponge and unleashed its contents on that exact day. Despite the overhang, I was determined this would be the year it changed.

My apartment was right on the Quays in the middle of Cork City, with only a short stroll to work. No matter what went on the night before, the walk always woke me up and shifted my mood. Seeing the river, watching the seagulls, nodding at the many people going about the day helped. The same people became familiar, even friendly. Wasn't that what a friendship was, when you broke it down? Friends were just random people you became used to seeing on a repetitive basis. Take white runner guy I just passed. Always in a suit. Always wearing pristine white runners he must scrub clean every evening. Every morning he walked on the bridge at the same time, with a cup of something in his hand, although that detail often changed. Sometimes the waft was tea or coffee, or in the summer, replaced with a protein shake or smoothie. Every week day we smiled at each other and made a nodding gesture that replaced a hello. He was about the same age, give or take a few years, at a guess thirty-two. We'd never exchanged a word. I didn't even know his name, yet my morning wouldn't be the same if I didn't see him. I missed him if he wasn't there, if he was absent, or if I worked the night shift. We never went further than a smile and a nod, never got flirty even though I would if he did. But it was just one of those things that the moment had passed by. The opportunity was no longer there. Unseizable. We had crossed into untouchable territory one time we kept walking, so White Runner Guy stayed a stranger.

There were other people I felt I knew, too. Take Busy Mum rushing towards me. Leaving so little time to get to work, the woman would have to groom while half walking, half running over the bridge. Either untangling her hair or shuffling in her bag or changing her flats mid walk to heels. Or speaking on the phone where words would float over to me: 'did you give her the medicine?' or 'there's rice cakes in the bag.' Or, 'you said you could do it.' Or, 'fine, I'll collect them.' One time there was a lollipop stuck to the hem of her skirt that I saw quick enough to bend and whip off. The woman had jerked in response, searching for the threat, but rolled her eyes and sighed when I displayed what was in my hand. The woman took the sticky lolly, rooted in that big bag of hers and took out a tissue, then wrapped the offending item and popped it in her bag. 'Thanks,' she mouthed, with only enough time to give a grateful nod, and then she was off again, trying to beat the clock. Up close, the woman was nearer my age than I'd thought, early thirties for sure, but there was a tight tiredness behind the made-up face. I shuddered at the responsibility of looking after a child. I couldn't even look after myself.

Dog Walker Guy was in the distance. Every day, the man and his Labrador would stop at the bridge and the dog would jump at the seagulls and then do his business at the busiest part, right on the apex of the bridge. In fairness, the dog always had a look of embarrassment, looking away if anyone caught his eye, a look that said, 'it's not my fault, I don't have a toilet, don't judge me.' His owner, a lean man in his fifties, carried the same type of expression, always waiting with a plastic bag covered hand and an expression saying: 'don't attack me, I'm ready to clean it up.' He always did scoop it up. If I was a little early, and the Lab, Jessie, wasn't busy doing his business, he would run over and greet me. On a good day, he would give me the paw. Jessie became my talisman. On the days I got to look into those chocolate brown eyes and rub his fur, feeling the softness of him, what happened after just seemed to go better. A few seconds of petting him made me lighter, lifted me on even the most miserable of days. Of course, today, the day it being, Jessie was squatting and didn't want to be disturbed. I carried on.

As I walked across the bridge, the docks' sparkling water caught my eye in the distance. The squalls from hundreds of seagulls pierced my eardrums as they gathered to fight and pick at the bits of bread a man threw over the railing. I screwed up my eyes at him as I ducked to avoid a passing bird; it would be typical if it shat on me.

Despite the daily possibility of hair covered in bird excrement, I loved living in town. The walk to work was handy for uncluttering my head and waking me up. It helped that the apartment was close to restaurants and more important the bars. The noises at night from a city were comforting. On the weekends, there was always someone wanting to crash after a night out or if I came home alone, it was bright outside, anyway. On the weeknights, the tiredness from work ensured I was asleep before my head hit the pillow. The car alarms or roars from drunk people brought their own type of lullaby, which was welcome. I didn't do well with silence.

The phone rang. I diverted it, not wanting to deal with her now. The phone rang again. I cursed my mistake, knowing I should have let the call ring out. By diverting, I let her know I was there. The woman wouldn't give up, she would keep pressing redial.

'Hey Mum,' I said.

'Happy birthday love. *Happy birthday to you. Happy...*'

I interrupted her mid song. 'Mum, can I ring you later because I'm on my way to work? I'm just going in the door.'

'Oh, I just wanted to make sure I got hold of you before you went in.'

Maybe if you rang a little earlier, I would have had time to talk.

'Sorry, I have to go now.'

'Will you call out after?'

'Tonight? I'm going out straight after work.'

There was a pause before Mum spoke. Her way of letting me know she wasn't happy.. 'Oh. OK.'

I sighed loudly, which was my way of letting her know I knew what she was up to. 'What is it Mum?'

'I just wanted to give you your present, that's all. How about I drive into town and meet you later for lunch?'

'No, don't do that.' I softened my voice. 'Sorry Mum, it's just it would be a waste of time. I'm getting my hair done then.'

'Didn't you just get it done?'

I exaggerated another loud intake of breath, playing my part in our oral games. 'As you know, I get it done every four weeks, Mum. I've told you before, blonde hair takes effort. I hate my roots showing.'

'I liked you when you had brown hair.'

'I know.'

And look like you?

'You were still my little girl when you had brown hair.'

I felt a pang of guilt at that, which annoyed me more. Mum made me feel guilty even when I'd done nothing wrong.

'I'm still your girl, Mum, just not so little. Look, how about I drop by the weekend for it?'

'Will you? You've said that the last three weeks and you haven't. And

I know what way you get on your birthday.'

'Are you actually having a go at me?'

There was a sigh on the line. 'No. I just wanted to give you a good day, that's all. I know you haven't had the best of birthdays in the past.'

'I know. Thanks. I promise I'll call the weekend, OK?'

'Great. I'll get a cake and you can stay for dinner. Sure, you could always stay the night.'

'We'll see. I've got to go, I'm at work now.'

'OK love. Have a great birthday.'

'Will do. Bye.'

I stopped outside a dress shop window and checked my watch. Despite what I said, I still had some time.

Don't feel guilty Dawn. You've waited for this moment for weeks. Don't let the phone call spoil it.

There was a dress I'd been starving for the last month to fit into. Today was the day to see if it would fit. Ten minutes which had the possibility of changing which way the day went.

* * *

Behind the counter of Greene's Deli, Kristin waited, giving me a nod as I approached and taking off her apron.

'That's me out of here. Where are we meant to be going again?'

'I booked Clouds but Peter got us a spot at that new restaurant on Oliver Plunkett St.'

'Cool. Text me the details.' She edged past me, then backed around. 'Sorry, long shift, happy birthday Dawn.' She leaned in to hug me but didn't commit, her hands hanging low at her sides so it was only a touch of chest and chin. I wrapped my arms around her and held on.

'You will come?'

Up close, Kristin's skin was grey. 'I said I would, didn't I?'

'Are you all right?'

Kristin took a moment to answer. 'I'm just wrecked, that's all. I've got to go,' she said, loosening herself from my grip and slipping past me.

'Why don't you ask to swap back to days? The night shift is wrecking you,' I called after her.

'It suits me,' Kristin called back before disappearing up the stairs.

Why though?

There were no customers, so I lost myself in the work. I checked the timers on the scones and rolls; the red countdown showed the alarm would sound in about five minutes. I left the counter and approached the salad bar, making note of what needed topping up, shaking my head at the near empty tubs. From the congealed mayonnaise on the coleslaw, it was clear Kristin hadn't emptied them overnight or cleaned them that morning. Typical.

Most mornings on my shift, I had to pick up the slack. The list was getting longer each time, with Kristin doing less and less. Layering the now useless trays and carrying them over to the sink, I searched underneath for the spare empties. Then, going to the fridge, I slopped egg mayonnaise, coleslaw, and potato salad into new stainless-steel containers.

Someone else might say she was doing it on purpose. I didn't know why or what I had done wrong, but somehow I had offended Kristin. Since she moved out of our apartment, there was an awkwardness as we exchanged information from the changeover. No matter how much I went over the events leading up to her moving, I couldn't work out a reason. There had been no angry words, no battles, no arguments, but Kristin made it known I annoyed her. Her voice changed when I was near; she spoke in a clipped tone, or used huffs and eye rolls. I never, ever said anything.

I liked to keep the peace and whatever had annoyed Kristin was my fault anyway, so bringing it up would only mean getting hurt. Or maybe I was overthinking and Kristin's attitude had nothing to do with me; Kristin always went distant when a guy came on the scene. I would figure out the reason at the dinner, keeping the conversation focused on her. I had learnt you couldn't go far wrong if you kept the conversation about the other person.

Spotting Mrs McGee heading towards the deli, I made my way behind the counter, already knowing what the woman would want. There was pleasure in performing minor tasks, comfort from cutting the meat. When I worked the machine, it would give a symmetrical piece of ham. The satisfaction when I pushed the meat across the steel and a thin slice landed in my other hand was almost zen like, giving me a sense of peace. I loved the rhythm of going back and forth, the motion, as the meat moved across the blade. It gave me a little thrill too, the element of danger, knowing I could move it too close to the bone, through bone even, if I wasn't careful. One wrong move and I could just slice the top of my fingers off. They warned us about putting the safety on, but who did? It took too long and if you had a steady hand you didn't need it.

A crowd came out of nowhere and a line formed. Of everything in the job, I loved this the most, when the place was tearing busy and I slipped into a flow. There could be twenty people wanting my attention and yet, time would slow enough that I could acknowledge everyone. If I recognised some people in the queue, I would pre-empt their orders and get them ready at the same time as the one I was working on. It was like I grew extra hands, buttering bread at the same time as ladling soup into a carton. A sixth sense of time management kicked in and I could break down the next move and the move after that. Just like now when I shouted over, 'Your usual, Mrs McGee?'

Cutting four slices of the honey baked ham now, knowing the woman behind Mrs McGee would ask for two as well. In those times, it felt like my feet lifted from the ground, moved with a glide rather than a run. It felt effortless.

'You would think with the much cheaper supermarket chains all over the place, that fresh, sliced meat wouldn't be popular,' I said to Mrs McGee as I handed her the ham.

Mrs McGee sniffed, as if offended. 'I would never buy ham from a packet.'

After I sliced and scooped and packaged and chatted, I wiped down the counter tops. There was solace in the smells. From the floury scent of baking scones and rolls in the early morning. Or the meaty wafts of cooked chickens. The gravy waft from the set dinners would come later. Even though I loved to cook, making the food wasn't my concern, as the kitchen handled that on the top floor. Once ready, they sent them down to be doled out. The deli concentrated on baking and maintenance. And serving.

The worst part, by far, was the heat. With no windows and plenty of ovens, in the summer it could get so hot, my scalp and neck would drip as if someone had turned a tap on. My top would dampen, then saturate, getting heavier as the shift wore on. If I complained enough, Mr Greene would send a fan down, only after I hung onto the counter to stop from fainting, his eagle eye catching the moment I weakened on camera, and he would cave because sending a staff member home cost more than the electricity. I didn't care what changed his mind as long as something did, relishing the glorious waft of cool air as it stuck wet fabric against my hot skin. Never a substitute for air conditioning, that suggestion shot down years before along with the lift idea, with a quick flick of his hand, swatting the ideas away as if they were annoying insects, explaining the building was too old to rewire and it would be easier to knock down and start again before doing any of that nonsense.

The other downside were the burns. Many crisscross scars laced the underside of my arms from the scorching hot trays. Loaded with cooked meats, they would get heavy, and rather than let the meat slip, and potentially have Greene dock the damage from my wage slip, my flesh would counteract the fall. Or, if I was too busy with a queue of people when the beeps went from the oven, rather than let them overcook, in the rush to take them out, it was easy to miscalculate the weight of what was being lifted or the space left to lay the tray down. Whichever way, it was my forearms that suffered.

I checked the chickens and clicked my tongue when I saw the number left on the timers. The pale meat turned on the rotisserie through the glass. The alarm would tell me once done, but Kristin should have started them the hour before. Was it on purpose? She knew I would hear about it later when the mid-morning lot wanted them. I checked the freezer, counted the trays of scones and rolls that needed baking. Scanned the ovens to see what was in and what I needed to go in.

Ten years ago, the place used to be packed. Queues would run from the deli to the length of the store, even to the outside. The builders loved the cheap, large portions. These days, there wasn't much available space for new buildings in that part of the city, yet there was still a steady flow of people from the shops and offices, enough to keep you busy. Also, as the customers lessened, the staff did too. Before, there would have been at least three deli assistants, whereas now, on my own, there was always plenty to do.

The intercom rang. 'Dawn, Sheila here. Greene wants to see you. Course, he chose the time that I needed to stay on the sauce. Give me five minutes and I'll come down.'

'Good or bad form?'

'He's his usual pleasant self.'

'Great.'

I took off my gloves and tidied my hair. It was the call I had been waiting on for days, yet now that it was here, I felt nauseous.

Five minutes as promised, Sheila appeared and, as she put on gloves, winked at me. 'Go on, get out of here. Good luck.'

On the way, I ducked into the bathroom and tried to breathe. Beads of sweat formed on my lip. I wet some tissue and dabbed under my arms. I wouldn't have long; Greene didn't like to be kept waiting. This situation was my worst nightmare. Interviews or assessments or one on ones or being put on the spot or disagreements or expressing my opinion, all caused the same reaction.

Only the week before, I had sat in the same office and interviewed with Greene for a management position. It had taken its toll. After practising every night for two months, I got through it. Just. The full timers pushed me to apply, insisting that the interview would only be a formality since I'd proved ten times over how hard I worked; they walked me through Greene's obligatory questions with such diligence I could have answered them in my sleep. The promise of extra money and their conviction persuaded me, but I wasn't so sure about the outcome after I went blank several times in the interview.

I knocked on the door.

'Come in,' he called.

A reflective glass wall in Greene's office faced the women's clothing so he could overlook everything going on. His desk was a few inches from being the length of the room, with ten big screens surrounding him that played live footage of the fun on each floor. Mr Greene liked to keep an eye on his staff.

Greene's store was over one hundred years old. His father had opened the building before he was born and the picture of Mr Greene as a child outside the front doors with the store's sign above him covered the entire wall behind and I would bet if there was a fire, Mr Greene would wrench it from the walls. The date of the picture suggested he must be in his late seventies, but he kept himself lean and spoke of his love of golf and if I met him for the first time, would guess he was in his early sixties. His work ethic was legendary, often not going home and spending all night at his desk if something important loomed. He was old school, expecting people to work hard for little money. He was firm, but rewarded his hard workers. Being in his presence was terrifying.

'Sit down Dawn please.'

I did. He gave me a moment to settle by closing the ledgers he wrote in. The side wall was full of those ledgers, with who knows what inside. 'So, I've made a decision about the floor manager role.'

'Oh, you have? That's great.' I smiled, trying to stay calm. Greene didn't look at me, instead he made circles on the expensive desk with his finger. My smile dropped.

'As you know, there were many applicants that went for the position, so it was a tough decision, but I thought it right to tell you in person.' He stopped circling and clasped those fingers in front of him. 'You were unsuccessful this time. The position went to Jill.'

The shock took words and thoughts and time. A blankness shrouded me and my mouth parched. I couldn't speak. My thoughts processed his words in slow motion: *You were unsuccessful. The position went to Jill.* The last sentence ran over and over for long enough to help me find something to say.

On my side of the table was a glass of water. I reddened. Greene had noticed how dry my throat became at the last interview, and expected I'd need it again. My stomach churned for how he thought he knew me, how by picking it up I was acknowledging he was right, but I took it anyway to wash over my desert tongue. It took a while to gulp, to force it down. Rehydrated, I spoke. The words came out soft, dejected, accepting even, and I hated that about myself even more. 'You gave the job to Jill?'

'Yes.'

'That Jill?' I pointed to the girl stood by the aisle in front of the window, texting on her phone. As if she was hiding and had forgotten that the boss could see her. A customer tried to get her attention, leaning over the counter to speak, but Jill turned her back on the woman. I said nothing. I didn't need to say anything. Instead, I kept my finger pointed as we both watched Jill finish the text and put the phone down her top, tucking it into her bra. 'That Jill?' I asked again.

Greene grimaced. 'Look, I understand you're disappointed, but you can always try again next time.'

My eyes welled. 'Did I do something wrong?'

He hesitated before he answered, clasped his hands. 'No.'

There was so much I should say but in that moment I couldn't think of one thing that mattered, that would matter to him. My stomach churned and my body squirmed, looking for an exit, wanting to get as far away as possible and forget the conversation even happened. A braver person would raise their voice, beat their fists on the table, tell him a few home truths.

Instead, despite the water, my throat constricted, and I went deep inside, to the place that felt safe. I bowed my head and begged my eyes not to let out tears yet.

'Jill is more suited to the role. The incentive will make her focus. What I need from you is to stay at the deli for the moment. Look, I can see you're disappointed.' He unclasped his hands and tapped his fingers against the skin of his chin, sizing up whether to speak.

'I'll be honest with you, so you can improve on what doesn't work.' His hands left his chin, committed to what he had to say. I braced myself.

'You're an exceptional employee Dawn, but you don't have any authority for a management role. You're a grafter, a great worker, but you can't correct people. I've watched you. When you need to direct staff, you crumble. If there is even a sniff of confrontation, you freeze. Can you imagine trying to get Jill to do anything?'

So Jill gets promoted?

On any other occasion, I would say sorry, or I would shrink back and say nothing, but whether it was because of the day it was, or because it was Jill or just the worst had happened, for once, I spoke.

'Mr Greene, do you know how long I've worked here?'

He looked to the ceiling, doing the math.

'Twelve years. All my adult life. At seventeen, I took a summer job here, and I never left. You convinced me to stay on instead of going to college, promising you would train me in all areas.'

He screwed his eyes, and when he spoke, he spoke slowly. 'Which I did.'

'But I thought the next step was promotion.'

Two bright red spots appeared on either side of Greene's cheeks. This was a warning sign. He enunciated every word, each one coming out sharp from his tongue, sharp enough to cut. 'I thought once I gave you a chance, you would step up. You had such potential Dawn, but no matter how many times I offer you a hand, no matter how I push, you fail. If I gave you the position, it would be a disaster. I've told you where your shortfall is. It's up to you to improve in those areas.' Greene's cheeks blazed crimson and he let a loud puff of breath. 'You had no work experience when I took you on, you didn't have a clue what a job implied.' He tapped on the desk. 'And be honest with yourself, you didn't sacrifice college, you didn't want to go. If you had, no job or money could have kept you here. I trained you from scratch. I invested money and time into your advancement so you could get employment anywhere in the world. You choose to stay. I kept you employed throughout the quiet times, through the cutbacks and layoffs and recessions, when I had to leave other good workers go. I kept you from the dole, when all the other shops closed down, when other workers, people more experienced than you, struggled to find jobs. But if you don't want to continue with this company, or if you think I owe you a favour, you are mistaken, my girl. You can leave right now.' The last few words came out in a growl. His jowls shook in indignation and he looked like steam could escape from his ears. I recoiled from his stare. Greene lowered his voice. 'I would give you a good reference, of course. You wouldn't have to worry there.'

The-words-wouldn't-come.

I searched for an answer, but all memory and thought faded to a blank wall. Not that I held back, there was only emptiness to grab onto. There were no answers, no solutions or flashes of inspiration. All I could feel was a shrivelling of ideas and brain and breath. Even if anything had risen from the void, words weren't possible, the connection broken from voice to brain, constricted the same way as if someone grabbed me and squeezed my larynx. The only thing left was confusion. This meeting was meant to end in a different way, and I was reeling at how the conversation had turned.

'Is that what you want, Dawn? I can have Sheila cover the rest of your shift if you want to leave today?'

He waited. I took another sip of water, letting the liquid coat my tongue and soften my palette, then cleared my throat with a cough, to kick my voice into shape. Greene stared at me. His question required an answer.

I shook my head. 'I don't want to leave.'

Mr Greene looked away at the shop floor, but I saw the upturn of his mouth. He loved to win.

'Good. Get back to work. Before you go back, can you sort out the incident on the drapery floor?'

Through the darkened glass, the customer's face appeared purple. She was gesticulating at a disinterested Jill. This was my time to back myself up, to refuse, to say, let your new manager do it. All I wanted to do was curl up in a ball and go to sleep or go home and climb under my duvet. What I did was nod and shuffle to the door.

'Dawn wait,' he called, his expression back to amiable now that he had won the conversation. 'How about we revisit it the next time a position comes up? Work on your assertiveness and you would be a done deal.'

I nodded again. *I waited two years for this position.*

Out on the floor, the customer's voice screeched. 'Never in my life have I been spoken to with such rudeness. I want to speak to the manager.'

'You're speaking to her,' Jill said with a grin. I groaned; this was all the girl needed; incompetency combined with a power trip.

'Can I help?'

The woman swung around and I knew I was going to get the woman's exasperation full force. And I would take it. I would nod and placate and wait for the woman to calm and then offer a solution. In those situations, I always found the words. In those times, I could separate my problems from the problem presented in front of me. When it wasn't a confrontation or an accusation regarding me, regarding Dawn Moloney, I could break down the layers of the problem and find the way out because that's what I always did; I took everything people threw and adapted to it. I pushed it down and moved on.

Party Time

Before going to the deli, I slipped back into the bathroom. Cubicles were often my saviour, a chance to gather my thoughts and resettle my nerves. There wouldn't be long under Mr Greene's now gunning for me, watchful eyes. Not enough time for tears, I took a few breaths, ran cold water on the back of my wrists and wiped at my dry eyes.

Back at the deli counter, I shook my head at Sheila and hoped she wouldn't push for more. Sheila wasn't one to mince her words. Sensing I couldn't handle a quizzing, she patted me on the back. 'Bastard,' she whispered as she walked away. This time, I had to agree.

The shift took forever to end. I did the expected; I nodded at the passer-by's, plastered on the smile, sliced the meats, served the customers, answered the mundane questions, took out and bagged the chickens, restocked the rolls and scones and breads and topped up the salads but inside, I was drained. As I wiped down the counter and replayed what I should have said.

I thought you were someone else. That you were firm but fair. I thought you were clever, but you just showed me who you are. You make bad choices and see me as only a cog in the wheel. I thought if you saw my potential, saw how hard I worked, you would promote me. You would see my worth, but you don't. What about all the times I stayed on when you had no one else to cover the shift? When Jill didn't show up. For the last three months,

I have been employee of the month. When my shift is over, I stay longer than everyone else. I've never taken a sick day. What about when I was the only volunteer to empty the basement for you when you needed it done with one day's notice? Do you remember how I lifted old tills and tables on my own to clear the room and got it done in time? Even though I couldn't walk the next day. I thought if I proved my loyalty, if I proved how hard I worked, you would reward me with the promotion but it backfired. Instead of seeing my potential and rising me up the ranks, you want to keep me grafting down below. The useless Jill gets more thanks.

And then I should have told him to stick his job and storm out.

Course the words came when they didn't matter. Course they fluttered into my consciousness when there was no one around to hear. Who was I kidding? I would never say those words or act that way. I wasn't that kind of person. What I was, was gutless.

What I wanted to say was he had just broken me. Or explain how he let me down. How if I was honest, the job distracted me from what I should do, but who was I to tell him how to run his company? Maybe I wasn't good enough? Maybe he could see that? He had a point about hiring Jill; I couldn't reprimand anyone. I couldn't even tell people what I was feeling, let alone instruct anyone about what they were doing wrong. Jobs *were* scarce these days.

I closed my eyes and went to my happy place, concocting a recipe I would make tomorrow. Only sugar would do in this scenario. I played out the motions as if I was at home in my kitchen. I would melt some milk chocolate in a Bain Marie and then with a brush, dip and layer it inside a cupcake holder and once even on all sides, with no gaps or holes, I'd pop the tray in the fridge. Once set, it would look like a little cup. Then I would slice strawberries in even layers and whisk cream until it formed peaks. Scooping cream into the chocolate cup, I would splay out the slices of strawberry and melt some more chocolate, drizzling it over the top. And then, I would devour one in two bites and life would be better again.

After the shift ended, I busied myself with my phone so I wouldn't have to answer any questions from the ladies in the canteen. I scrolled through the birthday notifications, twenty already, better than last year. Most were from aunties and distant cousins and an old school friend living in Australia, who I hadn't spoken to since school. It was the sole reason I stuck with social media, the birthday reminders better than any organiser. Scrolling made me feel like my life wasn't quite up to scratch. Without pictures of me in a bikini the size of dental floss wrapped around the perfect bum on the beach or blue white veneers or a plump lipped smile, without a partner in the frame showing the world how adored I was, even though those images seemed false and far from reality, they still left me with proof my life was a failure. It didn't matter what I posted; I would never measure up to that perfection. I always left my feed feeling less. Feeling like I wanted a hug.

It was the messages from my every day friends that made me smile. Peter's post was a picture of the two of us drinking from cock straws at a hen party. Ciaran had been the first to post, his words short and to the point. *Happy birthday, you deserve a good one.* Ber's GIF of a dancing squirrel doing shots was typical. Kirstin didn't post a separate one, adding to Ciaran's instead. *Happy birthday!*

I put the phone away. It didn't matter about the job, or the things Greene said, this time *the gloom* wasn't coming. This year was going to be different.

On the way home, I stopped at the supermarket and picked up a bottle of wine. On the bridge, the wind whipped at me. I tightened my jacket and hurried along.

Once in the door, I stripped off, leaving my chicken fat clothes where they fell and went straight to the shower, wanting to douse the conversation with Greene away. The warm water helped. It would be easy to close the curtains and climb into the bed and not move, the day already surpassing the expectation. Instead, I was determined to salvage what was left, and out of the shower, took a long time to style my hair. After what happened, I couldn't have made small talk with Antoinette, my hairdresser.

To change my mood, I turned on some upbeat music and opened the bottle of wine, and sipped at it while getting ready. *The gloom* hung around, brooding, waiting for the nod to coil. This time, I wouldn't allow it to ruin the night.

Applying my makeup was difficult; it was hard to meet the mirror when I hadn't stood up for myself. Why hadn't I fought my case? Applying eye shadow, I couldn't avoid my failure.

The image in the mirror wasn't the same as what I viewed earlier in the dressing room. Had they used thinning mirrors? I had drooled over the dress for weeks, eyeing it on the mannequin as I rushed past every morning. In the shop, the shimmering dress pulled me towards it. It was silver, but had an iridescent coating that meant it changed colour whenever it moved. I grabbed it from the rail and watched as the colour changed from pink to purple to turquoise. It was a challenge to even fit into the teeny changing room, but then the real struggle of trying to get the dress on, started. The fabric moulded and stuck to my skin around my breasts, not wanting to move further, the straps leaving red lines on my arms. I tried rolling the material and that did the trick, the dress squeezed my flesh like sausage casing that goes over the meat. Sweat gathered in my pits and beaded on my forehead.

In the shop my breasts appeared more rounded and pushed together and the sucked in fabric showed off my cinched in waist, giving the impression of the perfect hour glass. I had dismissed how uncomfortable it was, or that I'd never worn a dress that tight before, never even tried one on because of how unforgiving they were, with nowhere to hide your flaws. This year I'd promised I would try new things. It was the first day of my thirties, after all.

Now, the dress didn't sit right; gathering at the tummy. The straight lines going across my waist slightly curved, the dip highlighting my not so flat stomach. I would have to wear slimming underwear. It meant eating before the restaurant was out; the dress wouldn't allow it.

What I needed was a mood change. I messaged the group chat.

Anyone want to meet earlier?

Sorry still at work, can't wait for later. (Ciaran)

Got to collect my cousin at the airport, remember? (Peter)

Running late, catch ye later. (Ber)

There was nothing from Kristin.

With three hours to spare, *the gloom* was coming. I switched to water, hoping to fill my empty stomach. There was only one way I could reverse the way the night was heading. Tying an apron around me, I searched my fridge and cupboards and, spotting the usual staples, I set to work. First, I turned on the oven and set about making shortbread, creaming the butter and caster sugar until it was smooth, then mixing in the flour until it was a crumbly dough. Lining a tin with baking paper, I pressed the soon to be shortbread in and after twenty minutes, when the top had turned pale gold, I took the tin out to cool. Lobbing butter, caster sugar, golden syrup and the contents of a tin of condensed milk into a saucepan, I stirred as the mixture melted. This point was critical. I could not leave the pan until the sugar completely dissolved, even one eye off for a second could be the moment it caught and, learned from experience, bits of burnt sugar in caramel, were never pleasant. Once dissolved, I turned the heat and let it boil, stirring and soothing, being careful not to splatter as the sauce would stick to my skin and scald. The smells were torturous. The sweet scent of melted butter and sugar and baked biscuit wafted, making my stomach gurgle. I was starving; I contemplated chewing and spitting it out, just for the taste, but knew I wouldn't have the willpower not to swallow. When the caramel turned to darker and thickened, it was time. Caramel was notoriously difficult. Left alone, it would burn, left too long, it would turn rock hard once set. Pouring the caramel on the shortbread, I slid the tin in the fridge. With an hour needed to set, I rested my knuckles on the counter and inhaled the sugary perfume and smiled, allowing the bad turn in the day to leave me, then tidied up. Once the hour was up, I melted white and dark chocolate and swirled them on top, creating patterns. Allowing them time to harden, I topped up my makeup and fixed my hair before taking out my creation for the last time. Leaving enough for my visit with my parents, I cut the leftovers into squares and grabbing some tissue paper, wrapped the rest, securing them at the top with a ribbon. The thought of giving them away made me smile. I hated to pass the couple on the bridge; them hunkered close together, with their sleeping bags around them and me all dressed up, knowing they had nowhere to go. A tin of shortbread wouldn't change their life, but I hoped it might make their night a little brighter.

The doors of the restaurant opened in to a huge circular room with the bar running along the entire back wall. Music filled my ears and heat warmed my bones.

The place was bustling, stylish, and judging by the packed tables, the new place to be. My heels squeaked as I crossed a black marble floor that sparkled with flecks of gold and contrasted with the dark grey bar and walls. Every edge was rimmed with gold: table legs, chairs, banisters and bar taps.

I nodded to a girl in a black uniform. 'Hi, there's a table booked for Moloney.'

The uninterested girl checked a gold tablet. 'No Moloney,' she said and went to walk on.

'What about Devine?' I asked. *Of course, Peter would use his name.*

The girl sighed and tapped the tablet again.

'Up the stairs and to your right,' she said, giving me a quick smile and moving on.

The staircase was unmissable. Black marble steps, each with a strip of gold on its outer rim, paved my way to the restaurant. Up there, the grey velvet chairs were the exact match to the walls. Droplets of gold hung down from the ceiling with circles of light on their bottoms. The cutlery, of course, was gold. It was plush, modern and pure Peter.

Ciaran and Kristin sat at our table, and I broke into a spontaneous grin. Ciaran made anything all right and, being just the two of them, I might have time to talk to Kristin. Ciaran stood on seeing me, his dark hair flopping over those dark eyes, his smile all I ever needed to settle my nerves. 'Here's the birthday girl.'

He raised his glass and poured me a drink from a bottle of white wine. Kristin stayed sitting, but as Ciaran sat, she placed a hand on his thigh and snuggled closer. It was a blink and miss it gesture, subtle enough I could pretend not to notice. Ciaran flustered and brushed her hand away. Kristin drained her glass and poured another.

I looked away, feeling intrusive. Instead, I sat next to Ciaran and picked up the menu and pretended to examine it. I needed a second in case they confirmed what was going on. Everything slowed down.

They were together.

I felt nauseous.

'Where's the lads?' I asked. *What the hell is going on?*

'Peter's cousin arrived from Italy late. He said they'll be another ten minutes. And sure, you know Ber, she'll turn up and take over,' Ciaran said.

'True,' I said, this time reading the menu. It reflected the venue. Expensive. Extravagant. It would be all style over substance and small portions that would leave you starving and having to get a chipper after.

Peter rushed in holding the hand of a long-haired Italian that looked like she just came chiselled from a statue from the Renaissance. She was just exquisite. I took a slug of wine. Peter ran over and bear hugged me.

'Well, get up and let me look.'

I stood and curtsied. Peter bowed back, then took my hand and swivelled me round as he whistled, 'looking fine girl. You lost some of those Christmas two years ago pounds.'

I blushed. For Peter, that was a compliment. 'This is Vittoria. Be nice, lads.'

We all said hi. Vittoria nodded hello. When you were that beautiful, you didn't need words.

I sat, pulling at my dress.

'You'll love the menu, Petey boy. All flash and they'll take your cash,' Kristin said.

'Meow. I see we have Kristin in bitch mode tonight. I'm a meat and two veg kind of guy I'll have you know.'

'Yeah, you let us know plenty of times,' Ciaran said. Kristin placed a hand on his. 'Stop,' she whispered.

I stared at my menu again and tried to reason out what I was feeling. It wasn't just a new thing if she was touching him like that. How had I missed it? When had they progressed to hands on each other in public? Kristin knew me from work. Ciaran grew up with me and was my longest friend. Maybe that was all it was, a left out feeling because they were my friends, only knowing each other through me. It felt like an indiscretion, an infidelity even though Ciaran and I had never been a couple, I'd always thought of him as mine. My friend rather than theirs.

I ran my finger along a roll of fat that had popped out under the waist of my control underwear while cursing not going with the full-on body holding in. But the bead of sweat trickling down my neck reminded me why; I had guessed right that the restaurant would be hot and I would end up having to wrestle my underwear off every time I needed the bathroom. Just the thought of that was exhausting.

'I suggest with these prices we go straight for the mains,' Ciaran said, shaking his head.

'That's fine with me. With this dress, I wouldn't fit much food in,' I said.

'Leaves more room for drink,' Peter said, winking.

Ciaran was right, the starters were the price of a full meal elsewhere and I just knew the plate would be full of space. My stomach rumbled in protest.

The server appeared at the other side of the table taking orders. I blocked out the noise as the wine and the music and the bombshell of the new coupling made it hard to concentrate. Rejecting anything with potatoes, chips, pasta and bread because my stomach would bloat and dismissing everything over forty euros, as I wouldn't have enough for the club and drink after, left little else. Bass with fennel or chicken salad. The salad was cheaper.

'I'll go the chicken salad please.'

The waiter took away my menu with an efficient swoop.

'Any news?' Peter asked.

'Not really,' I said.

'Christ, someone give her a drink. It's the only way we get her talking,' Peter said.

Ciaran topped up my glass.

'So how old are you today, forty?' Kristin sniggered.

'Hilarious. You know how old I am.'

'We do. The Big 3-0. Time to cop on now, Dawnie. No more getting pissed. Time to bag yourself a man and start pushing out babies,' Peter said.

'Er, hello? You turned thirty last year and you're still partying.'

'True,' he wagged his finger at me, 'but I'm a man. So we don't age like ye women. And I don't have any ticking time bomb telling me to get knocked up.'

'Peter, believe me, I don't either.'

'Well, I'll drink to that.'

We both raised a glass and tipped it back. Kristin and Ciaran were whispering, so didn't notice. Vittoria flicked her hair. My stomach churned with hunger; it was so empty that when I drank, I felt the alcohol move down until it hit my stomach lining.

'Come on, something's at you. What's up? Don't tell me your stupid theory of *the gloom* has got you already?'

'Bad work day. Jill got the promotion.'

Kristin shrugged. 'Bummer.'

She *was* annoyed. Kristin knew how much I wanted the promotion and seeing as she was the only one who worked there, I thought she would understand. When she first started working in Greene's, she needed a place, and after spending enough time in the apartment alone to consider living with another person, I suggested she move in. Kristin became part of my life, enfolding and integrating between my friends until they became her friends also, but our home life together hadn't been ideal. She was untidy, like unhygienic untidy, leaving plates around until they had mould and new planets sprouting from them. She discarded her clothes wherever and whenever she got the notion and never picked up any, stepping over them as if they were objects meant to stay on the floor. It wasn't that she ignored normal household tasks, but rather she didn't see them, which left it to me to do everything. Another thing she often forgot about was paying her share of the rent. I never said it to her, reasoning I would have to tidy up the apartment or pay the full rent anyway if she wasn't there. For two years, Kristin's good qualities combated her inadequacies. When she went food shopping, she always brought home supplies for two of us and never forgot my favourite chocolate or bottle of wine. She showed me the right way to blend eye shadow and apply makeup, invaluable to a girl with no sisters and a mother who wouldn't dream of wearing mascara. Most of all, Kristin didn't challenge me when I quietened, waiting until I was ready to talk, listening when the words processed, without making me feel stupid.

At first, I felt closer to her than any other girlfriend I'd ever had. And then Kristin cooled, spending more and more time in her room. Or she would slip out of the house without saying where she was going. Those clipped tones appeared and I could feel I was losing her, losing the friendship, but every time I worked up the courage to approach the subject, I would go blank or talk about something stupid, like a show on the TV instead.

Three months ago, Kristin announced she was moving out, and within a week, she was gone. I didn't even have time to find out where. It was only then, once she left, after I scrubbed each room from top to bottom, after I walked through my sparkling clean apartment, as I placed my bits and pieces in the places I wanted, that I realised I was relieved for no longer having to bite my tongue or tiptoe around Kristin's erratic moods.

Straight after moving, Kristin volunteered for the night shifts, so apart from the daily handover, we hadn't seen each other since. Was Ciaran the reason? Had she distanced herself because she was sneaking around with him? Would they lie to me like that?

'That's lousy. Sorry,' Ciaran said. I nodded, but couldn't look at him. Even though I knew I was being unreasonable, I felt betrayed.

There was a commotion on the stairs. I didn't need to turn. It was Ber; it was always Ber. The girl was loud and messy and caused trouble wherever she went, but I loved her to bits.

'Just you wait, I'll give you the night of your life,' Ber shouted at a man, not caring that the whole fancy restaurant had stopped to listen. Been forced to stop, more like.

Ber approached the table. 'That's my night sorted, anyway.' She cackled. 'Happy birthday, bitch.' She grabbed me and nuzzled my neck, nearly sending me off the chair. 'Come here you, you're one of my favourite people ever!' She slapped the table so hard it wobbled and I steadied my drink just in time. The others had already lifted theirs off the table.

'What's wrong with ya?' she shouted, even though she was right next to me.

'Nothing,' I said.

Ciaran leaned towards Ber, 'Don't you know by now Dawn always gets sad on her birthday?'

'I do not,' I said.

'She does. Every year her face looks like a slapped arse,' Kristin said.

Ber shoved herself down on the empty seat next to me. 'Come on. Tell me the sca.'

'What is scaah?' Vittoria said in an accent made of honey.

'Scandal, darling,' Peter said.

Once explained, they all looked at me for an answer.

'There's nothing to tell. Things just happen. I have a history of things going wrong on this day.'

'Right, yeah, you have no involvement in it. You invite it! You look for it,' Kristin snorted. She screwed her eyes at Ciaran's warning and poured another drink from a fresh bottle of wine.

All eyes stayed on me. I took a sip of wine. Drink always made it easier to talk. 'OK. Here's what I've figured out. If I have any involvement in *the gloom*, it would be that the date reminds me I'm not at the stage I thought I'd be at.' The look of confusion on their faces told me they wanted more of an explanation. 'That another year has passed me by yet I'm still living with the same crap going on, that nothing has changed. It's like what happened today at work. I'll be fine. Maybe it will be the push I need to look for a better job. I'm just tired of the graft and slog. For working hard for someone that doesn't appreciate me. Aren't ye tired?'

'You're thirty, not sixty,' Kristin said, rolling her eyes.

Definitely annoyed.

'I suppose my birthday reminds me I haven't done the things I thought I would have done by now.'

'Like what?' Ciaran asked. I smiled at his genuine interest.

'I don't know.'

'Well, that's helpful,' Kristin said, sniggering.

Ber slapped her thigh hard. 'I know what we can do to cheer her up. Let's go around the room and tell Dawn why we love her.'

'Oh, good game,' Peter said, rubbing his hands together.

Ber shoved him too hard. One eye was half closed, which was a sign she was at least five drinks in. 'Whoa, hold your horses there, Petey. I thought of it, so I'll start.' She grabbed my arm to get my full attention. The grab would leave a bruise. 'I love you because no matter what state I get in to, you don't get mad and shout at me like this lot. And you always let me crash at yours or get me home safe.' She squeezed my arm harder. 'I mean it, girl. Thanks for looking after me.'

I nodded. 'That's the best compliment you could give me, Ber. Thanks.'

'I'll go next,' Peter said, raising his arm. 'As a man not one bit interested in you, I can say hand on heart, I would marry you if you promised to cook for me every night. Yum. You're wasted in that deli. Imagine they have someone like you baking for them and they don't even use your recipes. Those toffee muffins are to die for. Have ye tasted them? The one with the gooey middle?'

Everyone made agreeable noises or said yes. 'And we have a laugh,' Peter said, flicking his wrist, almost as an afterthought.

I smiled.

'I love that you introduced me to Ciaran,' Kristin said, kissing him on the cheek.

Everyone's jaw dropped. It wasn't just me that didn't know then.

Peter's eyes watered with the promise of a bit of excitement. 'What's going on here, then? Are ye at it?' Ciaran blushed. Kristin beamed. 'Ye are, ye dirty bastards. How do you feel about this Dawn?' Peter asked, his eyes wide, relishing the drama.

I looked around at the décor, ignoring the question. Why had they chosen this night to go public?

Instead, I changed the subject. 'This place is great, Peter. Thanks for choosing it.'

'Ciaran, your turn,' Ber roared.

Ciaran glanced at Kristin then dipped his head, thinking. I couldn't help it, I leaned in, desperate to know what he would say.

'I love how genuine you are. I love that we grew up in the same place.' He stopped when Kristin pulled away from him. 'All that history together, I mean,' Ciaran said.

Vittoria shrugged when it was her turn, eyed me up and down, and said after quite some time deliberating, 'I like your dress.'

'Thank you,' I said. There was silence. They had all turned in my direction, waiting for me to say something. I realised they wanted me to return the compliments.

'Thank you all for being here. I know how hard it is for ye to go out on a Friday night.' Ber slapped her thigh and cackled as if it was the funniest thing ever. I started with her. 'Ber, you just crack me up and there's never a dull moment with you. I could write a book on all the things you get up to,'

'Ah, but if you told anyone, I'd have to kill you,' she roared and slapped the table, oblivious to the disapproving glances from the couple at the next table.

'Peter, you keep me looking fab and entertained. I swear if you ever quit your job, I'm disowning you.'

'You were using me,' Peter whispered in mock disgrace. 'For that,

I'll forgive that thing you're wearing.'

I hesitated. *Was that a dig?*

'Kristin, there's been so many times you were there for me in the apartment and at work.'

'I know. I'm never clearing out your turn on the chicken fat again,' she said, grinning, with no animosity this time.

And then it was Ciaran's turn.

'Ciaran, what can I say? You are my oldest friend. You are the only one who knows what growing up in Knockfarraig and Crookstown was like.'

'Blow in,' Peter said, grinning.

I ignored the dig and carried on speaking; the wine loosening my lips. 'If it wasn't for you, I don't think I would have been brave enough to leave. I'd still be there on the beach, wondering when my life would start. You...'

'Jesus, enough with the love fest already. We get it, ye grew up together,' Kristin said, running her finger along her lip.

'Ber, you ordering food? We're just waiting on ours,' Ciaran asked, changing the subject.

'Nah boy. I'm on the liquid diet,' she said, winking at him and taking a sip of a bright red concoction.

'I have more to say.'

The table looked at me agape; everyone stopped what they were doing because I never spoke out of turn. 'I appreciate you all for coming out tonight. You could have gone to a million other places, so I'm very glad that you spent it with me. Thank you all for being my friend. Cheers.'

They raised their glasses and cheered.

As the table interrupted in chatter, I pretended to check my phone messages. I couldn't pinpoint why their comments and their good intentions had the opposite effect. They had said sweet things, yet my overthinking was turning it sour.

The food arrived.

The salad consisted of spiralised carrot, about four nuts and a fancy blotted sauce, several sheaths of lettuce and a shaving of chicken on the top. Just as I predicted, there was plenty of white space. I eyed the other dishes and salivated. 'Did I miss the memo on what to order?'

'Were you not listening to me? I said the steak was to die for,' Peter said.

The steak on everyone's plates was a huge lob of meat. It glistened on a bed of vegetables and I could taste the fat from there. It hadn't even been on my radar, the price tag over forty euros banished it. I forked a piece of salad and chewed a leaf of bitter rocket.

'So, we've got some news,' Kristin said.

Ciaran spoke in a low voice. 'We said we wouldn't do it tonight, remember?'

She slipped a hand in his. 'Why not? Sure, why wouldn't everyone be happy for us?' Kristin looked at me.

Ciaran went bright red. 'I'm sorry we didn't want to take away from your day. It's just been the first time we've all been around each other since we got together.'

Everyone was looking at me. I plastered on my best smile. 'I can't believe my two best friends are together. Congratulations guys, I'm delighted for you both.'

'Well, there's more. We're moving in together,' Kristin said, clapping her hands together with glee, then pulled Ciaran towards her for a kiss.

The table erupted with congratulations. I smiled as broad as I could manage, but the sadness was undeniable now. Why did that news make me feel broken inside? Maybe it was because, until that point, we had done everything at the same time. Same school. Same friends. We sat our exams together. Studied together. Went to the same Debs. Stood in the same line at our graduation ceremony at Knockfarraig school. Left Knockfarraig and Crookstown at the same time. Found and blended new friends.

The thing I had tried to bury for years couldn't be unsaid or un-thought any longer. Ciaran getting with a friend of both of ours meant a line was being drawn, with no ability for reversal. And then I understood why I was upset. Their relationship ended the possibility of us. From now on, it could only be them.

'Are you not happy for us?' Kristin asked, then lobbed a piece of steak into her mouth and chewed with slow, pronounced bites.

Lifting the fresh bottle of wine from the table, I poured a glass, ignoring the little spill. 'It's a lot to get my head round. This is a new thing?'

'Er, they've been with each other for months. Everyone knows that,' Ber said, missing her mouth so a dribble of red liquid ran down her chin.

I tried to work it out. 'I mean, I haven't seen you at the same time for ages. Every night out, one of you were missing. And Kristin, you've worked a different shift from me since you moved out.'

'Now she knows why,' Peter said in a singsong voice directed at his cousin, who nodded as if it was the most obvious thing in the world.

'You're jealous,' Kristin said, turning to Ciaran. 'See, I told you she'd be like this.'

I kept my eyes on my lap, and bit down on my lip.

I will not cry.

'Here we go. You are jealous. You're annoyed Ciaran won't follow you around anymore.'

Ciaran never followed me around.

'Everyone knows he loved you and you just ignored him. You played with him.'

Ciaran leaned into Kristin and spoke in her ear. 'No, I won't. She needs to know she can't play games with you.'

All the others stared at me, except Ber, who was licking the edges of her empty glass.

'I didn't,' I said. 'I would never. Ciaran never liked me in that way. We've always been just friends.'

Ciaran's head lifted and the way he did it, the way he hesitated, in the second it took for him to work up the courage, I saw the truth. It was in the way he looked right into me, in the way it made me feel when he did. That one look confirmed Kristin's insinuation. Ciaran had loved me.

In that noisy restaurant, all noise silenced, all alcohol evaporated, and I felt my heart break. Ciaran. My Ciaran. The Ciaran, I thought, that only ever saw me as a friend. The Ciaran I believed I had no chance with. All I wanted to do was cry. For lost opportunities. For realising my time had run out. For my foolishness and stupidity. Because hadn't I known it all along? Hadn't I, deep down, always believed we would end up together? That our lives linked and when our messing was out of the way, when we were both ready, we would join.

Kristin pointed at me. 'See! I told ye. She's always had a thing for him. I told you she was using you Ciaran. You think she's all sweet, but she's a bitch.'

'I'm a bitch?' I asked.

Ber put her hand up in the air to stop the conversation. 'This is boring me now.' She hiccuped. 'Hey, cutie,' she waved her empty glass at a man taking an order at the other table. 'I'm gasping. Top me up?'

He nodded, embarrassed, then carried on with his order.

'You don't want me to die of thirst now. Help a girl out. Pornstar for me. Anyone want something?'

'Yeah, you. You're a bitch.' Kristin spat the words out. 'All that time we lived with each other, you would laugh behind his back. You just strung him along.'

'That's not true.'

'See? I knew she'd call me a liar. You told me about how you kissed one time and it almost made you gag, that it was like incest.'

Ciaran looked like someone had punched him.

She's twisting my words. She's lying.

'We all know what you're like with guys.'

'What am I like?'

Peter whispered under his breath. 'Awkward.'

The only person I wanted to speak to was Ciaran.

'I'm sorry. I never meant to hurt you. Never would I want to. Ever. I loved you too.'

Kristin stared at Ciaran, who was pale and staring blankly at me.

'You're shameless. Even when we announce we're a couple, you try it on,' she said, her voice came out in a hiss.

'It's the girl's birthday. Give her a break. Start on her tomorrow,' Ber said, with one eye completely closed. She shoved her chair back with her legs, so it screeched on the marble floor and stood to take her drink from the nervous waiter. She swayed as she took a long slurp, then bumped into my shoulder when she bent to talk to me. 'You'll be grand.'

Ber's heel went to the side. Her ankle hit the floor. She lurched forward, tipping the slushy red liquid right down my neck and chest and arms, landing in a pool in my dress. I jumped up when the iced drink touched skin, hitting Ber's glass as I stood. The glass toppled in the air, unveiling the rest of its contents onto the floor and table. Vittoria and Kristin burst into laughter. Ber took a bunch of napkins and stabbed rather than dabbed at the ruined material. I pushed Ber's hand away but, already unsteady in too high heels, she fell backwards, catching the tablecloth and taking it down with her. Glass and plates and cutlery cluttered to the ground. Peter looked gleeful, loving the commotion. Vittoria tossed her hair and looked like she was bored and couldn't care less. I couldn't read Ciaran - his face was stuck in shock. Kristin was smiling. Ber splayed out on the floor. Whether it was from the fall jolting her stomach, or the shock or the ten drinks she consumed, as I helped Ber up, she projectile vomited bright red liquid. Warm, congealed, tomato coloured vomit landed on my feet. In revulsion, I let go and Ber fell again to the floor, into her own vomit.

Everyone stayed put except Ciaran, who ran to pick her up. The rest relished the train wreck of the night. Kristin stood with her arms folded, with a proud, smug grin, as if she took full responsibility for what had happened. As activity erupted from servers and managers rushing over, Ciaran tried and failed to hold a vomiting Ber up, as she flopped and slipped in her own sick, while his own shoes slid around the floor, trying to pick up a girl that was twice the size of him. Peter and Vittoria were no help. They were bent over, their heads joined, holding their stomachs, laughing at the chaos. In all that madness, the world slowed down. In that glitzy bar, I realized why I had felt such a sadness when they listed what they loved about me.

It had all been about them.

The truth I ignored for the last number of years opened up before me. It was all false. False friendships. False conversations. False love.

And then the world sped up again and Dependable Dawn took over. I picked up a turned over chair and grabbed Ber under the arm and with Ciaran deposited her on the seat.

I couldn't look at him. 'Keep her steady or she will fall. Order her a taxi.'

I grabbed a napkin and sidestepped the flapping staff, making my way to the bar, wiping the drink from my neck as I walked. Spotting a mop and bucket in a cubbyhole beside a hatch, I picked it up, putting my hand up to stop the waiter from approaching. 'You didn't cause this mess. Just please get something to dry it.'

I ignored Ber's cackles and drunken slurs as I slopped up the chunky red vomit. It stank. The water in the bucket was brown and as I dipped the mop in, the red formed a film on the top, like oil on water. I ignored the warnings from my own stomach as they reflexed from the stench, averting my nose so I didn't join Ber in vomiting. I was sick of cleaning up Ber's sick. I was sick of being the one to clean up all their messes. Being so busy worrying about their problems, I had forgotten about sorting my own and where did that leave me? After scooping up the worst, I saw a red glug on the side of that beautiful gold leg of the table. I knelt down, ignoring the wet floor and grabbing a napkin from the table, wiped down the leg.

'Please, you don't need to do that. We can clean it,' a man who looked like he might be the manager said.

'You shouldn't have to, though. We made the mess.'

'You shouldn't have to either,' the man said, placing his hand on my shoulder. 'Come on, we don't need another accident. Let go.'

I let him help me up. My knees were stained pink. I picked up my bag. 'You know, I'm exhausted. I'm going to head home.'

Kristin blocked my path. 'Here we go. Playing the victim.' She pretended to rub her eyes. 'Look at me, I'm poor Dawn and you've all ruined my birthday. Well, fuck that. I'll give you a reason to hate your birthday.' The fists changed to finger points, one of which jabbed me in the chest. 'You caused this. With all your stupid talk of *the gloom*. It's not even because it's your birthday. Shit happens with you, Peter and Ber say it all the time. They're allergic. You're just a miserable cow who drags us all down. We all had bets on how long it would take for you to ruin your birthday and here we are, another one for the record books. Well, go ahead and ruin it and every one of your birthdays but don't you dare ruin the happiest night of my life.' Kristin's voice ended in a screech. Even the staff who had rushed over to clean the mess stopped what they were doing. The restaurant stared at me and waited for my reaction.

The words wouldn't come.

All that was there was a blank, empty brain. I could not think of one thing to say. If you'd asked me my name, I would have been hard pressed to answer. Even if I could find the words, unlocked the block that came up between me and the messaging from my brain to my throat, an overwhelming sadness took over, I was afraid I would burst out crying in the restaurant. I took out the rest of my wages and placed a hundred euros on the table.

'Dawn, don't go. We can sort it out,' Ciaran said. Kristin turned to him, livid.

'What do you mean? You're sticking up for her?'

'Stop it Kristin,' he said.

'Stop it. Are you serious?' Her voice had turned so high pitch she was bordering on the frequency that only dogs and teenagers could hear. 'After everything she's done to you?'

In every other scenario that had happened in my life, I would have continued to be dumbstruck, but looking at Ciaran, seeing he believed I had meant to hurt him, was enough to shake me out of silence. For him, I found some words.

'Ciaran, I am sorry. All I wanted was for you to be happy.' I took a deep breath and fought away the tears. I wouldn't cry here. And then Kristen smirked, and it triggered me to find something to say. 'Kristin, you're right. This is all my fault. I'm sorry for my reaction. For causing this to turn out this way. But you've had a problem with me for a long time and I ignored it because I was afraid to say anything. I knew if I did, you would lash out at me, you would shoot me down. If your problem with me this whole time has been about Ciaran, about the way I treat Ciaran, and he agrees, then I promise I'll leave you both alone. You don't need to worry about me getting in your way.'

'See how obnoxious she is? She actually thinks she could get in our way.'

Kristin's shoulders rose up and down in anger. Ciaran noticed it too and put an arm around her, and my heart sank lower. Had I hoped Ciaran would take my side? Had I hoped he would choose me?'

With my last bit of strength, I held my head up as I walked through the restaurant. Any politeness left the patrons who hadn't already turned, the bright red blob coming towards them was too noticeable to ignore. No one followed. None of them tried to stop me. Their silence said it all.

Buttoning my coat, gave a chance to cover up. The material cloaked me and hid the mess underneath and apart from my red legs, I was safe to walk home without being stared at. In a daze, I listened to my heels as they click-clocked along the concrete, consoled by the sight of my apartment.

On that bridge I walked a million times, a familiar face stood out among the strangers passing by. A face I'd laid under before. A face I hadn't given a thought to an hour beforehand but now, desperately, instantly, wanted to lie under again. I smiled at him. He smiled back. We were at his house in fifteen minutes.

Naked

Eight days before.

Jed's back was the first thing I saw. His lean, beautiful, still unconscious, back. I counted the notches on his spine, resisting running my
finger down each one, knowing it wasn't allowed, knowing the rules.
Anything went the night before, but the morning was awkward domain.
Today, it would be too much to handle after the events of last night.
My head hurt. It was that time in the morning when it was still dark
but turning. I sat up in bed, not wanting to endure going through the
motions of having Jed pretend to care about whether I had breakfast,
when he really wanted to push me out the door.

All the times I had laid next to him in this bed. All the times I'd
looked at his back, wishing he would turn around. Wishing for more
than he could give. It wasn't even his fault. I knew what type of guy Jed
was. It didn't matter how many times I slept with him; I would never
make him love me. It didn't matter that he was the most attractive
man ever. Or on the nights I lay alone in my bed, I had to turn off the
phone in order not to ring him. It didn't matter that I'd tried to be what
he wanted, not asking too many questions, never probing or delving
too deep. Nothing changed the fact he saw me as a casual hook up and
would never see me as anything more, no matter how hard I laughed at
his jokes, how good I was in bed, how many times I said yes, he made

sure he kept the boundaries clear. It wasn't his fault I became attached. Like with the friends I had picked, the blame was all on me.

Last night had been different, though. Something had changed in me, like a switch or a snap. I couldn't go back to what I'd accepted before. As I'd taken off my jacket, he saw the massacre of a dress. He laughed and went to peel it off. Like he went straight to every time.

'Are you not going to ask me what happened?' I asked.

He looked at me with huge, bright blue, mischievous eyes and shrugged. Then got back to business. I turned away from him, rolled off my control knickers, which slipped off easier than normal due to being wet from Ber's drink. Once off, I kicked it under the bed, then offered myself to him, allowing him to take over and do the rest. As he stripped me naked, he stripped away something else as well; he stripped away my clothes as if lies shrouded them. I caught my reflection in the mirror on the wall of Jed's apartment. The angle of it was off. Instead of being straight, it tilted off to the side. Why hadn't I noticed before he had positioned it across from the bed?

'You all right?' He asked. He looked fearful, rather than concerned.

I nodded, still wanting to reassure. 'Hard night. Just give me a minute.'

In the bathroom, I closed the door and sat on the edge of the cold bath. Flashes of the last few years hit me.

Kristin hadn't just become snidey. If I was honest, if I was going to admit the real truth, her critical comments had always been there, often cloaked in friendship, enough to let the doubt of her words step in to my subconscious, taking it far enough that she would offend, the comment sometimes too subtle I wouldn't notice straight away but later, when I was alone and played over the words.

Stupid things I dismissed, like when Peter brought clothes over from the new collection and when I picked up my favourite, a blue dress, Kristin had whipped it off me and said, 'That colour makes you look anaemic.' Or when she sniggered when I ordered a frappe and said to Peter, thinking I couldn't hear. 'That's a deposit in the Christmas bank.' My world tilted for a moment, but then Kristin always pulled me back with her smile and a friendly remark that softened and confused and contradicted the words she'd just delivered. 'You look good anyway.'

Or when I caught her smiling when I told her about a horrible day.

Peter was Peter; his falseness was legendary. Before that night, I had regarded it as funny, or dismissed it as that anyway, but now I remembered all the times I'd rang him to come over and he hadn't answered me back. The times I'd listened when something had happened to him yet when I text with a crisis or just needed to talk, he wouldn't respond until days later when it was over. Ber could be a pain with drink, only a few more parties away from being classed an alcoholic. I tried to recall an occasion I'd met her outside of a night out. Thinking about it, I hadn't had one conversation between us without alcohol involved. What did I know about the girl? I couldn't even remember her last name.

Ciaran had been the true one. Yet he had kept his true feelings from me and now I had lost him. Jed knocked on the bathroom door.

'You dying in there?'

Poor Jed. He had thought his evening was a sure thing and here was a weirdo locked in his bathroom. I didn't look in the mirror, not wanting to see the carnage that would stare back. The best thing I could do would be to open the door and apologise, tell him I wasn't that girl anymore while I picked up my clothes and went home. But the alcohol was still in my system, and even though I knew that was what I should do, I was never very good at doing the right thing for myself.

What I did was rake a hand through my hair, squeeze a blob of toothpaste on my finger and rub, wash the vomit away from my feet and cocktail from my knees. Jed knocked again. I took a breath and opened the door and, putting on my best smile, pushed him towards the bed. Jed seemed more relieved his night wasn't taking a sour turn rather than for my opening my legs, but he still complied.

Slipping out of the bed, I got dressed. My head was banging from drinking more with Jed and only falling asleep a few hours before. I picked up my discarded pieces from the floor and left without a look behind. The shame came as I walked through town. Sleeping with him hadn't been right, but at least I knew why. I'd wanted to be wanted. When I closed my eyes, it wasn't Jed touching me, but Ciaran.

As I crossed the bridge to my apartment, the same bridge I met Jed the night before at, the same bridge I passed busy mum and white runner guy all those mornings, the same bridge I now tried to ignore the sniggers of two young fellas.

'State of her.'

'Bet she had a good night.'

They didn't offend; I must look a state. In my rush to get out, I hadn't even looked in a mirror, hadn't combed my hair. Because that was me. Wasn't that always what I did? I didn't choose the right choices. I didn't help myself. Checking my makeup in the mirror before I left Jed's apartment wasn't even an option because I never put myself first.

Kristin had known what would happen before she accused me of using Ciaran. My friends knew I couldn't move after a confrontation, that it shocked me into silence, they were used to me saying nothing, at most rocking to myself, with my mouth clamped shut. I could never speak, my body in shutdown, not able to move my lips or make words travel. Last night proved it. I was the one who went quiet if someone put me on the spot and asked my opinion. Who froze whenever I needed to fight my corner.

It was all messed up. I went to that restaurant thinking everyone was there to celebrate my birthday yet not one of them had wanted to stop me from leaving. Not one of them had left a message since or checked if I was OK. I was the one they called if they needed someone to listen at three in the morning when they were drunk and missed their ex. All the nights out soothing and ironing out their problems, then coming home on my own. And there was the truth. Even surrounded by my friends, I was lonely.

At the end of the bridge by my apartment I watched the early rowers practicing their runs on the River Lee.

Maybe it was just the hangover talking, or my assumptions about them would prove false. Maybe they'd surprise me. Still, I stood tall with a new resolve. I'd test them; they could prove me wrong. I wouldn't ring. If they loved me, if they cared, they would call. And if they didn't, then I had seen and called out their true colours.

The only one I hesitated about was Ciaran. It hurt too much to think of him. Why hadn't he stuck up for me? Why hadn't he rung?

Inside my apartment, before diving into the bed, I faced the mirror. The two young fellas on the bridge hadn't been wrong. Even though I had cleared some away the night before, the black mascara smudged past my eye sockets. My pale skin was blotchy from drink and the overexertion with Jed. I shook the falseness of how I had been with him away. Hoping to erase the night, I was a woman possessed, asking him to go rough, rougher, and he got off on it, whispering that he liked the new me, leaving me raw and chafed and as fragile as the rest of me.

The red stains splattered on my dress like cheap blood in a horror film, the whiff of stale, ejected passion fruit made my own bile rise. Before peeling off, I eyed the dress. Without the confines of control knickers, which were still lying under Jed's bed, the straight lines now made rounded curves from my bloated belly. My thighs stood exposed under the too short skirt; the false tan had settled and darkened on the dots on my legs where I shaved too hard making me resemble a plucked chicken. My hair, which before I left had felt glossy and smooth, now hung in sticky clumps. How could I have thought I looked attractive?

What was I thinking to even consider that type of dress? I wanted to be different for once, to step outside of the label of who I was and change, but no matter how I dressed up, I was still Dawn. And look where different had got me.

Still woozy, I held onto both sides of the sink. 'No more. I'm done with all of them. They are not my friends. They proved that tonight. Every time. Every time something is about me, they turn it. This is the last birthday they will do this to you.'

Naked, I hobbled to the bed, desperate to forget everything about the night before. If I hadn't stayed up most of the night, I would have lain there and fretted, but now I could feel myself falling asleep before I closed my eyes. *The gloom* could come later.

Walls

A beep woke me. Despite my protestations about not caring about any of my friends, my hand went straight for the phone. It wasn't a surprise. Will power had never been my strongest suit. If they text or called, I would act as if nothing happened and forgive them for everything. It was Mum, asking if I would still come for dinner.

I dropped the phone with a groan. Dinner in Crookstown was the last thing I wanted to do.

You promised. You've put your mother off for the last couple of months.

If I delayed a visit any longer, she would make a trip up to the city and that would be worse. A trip to the coast might help clear my head. I text back that I'd see them later.

The best part of going home was the journey. The long, meandering roads turned from city streets to coastal. I loved watching the scenery become greener, then sandy, the horizon lowering until it felt like the sky took over with only a sliver of land in front, reminding me of my insignificance, that I was only a tiny piece in an enormous planet. I always arrived early for the bus in order to bag a window seat on the left side, putting on huge headphones so the person sitting next to me wouldn't try to talk. It wasn't to be rude. Being quiet meant I was a good listener, but the journey to home differed from others and I needed the uninterrupted view. As the bus rounded the top of Knockfarraig Hill, and the sight unveiled itself, I always felt my shoulders drop. For that moment, before the descent down that steep hill, the whole of the town greeted me. The sea spread out and, in that view, it was as if I could see the entire world. Vertigo inducing, it always came as a shock, to see the water above and the land below from the apex of the hill. It always reminded me there was so much more I didn't know yet, so much more to see. Worth any journey to witness, whenever I saw it, it was as if I breathed for the first time since I'd last been, or rather, the quality of breath changed, becoming deeper, calmer.

As soon as the bus started the descent of the hill and passed the secondary school, once my secondary school, that joy at seeing the town's beauty dropped as the land straightened and righted itself in its correct order of land followed by sea, but the flat reminded of what happened before I left for good. It was enough to turn my mood, because every bit further the bus drove brought me nearer to Crookstown.

The hangover didn't help. Even when I didn't get *the gloom*, even on the nights that turned out well, drinking left me feeling vulnerable. It was more than a hangover, although all the signs were there: the dry tongue, the pounding head, the sore eyes and throat. It was the emotional massacre that bothered me. Today, I had reason, but other days, even when I didn't and had a good night, I still felt a shaky nervousness. Hangovers brought out my insecurities. If something I'd done coupled it, something I considered wrong, or out of place, or stupid, then the night stayed with me, replaying over and over the said word that should have stayed unsaid or the action that I wished I could unwind. It wasn't as if I insulted anyone, it was just that I became loose lipped, making declarations of love that I balked at the next day. Hugging people too long. Going home with the wrong type of people. Waking up in the wrong pair of arms. It was nothing new to feel shaky and vulnerable after a night out but just because it was an often occurrence didn't mean I became accustomed to it. There were only two ways around the next day: drinking more or staying in bed and sleeping it off until the horrors left.

I lay my head against the window, thankful for its coldness, but then took it away again as my head vibrated from the constant bumps. I wished for sleep, to forget about the night before. If ever there was a day to stay in bed, it was today. The assurance I felt this morning before sleep was well gone and now I just wanted to delete or rewind the night, to wipe it from my memory and pretend it never happened. The viciousness from Kristin bothered me. I could still picture her snarled up face, the pointed finger with those pointier words. They confused more. Hurt more. There was truth sown inside them about Ciaran that I couldn't bear. Had I strung him along? Never. There was no truth in that. Because to string someone along, I would have needed to have no intention of it going somewhere. What there was truth in, was I had kept the door open, left our relationship to maybe status, but that had been more in hope, that one day the timing would be right and he might see me for who I was, that he might want me and we could end up together. It never occurred to me he might already feel that way.

My stomach churned with the thought I might have hurt him. It made me nauseous that I may have, for even one second, offended Ciaran or slighted him. I could walk away from all of them, I could even give up the hope of never being together, of being a couple, but a life without him, I didn't think I could do. Had he thought I laughed at him?

Everywhere the bus passed in Knockfarraig reminded me of him. The green beside the bandstand, where we would lie on summer days cloud watching and chatting. The alley was next, the place we tried to smoke, after Ciaran robbed a cigarette from a pack lying around in his older brother's room. Him going first, he always was the more daring of the two of us. It took him two attempts to even light it, the first failing as his thumb slid off the lighter, the second doomed from the wind. I had leant over and shielded the death stick, cupping my hand over, blocking my view so I couldn't see if it was a success or not. We were so close to each other, and I had noticed the closeness, had felt something when his eyes met mine. Then the smoke escaped, spilling out from each direction behind my hand, and Ciaran exploded into a fit of coughing and waving his hand for me to take the cigarette while he composed himself. The moment left, I took the cigarette and tried to inhale, determined to show him how it was supposed to be done, to act cool. I remember that moment now, how Ciaran smiled at me as we leant against the wall. A secret between us, for only us, our shoulders edging closer. I remember feeling a shakiness then, in my legs, my first inkling of excitement about us, about the possibility of us, but put it down to the tobacco. The moment passed. Our one and only liaison with cigarettes ended with both of us vomiting behind the old scout hall.

Or now, as the bus turned onto the bridge, it brought back other memories. It was the point he walked me home to, the point where Knockfarraig met Crookstown. The very point we always said goodbye at. The middle of the bridge was the place I had searched his eyes so many times, hoping that night might be the night he kissed me. Sitting on the top of the wall, our feet dangling over, not afraid of the water down below. It was where we shared stories, where we were alone after spending the rest of the day hanging around with friends all summer. It was in that spot I realised he was my best friend and I would never push it further than that unless he wanted to.

And now I had found out he had wanted to. I had found out too late.

Each landmark after Knockfarraig bridge reminded me of why I dreaded Crookstown. The bus drove over Crookstown's little bridge, ridiculous in comparison to the other, so small you could class it as just a bump on the road. The winding wall that led from Knockfarraig to Crookstown had stones missing in parts from bored teenagers with nothing at all to do but to try to kick it in. I often wondered if the wall was built to keep the inhabitants out of the water, rather than keep them safe, as if the beauty of the sea needed protection from the town. Even the sign for Crookstown was small, a piece of stone tucked into the grass that if you didn't search for it, if it wasn't ingrained into memory, you'd miss. Every person, every building, reconfirmed why I had to leave. There was Mrs Corry with her hair rollers on under her headscarf, standing with her arms folded by her gate, as if she was waiting for some better occasion to take those rollers out, an occasion that would never come. As if all the people she met while she wore them didn't matter, irrelevant to whatever she was wearing them for. The same Mrs Corry who didn't go anywhere, standing at the gate was the highlight of her day. Or Mrs Callaghan, hanging her washing at the front of her house, when she had a back garden twice as big. Only done so she could watch the people come and go, could catch and gossip with any passers, bestowing her judgment with arms folded and head nodding.

Some things I'd done as a teenager came to memory, done to rebel against the town's confinement, pursued through boredom, things that didn't seem such a big deal then but if they came out now, would shame me. They were the things a small town never forgot. It was that mentality that I ran away from. The place-one-foot-wrong-and-you-would-be-sentenced-forever mentality. Even the thought of it was stifling. I had known from a young age I couldn't live there, that one day I would have to fail, and for that I wanted to be as far away as possible. In the city, you could fail and fail and avoid the people you failed in front of.

You couldn't even class Crookstown as a town when it was only one main street. That was why I had loved going to Knockfarraig, which was only a five-minute drive away and about a twenty-minute walk.

Still small compared to other towns in Ireland, yet it was a revelation to a just turned teenager, with its cobbled interlocking alleys that hid people that wanted to hide, that held corners you could disappear into. Knockfarraig brought Ciaran, and that had been the greatest gift of all.

The road winded along until I rang the bell for the next stop. Home. I wasn't sure I had the energy for it.

I caught sight of the pretty row of houses all painted in different colours and scowled. Pink balloons with the number thirty plastered in black for the whole town to see hung outside our bright yellow door. Tempted to walk past, I knew Mum would stand at the window, waiting. I didn't have time to ring the doorbell or root in my bag for my key, my mother threw open the door and grabbed me. I gave her a loose hug back, half in the house and on the street, trying to waddle her inside so we could close the door, wanting to get inside and stop making a scene. When it didn't stop, I removed myself from her tight grip but couldn't break free. Mum held onto my arms.

'Let me look at the birthday girl.'

'It's not my birthday anymore, Mum.'

I sidestepped her and walked through the hallway, peeking into the empty sitting room.

'Only by one day. I can't believe my little girl is thirty. Where did the time go?'

'Well, you had thirty years to get used to it.'

'When you have kids of your own, you'll see how quickly time flies, Dawn. How fast you grew. I miss not having children around. The house seems empty without you.'

'Sorry I'm lacking on giving you grandkids,' I said, entering the kitchen. I was in the door less than a minute and already she was getting the digs in.

'Time is ticking, that's all I'm saying. How was last night?'

I hesitated. What was the point in telling her? She would just say she told me so. Apart from Ciaran, Mum didn't approve of my friends.

'It was good.'

'Where did ye go?'

'Town. To a new restaurant that opened last week. Peter got us a table even though there was a waiting list.'

'Wow, fancy. What did you order?'

I sighed. The woman's enthusiasm was annoying.

'A salad.'

'Are you on another diet?'

I grimaced. 'No, the waiter recommended it.'

'Good, because you're getting very thin. You're always starving yourself. It's not good for your health.'

'I'm a size twelve, you could hardly call that too thin.'

Entering the sitting room again, I flopped down on the couch and turned the TV on just to drown out my mother's drones. Just because she summoned me to the house didn't mean I had to stay talking.

'Do you want a coffee?' She called out from the kitchen.

'Sure.'

I channel hopped and tried to ignore the sound of her fussing in the kitchen, of a kettle filled and flicked, the pulling open of drawers and banging. Every action grated. Every relic in the house annoyed me too: the old, ticking clock heard all over the house, the religious pictures in each room staring back, the tea cosy to keep the teapot warm. Who even had them these days? And that was not even getting to Mum, who was an annoyance all by herself. It bothered me she always wore a dress. God forbid she wore trousers. Equality in clothes was frowned upon by Mum. The dresses were never fashionable but sexless, shapeless frocks in some variant of brown or grey. With beige tights underneath and court shoes. She set her hair every Saturday in an aged shape that sat unmovable on top of her head. Only in her early sixties, yet the woman looked like she stepped back in time and arrived in the war era.

I hated that every time I came home I reverted to my youth, resorting to adolescence, the traits wrapping around me like a scarf, becoming this curt, unresponsive, secretive person. It wasn't my fault. Mum was a very irritating person.

She appeared, holding a tray piled to the brim. Apart from the clothes that looked like she lived in ration times despite not being born yet, or the outdated perm, it was the 'I know better' temperament, the relentless questions, her eagerness and the way she smiled at me as if I was the only light in her life that got under my skin.

'What did I do to warrant the fancy biscuits?'

'Your birthday only comes once a year. So, tell me all about last night. I'm dying to know all about it.'

I picked up a biscuit and thought twice before scoffing it.

'Mum, there's nothing new to tell. We went out, had something to eat and drink, and then went home. Besides, I'm too hungover to go into details, OK? I just want to vedge on the couch and watch crappy TV.'

Mum huffed. She eyed the crumbs I had spilt on my top. Some fell to the ground and seeing her horror, I made a big exaggeration of brushing them away.

'You're still not happy. I came, didn't I? Even though I could have stayed in bed, it's still not enough.'

'I just thought we could have a good day, that's all.'

'Five minutes in the door and you can't help but point out how I disappoint you. Sorry I'm not living up to expectations,' I said, standing. 'Where's Dad?'

'In his usual spot.'

'I'll say hi.'

'Of course,' Mum said, folding her arms and looking out the window.

My father's shed was an odd jobber's heaven. Rows of gleaming tools lined one wall. Everything in there was in order and Dad's favourite saying was: 'Everything has a place.'

He was tinkering with an old watch, his back to me. The hair was greyer since I'd seen him last.

'How's my girl?' he asked without turning. 'Out here for some space?'

'You know me too well,' I said, kissing him on the cheek. The grooves on his skin were deeper. He hugged me.

'Go easy on her, she misses you desperate.'

I picked up a screwdriver and pretended to examine it. 'Why does she have to dig at me so much, then?'

'She just wants what's best for you, that's all. She's looked forward to your visit for months.'

'That's because she doesn't have her own life, Dad.'

'You've been her life for thirty years. She gave you everything. Remember that OK?'

'I came out here to avoid a lecture.'

'Lecture over, I promise.' He smiled in the easy way I knew him for; my father wasn't known for a temper.

'Fixing as usual?'

'You know me, I'm happiest when I'm nose deep in a project. You staying tonight?'

'Not sure. We'll see how it goes.'

The smile left him. 'Sure,' he said and continued with the watch.

'If I've time I might go for a walk in the town, catch up with some of the lads.'

'Dinner's your mother's vicinity. Known her it will be five on the dot.'

'I'll go ask. Speak to you soon,' I said, and kissed him again.

'Happy Birthday,' he said.

Mum was checking some type of meat when I popped into the

kitchen.

'I'm going to pop out there and say hi to the lads.'

'Dinner will be ready soon.'

'How long is soon? Do I have ten minutes? Thirty? An hour?'

Mum shrugged in defeat. 'An hour, I guess.'

'See, that's plenty of time to walk down the road and back. I'll see you in a min.'

Crookstown being only one road meant there weren't many options for where the lads would be; unless they were at home or gone away, they would be in Regan's, the only decent bar on the street. I nodded at Mrs Donnelly, who waved me over from the door of her shop to stop and talk.

'Back home for a while Dawn? Your mother will be pleased to see you.' Mrs Donnelly said with a smile, but crossed her arms just the same.

'Yeah. Just for the day, Mrs Donnelly. How's Ian?'

'He's great. He got a huge promotion at work. Married last year. My first grandchild is due any day now.'

'Exciting times.' I walked on, hoping that would be the end of the conversation.

'Imagine, there was one time I thought it would have been you having his baby,' she called out.

'Sure that was a long time ago, Mrs Donnelly, twelve years feels like a lifetime. His wife is a lucky woman.' *Lucky escape for me, more like.* 'Tell Ian I said hi.'

I accepted the dig; the woman needed to tell me how well her son was doing. We had gone out for three months, right until the Debs. His family had never forgiven me for breaking it off on his special night. It didn't matter what caused the break or the many times before that they witnessed him putting me down or being downright mean.

'Will do. Any sign of marriage for you?'

I hid the urge to cringe. 'No. I'm enjoying the single life too much for that now, Mrs Donnelly.'

'Ah, sure, you always did. Not sick of the city yet?'

'No, I love the high-flying life, me. I better push on there, Mum only gave me an hour to say hi to the lads.'

'Sure, we might see you again in another year, so.'

'If you're lucky, Mrs Donnelly.'

Lucky escape. Lucky escape. Lucky escape.

The bar was empty except for an old man drinking in the corner. Leaning on the counter, I saluted Pat.

'Look who it is. My god Dawn, you're all grown up.'

'I'm officially old now, Pat. Where's all the lads?'

'Which lads? Yours' have all moved on now. Haven't seen them in years.'

'What, like Seanie and Tessa? Rolls used to spend night and day here.'

Pat wiped the bar with a cloth. 'You don't keep up? Seanie moved to Australia. Tessa is on her third child and only comes to the pub for either a christening or a funeral. Rolls doesn't go by Rolls anymore but Johnny. On a major health kick. Gave up drink. Buffed himself up. Apparently he has a huge following on the net.'

'Oh yeah? I'll check him out,' I said, typing his name into the phone. 'Jesus, you're right. Johnny got buff. Followed there.'

'Going or staying?'

'Well, I was hoping to catch up with them, but you're as good as any.' I checked my watch. 'And since I have forty-seven minutes until I have to go back for the last supper, I may as well have a drink. I'll need it if I'm honest, our Reena is in fine form today.'

'Your mother means well.'

'She does.'

'What's your poison?'

'Something strong. Not a short though, she'll see my cheeks from the window. Give me your highest percentage white wine, please.'

Every corner of the bar brought memories. Some good, some not so good. How many nights had I spent in here? After I moved to the city, I had stopped staying at home after Christmas Day. Outside the exit door, I had tried my first and last joint, then vomited down the side straight after, and finally learnt my lesson about tobacco then. At this bar, Ciaran held my hand and we made a vow to move to the city together. Crookstown reminded me now of what could have been.

The wine settled me, the hair of the dog running through my tense body, softening the effects of the hangover, the headache dulled from a pound to a hum. The second glass made me not care that I was sitting alone or drinking during the day or about what would come next at the dinner. Pat busied himself with something he regarded more important than talking to me yet he wasn't being rude, we had nothing in common anymore, the people we had known together were dead or moved on and even then, Pat had been quiet as it was. A third glass was tempting but sense told me it wouldn't do anything more than get me drunk and deepen Reena's resentment. Three wines in forty minutes was too much, even for me. Waving goodbye to Pat after I paid him, I left the bar, keeping my head down so I wouldn't have to make stupid conversation with the towns vultures who were out sniffing for gossip carcass. Today, I wouldn't give it to them.

As I let myself in, I straightened up and tried to find the balance of looking sober without trying too hard to look sober. The smell of roast dinner wafted and made me salivate, and my stomach grumbled. Apart from the one biscuit earlier, I hadn't eaten since the night before and one thing I could never deny about Mum, she was a great cook.

I heard a clucking of a tongue. 'Dinner will be ready in five minutes. Do you want to freshen yourself up?'

'For what? Is someone else coming?'

'No. But it's always good to look your best.'

I sloped to the bathroom, cursing her under my breath. Looking in the mirror, she had a point. I'd scraped up my hair in a ponytail and my cheeks were ruddy from the wine, my lips looked flaky and dehydrated and were almost bluish. Splashing my face with water cooled my face and while I dabbed it dry, I found a hairbrush and a lipstick in the bathroom cabinet. Pearly pink, at a guess Mum bought it in the nineties. I put it back on its shelf. Being bare lipped was an improvement than using that.

Back in the kitchen, Mum laid out the table like it was someone's wedding. Picking up a napkin folded like a swan, I pretended it was floating. 'Are you sure we aren't expecting someone?'

'It is your thirtieth,' Mum said, laying a pitcher of lemonade on the table like the cheap jug was precious crystal, before turning back to the kitchen.

'It was. Yesterday,' I said through gritted teeth, moving my hands over the holes in the tablecloth's lacework. It was older than I was. Everything in the house had a purpose, but the trimmings were outdated. Kept immaculate by my mother and useable by my father, its upkeep more important since they bought it back when they first married than the colour palette. Even in the seventies, the brown carpet should never have been popular. The moss green on the wall darkened and stifled the room and was another reason I wanted to bolt every time I sat down. The wood table was just like my parents: sturdy and pliable and lacking any style.

I sat in the chair on the long side of the table. My chair. It wouldn't bother me where I sat but my parents were creatures of habit and Mum would pass out from even the notion of anyone sitting anywhere else but our allocated seat. It had always been that way. The silent rules. The family laws you couldn't cross and the reasons behind them. Sitting in the middle so my parents, at the top and bottom end of the table, could make me the primary focus. Drunk enough to be braver, I decided it was the perfect time to challenge that rule; I didn't want to do it anymore. When Mum went out to the kitchen to fetch some condiment, I moved and sat in her seat.

'Dawn,' Dad said as he came into the room.

'I just don't want to be the piggy anymore.'

'The piggy?'

'Yeah, piggy in the middle.'

'Oh,' Mum said as she entered the room, looking at the empty chair as if it might bite her.

'Do you want my seat?' Dad offered.

Mum gaped, her mouth open as if her entire world had just crumbled.

'Oh, for god's sake, take the seat. I just thought we could do something different for once.'

I shoved the chair back with my feet, and the carpet, a little more worn in that area, couldn't take the pressure, toppling me back. To save myself from falling, I slammed my hands on the table. Mum placed a hand on her chest as if she was about to have a heart attack. After creating a scene, I couldn't stop, so I carried out my intention and sat in the middle seat and smiled, as if that had all been normal. Mum straightened her wool brown skirt and sniffed, but then sat down.

'You're drunk,' she said in a low voice.

'I'm not. I had two drinks. Without food, that's all and like you keep reminding me, it was my birthday. Just because you're teetotal, it doesn't mean the rest of the world has to be. Some of us want to have fun.'

Mum stood, smoothing the skirt again. 'I forgot to get the food.'

She rushed out of the room.

'Be nice Dawn,' Dad warned.

I took a calming breath. This place always did this. Turned me into a snarling teenager.

'I can't help it. I just react.'

'Your mother has gone to a lot of trouble for this weekend. Humour her.'

'Humour her? Isn't it meant to be my weekend?'

He rubbed a finger along the deep crease between his eyebrows. Up and down, soothing the line. 'Every weekend is your weekend, by the look of it. I would like just one visit of yours where I didn't see your mother left in tears.'

It was my turn to act shocked. 'It's not my fault she overreacts. Everything I do is a problem.'

He stopped rubbing to look at me. 'No Dawn, it's the other way round.'

'What? How can you say that?'

Mum came into the room carrying a large serving plate and ending our conversation. I plastered on my falsest smile. 'Can I help you with anything, Mum?'

'No, you sit and relax. It will only take me a minute to bring this out. Tuck in.'

She laid out the roast in the middle of the table. The slices of meat glistened with juices. My stomach rumbled loudly. As Mum disappeared back into the kitchen, I nudged my father.

'Sorry, I'm hungry.'

He nodded once, and I knew all was forgiven.

'We better get some food in you, so,' he said, gesturing for me to take the first serving of meat.

I piled my plate and smiled at Mum when she walked back in, this time not so false. 'It smells great.'

'Your mother makes the best roast in the world,' Dad said, popping an offcut into his mouth.

'That she does. Hands down,' I said.

Mum beamed, laying down a bowl of buttered salad potatoes, a bowl heaped full of creamed mash and another brimming to the top with dauphinoise. My mother wouldn't be one to use salads or to even consider ever going anti carb. She was old school, traditional Irish, where the potato was king and the staple of the meal and had to feature in every dinner. Potato three ways was not uncommon in the Moloney household.

'One more trip should do it,' Mum said, swivelling back again.

A few seconds later, she appeared with a huge serving plate of vegetables. I eyed the bowl. Divided into different sections, it was full of every bland colour in the rainbow. Muted yellow sweetcorn. Green peas. White cauliflower. Brown mushrooms. Terracotta orange carrots.

She sat down and jumped back up again. 'The gravy.'

If there was only one good thing I could say about my mother, it was that she was a fantastic cook. Even though she stuck to the basics, never wandering far from the meat and potatoes, the meat was succulent, timed to perfection, the veg just right, with food Mum had the Goldilocks touch. I sighed. If anything felt like home, it was my mammy's dinner.

Through chews, Mum spoke. 'How's the head?'

'I don't get you.'

'You look hungover. Like you had a good night,' Dad said.

'I drank a fair bit.'

'Ah, remember those days, John?'

'I do,' he said, smiling.

'What? When did you drink too much? Never in my life would I imagine that. I've only ever seen you drink a sherry at Christmas.'

Mum picked at a carrot with a fork but said nothing.

'When you came along, your mother knocked it on the head.'

'Why were you a bit of an alcho, Mum?' I said, sniggering at the ridiculous thought.

'I didn't want to drink around a baby. I wanted to give you all my attention.'

'But sure, I'm an adult now. Why don't you ever let your hair down? Live a little? Dad has a few drinks. He's fun.'

Dad lowered his head. 'Dawn.'

'On that note,' I said, leaving the table and going to my bag. After a rummage around, I waved a bottle of prosecco at them. 'Fancy a glass?' Silence. 'I was going to drink it tonight if I stayed, but as it's a celebration, why don't we have it together?'

'I don't think that's a good idea,' Mum said, coiffing her hair.

'Come on, celebrate with me.'

As I tried to wiggle the cork off, I turned, looking for a direction to point it, in case it went flying. The wall of porcelain in the open cabinet wouldn't do. Nor the window. Nor the TV. Nor the hanging picture frames. I pointed it at the ceiling instead. The cork made a loud pop and Mum shrieked.

'What's wrong? You knew it was about to happen.'

Instead of sitting, I plonked the bottle on the table and took out three glasses from a shelf in the kitchen. Mum blocked the mouth of the glass as I went to pour.

'None for me, thanks. You enjoy it with your father.'

'You won't toast with me, Mum?'

'I won't. It doesn't agree with me.'

'What do you mean, do you die after drinking it? Will you choke on the bubbles? Will you transform and turn green or something after a sip?' I laughed at my joke and took a sip. I let the warm bubbles hop on my tongue before swallowing.

Dad laid his napkin on the table and folded his arms, not touching the glass I poured. Mum picked at her food.

'What's this? You won't drink with me either? You don't have to copy everything Mum does.'

Dad banged the table so hard I startled.

'That's enough.'

In all my years, I was hard pressed to come up with an occasion when my father lost his temper. He was the calmer, the warner, but his threatening looks never went further. In fairness, they had never needed to. Used now, it had a sobering effect.

'I'm sorry.'

'I've lost my appetite.' He stood and left the room.

As I watched him go, I couldn't think of anything to say to win him back. Without looking at her, I felt Mum's stare.

'What happened to you Dawn? Why are you nasty to me all the time?'

'I'm not nasty.'

'Do you think I don't notice?'

Yes.

'You do.' She nodded. 'You think I'm stupid. That I will just take everything you throw at me, but I'm a person too. I don't know why you don't like me. We used to be best friends.'

I opened my mouth to speak but there was nowhere to start and too much to say and I was too drunk and hungover to have that conversation. If it was anyone else, I would stay silent, I wouldn't be able to scramble the words together, I wouldn't stick up for myself no matter what they said or did to me. No one else could make me angry except my mother, who always found the perfect way to piss me off. Even now, when her questions had meant to make me feel sorry for her, to shock me into apologising, I just saw her sitting all prim, looking smug, turning her nose down at me.

'What happened to you, you mean? You sit in your wool skirts judging me. Hanging on my words and then picking everything I say apart. It's exhausting. Why can't you have your own life?'

'That's not fair.'

'Is it not? You stopped living when I was born from the sound of it.

Do you know how exhausting it is to have a mother that wants to live through her daughter? You want to know all about my life because you don't have one. Get your own and stop wanting mine because mine isn't that great at all.'

'What happened?' Mum asked, the upset gone in an instant and replaced with concern, which pissed me off even more.

I couldn't do it. I couldn't admit what my friends were like, or explain how my real life was when she needed me to be happy, needed to believe in the life she thought I had. 'Nothing. Don't worry about it. Look, I'm sorry, I can't stay, I'm going home.'

'Don't go Dawn. Let's talk about this.'

'And say what? I don't know what is going on in my head most of the time, so how are you meant to figure it out? I'm a mess.'

Mum nodded. 'Maybe stop drinking for a while.'

And there it was - the condescension.

'Like you did? So I can become a bore like you? Do you want me to sit around all day waiting for life to come to me? Well, it doesn't work like that, Mum. You have to get up and make it happen, not sit in the same room every day of your life, in the same chair, watching the same TV programs, knitting the same ugly brown jumper.'

'Dawn.'

'No. I'm sick of your rules. I'm sick of being warned when I want to say something to shut up. You've made me mute! I can't tell anyone how I feel. You and Dad have made me push everything down rather than say a word to people. Because that's what we do in this family, isn't it? God forbid we'd say anything that may offend anyone. There were so many silences growing up. The three of us lost in our own tales, reading our stories. Silence was a companion then. Until the time for talking came, and I found words wouldn't appear when they needed to, they weakened from lack of use, wasted away like an unused muscle.'

I grabbed the bottle and my bag and headed for the door.

'Wait, please.'

I stopped to see what she would say. Mum hesitated, her mouth opening and closing like the words were too big to come out. 'Your father will give you a lift home.'

The moment had gone. Mum had her chance to talk, to break open the barrier between us, to rip it in two and get to the root and dig it up and she chose not to. The fight drained from me. There was no point arguing. I would get nowhere. Mum was the only person worse than me for finding the words.

'It's fine. I need to walk. I'll hop on a bus in a while.'

'But it's getting late.'

'I'm thirty and live in the city, I can take care of myself.'

'Wait one second.' She left the room, returning with a present that she held up to me. 'I know you're a grown woman, but I still worry about you.'

'You and me both,' I said, before closing the door.

Along the waterfront, I sipped at the bottle of prosecco and followed the road, heading for Knockfarraig. As the bus took the coastal road, I figured I could wait at any of the bus stops when I ran out of steam. In Crookstown, the water ran parallel to the length of the town, but there was no beach there and right now, I needed to see sand and waves but my body had other ideas.

My calves turned into dead weights and a tiredness belted me from head to toe, and I knew I wouldn't make the ten-minute walk to Knockfarraig beach. Instead, I sat on the wall by the bus stop and, turning my back to the road, looked down at the water. It would be easy to jump in. To give up and end the constant fight. To say goodbye to this painful life. Because what was it? Where was the joy? Where was the fun?

The disastrous birthday night and the scathing words from Kristin, the gaining Ciaran and losing him all in the same few minutes, the hangover, sleeping with Jed, the taking it out on Mum and the look of disappointment from Dad, ploughed on top of me. I looked up to the sky, trying to stop my tears from spilling, aware that at any minute the bus could come, I drank from the bottle as if parched. I felt hollow. Alone, with no one on either side of the road, bolstered up with wine and prosecco, and the contemplation that I could do it, I could just end it all now, I said out loud the words I was too afraid to say to anyone.

'What do you want from me?' I roared in a voice I didn't recognise as mine. A voice I didn't think I could sound like, letting spittle splatter everywhere. Yet it still lost against the water. Everything simplified as I watched the waves crashing against the wall. My body slumped. I waited until the adrenaline settled and my breathing calmed before I spoke again.

'I can't do this anymore. I can't live like this.'

It could all be over in a minute. All the pain could stop. The drop wasn't enough to do it; it wasn't enough to kill me. I would have to hold my breath for that. I would have to let myself drown.

Could I?

I couldn't jump. There was still a part of me that wanted to hold on.

'It doesn't get better.' I whispered. 'I keep hoping it will, but it doesn't. It's all pretend. It's empty. Don't you get that? No matter how hard I try, I achieve nothing. All I do is make mistakes. I've wasted my time on the wrong people. At the wrong job. I want my life to mean something and it doesn't. Who would miss me? My parents, but all I give them is worry. Ciaran maybe. What kind of life is that? I know what I am, what everyone sees me as. I am expendable. I'm weak and a coward. I am insignificant. I am miserable.'

My eyes followed a ripple in the water to a seagull floating on the surface. 'I want more. Wasn't I meant to do more?'

Saying the things I'd been holding on to for a long time, years even, helped. Although no one else had heard me, I got it out. I would not die that day.

A text beeped from Ciaran:

She was wrong. You never treated me badly. You've always been a friend. My best friend. I don't want to lose you.

A hysterical laugh escaped from me. If I had jumped a few seconds ago, I would never have seen that.

I don't know how you can keep me. Kristin hates me. I don't want to ruin things between you.

Had war with her, up all night fighting. She'll come round, don't worry. I'm outside your apartment, but there's no answer.

He still cared.

Back home. Had to get some space.

Straight after I sent mine, he sent another.

I'm here when you need me. Are you OK?

Not really, no.

Can we talk when you get back?

It's all so messy, Ciaran. I need time to figure things out. Give me time. I'll ring when I'm ready.

When the bus arrived, I hid down the back, avoiding all eye glances. Once home, I climbed into bed and stayed there until it was time to get up for work the next day. *The gloom* was officially there.

Jog

Work, home, bed, work. That was life for a week. No one rang. Even Ciaran didn't text, and I couldn't muster up the energy to message him. Everyone blanked me except Mum, who I diverted each time.

I immersed in work and completed everything that was thrown at me. Kristin shoved past me without a word when I took over her shift. What greeted me each day was a mess, so much so, I wondered how she got away with it from Greene. I wouldn't be the one to say anything.

Jill got a kick out of calling me out of the deli and giving me the dirtiest jobs possible; the jobs that were never meant for deli staff. If someone messed up the toilet. If the drains clogged. When the difficult customers arrived, she sent them straight to me or called me on the intercom. 'Dawn needed on floor two' became a common sound. There were no protestations. A quietness quieter than I had been before came over me, a quietness that rendered me voiceless because words didn't matter, words only got me in trouble. I took my new manager's goading and the extra work Kristin left with a smile, and hated myself for it.

Being without friends made the nights longer and quieter and instead of ignoring it or drinking, I sat in my silence. There had to be a reason for all this, but for the life of me, I couldn't work out what it could be.

There were years in my life that if I compartmentalised them into chapters in a book, I would have titled them, 'Wasting'. A decade of drinking and late nights. Of rolling out of bed hung over just to go to work and after, lying on the sofa to watch unchallenging TV. Being swayed whichever way life swayed me. Directionless and knowing it. Feeling it. There was always an undercurrent of panic, a nagging that I should do something, that I was wasting my life, but what? I had no want for a particular career, no confidence to back up an idea, no talent to speak of. I was stuck, and I knew I was stuck, but had no clue how to fix it.

My friends had served what I needed in my twenties and fulfilled the requirements. They were drinking buddies, which meant fun nights and company, and it hadn't mattered that the relationships always felt more on the surface and lacked meaningful, deep conversations. At thirty, I couldn't shift the feeling I needed more.

A week and a day after my parent's dinner, I woke up sober and with a different mindset. Instead of reaching for the drink the night before, it was the first Sunday in ten years that I woke with a clear head. A clear head made everything clearer. A bird sang outside my window, calling me to get up, to seize the day. My eyes snapped open and with it came a decision. I was tired of being sad and couldn't wait any longer for some miracle to change my life, like I asked for as I sat on the wall in Crookstown. Nothing had changed, if anything, life had become worse.

There was nothing coming to save me, and if I wanted my life to change, I would need to be my saviour; I would save my own life.

Whipping the duvet away, I leapt from the bed and charged to the mirror. In my t-shirt worn for bed, a slight wobble showed through the sheer white fabric. My change would start with my health. That could be immediate, something I could do straight away and see results from if I committed to some form of exercise each day. Apart from the physical toll from work that left me exhausted, and not having a car which meant I walked everywhere, I didn't do any exercise. It hadn't been like that in Crookstown. Growing up beside a beach had insisted on fitness. The walk sniffing in sea air and dipping my feet into cold water always helped clear my problems away.

So, fitness was in and false friends were out. I brushed my hair back into a ponytail and opened the curtains. Even though it was early and the air was cool, the sun was already shining outside. With no excuses, I changed without thinking, into a worn out five-year-old pair of jogging pants tucked away at the bottom of my wardrobe. Keeping the t-shirt on, I threw on a fleece jumper, reasoning I could wrap it around my waist if I got too hot. The lack of running shoes was an obstacle, but I didn't let it deter me; I could buy some later when the shops opened; my flat shoes for work would have to do. Grabbing my keys, wallet, earphones, and phone, I left the house quickly so I wouldn't talk myself out of it. With a deep breath and no direct route, at first, I just walked to warm up, heading towards the bridge in front of my apartment and the street ahead that led to Patrick Street. Town was quiet; it always was on a Sunday morning, when the shops wouldn't open until twelve. It was rare for me to be out this early, or if I was, it was coming home rather than going to. There was an eeriness to the streets, I couldn't shake the feeling like there was something wrong, like I'd snuck outside when I shouldn't, seeing the city when it didn't want me to, when it wasn't ready to be seen or betraying the thought of it somehow, cheating on the memory I remembered. But wasn't it true that a place could be different things to different people? I picked up the pace and turned my walk into a jog, hoping to shift the fear. Couldn't this be a runner's nirvana? The streets to themselves, alone with only the occasional passing car and my thoughts. I inserted my earphones and cut the noise from the outside world, selecting a fast song, with a tune that built up to a crescendo that I hoped would encourage me to move fast.

My feet hit the pavement as if bare; those work shoes would have to go, they weren't sturdy enough on the uneven cobbles. After a few seconds, I got a flow going. The river by my side made it the perfect setting. I smiled. I was going to do it, I was going to get fit.

Each leg pounded on the ground as I found a rhythm. The motion sent a shock up my body. It felt good to do something, anything, to aim for a goal and reach it. Each step further made it clearer; if I just made the effort, if I ran every day, I would grow stronger.

As I passed the second bridge, I promised to sort my life out. The world was open to possibility and from now on I was going to grab opportunity with both hands. I could see the steps I needed to make, and the path laid out in front of me in a clear line. After a few weeks of getting fit, I would tackle Greene again. If I worked on my confidence from the outside in, maybe I could work up the courage to stand up to him and Jill. If I wrote all I'd helped with throughout the years and practiced what to say, the time would come when I was ready to return to his office and tell him. There would be no shaky voice or no forgotten words and when I spoke, my voice would travel to his ears and the tone would demand he respect me. I would show him I could have authority. I would show him I could be who he wanted.

I upped the pace; the air swooshed past me, my heart thumped with the surge of adrenalin. It had been a long time since I'd ran, not since school at least. I'd forgotten the freedom, the lightness of my body, and the energy it gave. The river sparkled in applause for my new venture, each flicker of sunlight like silent claps on the surface. The end of the road led to a crossroads, a left turn onto the last bridge or a right turn for a curved slip road. Seeing the bridge had several people sitting on the bench just beside it, I turned right to avoid them. Caught up in my thoughts of my new life, I didn't contemplate the turn, didn't think for one second about the road I'd turned to run into. A road that wasn't a road but an alley, a particular alley I would always avoid. An alley known as a spot for drug dealing. It was only when I was already halfway down and saw the shoes hanging off the electricity line above and the swastika graffiti sign on the wall that I was alerted. It was the same alley I crossed to the other side of the street if I walked by at night. The same place I saw the girls stood at the corner, hiding behind shadows, eyeing for business. I kept running, not wanting to stop halfway and turn back, deciding the other end was nearer. Yet the feeling in my stomach changed to fear, a gut feeling, giving off a low warning in the pit of me, enough to make me pull out my ear phones but it was too late. My new attitude, coupled with the sun, had made me braver, but it had also distracted me from the things I should be wary of. As I saw a flicker of a person emerging from the shadows, I realised I had run towards that alley full of hope, and been blind to my surroundings. Even then, I wasn't ready for what would happen next. I couldn't imagine I wouldn't come out of that alley the same or what would happen next would be life changing. We never know though, do we? We never know when something is going to come and upend our world.

The Long Walk

It was the concrete that woke me, cold and wrong against my skin; the years of layered urine making its own brand of smelling salts. When I opened my eyes, I didn't recognise the images. The decaying, window smashed, graffiti covered buildings towered over. They hung above, unsettled, giving the impression they could collapse at any moment. At first, I didn't remember how I'd ended up on the floor. The bright sky was all wrong. Why was I waking up here? There was a slight, sweet reprieve before the pain and painful images came.

I slid my hand down to my legs and nearly cried in relief that my clothes were still intact. My head hurt where my hair had been yanked out of my scalp from behind. My face throbbed from the punches. My head hadn't taken the impact from the fall, it was the pain in my back that burned from that. Laying face up, I was afraid to look around in case the man was still there. My legs were splayed in funny angles from being thrown on the ground. I tried to straighten them, but a searing pain ran through my back and down my leg.

I tried to lift myself but I couldn't move.

Get up. It isn't safe to stay.

My phone and earphones were gone, taking with it the opportunity to ring anyone for help. The thought of the man coming back, of him appearing again from one of the shadowed doorways and finishing what he started made me move.

His eyes.

I touched my face to access the damage. One eye had swollen and forced closed already. The arm movement wafted a smell of urine that burned inside my nostrils and brought bile up my throat. I touched my jumper; it was sopping wet on the front.

He pissed on me.

A pain as strong and as shocking as an electric current ran from my ankle to the left cheek of my bottom. This wasn't the time for tears. I was never so glad to open the hidden pouch on the inside of my fleece and touch the cold metal of my house key, small enough to not notice, placed there to stop the key from jiggling around while running and being lost than for any other reason. Everything else was gone. I tried moving my feet, tentatively tapping the ground. Movement was possible. Next, I wiggled my fingers; my arms could lift, but then I moved too much, and a noise came out of me like an animal, primal and defensive. The pain was strong enough to pass out from. It would be easy to close my eyes. Yet somehow I knew it would only get worse the longer I stayed still, that unless I kept moving, I would get too inflamed or seize up. Or he could come back.

What are you going to do Dawn?

What could I do? I accessed my body. The worst pain was coming from my lower back above my hip. Lifting each side was impossible, even a millimetre of movement brought the flash of agony. Something was wrong there; I would have to work around it. I ran through what body parts were workable. As long as I kept my back to the ground, my limbs could move. If I rolled onto my stomach, I could move my legs and arms into a standing position. A rustling from the far end of the alley made me move. Pure panic kicked me into action.

Keeping my back poker straight, I pushed off the floor with my left arm, shifting my body onto its side. The pain ripped through me and for a second, I caught my breath, trying to stop from passing out. The rustling moved nearer. With all my weight, I tipped until gravity took over. My arms caught the impact before my body hit the floor, but not enough to stop me from crying out. For a second, the pain was worse than what any man could do to me. It took a minute to regulate my breathing. I closed my eyes and unconsciousness threatened.

I could taste the piss; better than any alarm, it was strong enough to keep me awake. I inched my legs up, up, up along the concrete floor until my knees touched ground in a kneeling position, but as much as I tried, I couldn't straighten. The muscles in my back had tightened, like an elastic band wound around a finger, turning unmoveable. I pushed my hands straight and raised until I was on all fours. Moving one hand, I followed it with a knee, doing the same on the other side in an awkward crawl. The movements had to be small enough to keep my back straight, confirmed by the tweaks of warning that ran through me if I even made a slight sway off course. The rustling got nearer. What if he was just watching me? What if he was just waiting until I was on my feet again? I couldn't look, instead I sped up and bit down on my lip to keep from screaming or fainting and shuffled one hand, then the other, one knee at a time, until my forehead rested on the concrete of a building. Sweat ran down my face and neck, pooling in my breasts. Still on all fours, I lifted my right arm and felt around the wall for any groove or chance to pull up to standing. I caught hold of a cobwebbed ridge, its soft cotton wool resemblance so welcome I let out one sob and, using the ridge as an anchor, I tipped back and moved my knees to a crab position. Standing, I couldn't help but roar. Someone shouted from the other side of the alley.

Get out now.

The bones in my lower back welded together. Stiff and unbending, it was as if a poker replaced my spine, but no matter what, I couldn't stay in the alley. Snot and tears and blood expelled from my face. Sweat ran down the back of my neck and my underarms from the effort of putting one foot in front of the other. The river Lee came into sight and it took all my strength to hold it together and not cry out or collapse when I saw a group of teenagers around a bench. One of them, a girl, looked in my direction. She said something to the others and left the group, running towards me.

'Are you OK?'

'I hurt my back.'

'Yeah. And the rest.'

With only one open eye, whether from the shock or just relief, I took in everything around me, the river and the sky seemed more vivid, every detail around me popped, the girl looked like she glowed. She had gold hooped earrings and a nose piercing. An open white bomber jacket with a crop top underneath that showed off her flat, perfect stomach. It was the outfit of youth, before drink or babies or gravity took a figure, my thoughts drifted, becoming floaty. It was an outfit I would have worn.

The girl waved her phone at me to get my attention. 'Will I call an ambulance?'

'No.' The last thing I needed now was a load of questions. 'I just need to lie down. My apartment's on Lear Street. Could you help me get home?'

'Sure,' the girl said, as if it was understandable to not want to get services involved. She looked back once at the other teens who craned into their phones or faced the river and pretended there was something else more important to do on the bench.

The stares of strangers didn't bother me. For once, I didn't care what I looked like or the attention I brought, all I wanted was to go home. Instead of worrying, I used what scrap of effort I had left to let the girl catch and drape my arm around her shoulder. Up close, she smelt of lip gloss and despite the heavy eyeliner, she must have been no older than sixteen.

'Thank you for this,' I said.

The girl just nodded. Every step was conscious and braced for. My apartment, in the distance, never seemed as far away. The girl stopped. 'Wait a sec.'

I had no choice; I wouldn't make it without help. The girl turned in the bench's direction and whistled. She pointed at me and shouted. 'A little help here, guys.'

Two lads shifted, deciding, but then walked over. At a guess, they were seventeen. They walked with a swagger, a ready for a fight expression, which if it had been in any other scenario would have caused me to run the other way.

'What's up?' The taller, stronger guy asked.

'Wilkie, help her get to the end of the road. Her apartment's over there.'

Wilkie shrugged and slipped his arm around my back, tucking it under my armpit. The other guy put his hands in his pockets and rocked back. 'Looks like the two of you got this.'

'Thanks, Laney,' the girl said, full of sarcasm. She replicated Wilkie's actions and once in position, both their arms raised me a little, taking the pressure off my legs and back. The relief made me want to kiss them.

'What happened?' Wilkie asked.

'She came from the alley,' the girl answered.

Wilkie made a sucking noise. 'You went down there? That's well dodgy.'

'I went for a run.'

'Why down there, though?' The girl shook her head.

I was too sore to blush. 'Because I'm stupid.'

They carried me in silence past the second bridge, then the first, only stopping at the end of the pavement across from my apartment and waited for the traffic lights.

'It's the blue door across there,' I said.

The green man flashed to walk and, knowing they would have only a minute to get across, they picked up the speed. My body screamed in protest and halfway through, my legs buckled in pain. The girl and Wilkie caught me and without having to say anything, with no need for speech or any instruction, they both raised their arms and hoisted me until I glided across the road; my feet, as pointed as a ballerina's, scraped the floor. At the other side they put me down, acting unbothered but their chests raised and dropped after the extra effort.

'Can you walk with us the rest of the way?' The girl asked.

I nodded, too wiped out to speak. The walk was slow. They said nothing more either, the awkwardness of three strangers being forced together, holding and helping a battered woman struck us all silent. I saw the sliding glances of passersby and figured I must look worse than I even felt, but I didn't have the energy to feel anything. I needed all my strength to get through it. When we reached the door, they didn't let go.

'Where are your keys? Can you reach or do you need me to get them for you?' The girl asked.

'I can manage, thanks.'

I tried to think of a way to thank them for what they had just done. These teenagers, who probably got grief everywhere they turned, who couldn't do right by parents, who teachers gave out about, looked down on by passers-by, yet were now my saviour. 'Can I give ye something? I have no cash on me. If you want to come up to the apartment, I'll give you some? I don't think I'd make it back down here.'

'Nah, we're grand,' she said.

'We better get back,' Wilkie pointed over to where we'd started and walked away, desperate to remove himself from the uncomfortable situation.

'Thank you,' I called to him.

'No bother,' he shrugged, and I saw the boy still in him then. He strolled away, then ran when the lights turned.

The girl retreated, but hesitated and took a step back. 'How will you manage? Is it far inside, like?'

'There's a lift. I'll be grand.'

'You sure you don't need a hand? Or for us to call the guards?'

'You didn't see anyone come out of there? Before me, I mean?' I asked.

'I've only been there ten minutes. I saw you come out, but no one else.' She glanced back, even though the bench was too far away to see.

'You could have just left me, others would have.'

The girl shrugged it off. 'Gave me something to do. It was boring there anyway.'

I remembered the years I spent in my teens hanging around. Waiting for a life to begin. I'd love to tell her it got better, but all the girl had to do was look at me to know that wasn't the case.

'I better go,' she said, embarrassed. Her walk turned into a run, and I didn't blame her for wanting to break free. If I could, I would run away too.

Closing the door took effort. I leant against it to regain my strength. The lift had a handwritten A4 stuck to it.

Lift broken.

Course it did. I surveyed the Everest that hovered above.

One step at a time. You are safe now.

I worked out the hard way that keeping my back as straight as possible, at a bent 75 degree angle, was better than any other position. Sliding my arm as far as it would go up the metal banister, I used it to harness my body weight, then lifted one leg, the least painful one, onto the next step. It took a moment to rally back and brace myself for the next, then I hoisted the other one. A bare touch of the step brought the pain. White dots floated in front of my eyes, warning of the potential to pass out. Time left me on those stairs. Instead, seconds and minutes broke down to every movement, every step its own mountain, taking every bit of concentration. If you'd timed the haul from the bottom to the top, it must have taken over an hour to reach the end of thirteen steps, but it took much more than time from me. When I reached the top, there was nothing left in me for trying to stand. All I could do was shuffle on all fours again like I did in that alley, like I'd regressed to a baby, like a dog. When I made the door, I didn't care who heard, I let the bawling come. By the time the key turned in the lock and I crawled through the hall, there was no question of what room I would end up in. All I wanted was my bed. It didn't matter that the snot and tears and piss would seep into my sheets and pillow, or that the guy who did this to me would have more chance to get away if I didn't ring the guards straight away. I didn't care about any of that. What I needed was a break from the pain. There was just no more energy left in me to fight passing out. My body gave up before I closed my eyes.

Sheets

I woke in the middle of the night to the image of a man I had no wish to see. Opening my eyes brought me back to the room, which was night time dark, meaning I must have slept for at least twelve hours. My mouth was parched. My face throbbed. Every cell and surface ached, and movement was impossible. It felt like a car had hit me. Maybe there was something more serious at play, maybe I'd hit my head and needed to go to the hospital, but the pain and tiredness won out to movement. Even trying to lift my head was too much. Thirst lost to staying in bed. I cried in the dark, and by angling my head, I let the tears run into my mouth.

The night was long and sleep didn't come again. By the time the morning arrived, I had no choice but to ring the doctor. With no phone, I lay awake, trying to work out a way to contact the clinic. Walking there wasn't an option, even though his surgery was only a few streets away, the bathroom in my apartment was too far, let alone there. I spotted my laptop. I could email someone, but I didn't what to explain what happened to the clinic.

The first person that came to mind was the only person I wanted. Ciaran. My parents would come in a heartbeat but telling them would cost too much; I couldn't cope with their pain from seeing me this way, on top of everything else I was trying to process. I ran through the list of other people I knew. There was not one of them I would ask or want in the room with me.

The doctor wasn't that far. Maybe I could get there, I could deal with people seeing my face. I tried to shift my position in the bed and nearly vomited from the violent spasm. I was staying.

Ciaran was my only option. I reached my bedside locker and said a silent thanks to the show I had watched two nights ago, as it meant I had left my laptop there.

I typed a message without overthinking:

I know things are awkward between us, but I need your help. I injured my back and need a doctor asap but I can't walk to the surgery. My phone is gone. I go to Cork Medical Practice on Oliver Plunkett St. Can you ring them and see if they'll do a call out or something?

Labelling the email urgent, I pressed send. Within seconds, there was a reply.

I'll sort it. Rest up and I'll see you soon.

I lay my head on the pillow. It was true, Ciaran would sort it. Even with everything that had happened, he would be there for me.

The pain took me to another place, similar to what I thought drugs must do, must bring you to or feel like. A throbbing covered my whole body, from my pulsing clogged nose to my swollen, unopen eye which stung like a million tiny needles piercing my eyeball. My knees burned against the sheet, from where they scraped against glass and pebbles to get to a wall, any wall and get away from whoever was coming, but I didn't have the strength to pull the cover back to examine them. And then there were the images, the things I didn't want to see, the sensations I didn't want to feel. The flash of eyes, the smell of urine, the fear of what he might do, the sad discovery that another human could do that to someone.

Please Dawn, please sleep.

The only way was to give in. I let the pain take over, from my fingertips to my toes, to envelop me in its fullness, until it covered the entirety of me and pushed me out of my being. And then I was floating, floating away, and it let me drift.

A knock at the door woke me. 'Dawn? Are you there?' I lifted my head. Ciaran.

To my shame, my first thought was about how I looked. Despite the pain I was in, the state of me was my priority.

'I have Kristin's key. Can I let myself in?' He shouted.

I laughed at the irony of their relationship helping me. 'Yes,' I shouted back, whelping at the pain from moving.

And then he was there, striding towards me, then next to me, his eyes wide in shock.

'I'm sorry Ciaran.'

He sat on the bed, on the edge, afraid his movement would trigger pain. He hovered his finger in the air for a second, then stroked my battered face along the jawline.

That gesture, that touch, unleashed everything I had tried to hold together. The relief from seeing him, my best friend, of him still caring, of him still wanting to be around me, made everything matter. I folded into him, not caring how sore it was. He cradled my face so he could see me.

'Your eye.'

I covered my closed eye. 'It's not the worst. My back is giving me the most trouble.'

'What happened?'

'I ran down the wrong street.' Tears brimmed. It was too much to say.

'It's OK. Everything is going to be OK,' he said, and then he lay his head just beside mine on the pillow and placed his arm around my sore body, a hug soft enough that it said multitudes: he cared enough not to be rough, that he was there for me. I smelt him, inhaling him, a mixture of mint and a cologne that was pure Ciaran, a smell that had the same effect as a whip of wind at the beach. It brought me to my senses, it brought me home. I didn't want him to let go.

'Whatever has happened, I'm here. You won't be alone. OK?'

'I can't move,' I said. Those words ripped something inside me, and I couldn't stop the tears. There was silence from him. My sobs echoed back against Ciaran's skin.

'I'm sorry.' My voice cracked. 'I'm just in so much pain.'

He took out a paper bag from his pocket. 'I have drugs. The doctor told me what to get. He said if it's a back spasm the best thing you can do is rest, take the painkillers and he'll see you when it eases, but I didn't realise you're more hurt than that.' Ciaran sat up. 'Give me a second.'

He left the room, and I listened to the sound of opening presses and pouring water, of popping tablets from a sleeve. He came back with a glass of water and a hand splayed out, like an offering, with two bright white tablets that glowed with the promise of resurrection, in the middle of his palm. I tried to sit up and winced.

'Wait,' he said, cupping the back of my head so my face tilted. He placed the tablets in my mouth and touched the glass against my lips. Cold water caressed my tongue. He didn't flood my mouth, only giving enough to cover the tablets. I let them wash away, hitting the back of my throat, and swallowed.

'That will help,' he said, placing my head gently back down on the pillow, slipping his hand away.

'Sleep now,' he said, stroking my hair. The repetitive movement as effective as a lullaby, I needed no more instruction. I closed my eyes.

* * *

The pain was different when I woke. It was hazy and closed inwards, tunnelling my vision. My eye didn't help; it had swollen to a slit.

My lips were cracked from dehydration and my nose throbbed and I wondered with a distant thought whether it was broken. I heard a one-sided conversation coming from the other room. Ciaran's voice spoke in mumbles at first, then raised louder. I caught some of what they said. 'I won't... she needs me... she's meant to be your friend too... I don't know Kristin, as long as it takes.'

I picked at my duvet, then seeing the glass of water from earlier on my bedside locker, pushed myself up on two hands until I was sitting, the painkillers made movement possible but still noise escaped from me, my body betraying my constant need for silence. The other room fell quiet, and then Ciaran spoke again. 'Look, I've got to go. I'll ring you when I know more.'

I took a drink of water, coating my parched tongue. I punched out two more painkillers even though the required four hours between mustn't be up. The stagnant water slid the tablets down my throat, and I smiled at Ciaran as he entered my bedroom.

'How's the patient?'

'Embarrassed. Guilty.'

'For what?'

'You wouldn't be fighting with Kristin if you weren't here.'

Ciaran's brows knitted together. 'Kristin needs to remember you were friends with both of us before me and her. And embarrassed? You're forgetting I grew up with you. I've seen you with braces and spots or when you couldn't stand up after a naggin of donkey's ass.'

'Don't remind me.' I snorted, then regretted the movement. 'It is my fault. I shouldn't have put you in this situation.'

'I'm glad you did.' He took my hand in his. 'What happened?'

'I can't.'

'Were you drinking?'

It was a plausible question. Still, it stung enough to make me take my hand away from his. 'No, it happened yesterday morning, when I was out for a run.'

'What? Did someone do that to you?'

I nodded. I couldn't meet his eyes and see how that answer would affect him. 'Jesus, did you go to the guards?'

'I couldn't even walk. The guy took my phone.'

'Did he... did he?'

'No,' I said, cutting in. 'Please Ciaran, I can't.' My voice cracked.

'I want to hug you, but I'm afraid I'll hurt you.'

'Then I'll hug you.'

In his arms, I broke. I cried for the pain that ramped up in my back again despite the extra painkillers, and for the unfairness of what had happened to me, I cried for the fact he loved me enough to drop everything to help me out and for the release of telling someone because that made the attack real. Most of all, I cried because of how right it felt to be in his arms, knowing it was too late.

We held each other for a long time, long enough to let the extra tablets kick in. By the time we broke apart, my head was lolling and felt wobbly on my neck. My arms and legs felt heavy. Sleep was calling again, but I had other pressing matters first.

'Ciaran?'

'Yeah?' he said, his face hovering so close to mine I could see the fullness of his lips, the stubble on his chin, the worry in his eyes.

'I really need the bathroom.'

He straightened, got off the bed, put his hands on his hips. 'Right. Let's do this. How are we going to do this? Is standing worse than sitting?'

'Yes.'

'Right then.' He knelt one knee on the bed. 'Put your arms around my neck.'

'Ciaran.'

'Just do it. It's not like I'm proposing or anything.'

I didn't move.

'Trust me, Dawn.'

Ciaran stood as close to me as was possible and, with tentative, slow movement, I wrapped my arms around his neck. He slid his arm under my upper thighs and lifted me as gentle as if he was carrying a baby. Cradled into his body, I didn't feel any spasms. His grip was steady, and he carried me to the bathroom without a struggle.

'I'm sorry, I'm too heavy.'

'You're not. You're perfect.' He stopped to look at me. I could tell he was going to say something, something irreversible.

'I'm going to wet myself if you don't hurry.'

He lowered me by the toilet bowl and hovered, 'Do you need me to pull down your underwear?'

'No, this is degrading enough, thanks.'

'Call out when you're ready.'

After spending far too long trying to get my trousers back on, my fingers looped the waistband. It moved up a fraction and then loosened from my grip. My breathing was heavy and laboured and it took me a second to try again. This time, my two fingers pinched the material and, in one go, pulled it up to my thighs. The pain from standing would be worth Ciaran not seeing me naked. With one hand holding the sink and the other behind me on the seat, I pushed my body to standing, then hovered and pulled the material up. I didn't shout out. The desire for Ciaran not to rush in and see me was greater than even the pain.

'Ready,' I called out.

As Ciaran scooped me up again, I likened it to transporting a precious, fragile gift. Any other time, if I so much as shifted position, it would unleash a pain on me that would make me cry out, but not a sound escaped me in his arms.

'Do you want to sit in the living room or is bed better? At least there you can sleep if you need to.'

'If I sit, I might not get back up. Lying I can manage.'

'Bed it is,' he said.

He lay me down on the bed as if he was depositing me on cotton wool.

'Hold on,' he said and disappeared out of the room. He came back a few seconds later with some cushions.

'I'm going to put one of these under your knees,' he said, slipping his hand under the gap between my knees and the bed, raising them a fraction which caused a spasm, but he stuffed a cushion under which helped.

'This one I want you to place between your knees.' He handed me another cushion, and I did as told.

'How do you know all this?'

'Done an internet search while you were asleep. It's when you try to bend the pain will come.'

'Good to know.'

He folded his arms. 'Now we have to get you out of those clothes.'

'No, we don't.'

'Your knees are messed up and you're covered in muck and I hate to say, but you smell.'

'It's not my smell. It's from the alley I fell in.'

Because he used me as a toilet.

'Where do you keep your clothes? Something that will pull over your head easy.'

'There's a shirt type pyjamas in the second drawer next to the wardrobe.'

Ciaran busied himself, pulling tops out of the drawer, then after selecting the right one, he walked out of the room, coming back with a bowl of water and a sponge in his hand. He set it on the floor and left again. Then returned with a towel.

'What are you doing?'

'I take it you're too sore to stand in the shower, so we'll make do with a poor man's wash.'

'Ciaran, it's fine, I'll do it later. I've taken up enough of your time.'

'Shush.' he said, sitting carefully on the edge of the bed. 'Let me take care of you, Dawn.' He squeezed the sponge. 'Close your eyes.'

With soft strokes, he wiped the grit away from my face. The warm water soothed my puffy skin. He unzipped my fleece and first, pulling my arms free, then stretching the neck of it wide, slipped the jumper off me without touching my face.

He looked at my t-shirt. 'Is that a favourite?'

A man I'd never forget flashed in front of me.

'I'll never wear it again.'

He nodded and left the room. I heard him pulling at drawers in the kitchen and he reappeared with a pair of scissors. Carefully, he snipped the neck on both sides, cutting until he reached the sleeves, and the t-shirt fell away into two halves. Unlike in the bathroom, he didn't avert his eyes from my body. He dipped the sponge in the water and cleaned my chest in circular motions, only stopping when he reached my bra, then worked down my arms, dabbing them dry with the towel. Holding me at the front, he tipped me slightly forward to slip the shirt behind my back.

'Oh Dawn, you're all bruised.'

'Don't worry.'

He tied my buttons as if I were a child, his breath and body closer to mine than it had been in years but he didn't stop there, he rolled down my leggings and cleaned my knees, working methodically, dabbing and stroking with precision and care. Once finished, he kissed my right knee and, cradling one foot in his hands, he slipped the pyjama pants over it, then did the same with the other foot, pulling them until they reached my bottom. In all other circumstances, I would have a different reaction to where his hands lay, but the pain meant sex was the furthest thing from my mind. Ciaran held out his hand. 'Grab hold of me and lift your bum.'

I did as told, crying out, and Ciaran pulled the pants up into the right position.

'Thank you,' I said, my eyes watering.

'You would have done the same for me.'

'I don't think I would have had as much luck carrying you, though.'

'You would have still tried.'

He ran his finger along my hand. It sent currents up my arm.

'Ciaran, I'm sorry.'

'You have nothing to be sorry for. I'm sorry I didn't tell them all to fuck off that night. We can talk about that later when you're not so out of it. Let's get the pain sorted first. Why didn't you ring me after it happened?'

'Because I'm not your problem. And I didn't have a phone.'

'I forgot. You do.' He rummaged in his pocket and pulled out a phone. 'It's only a cheap ready to go I had around the house, but at least you'll have a way of contacting people. The number is on the back there. I've put my number in and added credit.' He let the bag go on the bed and sat next to me. His next words came out full of concern. 'You were never a problem.'

'Tell that to Kristin.'

'Ignore Kristin. I want you in my life.'

'You say ignore her, but you love her, don't you?'

Ciaran looked distraught. I didn't wait for an answer.

'Which means I can't be around you. She won't let it go. I won't be the reason you fight.'

'What do you want, Dawn?' His eyes searched mine for the answer and I knew if I leant forward, or if I asked him to kiss me, he would. But I couldn't do that to Kristin. It wasn't the way a relationship should start. What if he was just caught up in the moment? If seeing me this way made him protective, igniting the need to soften my pain, to soothe me with love. I'd never know if we only got together through pity.

'Did you mean what you said on your birthday? About how you felt about me?'

Whether it was from the medication or the blanket of pain that shrouded my thoughts, something made the future flash before me. If I answered yes, Ciaran would draw me to him and would kiss away my tears and I would get everything I ever wanted. If I said no, a line would cross, never to be passed over again. I would hurt Ciaran, and I would be a liar, too. But I was too drugged and too sore and too afraid. So I chose neither.

'I think you should go. It's not fair on Kristin.'

'I wish Kristin felt as loyal to you as you do her,' he said, moving an inch away to examine my face.

I shrugged, then winced at the movement. 'You looked happy with her that night before everything kicked off. Happier than I've ever seen you. Ye need to see where it goes and give it a chance. I'm not going to be a part of breaking ye up.'

'If there's a chance between us, though.'

He hung on my next word. A word I couldn't say. I couldn't think, couldn't talk. And then I thought I shouldn't have to. Through the haze of pain, I felt something brewing.

'Why are you doing this now?'

His body curled inwards, as if I wounded him. 'I'm sorry, it's just you wouldn't meet me, or let me ring. It's the first time you've let me talk to you.'

'My head is all over the place. I need to get my thoughts together. I need to think straight. Please go.'

'It's you I want.'

I closed my eyes. He had gone there. He had opened the door, and I either had to walk through it or slam it shut. As my body throbbed, with my head clouded, at my lowest ebb, here was Ciaran pushing me. He was always pushing me and I loved that about him, but this time, it was too far.

'There's no chance Ciaran, not now. Kristin needs your chance, not me. I fuck up everything I touch.'

'That's not true.'

I rolled my eyes. He just wasn't getting it. What could I offer him? My body was broken. Even before my back went, I was broken. If you are in pieces, another person can't mend you. Even if they are whole, even if they want to put you back together, they can't fix you. And you'll just end up chipping away at them, clawing pieces from their being, looking for yourself. I couldn't do that to Ciaran. Yet he wouldn't give up. He would want to look after me. He would want to help.

There have been many times in my life that I've known I would regret doing something beforehand, but I still did it, anyway. This was one of those times. Call it a death wish or self-sabotage or a need to feel pain or just being dumb or in this case, the influence of too many painkillers, whatever the excuse, I always made the wrong choice, flicked the wrong button, opened the wrong door, and dealt with the aftermath. Before the words left my lips, I knew I was making the biggest mistake of my life.

'Kristin was telling the truth. I used to laugh at you.'

Ciaran laughed, but his eyes were unsure. 'I know what you're doing.'

'You're wrong. You're not my type and never have been.'

He cocked his head, still smiling, but his laughter ceased. 'Stop.'

'You've seen the guys I go for. I'm sorry, but you don't measure up.'

Ciaran shook his head no, but his eyes believed me.

'Kristin wasn't lying. I did say I'd puke at the idea of being with you. The very thought of us disgusts me.'

To the day I die, I'll never forget his expression, a contorted mixture of confusion and pain. His jaw slackened and his face softened to a droop. He looked at me for a long time, waiting for me to change my mind, or tell him it was a joke. I hardened my features and met his searching with a stare.

His head turned away, getting as far away from me as possible. He stood. 'I need to leave.'

Digging his hands into his pockets, he walked to the door, but instead of opening it, he turned back. Through my open bedroom I had a direct line of view and as he walked closer, my heart quickened with the realisation I didn't want him to go, I wanted him to fight for me, to tell me he wouldn't accept it. I opened my mouth to tell him I'd lied, but how could I find the words to take away the cruel things I'd said?

He didn't look my way. Keeping his head down, he fished inside his pocket and placed something on the hall table. The spare key made a tinny clunk as it hit the wood. That key said it all. There was no coming back to the apartment, no coming back from this, Ciaran was done with me once and for all. As his hand reached for the door handle, I clasped a hand over my mouth to stop me from calling out. What would he gain if I asked him to stay? I would destroy his relationship. I would dangle our friendship on the edge just to take a chance, and with my track record, would destroy that relationship in about five days.

So, I said nothing, and I watched him leave and I waited until the door clicked before I let any sound omit from me. What came out was pure pain, worse even than what I had experienced in the alley or since, the pain came from inside my chest, deep and raw and irreparable. Only then it hit me, by lying and then saying nothing in order to keep my friendship with Kristin, I had destroyed the only one I cared about.

Answers

I sat upright in the bed for a very long time until my skin was raw from crying on bruises. For two days, I stayed in that position, falling in and out of sleep, toying with the phone and typing out a text I would never send to a man I would never tell I loved. Hours flitted past, day became night and night crept away from me and day shocked me with how fast it came around again. I kept the pills next to me and popped them every time the pain ramped up, wanting the tablets to knock me out. When I woke, I was still tired; the sleep I had was fitful and immersed in pain; with breaks in waking to a man that hurt me or of Ciaran with a look on his face like just before he left, but in the dream, he wasn't in the apartment but left me lying on the floor of the alley.

After two full days of no real relief, spurned on to action by the empty packet of painkillers on my locker, the time had come to go to the doctor.

Best intentions were one thing, action was another. It took me ten minutes to brave any movement. Every slight nudge attacked. Moving my legs brought surges of red hot burning from my lower back that blazed right down my leg to my toes. Even the slightest move was like being stabbed.

By the time I reached my kitchen I had given up all idea of cleanliness, I didn't care less about makeup or running a hairbrush through my hair, what mattered was making it to the other side of the apartment to open the door. Everything else - getting fed, showering, even brushing my teeth were secondary, nothing was being done until he prescribed some painkillers, but before even that, I would have to find the strength to get there. Holding on to the counter top, I reached up with one hand, as slow as I could, keeping my back still, until I reached the overhead cupboard. I pulled the medicine box down, hoping to find some anti-inflammatory pills left from my period, and stopped from doing a celebratory dance when I found the sleeve; there were two left. I popped them into my hand. Reaching for a glass, my lean was too enthusiastic, so my back spasmed and made me jerk and the precious pills came loose and dropped. I scanned the counter top. No sign. I stepped back and spotted one on the floor, lost to me now; there was no way I would risk bending. One could still help. On top of the scum of four-day-old dirty dish water, floated the pill.

'Forgive me,' I said and scooped it into my mouth before I could stop myself because cholera was a better option than pain. With an hour to go to the appointment, I made a cup of tea and let the medicine kick in enough to get dressed. By the time I reached the apartment door, I needed to lean against it. My skin, hot with effort, welcomed the cold stone wall.

The walk would be slow and laborious. I eyed a cab parked up, but getting in and out of the car would be harder. It was only three roads away and once I kept my back straight and steady, hoped I would find a rhythm, and my body would loosen out.

My body did not loosen out.

It was bone on bone, tight muscle straining against tighter muscle. It was burning darts and shooting stabs until my whole body felt like it was throbbing.

Once there, I cursed my stupidity. At home, I was horizontal and comfy on my mattress, so what if I had no pain medication? I hadn't figured on what to do once I reached the clinic. Two flights of steep stairs peered over me.

With more than a sense of déjà vu, I clung to the banister, hauling my body up each one, keeping my legs straight and through breaths, took each step one by one.

The clinic was one square room for a waiting area, with a receptionist sat behind a curved desk on the left and uncomfortable chairs surrounding one small coffee table on the right. It had magazines older than me splayed out on top of it. The carpet was clean but worn, my feet padded parts that were almost hard floor. The chairs were full of people. A young man held his bruised jaw. A woman shivered in the corner. An older man with frizzy hair rocked in the chair next to the only available seat. I stifled a sob as I landed on the chair by pretending to cough.

I nodded hello at the shivering woman, hoping what she had wasn't contagious. The lady gave me a tissue covered nod back. I didn't look at the rocking man.

Desperate for a distraction from the stares of the waiting room eyeing up my bruises, I scanned the coffee table. If I leant across for a magazine, there was no guarantee I'd make it back. Instead, I opened my bag and took out a book. I carried one everywhere, even though the weight of one wouldn't help my back, but for me, it was the only comfort in a sea of darkness. Since the injury, I hadn't been able to read, the pain overtaking everything. In a social situation, a book helped to cut the chance of conversation and I figured it was better to stare at a page and get nowhere than to attempt to talk.

The book often reflected my mood, and this one was no different; horror wasn't my thing, especially since living alone, but I was working my way through the thousand books to read before you die list I found on the internet and from the library pile I had on my bedside locker this one jumped out. Bram Stoker's Dracula was beautiful, in its prose but also in the underlying story; which wasn't horror at all but a love story that beat all love stories. I loved when a book did that, when I looked at a cover and thought I knew what I was getting but then as the pages turned, gems of vocabulary popped, and it guided me along a story I didn't want to end. Even though it was years before, in another age, I was proud to discover Stoker was born in Ireland. It pleased me also to find he was bedridden until the age of seven, seeing him as a kindred spirit, stuck to the bed like me. According to the article, he said the long illness gave him the opportunity for many thoughts that proved fruitful. That statement gave me hope, because if it helped Bram Stoker, maybe this injury would help me.

I selected the right page and settled in. With a book, there was always a distraction. I could get away from the pain, or ignore how long I waited or not notice the other patients as they sneezed in my direction or went in before me or stared at my bruises. With a book, I could blend into the background and melt away from the world I hated and get lost between the words.

'Dawn Moloney?'

Dr Murphy's smile was perfect. It said don't worry, I'll sort you out and brought up such powerful emotions, I had to resist from hugging him. He wore a cravat and suit even on a summer's day and oozed patience. He waited at his door while I struggled to get up from the chair.

'Well, it looks like you're after getting yourself into some fine mess.'

Holding on to the door frame, I pivoted in to the room and hobbled to the chair by his desk, biting my lip in order not to cry in front of him. Dr Murphy caught my arm and helped me to sit.

He pointed to my eye as he sat. 'Do you want to tell me what happened?'

'I fell.'

He tapped his pen against his chin.

'You hit both your face and hurt your back when you fell?'

I thought about lying. Speaking about what happened made it real, but he needed all the facts. I looked away from him before I spoke.

'I was attacked. A stranger grabbed me by the hair and pulled me onto the floor. He punched me in the face and robbed me.' I stopped, not able to say anymore.

Dr Murphy pursed his lips together, closing his eyes and nodding, he sat back in his chair as if the thought of it hurt him. He went back to tapping the pen on his chin. 'I'm sorry Dawn. That must have been very frightening. Have you contacted the police?'

'What's the point?'

Dr Murphy stopped tapping and eyed me with such scrutiny it demanded I meet his look.

'He may do it to someone else.'

I nodded and examined my hands, hoping he would pick up the sign to drop it.

'Have you had any loss of vision? Any dizziness?'

'I've felt like passing out, more from the pain in my back, I think.'

His fingertips padded my scalp, barely making contact.

'Did you hit your head?'

'I don't think so. My head is sore from where he pulled my hair. It doesn't feel like I got a bang.'

'There are no bumps or cuts. Does it hurt to bend?'

'That's when it's the worst.'

'Where do you feel the pain?'

'Everywhere.'

'Is there a source? A place it feels it originates from, or is more intense?'

'Right here,' I said, pointing to the middle of my left side. 'On my back, the same height as my hip.'

He nodded, as if that made sense.

'Standing, OK?'

'Getting up is hard. If I keep straight I can manage, if I only try for short spurts.'

'Can I touch your back? Is it too sore?'

'You can try.'

His hand only tipped against my lower back, yet a loud moan rushed out of me. His nose wrinkled, and he shot his hand away as if I'd burnt him. He helped me sit and matched my movement.

'Like I thought. For the moment, you're too inflamed to even touch, I suggest strong medication and rest. When the pain eases a little, we'll give you a more thorough examination. From what I can see, it is more bruised than broken. I'm hoping your back injury is muscular, but if the pain persists past Monday, call or drop into me and we'll examine you and get an Xray. I'm going to write you a prescription for a strong anti-inflammatory and painkiller.'

'Thanks Dr Murphy.'

'Do you have anyone, Dawn? Anyone that can drop in on you? You are going to be quite restricted in your movements for a while.'

Ciaran.

'My parents live in Crookstown.'

'Would they come for you? You could probably do with being looked after.'

'You don't know my mother.'

His eyes bore into me with concern.

'I'll ring them.'

'OK then,' he said, satisfied.

'I don't know what I should do about work. I'm meant to have a shift tomorrow.'

'What is it you do again?' He checked his computer screen.

'I work in a deli.'

'That's not feasible. You'll be on your feet all day. Just ring them and explain that I examined you and that you'll need at least a week off, two, even. I'll write you a cert now just in case they need it. Unless you have any other questions, I better keep moving, there's a clinic full of people this morning and Gemma will kill me if I run behind.' He stood and held out his arm to help me up. As he walked me to the door, in almost a whisper, he said, 'Please go to the guards.'

I shook my head.

He stopped and didn't speak until I looked at him. 'It's important for you more than anything, they have the right people to talk to, to refer for counselling.'

I looked at the floor. 'I just don't have the energy. Even the thought of standing in the station exhausts me.'

'You can ring them and they will call to your door. What if the person who did that to you has decided now they've got away with it once, they can do it all the time? What if the person they hurt isn't physically as strong as you and isn't able to get up?'

'Strong? I don't feel strong at all.'

He squeezed my arm. 'I know you're scared, but it can be a way to claw some power back from a situation you feel powerless about.'

* * *

There were two Garda stations in the city centre. One for the public, which was the one I stood in now, the one for the pleasant on the surface, mundane matters: the signing of photos for passports, the stamping of forms, or the reporting of lost property. It was high ceilinged and brightly lit with Gardaí who didn't mind their job and might smile back if you smiled at them. The other station was different. Growing up, everyone heard the rumours of what happened there – you didn't want to end up in a cell in that place for long.

The queue nearly made me turn around and give up. Only around the corner from the doctor's surgery, yet it had felt like I'd walked the length of Ireland. I eyed a bench beside the last person standing, and sat and took the pressure from my legs, not even caring anymore when I whelped on sitting, I couldn't stop it, only suppress, just reduce the noise from a yell to a whimper.

I didn't want to be there. I played around with excuses. The queue was too long, they would take ages to get through it. I was wasting my time. They would tell me I was in the wrong building. Anything I could grasp at that would be reason enough to leave. For every excuse, the doc's words counteracted.

The man could do worse to someone else. If I heard or read about someone else being attacked in that alley, I would never forgive myself. It wasn't about helping me; talking about it wouldn't help. The only reason I sat there was because it was the right thing to do.

The pain was a hot poker sticking into my bone above my left hip. Bile salivated and gathered on my tongue. I had carried it since the doctor's and it had no intention of going away. I considered going home and resting for a while or just ringing like Dr Murphy suggested, but, I knew, if I didn't do that very moment, I would put it off or talk myself out of it.

In fairness, they were ploughing through the queue; the last person was now the first person. Before anyone else came in and nabbed my spot, I pushed on.

When it was my turn and I reached the counter, I leant on it for support. The Garda was a woman, similar to my age. I felt the shame of that, how it could have been me behind that glass, if I'd made different choices, or walked down a different path. Her smile got to me. Whether it was the uniform, of the thought of safety that she represented or whether it was because of all the pain I'd been through, all the trying to keep it together, all the fear I'd felt since he done what he done, or because of all the nightmares after, staying strong waned and disappeared and not caring who saw me, I cried. In between sobs,

I got the words out.

'I want to report an assault.'

Inviting The Dark

Dr Murphy was wrong. He implied it would feel cathartic to talk to the Guards and open up about what had happened, but it didn't; coming away from the place, I felt dirty and defiled. Speaking about it hadn't helped; by talking, I had admitted my experience. It was better to shove it down; it was better to deny.

The Garda had been kind and had brought me into a room and took my statement. She had given me a card for a counsellor, suggesting she could help with trauma. I wouldn't call; I already knew what the woman would say; that it wasn't my fault, that it was just bad timing, that I'd done a good thing by coming blah, blah, blah. None of it mattered; and I did not want to hear it. I knew the mistakes I'd made; I should never have ran through that alley. It happened because I ignored my instincts and no matter what anyone said, my opinion on that wouldn't be changed.

After going to the doctor, and braving the Garda station, there was one more thing hanging over me and since I was upright and only one street away and if I was on a mission to do the right thing, I needed to go to Greene's. The first person I met was Jill, who broke out laughing when she saw me.

'Who did you piss off?'

'What?'

'What happened to your face?'

'I fell. Is Mr Greene there?'

She folded her arms, acting uninterested, but her eyes glistened with the hint of gossip. 'Why?'

'Jill, honestly, I haven't the energy to explain. Can you just get him for me?'

Jill examined her nails. 'You know where his office is.'

'I won't make it up the four floors.'

Instead of going for the phone at the back wall, Jill moved in the opposite direction, standing behind the counter, and picked up some paperwork. Right then, I hated her. I hated giving her the satisfaction of pleading for her help, but if I didn't quicken things up, I was afraid I'd faint. I laid my hands on the counter and meaning to lean towards Jill, underestimated how much it would hurt, and collapsed onto it. Even though Jill didn't look up, a smirk betrayed her disinterested stance. The girl was loving it.

'Jill, I'm about to pass out. I need to explain to him in person what's going on. Can you help me out?'

Jill's hesitation riled me. I had never treated her unfairly and been nothing but helpful. Her lack of compassion hurt and in that moment I couldn't think of one good quality the girl possessed. If I'd met anyone else on the shop floor, they would have rushed to get me a seat, then ran to get Mr Greene. Not Jill though, it all came down to whether it was of benefit to her.

Sweat beaded on my lip. I felt foolish standing there, for trying to do too much.

'Please Jill.'

It was the closest I would get to begging. Jill, pleased to have the upper hand, gave it another minute, then sighed and sloped off, going to the internal phone and ringing up. I straightened, not wanting to cause a scene, but still felt a hundred eyes on my back. Customers passed not even trying to hide their blatant stares, all checking out what was wrong with the girl hanging onto a counter with the messed up face.

Scumbag. Trouble. No smoke without fire.

They judged and wrote me off with a flick of an eye. Even though I shouldn't, I cared what those strangers thought, wanting to approach each one of them and explain I wasn't the type of person who deserved a black eye. Or the kind who hung over a counter because they couldn't stand. With one quick evaluation, they labelled me a loser and the thing was, I agreed. I had lost at everything in life and now, even my body had given up on me.

Mr Greene took forever. Jill didn't come back to the counter and after ten minutes of waiting, I wondered if the girl hadn't just left the floor to go on her lunch. It wouldn't be a surprise. Standing was making me nauseous, and there was a queue forming behind me with no staff around to deal with them. I thought about leaving, just shuffling off and ringing the shop when I got home, figuring Greene could check the cameras after, see how sore I was. But then he was there in front of me, looking concerned.

'Dawn, what happened?'

Even though our last meeting hadn't gone well, he was such a familiar face, knowing him all my adult life, I couldn't help it, the tears welled.

He looked at the queue. 'Can you walk?'

'A little.'

'Come to the side here.'

He guided me into the small returns room and rolled out a computer chair from behind a desk and a fold up chair underneath. He offered me the computer chair, and I had to look at the light to stop the tears from falling.

'Give me a second,' he said, picking up the intercom. 'Can a staff member go immediately to checkout three, please,' he boomed.

I couldn't stop the smile. No matter what, Greene's mind was always on the job.

I placed the medical cert on the table and he nodded in recognition. Mr Greene would be too stingy to supplement my pay while I took leave, or even show any thanks for my many years of service. Known for his ability to turn ruthless, from now on he would see me as surplus and as soon as I walked out of the store, no longer beneficial until I was better.

I clocked the look of relief when he heard it happened outside work, his primary concern when he saw me being whether it was something with ramifications. I knew all that, but that flash of concern, that show of care, that fraction of kindness was enough for me to crack with emotion. He listened and consoled and gave me a tissue to wipe away my tears. He rang Sheila, asking her to bring down three coffees, and stay. Sheila, the mother of the store, the woman who worked there before I was even born, held my hand as I detailed what happened, what I knew so far. Afterwards, he asked Sheila to help me home. As we walked out, with Sheila's arm around my back, supporting me, I looked around. It felt important to take the details in, as if it was the last time I would. Even if I got better overnight, even if I woke up and all my pain left, something had become irreversible about working there, something had changed and couldn't be unchanged. He would leave the job open, yet I couldn't shake the feeling that when Greene said goodbye, he was saying goodbye for good.

On the way home, on Sheila's insistence, we stopped at the super-market two doors down from the apartment and stocked up with as much alcohol as she could carry, as well as tons of ready meals, a loaf of bread, milk and cheese and a multi pack of cheap tins of tuna that would do me a week. I nearly wept when I saw the lift was working again. In my apartment, Sheila helped me into bed and, tucking me in, assured me she would put away the food and let herself out.

Free to wallow, I barely moved from the bed for days, only leaving to empty or fill myself. I entered a dark state of mind that could only be described as giving up. I didn't wash. Or want to. There was no wish to talk to anyone, and it felt good to turn off my phone. I let the dark take over and the pain complied. Pain reduces you. It reduces your world, suffocating it to a bare existence and destroying how you used to see it. Your life shrinks to restricted movements and laboured talking and disinterest. It takes you over. It doesn't seep, but is a violent visitor who pounds on your door and outstays its welcome. It won't leave, no matter how much you try to make it. No matter your resolve to force your body to get better. No matter what you wish for. The pain appears in sharp shocks; the major blows do anyway. Then the burning muscles come. The sizzle starts on the surrounding areas: down the back of the right leg, the inflamed muscle around the bum and lower back hot to the touch. It exhausts you. Makes you woozy. Makes you wonder if living is too hard to continue. Or if it was ever worth it. It amplified and grew bigger, bigger than me. It created a bubble and nothing I could do or nothing anyone else could say would penetrate or get rid of it. I hated it, yet I had never felt a love like it. A love that never left. It stayed night and day; it gripped on to me like an abusive lover, warning me if I tried to change even a small detail like what position I lay in, it would rain down on me an existence of suffering.

The drugs made me woozy, but after a few hours, I found I could walk about a little. It was hazy. My limbs took on a floaty feel, not painless, but it was a win that I could make it to the bathroom.

Drugged up days passed by in a loop of never-ending agony. The pain was still as present even though I devoured the pills as if they were sweets. The pain stayed, but caring about it vanished. I numbed to time, to eating, to the outside world. Life reduced to survival. The edges of my vision took on a black fog, seeing things through a veil. My thoughts softened and blurred until I settled into a dreamlike state, finding it hard to differentiate between day and night, or to determine between layers of sleep and wakefulness. My nightmares matched reality. There was only so much TV I could watch, yet I left it on, anyway.

There was no phone call made to my parents. I couldn't deal with Mum's judgment or worse, their pity. It would only be another thing for them to worry about, for them to see how much I failed again, and I didn't have the energy for explanations.

On the third day of being holed up, I turned on my phone and ten messages came through, each one increasing in worry. My poor mum. If I ignored her any longer, the woman would pound my door down. I sent a quick text. *Sorry mum, in bed with the flu, just going back to sleep now. Will call when feel better. Don't worry.*

On the fourth day, I stopped taking the painkillers, in part because they never took away the pain anyway and the cramps in my stomach caused only added discomfort. A warped part of me liked it. I had always been the kid who, after a fall, when the cut scabbed over, I would pick at it until the blood oozed out and the cut became raw again. For a reason, I couldn't understand, I liked to prolong the soreness.

No fresh air passed through my nostrils for days. I was glad I didn't have to go anywhere, glad that the visit to Greene's had bought me two weeks. There was paperwork for the Social Welfare to fill out and I would need to go back to the docs, but for those couple of days I didn't have to worry about any of it. I could stay in. The very thought of going out was enough to send me into a panic.

Everyone will stare at you. You'll go out and your back will lock and you won't be able to move. You'll embarrass yourself. You don't have the energy. Just stay in and get better. Just lie down and heal.

And I would lay my head back down, convinced I was helping my back, satisfied I was doing what my body wanted, even though a part of me knew I was giving up.

Night time was different. From sleeping during the day, I was wide awake and being awake brought the images I didn't want to see. It brought the fear of what had happened back, of him finding out what I said to the guards and where I lived and turning up to finish off what he started. It was the perfect excuse to open a bottle; the wine going down all too easy. It helped to numb more than the painkillers. I understood why alcoholics existed if it started as pain relief.

In my apartment, a text beeped with the only number inside. Ciaran.

Can't stop thinking about you. I'm worried you haven't asked anyone for help and are wasting away with no food or painkillers. What can I do?

Even after what I said, he still cared. That was Ciaran, that was the Ciaran I loved. It would be so easy to lean on him now, to let him take over and guide me to getting better, like he had done over the years. Before this injury, I would hand over my problem and Ciaran would always know the way to figure out the solution. This time was different. He couldn't do this for me, he couldn't sort it. The only person who could fix me was me. But also, I didn't have the energy to pretend anymore. To pretend that I didn't love him, or to listen to him talk about his relationship with Kristin. There was nothing left in me, I used all my energy reserves up for conversation, for enthusiasm, for wit, and now depleted, anything scraped together could only be for survival. I had to let him go.

I don't deserve your friendship. There's nothing you can do. You can't take away my pain. I have to do this on my own.

On the fifth day, I made a phone call and for the first time since the morning I ran down the wrong alley, I felt a fraction of hope.

Terri

The physio was a tiny little thing. Too small altogether to do anything substantial with my bigger frame or win against my mound of twisted, sore flesh. What she had was a likeable face and a smile that wasn't condescending and she lifted off the seat when I winced on sitting, prepared to jump up and help me. For that reason alone, I would give the dot a chance.

'Dawn, I'm Terri.'

I nodded; it was too painful to speak.

'I've looked over your notes and from what I've read, you're in a hell of a lot of pain. Can you tell me a bit about it? Between one and ten, ten being the worst, how's your level today?'

'Being optimistic, I'd say eight going on nine.'

'What we are going to do today is a stress test which involves some movement to see where you are at. Sometimes when you have pain, that isn't just where the problems lie, so I need to do a full body examination to assess.'

I nodded.

'Can you stand for me?'

She touched my hips, and I cried out.

'Can I lift your top a bit, Dawn?'

'Yes.'

'There's still a lot of bruising there.' Her touch was light, yet it may as well have been a karate chop. I grimaced.

'Is the pain higher or lower?'

'Both.'

Thumbs pressed on the skin below, moving along the top of my bottom. There was no way to stop the tears, they were involuntary reactions. As Terri's hands kneaded along on either side of my spine, my legs buckled. Terri caught me.

'You're OK, I've got you. That part's over now. Do you think you can walk?'

'Slowly.'

'Walk as slow as you like. It doesn't have to be much. Say ten steps forward.'

Ten steps might not be much for you, but it's a marathon for me.

I did as asked. Terri touching my back had set my skin alight, and each step caused waves of torture through my joints. As I neared the door, I resisted the urge to open it and go straight home.

'Almost there. Can I get you to sit on the bed? I want to check your reflexes.'

It was a relief to sit.

'Right. Can you lay down?'

'I might need your help.'

'That's what I'm here for. Try first yourself, as I want to watch how you manage, how your body reacts.'

'Do you want me on my stomach or back?'

'Stomach, please.'

'OK, here goes. It may take a while.'

Keeping my back as straight as I could, I grabbed the edge of the bed and tipped my body sideways, so I stayed sitting, but my upper body moved towards the bed. Once the motion had started, I let my lower body follow as if a lever pulled me and at the same time, lifted my legs up to the bed, until I was lying on my side. The usual grunts and groans dispelled but as far as motion was for me now, it wasn't as bad as I braced for; I had learnt the ways to provoke or avoid. Grabbing the underneath of the table, I used my arms to lift my body slightly from the bed and twisted to lying on my stomach.

'I'm impressed. You've mastered that.'

'I'll have arms like power lifters. Wait till I try to get up. That's the one I haven't worked out yet.'

'I can show you some tips.'

Terri's hands were soft and warm, so I didn't flinch when she placed them on my skin.

'I'm just going to work my hands around your back. It helps me determine what's going on. I won't give you any surprises. I won't work on an area without telling you. Just try to relax.'

Terri's finger tips moved along my lower back, in soft circular motions that were too light to hurt, skimming only the surface. Still, when Terri moved to the spot just above my hip, I let out a moan that could have been a scream. Terri moved on while I tried to find my breath. After moving over my entire back, Terri asked me to turn over, holding one hand out to hold me and another to stop me from falling from the bed.

'I'm just going to move your legs and check your range. Tell me if anything hurts.'

She lifted my leg and moved my thigh to my stomach. Once my back stayed straight, I was fine. While my leg was still bent, Terri rotated it to the side and back. After she tried the other side, she sat next to me.

'If you're screaming out by just my touch, then I don't want to do too much work in that area. There's inflammation in other parts too, so what I suggest is I'll work on those areas first and then we'll see if we can help the main.'

It wasn't pleasurable what came next, but the pain had purpose; I already trusted her with that.

Terri worked on my neck with fluid motions. Massaging and moving, getting into the muscles and tissue. As she moved lower, I tensed. It was getting sorer, uncomfortable. As she lay her hands on my lower back, I swooned. Terri stopped.

'Dawn, you're too inflamed for me to continue. What I suggest is taking some rest for two days. Take a hot bath. Relax. Don't move around too much.'

'But the doctor told me to keep moving.'

'Move around every hour or so, but otherwise rest. It isn't the time for exertion. Your body needs to heal.' Terri's face twisted in thought. 'Can I get you to take your top off?'

I stripped, glad I chose something easy to remove.

'Hmm,' Terri said again. 'Can we move you over to the mirror?'

With her hands on my shoulders, she slid along with me to the full-length mirror on the wall.

'Look at your hips. Can you see anything?'

One hip was at least two inches higher than the other hip. My whole middle body was lopsided.

'One is higher than the other.'

'You can put your top back on.'

Terri picked up my top and, looping the arms with her hands, dressed me as if I were a child and guided me to the chair.

'Sit, take a rest.'

I caught my breath. Even with help, dressing was exhausting. I felt a hundred years old.

'Your hips shouldn't tilt like that. I think your problem is more a disc than a muscle.'

'What does that mean?'

'It means I don't think I can help you.'

My eyes welled. 'But how can you know that after one session? You're the first person who made me feel I could get better.'

'If I were you, I'd go back to my doctor and ask him to book an MRI. That is the only thing that will confirm what is going on.'

'Terri, you know I would have kept coming to you if you said you could help me.'

'I know.' Terri rubbed my arm. 'But what you need is someone who can fix you. I couldn't keep taking your money when I know I won't make you better.'

It didn't matter that I believed Terri. Or that I knew she was right to discontinue treatment. I thought of that girl I'd once been, who seemed a lifetime away now. The girl who sat overlooking the water and cried out for a better life. I wished I could travel back in time and slap her. She *had* lived a better life. Or at least an opportunity for one. I wished more than anything I could tell that girl to soak every second of life up because you never knew what was around the corner. To tell her to stay in bed that bright morning, to not want to change the life she had, to not want to better herself and, above all else, to never, ever run down that alley.

News

The buzzer went. I checked my watch; it was early, earlier than I had woke anytime lately. I shuffled over to the buzzer.

'Hello?'

'Dawn Moloney?'

'Yes?'

'It's Garda Tom Leahy and Garda Ann Kearney here. We'd like to talk to you about the incident you reported. Can we come up?'

'OK.'

I buzzed them in and took the few minutes to brush my hair back with my fingers. I stood at the door, waiting. What was it about guards that made you stand taller? Was it the uniform? Or the threat? Or the serious faces? Even though I knew I wasn't in trouble, I couldn't help feeling like I had done something wrong.

As they approached, they took in the corridor, the lift, me.

'Sorry, I'm having back trouble and haven't been sleeping well at night, so I'm only just up.'

'That's understandable. Can we come in maybe and sit down?'

'Course. Please. Would you like a tea or coffee?'

'No thanks,' Tom said. They both sat on my couch.

I sat opposite them as it was a required move; the guards expected me to stay at their eye level.

'We wanted to speak to you in person, to talk to you about the incident that happened. From what we heard, you had a bit of an ordeal.'

I nodded. *Please don't make me talk about it.*

'We just wanted to keep you in the loop. Two plain clothed guards on duty went down to investigate the alley and found a man hiding in an alcove. He tried to attack the officer with a knife. He fits the description you gave Dawn. Can we show you some pictures?'

I nodded. The woman stood and handed me a file. It contained photo shots of various men similar to the person I described. I flipped and flipped and flipped. The eyes were off. Or the nose was different. There was no scar on the lip. I stopped mid flick. The eyes staring back were his exact eyes, and the picture transported me back to that floor, to that alley. To the vile smell of his breath, how could I have forgotten that? The smell imprinted on me, a smell that told me something had died inside, rotten and decaying. I saw the thin lip with a scar between the bow. The welt by his temple that looked like a burn. My hands shook.

'That's him.'

'Are you sure?'

'I'll never forget his face.'

'Thank you, Dawn.'

'Do you need anything else?'

'For now, that's it. We may have to get you to come to the station again, but as you're in a lot of pain, we can do it another time. It was a brave thing you did coming forward. He would have attacked again. You've stopped him from doing to someone else what he did to you.'

They made further pleasantries, all of which I zoned out and only nodded for. I wasn't there with them anymore, but back in that alley, with his breath on me, with his arm ready, the bright sky wrong and displaced. I didn't hear another word said until I closed the door on them. My back rested against the wood, and I breathed as if for the first time since the attack. They knew who he was and now I was safe. He couldn't come after me now.

'Oh, mother of god, has something happened? Has she been murdered? Is this a crime scene? I knew something was wrong when she wouldn't pick up the phone.'

The two guards were trying and failing to get past my mother. 'Mum,' I hissed. 'Would you stop it? I'm sorry,' I said to them.

Tom waved his hands. 'No bother. We're glad you have someone with you who cares. We don't always see it.'

For another second, Mum stood still and clutched her bag before attempting to touch me. Unused to the intimacy, the hug was awkward. It was a lot for the woman to take in.

'I'm sorry Mum, I didn't want you to find out,' I said, feeling the guilt of not telling her. Yet the judgment I expected from her wasn't there. She didn't break away, instead she stroked my hair back. 'Look at your face. What happened? Is your phone broken? I've been ringing and ringing.'

'Mum, calm down. Come in and I'll explain.'

As I limped in, she didn't let go, and I was grateful to have her to lean on. She didn't say a word, which must have killed her, waiting for us to both sit.

'I didn't want to worry you.'

'What do you mean? I've been out of my mind with worry. Whatever happened can't be worse than what I thought about.' Her expression changed then. 'Can it?'

Mum stayed still as I told her everything. The only motion was from her bag, inching closer to her chest with each sentence. The woman didn't cry, even though I could see the welling, and the worry and the urge to grab me. I appreciated the effort because that would have been the end of keeping it together. After I finished talking, the quiet moment before she spoke took forever.

'You're coming home.'

'I can't. I have to go to the doctor tomorrow.'

'Fine, then I'm staying here until then and after that you're coming home.'

'Mum, there's no need.'

'You're not dealing with this on your own. I'll come with you.'

There was no point in fighting. Once Mum made her mind up, it wouldn't alter. I was relieved. I wasn't alone anymore. Now someone else would cushion the blows.

Closed Spaces

I smiled at Mum as she parked at the entrance to the hospital. She had been a godsend when she'd heard about the need for an MRI, insisting on ringing Dr Murphy and demanding he book one straightaway. From the gist of what I could make from that side of the conversation, this was how it went:

'No, she has no insurance, even though I told her for years you never know what's around the corner, but sure, the young these days don't listen.'

Brief pause.

'Public so, yes.'

Long pause.

'A wait of how long?'

Brief pause.

'Two years!'

Poor Dr Murphy's eardrums.

'How much if she goes private?'

Long pause.

'Book it for as soon as you can doctor.'

The hospital was old but still held some of its grandness from years gone by. It was also private, used only for patients with insurance or people paying for procedures. I followed the signs for reception and a girl pointed to the MRI department.

As soon as I got there, a nurse handed me a gown. There were no long queues, no bristling, overworked nurses, no not knowing how long you'd be there. Money got you somewhere in the Irish health system and being poor could get you killed, I thought with a guilty pang.

'There's a room there to change out of your clothes. Can you remove any bra, any jewellery, any item on you that may have metal?'

'Metal?'

'Yeah, the MRI is like a giant magnet. It's how it gets the images. It's noisy though from the magnet taking the images. If you'd like, you can pick some music to listen to?'

'Does it help?'

'Some people find it distracts them, others prefer not to.'

'No, I think the music will only add to my anxiety.'

'I'll give you earbuds to help block out some of the noise. Pop into the room and get changed and I'll see you out here and we can go in, OK?'

As I unrolled my leggings and slipped off my shoes, I thought back to another room I undressed in, when I had looked at my dress in the changing room mirror on my birthday. A different person's life now.

Stepping out in just the robe left me exposed; the gap at the back didn't help.

The nurse waited. 'Ready?'

I nodded. She opened the door and guided me in. There was nothing in the room except for the machine. It looked like a bed jutting out of a circle with a plastic cube behind it. This was going to hurt. I gulped.

'Don't worry. All you have to do is lie there. We won't start till you're comfortable. How are you in enclosed spaces?'

I couldn't stop looking at the hole in the circle. That's where I was going. 'Not the best.'

The nurse picked up a little box attached to the bed. 'If you feel claustrophobic, there's a little button you can press here, and you'll be able to talk to me.'

'You won't be in the room?'

The nurse pointed to the window behind which separated the rooms. 'No. Sorry. If I stayed in here, I wouldn't be able to work the machine.' She smiled. 'It'll be grand. Honestly, there's no side effects from MRI. It's very safe. All set?'

'I guess.'

'You just need to lie down.'

Used to people in pain, she helped me, holding out her arm so I could lever myself rather than pushing me into position.

'Once you're comfortable, I will leave the room and the bed will move into the tunnel. See the lever with the button? If you need me, you just press that and I'll talk to you. Just remember not to move. It can blur the images and we would have to do it again another day.'

'No pressure then.'

'You'll be grand.'

The room felt very empty when the nurse left. Being alone has a sound. A room senses space, reflects the hollowness, echoes and amplifies the silence against the walls.

After a minute, the bed moved until a tunnel of plastic covered my head.

'Are you comfortable?' came through the speaker.

'I guess.'

'Remember, no moving.'

'Yep.'

The plastic was hard and flat, which made lying on it unnatural. I cursed myself for forgetting to ask how long I would have to lie there. The inside of the MRI was artificial, closed in, depressing. A spasm of pain ran up my leg.

Please, not here.

The lights went out in the room. The machine fired up. As it did, it clattered; making loud jutting noises, infiltrating my brain. The earbuds did nothing. Not picking music was another thing to curse myself for. As if knowing I couldn't move and wanting to test me, the nerve in my leg burned. Shooting pain sizzled down in a line from ass to toe. The burning had a motion. A rhythm. Spreading outwards along the rest of me until my muscles hummed and begged to shift position.

I will not move.

My body wanted to stretch out the spasm. The unnatural position of staying straight, staying still, contracted my muscles, and afraid to relax them in case any movement ruined the images, tensed every other part of me. My neck ached. My upper back prickled. Holding the position made my arms tremble.

Don't move.

I felt the sinking into a new low. Every single part, every single cell, every organ and tissue and piece of skin and nerve screamed at me to itch, to move, to smooth, to soothe, to get out of there.

Please, don't move.

A tear escaped, running down my temple and dampening my hair. Could water mess up the MRI? Whatever I did, I had to hold on, not move, stay still, do anything to not repeat this, yet the time went on and on. The noise kept on clattering, adding to the claustrophobia. It made me want to scatter, to get far from there. Panic clawed at my chest and throat. Plastic walls and noise surrounded me. Until, I couldn't take it anymore. I was going to faint. Or scramble out of the tunnel. I felt for the button, deciding to call for the nurse, to tell her I needed to stop, that I couldn't do it, that I had to go. It didn't matter how much it cost, how much money I'd waste, I couldn't stay any longer. Mum and Dad would understand. But then I would have to go through it again and I couldn't do that and I needed answers about what was going on; to fix the body, I needed the information the MRI would give. Why hadn't I taken the painkillers Mum offered beforehand?

Because I wanted to be at my worst, because I wanted the MRI to prove the pain I'm in.

Now I saw how foolish that was. It wouldn't have changed the results, all it would have done was help me get through it.

And then it was over. The noise stopped, and the lights came on. The door opened, and the bed slid out and the nurse helped me up and it was time to go. On the surface, nothing had changed. I was still in pain, wearing the same clothes as when I walked in, but I left the hospital altered. The experience had taken something from me I couldn't explain; something I couldn't get back. Every step hurt. Every motion meant pain. Once I rounded the hospital grounds, I took two painkillers from my bag and swallowed them down with some water I kept in my bag. I kept going, kept walking because stopping for a minute was harder. At that stage, I couldn't straighten my body. My neck, in retaliation for keeping straight for that long, only gave some reprieve if I angled it. My lower back spasmed if I straightened. The only way to walk was to stick my bum out and bend my back forward; positioning my body in a wonky r shape. Strangers stared but didn't help. I wasn't walking but waddling, a human duck.

The car was in sight, but was still far off. I saw my mother reading in the car and willed her to look up, to spot me. To catch my breath, I held on to a streetlight for a moment. I couldn't let the tears come. I needed my bed. Needed the safety of my duvet. The sadness clawed and dug its nails inside my skin and the hooks would not release by itself. The only way to survive would be to shake it off. I did not want to shake it off.

'Mum,' I cried out.

As if waiting for a sound, Mum was out of the car in a shot and running. Her face fell when she saw the way I was standing. Mum cupped an arm around my waist.

'My poor girl. It's over now. Come on, I'll help you to the car.'

That arm was everything. A person without pain can't understand how a simple gesture of an arm wrapped around someone suffering can save them. How it anchors them back to this world. How it reminds them they are not alone. I wouldn't admit it, but the only person I wanted was her. Because I could let go now. Because she would fuss over me. She would take away all the responsibility of having to act like I could cope. She would look after me.

In the car I closed my eyes and it was only as the journey continued I realised we weren't going to the apartment but driving to Crookstown. I didn't argue, there was no fight left. I closed my eyes and braced for the bumps in the road.

End Of

I had gone back in time. Untouched for ten years, the neon pink walls were the coolest back in the day, but older now, it made me wonder how I studied in the room at all. A bunch of photos broke the bright colour on the main wall. The one in the middle was the biggest, blown up to A4 size, while all the others surrounding it expanded out to a massive square. The main one was clear even from the bed, Ciaran and I, our heads dipped touching each other, smiling big toothed grins. How young we looked, how happy. It hurt to look at him.

Dotted around the room were sketches of friends long gone from my life, suspended now in past tense along with paintings of Crookstown, and Knockfarraig beach. Some of them were passable as decent pieces, but they were like looking at a stranger's work. When was the last time I picked up a pencil? What had I done in those ten years since I left this room? The question depressed me. The pain enclosed on me like a predator waiting to attack from the shadows. I closed my eyes and blocked out the world.

At some stage, Mum came in to the room and sat on the bed and brushed away the hair from my face.

'How you feeling, love?'

I kept my eyes closed.

'Don't want to talk?'

'I'm following the saying if you've got nothing good to say, say nothing at all.'

'Do you want to get up and have some lunch?'

I opened my eyes to a bright day. 'Lunch? I missed morning?'

'I figured it was better to leave you sleep.'

'I don't feel too bad lying here, if I move around, the pain will come and I can't cope with it today. I need a day of just staying in bed. Can I Mum? I'm exhausted from trying.'

My voice broke on the last word. Mum patted my hand, unsure of what to do and I knew that was my fault, because I had pushed her away every time she'd tried to hug me.

'How about I bring you up a cup of tea and a toastie and if you want anything else, you just ring down from your phone?'

'Tea cures everything.'

She ignored my sarcasm.

'We'll get you right again Dawn, don't you worry. Cup of tea coming up, then I'll drive you to the doctors,' she said and left the room.

There are limits to what you can do from your bed, stalking was a recent pastime I'd taken up. There had been five new posts since my birthday night. Five nights out without me. As I'd guessed, apart from Ciaran, the group hadn't contacted. Ciaran, I didn't and couldn't blame; I had ignored every text and diverted his calls because as much as I needed to talk to him, I didn't have a clue what I would say. My finger hovered over his face and I scrutinised each photograph for way longer than was healthy. Kristin in one, with her mouth wide mid laugh, her head tilted down, her black hair half covering her face, looking straight to the camera, her hand on Ciaran's chest as if sending the world a message that he was all hers. Or just sending me the message. What killed me most was how happy Ciaran looked. His brown eyes twinkling in her direction. Their relationship status changed making it official. Her profile pic of the both of them mid kiss.

Another picture was of Ber on a table, shoe less and looking like she was getting ready to remove other clothing. Peter licking a random guy's face. All typical nights out, telling me nothing new except they weren't missing me one bit.

I closed the computer. What else had Kristin told Ciaran? Would Ciaran stay with her if he knew she had lied about how I felt about him? But telling Ciaran might destroy their relationship, and didn't that make me just as bad as Kristin if I was trying to ruin his happiness? I couldn't be that person. Or hurt Ciaran any further than I had done.

* * *

The temp doctor clicked at his computer, he didn't even look up.

'Dr Murphy explained you would drop in for your results when they came in. He apologised he couldn't tell you himself.'

'Well, even he is entitled to a holiday.'

The doctor didn't laugh. His full concentration went on reading the screen. 'The report states you have a disc herniation, a couple of them actually, in your lower back.'

So Terri was right.

'It also mentions degenerative disc disease.'

'What's that?'

He blew out a breath, thinking. 'It's like, how would I describe it? A bit like your spine is crumbling.'

How can you fix a crumbling spine?

'But I'm thirty.'

He shrugged. 'We can put you on stronger painkillers.'

'The painkillers aren't killing the pain. What they are doing is killing my stomach. Then I have back pain *and* stomach pain. It's effecting my whole life, I don't want to get up in the morning, I can't sleep at night. I lie awake, not able to do anything.'

'I'll give you suppositories. They are lighter on the stomach and are very fast acting. I can also prescribe anti-depressants.'

'I don't have depression.'

He tapped on the desk but this time looked up. His eyes were hazel. 'You are showing signs of depression.'

'If I get rid of the pain, I'll get rid of being depressed.'

I heard the stories of people having more problems weaning off anti-depressants. That wasn't a road I wanted to go down.

He kept tapping. 'If you find it too hard, I can prescribe something to get you through. What I recommend is rest. This type of injury isn't going to just go away. I'll be honest, back pain isn't my area of expertise, so I think it might be best to refer you to someone who knows a lot more. He's private though.'

Mum's words ran through my mind. *'Don't worry about how much it costs. Whatever they suggest, we'll do. That's what me and your dad are for.'*

'That's fine, book him.'

'I'm going to arrange a consultation with Barry Nevin. He's up in the private hospital in Carrigaline. He should be able to tell you what's best to do next.'

'Good.'

I had batted away the suggestion from Mum that she come with me, asking her to wait instead, pretending not to see her disappointment while she pretended she was fine with that, saying she had to pick some things up in the shops, anyway. At the time, I thought it would be easier to concentrate on what was happening if I was alone, but now I wished she was there with me. She would have asked questions. She would have found out exactly what it all meant. Outside, I didn't ring straight away but walked to the end of the street in a daze.

Degenerative disc disease. Spine crumbling.

As I hobbled beside the river, the water invited me in. My life was over. Just thirty and the body I'd abused was disintegrating. *Crumbling.*

What was in front of me? I couldn't live a life in this pain when even the idea of another day of it was an ordeal. There was no reason to live. There was no life in me for living.

I wanted alcohol. It was the only thing that took the edge off. Not that it took away the pain; it just made me not care so much. What was going on wasn't fair. I didn't deserve it. I missed my life. I missed the opportunity of being able to do with my life what I wished. I missed white runner guy. Dark and violent thoughts bombarded me.

End it now. The pain can be over in a few seconds. I can't live like this.

Peering over the railings, the water was low and the tide was out. The drop was high, at least twenty feet and I hated heights. The street was busy so if I did jump I couldn't guarantee a have a go hero wouldn't dive in and try to help. And that was after I climbed over the rails, which in my current condition would take so long, ten people would have enough time to notice what I was up to. Instead, without overthinking, I rang Ciaran, needing to hear his voice. The phone went to voicemail, course it did, it was a weekday, he'd be at work. Still, hearing his voice was enough to trigger the tears. My message was a mumbling mess.

'I know I shouldn't call. You probably don't want to hear from me, but I just... nothing's gone right since that night. I'm sorry for what I said in the apartment. I was in pain and wanted to hurt you. Ciaran, I miss you so much.'

After explaining what had happened in as little words as possible, Mum drove home and let me slip into silence for the rest of the journey. Back in the house, I took up residence in bed and planned to stay there for a long time.

Later that evening, Mum knocked on my bedroom door and entered with a bunch of flowers wider than her.

I smiled for the first time that day. 'Mum, they're beautiful.'

'They just arrived. Who are they from?'

'What they're not from you? Must be from Dad then.'

'Read the card.'

You are stronger than you think. It will get better, I promise.

Love you, Ciaran.

'How did he know I was here?'

'Didn't I tell you? Ciaran's the reason I came to the apartment. He rang me saying he was worried because you were in pain and wouldn't answer his calls. He thought you might need help. I drove straight there.'

In the night, when sleep alluded, I pulled myself to sitting and typed. Wallowing was over. It was time to understand what I was dealing with.

The search results for degenerative disc disease produced over a million articles.

'Degenerative disc disease is an age-related condition that happens when one or more of the discs between the vertebrae of the spinal column deteriorates or breaks down, leading to pain. There may be weakness, numbness, and pain that radiates down the leg.'

Another article stated:

'Degenerative disc disease is frequently the cause of low back pain, especially in young adults. Although this condition can cause lower back pain symptoms over a long period of time, the good news is that the pain is usually manageable with various conservative treatment options (meaning back care that doesn't involve surgery).'

Not crumbling then. I cursed the doctor for his use of words. For the carelessness of explaining about something he knew nothing about. About the needless fright he gave me. These pages were hopeful, suggesting different ways to treat it. I wrote them down, one underneath each other on an A4 page. Some I had already tried, the rest I would try, all but one.

Searching had made me feel slightly better. My life wasn't over. The flowers on the bedside locker proved Ciaran still cared. Mum and Dad would support me no matter what happened. That was enough. Yes, the pain was still there, but now I knew what was going on inside. Now, there was an actual documented reason. I wasn't crazy or imagining it. There was a diagnosis with solutions to try. What spread out in front was a long road. A road I would have to hobble down until I found a way to walk again. There was no choice but to try.

Nevin

A polished oak desk took over most of the room. To the right of the desk, expensive leather hardbacks lined according to their height on shelves. The left was shelfless, spared for credentials. Each one framed and placed side by side, so they took up the length and height of the wall. It was impressive.

Mum fiddled with her bag; her nerves were more obvious, which annoyed me even more; what did she have to worry about?

'Hello Doctor, thanks for seeing us,' she said.

'It's Mr Nevin, Mum. Consultants don't answer to Doctor.'

He was tall and thin, with a hook nose and eyebrow hair that couldn't decide what direction to stay in. He brushed the comment away. 'It's fine. I don't mind.' His expression said the opposite. He clasped his hands. 'So, Dawn, I hear you've been having a bit of trouble. Where are you feeling the most discomfort?'

Discomfort doesn't quite cover it.

'My lower back. That's where it started, but now it goes all along my legs too. Also neck pain. The back of my shoulders hurt, but I think that is more to do with how I'm walking or when I stand. I can't stand straight, so they get sore.'

He nodded. 'Right. Have you brought your MRI?'

I handed over the large envelope.

'Ah films. Most people bring discs these days, but I love to examine them from a light box. It draws the eye in.'

He pulled the black blue films out and held them to the light. He smirked and waved them at us.

'Did you take a look?'

How did he know? Did the light change the image? I'd been careful not to leave fingerprints. Wanting not to seem bothered, I shrugged, but my blush betrayed me. 'I wanted to see.'

'People often try to diagnose themselves these days. Better leave it up to the people who have studied and know what they are talking about. Right, let's see what they tell me.'

Condescending dickhead.

He walked over to the light box and attached the film to the top. I used the second his back was turned to grimace at Mum in a silent: 'Who does this guy think he is?'

Mum tipped her head to the side. It said: 'Let's see what he has to say.'

'I can confirm you have three disc herniations in the lower back at the L3, L4 and L5. Your spine has lost some curvature.' He ran his finger down the image. 'See here, it is quite straight. It may have been in spasm.'

'I was in a lot of pain on the day of the MRI.'

'How is the pain now?'

'The same.'

'What I would suggest is an epidural to reduce the pain.'

'Like what they give women in labour?'

'Something similar. In labour, it works by anesthetising the area, whereas an ESI has a corticosteroid in it to take the inflammation down. From looking at your X-rays, I think it is best to perform an interlaminar injection.'

I had seen those needles on the TV. They were long.

He stroked his chin, assessing me. 'The other thing we need to address is your weight. Every excess pound places added pressure on your spine.'

Mum straightened. Her friendly face changed to her stern one, the one usually only reserved for me; never an outside face but she must have remembered where she was and changed it back. Before it turned again, I spoke.

'I've put on over two stone since the injury two months ago. Before this, I was very active. If I could exercise, I would.'

He flicked my words away with his hand. He used those hands constantly. 'Well, that's where the epidural comes in. It will take the pain away but then you...' pointed finger '... have to take responsibility for making the pain-free permanent.' Clasped hands. 'An exercise like swimming is good. It takes the pressure off the joints.' He wagged his finger at me. 'I can't stress enough how much weight amplifies a back injury.'

Tears prickled in my eyeballs. I would not cry in front of this man.

'A man threw her down on the ground after attacking her. Her weight gain had nothing to do with causing her injury,' Mum said, clutching her bag to her chest as if she was the one being attacked.

Way to go Mum, I didn't think you had it in you.

His hand went back to stroking his chin. 'I'm sorry to hear that happened to you. I understand it must have been traumatic. And you're right, Mrs Moloney, her weight had nothing to do with the cause of her injury, but it has a lot to do with her staying in pain.'

I gulped back the retort. It stung. Mum was bright red in the face. I braced myself; there was a question coming. The woman looked around, checking if there was anyone else in the room. As if what she was about to say was top secret.

'What about pregnancy?'

'Pregnancy?' He blinked a few times as if he couldn't even process the absurd question. Then he laughed. 'A disc herniation won't affect her fertility.'

Mum's blush turned deeper, almost to a shade of purple. All my life I had been taught never to answer a person back in authority but looking at this man with his smug attitude and his expensive clothes and the way he looked down at me for my weight and my mother for an innocent question was the last straw.

'That's not what she meant. She was asking if I got pregnant, how that would affect me?'

He batted the misunderstanding away with his hand. 'Like I said, any weight gain will cause you major issues. With your type of injury, you could guarantee you would need to be bed bound for the duration. Are you pregnant?' He raised an eyebrow. The way he looked at me made me squirm. It said, 'Who would even consider looking at a fat lump like you, let alone make you pregnant?'

'No.'

'Well then, I wouldn't advise it. You need to get the weight off, not put it on.'

He was right.

He tapped on his computer. 'I have a slot available next week. Let's get you in and start getting you better.'

'How much is it going to cost?' I asked. This appointment was over two hundred euros as it was.

'My secretary will go over all the prices with you outside,' he said, now studying his computer. He slid the MRI envelope back.

Mum picked them up. 'It doesn't matter how much it is Doctor, just book her in.'

As we walked out, Mum linked my arm and this time I didn't break away.

'Well, he was a pompous thing, wasn't he?' Mum whispered, fiddling with a curl in her tight perm.

I smiled. For once, we agreed over something.

* * *

A week later, I stood in the same building. This time they led me to the hospital section with lots of artwork displayed on the walls. Like the private hospital where I got my MRI, there was no waiting. My appointment time was mine. If you paid, you got first class treatment. Cash got you somewhere fast.

A nurse led me into a small room with an examination bed in the middle of the floor. It smelt of bleach. Scrubbed up and waiting was Barry Nevin.

'Morning Dawn.'

'Morning.'

'I know Sandra has already gone through what to expect when she booked you in, but I'll just remind you again. I'm going to give you a local anaesthetic first and wait for five minutes to numb the area. Then I'll give you the epidural and get your recovery on the road. After I've administered the medicine, you'll have to lie still for at least two hours. We will move you to a room where you can relax. That's very important Dawn, no movement. Understand?'

'Understood.'

He clapped once. 'Right, let's get you better.'

He unpackaged a sterile needle, then, walking behind me, rubbed the area on my back with some type of cleaning wipe. It was cold. The anaesthetic felt like a pinch. Of all my fears, being afraid of needles wasn't one of them, yet I couldn't shake off an uneasy shakiness. I didn't know why, but I didn't believe he would heal me. Putting aside his condescension and smugness or that the man was a horrible human being, it didn't mean that he wasn't great at his job. It seemed too easy though, too clear cut. I hoped he was right. Nevin was saying he could help; that this was the only option to take the pain away. I had to try it. Even if something felt off. Even if the man annoyed me and acted a dick. He could be a dick and still excel at his job. Anyway, my parents had paid for it now.

He stood by the sink while he waited, with his back to me, and I was glad because I couldn't stand facing another of his disingenuous smiles. Maybe it was just me. Maybe the pain just made me brittle, made me annoyed by the little things that wouldn't have bothered me before the injury. Pain changed people.

After what felt like a minute, he checked his watch and, satisfied, approached me. He tapped the spot where he injected the anaesthetic.

'Can you feel that?'

'Yes.'

He frowned. 'We'll give it another minute so.'

He didn't wait by the sink this time. Instead, he got the epidural ready. I looked away; I didn't want to see the needle. The fear was rising. What if he damaged my already damaged spine? What if he calculated wrong, and the needle entered bone?

Mr Nevin stood over me. 'Dawn, can you lie down on your stomach?'

It was a struggle. The pain pulsated the nerve along my leg with enough force and frequency, it shook. He didn't offer reassurance or help. I wasn't even sure he noticed.

'Remember now, no moving as the needle goes in.'

I kept my breathing shallow and tried to imagine I was somewhere else, although there weren't many places classed as fun while lying on your stomach. The image of the needle kept flashing in front.

What could I turn that in to? A tattoo needle?

I could imagine I was getting a tattoo.

What tattoo would I get near my spine?

THIS IS WHERE I FELL.

or even better, but not true.

WHAT DOESN'T KILL ME MAKES ME STRONGER.

Flashes of my injury came then, which didn't help, so I switched the image to lying on a beach waiting for a masseuse to apply a new treatment. Anywhere but the harsh lighted, shiny floored room where I could see the assistant's gowned up legs and the plimsolls on her feet. I couldn't see his feet but felt him nearing, then sensed him looming over. Time to go somewhere else. I breathed. Tried to calm. Beach. Sun. Calming waves.

I heard the opening of the needle.

It's just a tattoo. Do I want a palm tree? A butterfly?

The lid of a bottle popped.

A butterfly. A bright blue one.

I had seen 3D ones that looked like the butterfly had just landed and then the thought left me because all I could feel was burning hot, excruciating pain. There was no numbness. Metal piercing skin. The needle driving in to me. Touching bone. The needle touched the exact spot, the source from where the pain pulsated and ramped it up a thousand times more. It needed to stop. I was going to vomit. I couldn't take it any longer. And even though I had been told many times, I pushed with my arms to lift my body from the bed, trying to get away.

'Please stop. I can't.'

He pushed me down. 'Don't do that. It will only make it worse.'

The assistant's shoes moved nearer. Hands held my shoulders in place. 'It will be over soon. Just one more minute.'

The pain was too much. I made a sound that was louder than any sound that had ever come out of my mouth before.

As it was at the MRI, at the point of not being able to take any more, just as consciousness left, a reprieve came and the needle left my body. A different pain replaced the one before. Even if I wanted to, I couldn't get up from the bed. They slid me onto the gurney and wheeled me into another room, where two smiling nurses greeted us. The room held at least five others. All white haired, past seventy-five years old type of people. None of them looked like they were experiencing the same pain or that they would have screamed out on the table. The nurses stopped at an empty bed and lining the gurney alongside it; helped shift me onto the bed. They flapped about and made me comfortable, but all I wanted was for them to leave me alone. I faced the wall; I couldn't deal with people watching me or, even worse, trying to make conversation.

'Do you want me to pass you anything?' One nurse asked.

'My bag please.'

After a few seconds, the nurse placed it on the bed between me and the wall.

'Remember now, no getting up. If you need anything, just press the button. We'll call you when the time is up.'

I couldn't speak. I had felt all different types of pain now. Throbbing. Stabbing. Burning. Aching. This was worst of all. My nerves were not burning but were lines of fireballs blazing throughout my body. The pain was expanding out, out, out from the site of the injection and then zooming back in. It was knocking against me in a THUD, THUD, THUD. The normal pains would not be outdone, either. The sciatica down the leg throbbed to the thudding beat. I was nauseous from the pain and fasting didn't help. I tried to focus on the uneven raised parts of the wall. The hospital bill might have been ridiculous and the rest of the hospital looked fancy, but it was still an old building. The place was silent except for two women's voices.

'How many times have you got it done?'

'It's my second. The last one kept me going for six months.'

'It's my third time. I'm hoping this one will work better. The first one was fab, but the last didn't have the same bang.'

'What do you get it for?'

'Arthritis.'

'Same. It's a curse, isn't it?'

A tear rolled onto my cheek. The low sank lower; life just kept on getting lower. I should be those women's age before I needed a place like this. The women and men here had earned their pain. They had lived years with healthy bodies that did what they were supposed to until they had ground themselves down, until it was normal and expected to get the aches and pains. It wasn't supposed to happen to me, I was too young.

The unfairness throbbed as bad as the pain, with nowhere to go and too intense for sleep, I let myself feel the full scale of what happened. For the attack. For the shock of it. For the pain I felt since. For having to go to the guards. For the fear I felt walking anywhere now. I didn't trust Cork City anymore and saw the man that hurt me in every stranger.

I thought about texting Mum, but what would I say? The truth would only worry her more. Flipping open my book, I tried to read, but the pain wouldn't allow it; the words jumbled and blurred. More than anything, I wanted to shake it off, to get positive, to find the belief inside that I would get better, but I couldn't. This injection was meant to be the answer, the start of getting back to me, and it wasn't. It wouldn't be the answer. Instead of going with my gut instinct, I was over a thousand euros down and in more pain than what I started. For those women talking, for those around the room that suffered with the likes of arthritis, for injuries associated with wear and tear and the wearing down by old age, I could understand how it would be of benefit. How could sticking a needle into a part of the body that was hurting help? How could piercing the source of pain, the part that was inflamed and already sore, take it away? It was like stabbing a knife into a healing wound; it didn't make sense.

Along with the pain, I started feeling a low pressure in my pelvis. Not pain. It stayed long enough for me to realise I needed the bathroom. There was no nurse around. What was it with me and going to the bathroom? That's what my days had reduced to; bodily functions ruled my life. This time I wouldn't leave it too late. I shifted my position to my opposite side. The bathroom sign pointed to the wall opposite. They had told me I couldn't move, but the injection hadn't worked; I could move. I pulled off the blanket. One of the talking ladies noticed.

'I wouldn't do that, love. Let me call Eileen for you. Eileen! You've got a walker.'

The nurse, Eileen, came rushing in. She looked at the woman, recognising the voice, then followed her pointed finger in my direction.

'No. Don't do that. Stay where you are.'

She rushed over.

'I need the bathroom. I can walk.'

'Yes, but the medication needs to settle. I'll get you a bedpan.' Eileen waggled her finger at me. 'Promise me you won't move.'

'I won't move.'

Because I'm an obedient fool.

Shuffling

Mum's hands went to her face when she saw me struggle to walk to the reception area.

'Jesus, Mary and Joseph, what happened to you?' She swivelled behind me. 'Wait and I'll call the doctor.'

I grabbed her arm. 'Mum please. I just want to get out of here right away.'

For once, she didn't argue or resist. Instead, she half hugged me, her arms hovering around, not touching except for one hand laid gentle on my back, she whispered in my ear.

'All right, love. Don't worry, we'll get you home.'

As we rounded the corner, Mr Nevin opened his office door and stepped out. I saw him take in my hunched over position, how tightly I clung to Mum's arm; the sheer agony radiating from me. He took a step forward and then averting his eyes, pivoted back, closing the office door behind him. That told me everything I needed to know about the man.

'Can you hold on to the counter?' Mum asked.

I nodded with closed eyes. The skin on my face screwed up, forming new lines, contorting to cope.

'Wait here. I'll get your father.'

A moment later, both parents came rushing in. My father tried not to look bothered, but his widening eyes betrayed him. He took the weight of me without an issue, he shouldered me as if I was still the little three-year-old he would lift and swing in his arms. My daddy. Who I was never so glad he had come to Cork to buy some tools. Mum took my other side.

I didn't walk out of the expensive hospital like the new woman Nevin had promised, or hobble like I had walked in. This time, I had to be carried.

Dad pushed the front seat as near to the dash as possible but even if he'd cut the seat out, getting in to the car would be a challenge. If I'd heard the sobs and moaning from someone else, as I tried to bend and shift my legs, I would have thought the person was being murdered.

Once settled, the journey was a nightmare. Every bump, every stop, every hill brought fresh, raw, screaming out pain. Lying down across the seats didn't help. I sat up and found if I stayed ramrod straight and braced for any bumps; it eased a little.

Mum huffed and crossed her arms. 'I'm going to ring that man up. It's worse you are. It was supposed to help.'

Dad kept his eyes on the road. 'Now Reena, maybe it needs time to settle. You'll be as right as rain tomorrow, Dawn. You wait and see.'

I saw him look at me through the mirror. The furrowed brow furrowed deeper.

The guilt. The pain. The exhaustion was too much.

At home, making the stairs and lying in my bed wasn't an option, all I could manage was a shuffle. The minute I tried to straighten or lift my legs, it brought spasms and involuntary shrieks. Instead, they settled me onto Dad's old, battered recliner. After multiple failed attempts at getting me comfortable, we found a position with the recliner legs splayed out and a pillow under my legs that didn't aggravate it. My chin collapsed onto my chest, safe that I didn't have to make any effort or have to deal with movement for a while. While Mum covered me with a blanket, I could already feel the slide of sleep.

I stayed there for two weeks.

After sleeping and eating and trying to live on that chair, I'd had enough. My parents had carried me when I needed the bathroom, served me dinners and painkillers and drinks, shifted my position, propped up my pillows, stroked my hair. What if I'd been alone? What if I'd had no one to help me? The injection left me totally incapacitated, a lump of useless flesh, that moaned and cried so much even I wanted to get away from her. As the days went on, a prickling started that grew stronger until I couldn't ignore it. It wasn't right that I'd gone for treatment and was worse. It wasn't fair that he'd seen me and hid. Spending money on a treatment that left me unable to walk, unable to even wipe myself without screaming in agony. I needed to say something. I needed to find a voice. Silence got me nowhere. Riled up, I finally made a phone call.

'Mr Nevin's office, Sandra speaking. How can I help?'

'It's Dawn Moloney here. I had an epidural two weeks ago with Mr Nevin but I'm worse.'

'Hold on, I'll see if he's available.'

I closed my eyes while listening to the tinny, automated music.

'Dawn, I hear you're having a little trouble?'

Little?

'Ever since the epidural, I can't walk or even lie down. The pain isn't better, it's worse.'

A click of the tongue came over the line. 'Right. Take anti-inflammatories for the moment. Every four hours. You can take a painkiller in between. Sometimes patients with acute back pain need another go before they work.'

'Another epidural?'

'Yes.'

I laughed. It came out maniac and high pitched and not like any laugh I had ever used before. 'Are you serious? If you think I'm ever getting another one of those, you are mistaken.'

I can't believe I just said that.

'Dawn, it is the best thing for you.'

'It was meant to take away the pain I had, not increase it. I'm worse. Do you understand what I'm saying? I trusted you when you said it would take away my pain. It hasn't, though. I am worse.'

I shook.

Oh, that felt good.

'I understand how you feel, but my recommendation is that you continue with a second injection. What you have is incurable without surgery. All we can do is focus on pain management.'

Incurable?

'I can't afford another one. My mother gave me a loan for the first and I've exhausted my savings. I'm not going to pay for something that might not work.'

'If that's your decision, I understand. You know where I am if you change your mind. How about I send you an appointment in a couple of weeks for a follow up?'

I hung up. My chest heaved; it felt good to get angry. To Nevin, I was just a paycheck. A person he dismissed and blamed my injury on my weight. He summed me up by just looking and judging and making it my fault. I would figure out the next step. Not him. I would become my own saviour, doctor and expert because all these labelled experts didn't have a clue. I would show him.

Then the darkness took over.

Every gamble I took, I lost. Every time I tried to get on top, I ended up on the bottom. My life was a succession of failures. I was a loser.

Crawling up the stairs, I moved to my old bedroom and stayed there and let night blend with day, pain blend with existence, hope evaporate to acceptance. I faced the fact that just like the injection hadn't worked, nothing would. There wouldn't be a brighter day. My injury was permanent, and I was never getting better. I let plates pile up with food, managing bites here and there. Sleep called to me day and night.

And then one day I woke to curtains pulled open and sunlight bursting in.

'What are we going to do with you?' Mum asked as she plopped down on the bed. I grimaced from the movement and wiped away crust from my eyes.

'You're not even trying anymore.'

'I can't even walk. You tell me I'm not trying, but carrying on is trying harder than I ever had, and where is it getting me? Nowhere that's where.'

'I didn't mean it as an insult.' She closed her eyes and let out a long breath. 'I'm always getting it wrong, aren't I? How I talk to you, I mean. Believe it or not, I want the best for you and you're not the same and I don't know how to help you get it back.'

'I don't know how either.'

She rummaged in her pocket. 'I saw this article and thought it might be an idea. Don't dismiss it straight away. It's in town. I thought you might give it a go.'

It was a newspaper article with a picture of a long-haired woman standing in front of a building. The headline read: Happy place under threat.

I shook my head at Mum, handing it back. 'What's that got to do with me?'

'You couldn't have read it all. It says it holds classes for unemployed people, more than that, it helps people get back on track.'

'Sounds delightful.'

'I thought it might be an idea.'

'Mum, I haven't the energy. How can I go for a class when I'm finding it hard to even sit? Anyway, I couldn't travel from Cork every day.'

'Well, that's the other thing I wanted to talk to you about. Your dad and I think you need to stay here.' She held her hand up to keep me from interrupting. 'Not for forever, just do a few classes, take away the pressure of looking for work and concentrate on getting better.'

'What about my apartment? You want me to give it up?'

She sighed, moved on the bed.

'I don't think there is any other choice, is there? If you keep paying rent, you'll have nothing leftover and I'd prefer to help you out with treatments than pay for a place you can't get around in. The way you are at the moment, we'd worry sick about you being on your own.'

'I'd manage.'

She closed her eyes and took a deep breath. When she opened them, they were filmy, ready to spill.

'You're getting sucked in. I can see it and I know what happens if you give in. A black hole opens up and swallows you. If you catch it in time, you can climb out, but if you let it get you, if you let it close its mouth on you, it's harder to escape. You have to keep on looking for an answer. You have to keep fighting.'

The way she said it made me wonder if she was talking from experience. Did she have to do this herself once?

'I don't think I can.'

'I'm worried about you. I'm worried you may do something desperate.'

We met each other's eyes.

'Promise me you won't do anything desperate?'

It took me some time to answer, which itself was an admission of contemplation.

'I promise.'

Mum placed a hand on mine. 'Good. Because I wouldn't be able to carry on without you.'

I fiddled with the sheet. 'I know.'

'So how about we contact your landlord and give a months notice?'

I nodded, my eyes welling. *Oh, the relief of not having to worry about it anymore.*

'And will you think about going to that place?'

'We'll see.'

Once given that assurance, Mum reverted to normality. 'One step at a time, so. First things first Dawn, I'm going to be honest, you smell.'

I burst out laughing.

'I'm serious. You're stinking. Everything feels better when you're clean. Get into some fresh clothes, brush that matted hair. Do you want me to book you in to the hairdresser?'

'Your hairdresser? No way.' Mum recoiled. 'No offence. I couldn't sit in any hairdressers for three hours. I'll have a shower, OK?'

'Good woman,' Mum said, fixing the bed sheets as I stood.

'Stop Mum,'

'Sure, you're not able. I can't help meddling, it's my job to want to make life better for you.'

The shower felt good. As the hot water cascaded over me, it soothed the sore muscles. I couldn't stand for long though without the pain in my lower back returning with a vengeance. After drying, I dropped the towel and surveyed the damage. I thought of how only months before the attack I had been getting somewhere. But at what cost? The cutting meals, the constant stage of hunger, the guilt if I ate anything with calories at all. And for what? It still hadn't made me happy. Now, injured and overweight and unhappy, could I go through all that effort again? All that hard work seemed too exhausting now.

How life changed. The life I had thought was permanent and fixed, had uprooted and ripped to shreds. Nothing was constant, everything was changeable, I learnt. From where I lived, to having friends I could speak to, to not working and being on the dole. Even if I could have those things again, I would give them up in a second if I thought I could have a day without pain. Life means nothing if you can't live it.

I picked up the newspaper article and I couldn't understand why, but I felt drawn to it, like it was calling me, like there was something right about the place. The woman stared out of the page; her face defiant, her eyes dared me to be brave, too. I put the clipping on my bedside locker.

Rooting through my clothes, I could tell the items were going to be uncomfortable or not fit anymore, so I resorted to wearing a pair of leggings that were so stretched when I pulled them on, little holes appeared at the seams. My blonde roots were not blonde anymore. The brown ran down the strands, ending two inches from my scalp. I thought of the money I had wasted now that I was broke. On nights out, the constant round of shots bought that at the time made me feel powerful, made me feel important and only regretted the next day when all I had left was an empty wallet and a hangover. Or the new outfits I bought every week because, God forbid, I would wear the same clothes twice. The manicures, the facials, the newest make up products that promised a way of turning back time. Which would have been fine if I enjoyed them, but I hadn't. It was about being out there, looking good, impressing the people who turned out not to care, anyway. I tried to remember the last time I wore makeup or thought about my appearance. None of that mattered when your face scrunched in pain, when you couldn't bear to look in a mirror, when you couldn't stand straight to wash. After wallowing for so long, after allowing myself to lie in the bed, I knew Mum was right. I had to force myself out of it or give in and die by staying there. No one was coming to save me. Nobody else could do it for me. Only I could do it. And now it was time.

I sat at my old homework desk and, taking out my makeup, made gentle strokes with the brush, applied for Mum more than for me. I would show her I could try.

Afterwards, even though my back was throbbing, I put on a smile as I hobbled into the kitchen. Mum pretended to clean an already clean counter top.

'I was thinking of a way you could help.'

Mum put down the cloth.

'Could we maybe go into town and buy some hair dye? If I go back to brown, I won't have manky roots anymore and I won't have the upkeep. I know I'm asking for enough what with being here and not paying rent and you paying for the epidural, and my rent in town but if you could hold off on me paying you back for a while, I haven't touched my benefit and could do with some clothes. Nothing fits.'

I blinked away the threatening tears. Mum didn't miss a beat.

'Go away with the talk of paying rent. For as long as I live, I will never take a penny from you for staying here. Sure this will be yours when we're long gone. I didn't want to say anything, but you could do with a new wardrobe.' She grabbed her keys from the hook. 'Ready?'

I nodded, and this time didn't have to force a smile. 'Ready.'

Frames

Brown hair made me different. From every angle, I'd changed. After a decade of being blonde, going brown was like stepping back in time, or rather, brought me back to a former person, the one I had tried to run away from. I recognised her.

'There's my girl,' Dad said as I walked into the kitchen.

'At least I'm not two tone anymore.'

'It suits you. Your dark eyebrows stood out too much when you were blonde.'

'That was the point. I wanted striking. Anyway, why are you telling me now and not when I had them too dark?'

'Because you seemed happy with them, and what do I know? I can say it now because you changed it. And it confirms what I believed. You're better as a brunette. You're the image of your mother.'

My mouth gaped open. *That is not the look I'm going for.*

He laughed. 'Don't look so horrified. Your mother was a lasher, I'll have you know.'

'Is that right?' I arched my eyebrow.

'She's still gorgeous. It's just that you never look at her, not properly. All you see is what she is to you. You never see her as a person.'

'Ah, go away.'

He walked to a drawer and pulled out a photo album and brought it to the kitchen table, tapping the seat next to him. I followed. He flicked through the pages until he came to the one he was looking for.

The photo could have been me.

'Jesus, I see what you mean,' I said, leaning closer to the picture. 'I could be her twin, well, if the twin stepped back in time and changed into dodgy clothes. What was she wearing?'

'Don't do that,' Dad said, grimacing, his hand moving the page as if he was about to close the book and abandon the talk.

I placed my hand on his. 'I'm sorry. It's a habit. I'm trying.'

He nodded, placed the page flat down again. 'What she was wearing was the height of fashion at the time. Believe it or not, she was pregnant in that photo.'

'What? Her stomach is flat.'

'I know, she didn't show till she was about six months. I remember that day well. It was the day we told our parents. Your mother was ecstatic. She'd had a hard time of it, you know?'

I didn't know.

He stared at the picture of Mum, his eyes taking on a blankness, going back, remembering. I sat quietly, waiting until he was ready to speak.

'We had many losses. Each one chipped away at her more, made her go further into a depression. We thought it wouldn't happen.'

'I never knew that. Why hasn't she told me this before?'

'You should know better than anyone how hard it is to talk about the things that matter. It's too hard for her to say the words. Especially to you. She wants to shield you from anything that could hurt, she'd never unburden on you. After you were born, the doctor told us he thinks the reason she lost so many was she couldn't carry boys. Do you know the back of the garden, where the flower bed is?'

I nodded.

'Your mother planted a different rose for every baby she lost.'

'But it's full of different bushes.'

He nodded, kept his eyes on me as I made the mental count.

'There must be at least five.'

'Seven. That's why you should go easy on her. You were so wanted. We both were desperate for a child and then because of complications at your birth, the option to try again, to have a brother or sister for you, left.'

I looked at the mum version of me, her face cocked to the side, her broad smile, her eyes hinting at untold secrets.

'I don't know what to say. That must have been very hard.'

'We all get handed our own cross to bear. For your mother, for us, it was losing our baby boys. For you, it's what you're going through now. Sometimes I would look at your mother, when she would take to the bed and she would just lie there. It was as if she was in shock. Her whole body would go limp. I didn't know how to fix her, this fragile, broken thing that wasn't my wife. She got herself out of that bed. With slow steps, my Renee came back to me. And then she had you.'

'Should I have a baby then?' I smiled.

Dad nudged me. 'No, that's what your mum needed. You need something else. My point is, you are more like your mother than you think. I see you going the same way she did in that bed and I want you to know, even though life is hard for you now and it seems like nothing will ever get better, I want you to know it will. Life will get better and you'll be stronger for it. Your mother has always said life began for her the day she became pregnant with you.'

'Maybe that's the problem. All my life, I've felt the pressure of being an only child, missed not having a brother or sister, resented it even. I thought ye choose that. I thought ye wanted to focus all the attention on me.'

He shrugged, gave me a smile full of sadness, but truth too. 'Life is never that clean cut.'

'No, I guess not.'

I rubbed my finger along my mother's arm, forced still in a picture, frozen in time. That woman looked friendly and open and fun. That woman looked like someone I could have been friends with.

156

Alayne

An impressive wooden plaque signified it was the place. The engraved words looped like handwriting; the grooves of each letter descended until it blended into the background block of wood. I rubbed my finger along the smooth surface of the letters, then felt the grooves; each ridge deliberate. What it read was another story: The Happiness Initiative. I hesitated. The name brought to mind some hippy place where everyone talked about their feelings and was the worst thing I could think of doing. Mum made shooing motions with her hands from the car. The woman's excitement made her almost bounce in the seat, my instinct was to leave, to hobble away, but instead, I pushed open the door.

I stood in an empty corridor. There were lots of open rooms, all seeming to omit noise. I walked, looking for a reception. The first open door was empty. The one across from it had a woman with wild hair sitting on top of a desk. There must have been ten others in there, all playing various instruments. The sound wasn't pleasant. The woman jumped from the desk when she noticed me and came to the open door.

'You OK?'

'Yeah, are you Alayne?'

'No, I'm Bex. You'll find Alayne further down at the end of the corridor. Dawn is it?'

I reddened, surprised.

Bex smiled, then winced at a rather loud, overenthusiastic squeak from a tin whistle. 'I better get back. She's expecting you. Welcome, and don't worry, we're good people here.'

An old lady with bright pink hair blew a trumpet badly. The sound was more like from someone breaking wind. She waved. The next open door looked like an art studio, with chairs circled around a person modelling in the centre. Easels and artists dotted around the room. A black-haired girl was pinning paintings to a line, as if to dry, but turned as I walked past. Even from across the room, the girl's iris were so light they almost appeared white. The girl smiled. My cheeks burned from getting caught being noisy. After that, I didn't dare look in any other room.

The end of the corridor opened out and I could see now multiple other rooms. The outside was deceiving, inside was huge. To the left was an open area with couches and comfy looking seats. Seated on one was a woman reading some paperwork.

She looked up, unsurprised. 'Dawn. You came.'

Mum gave me no choice.

'Would you prefer to go into the office or talk here?'

Anyone could hear the conversation in the open space. 'I'd prefer the office.'

'The office it is.'

Alayne pointed to the room to the left. The room was bare except for two chairs facing each other and some art on the walls and a desk in the corner with a kettle and tea and coffee supplies and a few wire racks with paperwork.

'I don't use this room much. It's here if anyone wants a quiet place. Or somewhere to talk in private. I prefer to be around, out where the action is. You'll see.'

It annoyed me that the woman assumed I would stick around. That I was such an obvious candidate for the place.

'So, Dawn, why are you here?'

'My mother read about you.'

'Why are *you* here?'

I gritted my teeth. 'Because my mother made me. Since I'm failing at everything else, she thought I needed to do something.'

Alayne furrowed her brow. 'Do you think you're a failure?'

'Well, I've moved back to my parents' house because I can't work or pay the rent on my apartment any longer and I've spent the last couple of months in bed with a back injury and spend my whole day in pain. Besides that, I fell out with all my friends and have nothing to live for, so yes, I think I'm a failure.'

I sat back, a little shocked. The outburst felt good, but I couldn't understand why I had said it, why I had unleashed on her.

Alayne nodded. 'Yes, you're right. You are a failure.'

What?

She leant forward, putting her elbows on her knees. 'You didn't expect that, did you?' She grinned, amused. 'You expected me to disagree, but let's look at your reality. You have failed at living alone and keeping the rent up. At keeping a job. Your body gave up on you.' She splayed her arms in the air. 'You failed.'

Hearing those words felt the same as receiving a blow to the chest. Saying those things to myself were normal, but I hadn't expected this stranger to think the same, or at least say it to my face.

'If you examine the facts, then the facts indicate you have failed.' She sat back in her seat. 'Facts only tell half the story. You only fail if you stop or give up. Failure is not permanent, accepting failure is. Failing is just an indicator of what isn't working, a marker for changing your course of action and carrying on. Were you happy in your apartment?'

I thought for a moment. 'No.'

'Are you happier where you are living now?'

'I wouldn't say happier. My injury makes it hard to do simple things like cooking or cleaning, so unless I'd wanted to starve, I had no choice but to move back.' I shrugged. I wouldn't give her the positive she was waiting for.

'Would you say you are failing with where you live now?'

'Other people my age have bought their own houses, yet I can't even keep up with my rent.'

'Is that a goal of yours? It can be if that's what you want, Dawn. A goal means you aren't failing. Failure only happens if it's over, if you give up. Were you happy at your job?'

I thought about Jill and her promotion, about the fact not one of them had called since to check how I was. 'Some parts.'

'Leaving your job and spending your time somewhere else, even here, is it better or worse?'

'I don't know yet.'

'I'll reword that. Being here or at your work, which one has more possibility for opportunity?'

I looked at the open door. Listened to the sound of classes coming from down the corridor.

Here.

'I don't know yet.'

'I think you do. Funny how something you failed at brought forward more chances for opportunity. How is your pain today?'

'All I've done for months is exist, but what kind of existence is it? I can't plan anything. It gets me down. There are days I can't even stand, let alone work. Even if I wanted to, I don't know if I could stay in a class. The consultant said I will have this for life. He said I will have to learn to manage it.'

Alayne swiped at the air. 'Consultant smultant. Don't concentrate on someone's labels. Facts can be changed. Facts can bend. Be careful of any statement given to you, about you, as a fact. Just because he has credentials behind or in front of his name doesn't mean he knows everything. He doesn't know you.'

I felt an unreasonable flash of anger. 'You don't know me.'

Alayne's eyes widened first, then she beamed. 'He doesn't have all *your* facts. He has no clue how resilient you are. How strong. How determined. He doesn't see what you're willing to do to get better. I do. I see it all. And so do you Dawn. *You* know. Give yourself time to work through this. You have no idea what you'll be doing this time next year. Where you'll be. How you'll be. But I promise you whatever the outcome, if you decide to start here, I will be with you every step of the way to find out. Have you ever seen those mugs that the images appear when you pour hot liquid into it?'

'Yeah.'

'Those images are always there. It's only when you add heat that they unveil. When friction comes into your life as pressure or conflict or pain, it causes you to discover whole layers of yourself you didn't even know you had. They were always there, but the pressure causes them to appear at the surface.'

'So, I'm a mug?'

Alayne grinned. 'Yep. You're a mug.'

'I feel like a mug.'

'Like how?'

'Like my job. I sent in my notice today.'

'That's a blow.' She nodded, then leant in again. 'I'll let you in on a little secret. That job wasn't meant for you. The life you lived isn't yours anymore. I'd bet a million euros you were miserable there.'

'At least I wasn't broke.'

She shrugged. 'Being broke brings a willingness to try things you may have dismissed before. It can also bring clarity if you allow it. This will lead you to search for what's right for you. You say you can't go out, so even if you had money, you wouldn't be able to spend it. Moving back in with your parents means the pressure of paying rent and house bills is gone.'

'Now I'm a dosser, a layabout. I can't even pick my shoes off the floor, let alone work. I was always dependable, always a grafter. People came to me if they had a problem. Now I can't even sort myself out.'

'It won't be like that forever. You will heal. Is that what is doing it, or is there more?'

'Isn't that enough? The pain. The lack of choices. The being stuck. If I'm lying on my back, I can't improve.'

'That's where you're wrong. That's when you can change every-thing.'

'How?'

'You lie there and plan. You imagine and daydream. You get clear on what you want to achieve.'

'I just want to get better, but the pain means I can't even think straight.'

'That's a start. Focus on getting better.'

'Yeah, it's that easy. I'll close my eyes and then I'll wake up and jump out of bed.'

'Well, it's good to see there's a bit of passion left in you.' Alayne grinned. 'What I mean is, we'll break that down into measurable goals. Each day, we'll try to achieve something. You spoke about your pain. How are you coping with how the injury happened?'

'I'm scared all the time.'

'Because of the attack?'

I nodded, but avoided looking at her.

'Do you want to talk about it?'

I rocked my head.

'Another time.'

Never.

'How's life since?'

'Sometimes I wonder if life is worth living.'

'Is that a new thing?'

I flicked my eyes at her. I didn't know if it was because she was a stranger or because she showed a genuine interest or the way she asked questions made me open up, but whatever it was, I wanted to talk to her, I wanted her to understand me.

'I've always had moments of feeling overwhelmed. Times where I felt life got too much. When things would stack up and just all fall on top of me and all I'd want to do was climb into bed and stay there. But that was usually over something I did when I'd drunk too much or if someone turned out to not be who I thought they were.'

'How would someone turn out like that?'

I'm here to do a class not get the third degree.

Alayne stayed still, waiting. She gave the impression she was comfortable with silences and wouldn't move on until I answered.

'Like, I don't know.'

She settled back in her chair. 'Take your time.'

'When people have let me down or they've turned on me about things and I didn't stand up for myself, I'd run over those things after and they would get me down. Anyway, this time, this is something different.'

'In what way?'

'Because I'm wasting my life. And it's not getting better. I'm not getting better. Sometimes I have to go to bed and as soon as my head hits the pillow, I pass out. Yet no matter how much sleep I get, I wake up tired. The day exhausts me even though I've done nothing.'

'I know you can't even think about this now, but every day you do get through makes you a day stronger. At the moment, the best you can do is survive. That IS something Dawn. Those days, as bleak and as dark as they are, will end. I promise you that. Pain forces growth.'

'Well, I've certainly been growing. Outwards.'

She dipped her head, and I liked her for not appraising my body. 'Does that bother you?'

Tears prickled. 'Course it does. It's embarrassing. I hated my body before all this anyway, now I've added another two stone to the mix. The joke of it all is I went out that day to change myself, to get fit. Now I can barely walk, let alone exercise.'

I felt exposed, expecting the woman to scrutinise me now.

Alayne's head made a slight turn, not missing the beat. 'If that's the way you talk about your body, no wonder it's giving you grief. Stop being so hard on yourself, Dawn. You survived an attack. Your body is doing what it needs to do to heal you. It takes time to do that. Don't force it. Don't worry about weight gain, it's making you feel worse. You are strong.'

'You don't know me.'

She shrugged. 'I don't. Call it a hunch.'

'Well, your hunch is wrong. You don't have a clue about me. How am I strong? I'm weak. In my body and my mind. If someone attacked me today, I couldn't run away. If I needed to fight back, I couldn't even wave my arms without getting a spasm. I'm not strong at all, all I'm doing is breathing and dragging my lump of a useless body around.'

My chest heaved with getting the words out.

'Did you get out of bed this morning?'

'I'm here, aren't I?'

'Despite your injury, your lump of a body got you to this building. Small steps Dawn. Give me a few seconds.'

Alayne left the room. A printer whirred, then a sound like paper being spat out. The biggest canvas on the wall caught my eye. It was of a woman's face, with a turquoise teardrop earring draped down almost to her neck. At first I thought it was a photo but then realised it was one of those hyper realistic pieces. Despite the pain of standing, I had to get closer. Nearer, you could see the shine from the earring, the pores on the woman's skin and I stood and wondered how anyone could have the insight to draw like that. Just then, Alayne came back and smiled when she saw me standing. I felt like she caught me mid snoop. Embarrassed, I dragged my legs back to the seat. Alayne handed me a sheet.

'Is that you in the painting?'

'A better version of me, I think.'

'It's brilliant.'

'It is, isn't it? A friend painted it. You'll meet her at some stage. She teaches art here sometimes.'

The woman kept beaming. Embarrassed, I examined the page. There were pictures of people in various positions.

'These are safe stretches for people with a disc herniation. My friend, a chiropractor, sent it to me when he helped me with an old injury.'

'A back injury?'

She nodded. 'If you like, I could arrange a consultation.'

'My funds aren't doing too well at the moment.'

'Dale is a nice guy. I'm sure if I said it to him, he'd give you a quick consultation for free. You don't have to. He knows his stuff, though.'

I took the card, but knew I'd never make the call.

'I know it seems terrible at the moment and like the hard times will never end. It will end. Nothing stays the same. You get to have a choice here Dawn. If you make bite-size goals, you can tick them off and when you do, when you acknowledge the achievement, you will feel a little better. It could be putting socks on. Tiny to anyone else but huge to you when you couldn't before. Celebrate when you achieve them. That's what we are going to work on here. If you can, try to do those stretches each day. If you can only manage one the first day, that's OK. Build up until you can do more. When that becomes easy, you could join the gentle yoga class we have here. Or do short walks. There will be a day when you look back at this and it will only be a memory. An unforgettable one, but it will be your past. It won't be your present.'

'I wish my past would hurry up.'

Alayne smiled, 'Don't rush it. There's lots to learn. There will be times when your recovery will be up and down. If there's days the pain grips you and it's too much, you rest. We'll see what can be done. Do you know how this place got started? How I came to open the Happiness Initiative?'

I shook my head.

'In what seems like another life now, I was a teacher. A teacher frustrated about what I was teaching. We focused on subjects most students would never use for the rest of their life. Exams and point scores and the curriculum took over when what the students sought and needed was to be tutored about life. One day, the principal of the school asked for some volunteers to help run a series of detentions for some students. I was a substitute waiting for maternity leave to kick in for the teacher that I was taking over for and not using the full school hours yet, so I offered to do all of them. Twelve weeks of Saturdays. That first day, I could see they all were struggling, all in different ways, and then I found a note one of them wrote. It changed everything. From that day on, I taught them what I wished I'd learnt when I was their age. From those lessons, this place was born.'

'Did you help them?'

'You'd have to ask them that. You'll see a few of them while you're here.'

'What's with the name?'

'The Happiness Initiative?' Alayne chuckled. 'It's full on, I know. When I first began the lessons, I used a book called The Kybalion by The Three Initiates. The book talks about when the student is ready to learn, the teacher will appear. From then on, they called themselves Initiates too. Based on those lessons, I wrote a book called The Happiness Initiative. When I opened the centre, that was the first name that came to mind. The Initiative, in homage to my first students and the other, the happiness, because, well, as corny as it sounds, that's the aim.

Let's be honest, it's not a great name. Everyone calls this place The Centre. Maybe I should change it.'

'I don't think you can help me.'

'I can't.'

We stared at each other.

'This place isn't about me. It's about finding out what you want and working out how to get it. Alongside counselling and meditation workshops, we also offer lessons on several life skills. Gardening and growing your own produce. Art. Woodwork, music and other subjects you wouldn't learn in school.'

'Is it where the trouble kids get dumped?'

Alayne squirmed at my choice of words.

'No. We have people of all ages here. Lot of characters, all people that want to better themselves. It's a positive place. No judgment allowed.'

'And it's free?'

'We rely on donations. There's also a carry it on policy. If you're helped, you volunteer. Doesn't have to be your life work but a few hours teaching people the skill you learned is enough. Any life skills you could pass on?'

I shook my head. *I've got nothing.*

'We'll find them.'

Alayne stood and walked to some wired racks on top of the desk. Trailing her hand along the metal spokes, she selected the top one and rooted through some paperwork. 'Here we go,' she said, taking what looked like a book from a pile. She handed me two books. The top one was a pocketbook with intricate swirls in the leather.

'If you want to try what we offer here, my only ask is you read The Happiness Initiative and follow the tasks. I won't force you. We don't make anyone do anything. You have to want to better your life or your choices. If you want to go away and think about it all, come back when you're ready.'

'What lessons?'

Alayne smiled. 'The first task is to write where you are. I suggest you go home with the journal and see if you can write anything down. If you're still interested, come back, sit in a few classes and get a feel for what to expect and go from there. No pressure. This place isn't the right fit for everyone.'

I eye rolled at the reverse psychology. Did she think that would get me interested?

'Whatever you choose, remember, every day you get through makes you a day stronger. At the moment, the best you can do is exist, to survive. That is something Dawn. These days, as bleak and as dark as they are, will end. Do you believe the pain will last forever?'

'If I believed it was forever, I'd walk into the river.'

The Centre

I caught my breath outside and tried to figure out what had just happened. Never in my life had I confided in anyone the way I just had with Alayne. I couldn't understand how I hadn't clammed up, how my words hadn't dried on my tongue. Was it down to Alayne, or that I had nothing to lose anymore by talking? Mum sat in the car like a puppy spotting its master.

'Well?' she asked.

'Well, what?'

'What did you think?'

'I think it's a woman promising a lot of things she won't be able to follow through on.'

Mum bit down on her lip. 'Is it a place you could go to?'

'They do art. Maybe it would be good to get out of the house. It's just, she wants to get into my head as well and you know how I am with talking about things. I don't need counselling. What I need is to get better.'

'Wouldn't it be good to talk?'

'Talking is overrated.'

And she already got more information out of me than I'm comfortable with.

'To you, maybe.'

I looked out the window. Conversation over. I ran my finger down the groove of the journal. Even the thought of writing where my head was at was scary. I wasn't where I wanted to be. My life was a mess and if I wrote it on a page, it would become real, documented as evidence of how bad my life was.

Yet here was a woman saying she knew a solution when I didn't have all the answers. Or any answers. I ran my fingers along the spine of the book for the rest of the journey home and once there, went straight to my room and opened the journal and wrote. The words came out in a scribble.

My life is a complete train wreck. I don't like who I am. I am unhealthy. I am failing in life. My body doesn't work. I am miserable and if I had a choice, I wouldn't be around me either. I am an embarrassment. I am useless. I am broken.

I had to take huge gulps of air as I stopped writing. How could this help? All it did was make me feel worse. This was Alayne's fault. I picked up the book and fired it across the room.

As I tried to get comfortable that night, sleep wouldn't come. All day, what I wrote in that journal bothered me. There was nothing I had written that wasn't true, so I couldn't put a finger on why it troubled me so much.

Because it is the truth.

I shifted my thoughts to something that would distract, something that would relax me enough to let me sleep. In the morning, I would make pancakes, adding chocolate chips to the batter. I would whip some cream, slice fresh strawberries and blueberries and, setting some aside, would use the rest to make a coulis. As I pictured the motion of stirring, my food lullaby worked, and I felt the drift of sleep.

* * *

Not to show eagerness, I left it a couple of days before I made contact.

One minute I hated the centre, the journal and everything Alayne stood for and then in an instant caught myself hoping it was the answer. I had never played hard to get with a guy, but I had to play it right there. If I was going to reinvent myself, if I was going to change my life, I would do it correctly. On the day I returned, I took an anti-inflammatory an hour before, sacrificing my stomach for the chance to walk without looking like a complete victim. The plan to stay unaffected changed when Alayne greeted me at the entrance like a long-lost friend, with her arms open, wrapping me in them. I couldn't help but smile. Alayne offered me an arm and even though I hesitated at first, I took it.

'I'm so glad you came back,' she whispered in my ear.

I looked away.

'What I was thinking for today was a tour of the centre and if you're not too tired, you could try out the art class. I know you put that down as one of your options.'

'Sounds fine.'

'Right so, we use the left and right rooms for various studies. We help people to get their Leaving Cert, or learn English so we teach the more academic classes in these. Oh, and music.' She carried on. The next door was closed. 'That's the art room in there. The next class is in about an hour if you're up for it.' She pointed to the open area.

'You already know this spot. Across there is the canteen, go in any time you want a rest, I'll show you down the corridor here.'

There was a massive room laid out with benches and equipment.

'This is the workshop. Everything from woodwork, jewellery making or teaching people how to fix motorbikes happens in this room.'

There was a room decked out with bulky computers that had seen better days. At the end of the corridor was a black wooden door that stayed on the latch. 'Here is our masterpiece,' Alayne said. 'We make all our own produce, some ladies have a jam class and we sell them and all the veg at farmers' markets to raise money.'

'You need money?'

'Always,' Alayne said.

A guy about my age was hunched over some lettuce in the garden. The guy wasn't topless, but he may well have been, for his t-shirt was translucent from sweat. There was just enough lean to see muscle movement. He was not bulky, just muscular. As we walked around the back to the bins, he glanced in our direction and smiled. His hair was long and blond and he had tanned skin. He stunned me with his beauty, with the freedom in his smile. I looked away. New Dawn averted her eyes, not wanting a guy like him to look at the state of her. Old Dawn wasn't shy with men. She hadn't needed to talk to get them. Subtle signs had been enough to give her what she wanted. It was when she wanted to talk to them she got in trouble.

'This looks like a lot of work. Who looks after the garden?' the question came out a lot less casually than I wanted.

Alayne grinned. 'That's Sam. He's not here long, but he's a dab hand at getting things to grow. He's quite a way with him. Are you interested in gardening Dawn?'

Alayne pretended to be serious but couldn't keep her mouth straight.

I couldn't help to take another quick glance at Sam. 'I've always wanted to learn. I don't think it's the best idea at the moment. If I bent, I wouldn't be able to straighten up.'

'We could get you a chair so you could just sit and watch.'

'I would love to know how to plant a flower.'

'Right.' There was that annoying grin again.

'I mean, I know it just goes into the ground, but how do you prepare the soil? What flowers to choose and when to plant it, like what season or how to look after it, things like that.'

'I can show you that Dawn, we can hold our next session out in the garden.'

I tried to hide my disappointment. Alayne noticed. Her eyebrows knitted together.

'Or I can check with Sam. Just be careful there.'

'What do you mean?'

She scrunched up her nose. 'Sam is lovely. He's funny and very charming. I just don't know if that is what you need right now.'

'And you know what I need?'

'No. Not at all. If you think you're able and you decide to come here, we can select gardening as one of your options.'

Alayne's phone rang. She frowned at the screen. 'I'm sorry, I have to get this. Do you think you could go back yourself and I'll show you the rest after?'

The phone continued to ring.

'I'll be fine.'

'Will you stick around for the art class?'

I nodded.

'Just head to the canteen and help yourself to a coffee.'

As I took slow steps, I peeked into the workshop as I passed, focusing on the people rather than the layout of the space, in groups chatting or taking notes. They seemed relaxed or were too busy concentrating to look up. The sound of laughter travelled through the centre. What could I learn here? I doubted it could help me. It wasn't like it was going to take away my injury, but it might give me something to do.

My back was throbbing, begging me for a seat, so I followed the handmade wooden sign with the arrow pointing the way to the canteen. It was a large space with circular tables dotted around and a long industrial style stainless steel counter near the entrance. Behind that was another counter with a coffee machine and tea facilities. There didn't seem to be anyone working.

A woman sitting at the nearest table noticed me and stopped mid conversation with two other elderly women. 'It's help yourself here. Just go behind and poke around. You'll find loads of treats on the top shelf over the sink. Come and join us if you like.'

'I've a few forms to look over,' I mumbled, not sure if I wanted company.

'Fair enough, we're leaving in a minute, anyway.' The woman smiled and went back to her conversation. I stroked the spotless stainless steel as I rounded the counter, imagining rolling pasta out on its smooth surface. I filled the kettle and kicked myself for how I automatically dismissed the woman.

'Is the offer to sit with you still open?' I asked the three women once my tea was in my hand.

'Course,' the woman smiled up at me. 'Did you find anything?'

I shook my head. 'I didn't want to root around.'

'I'll get them for you, gives me an excuse to rob one myself,' A woman whose grey hair was down to her shoulders said, getting up.

'I'm sorry if I seemed rude there, I get back pain.'

'You poor thing.'

'You're so young,' the other woman said, then tutted.

'I don't feel young, I feel like I'm about a hundred years old.'

The lady who had called me over pointed to herself. 'I'm Maree, this is Jean and the lady currently robbing all the biscuits is Mo.'

'Excuse me, the girl might be hungry,' Mo said, coming back. 'Anyway, I brought them, so I'm allowed. We take it in turns to bring snacks.'

'What's your name, love?' Maree asked.

'Dawn.'

'Is it your first time here?' Jean asked. They were about my mother's age. In fact, they were so like her, I could picture Mum sitting right in the middle. I tried not to hold that against them.

'Second. Alayne was showing me around, but she had to take a phone call, so she told me to check the place out and see if I want to start.'

Maree leaned in closer, spoke lower. 'It's a great place this. A lifesaver for me, if I'm honest. When my husband Joe died, I went a little off the rails.' She tipped an imaginary bottle to her mouth, as if drinking from it. 'My kids were travelling or up in college, and suddenly I had no one.'

I nodded. That feeling was way too familiar.

'Alayne spotted me in a car park at the back of an off licence. I was so desperate for a drink I didn't even wait till I got home. I unscrewed the cap off the whiskey and took a slug, thinking no one could see me. It wasn't enough. I took another and another, then burst out crying. Did you ever get so tired from trying to keep up holding it together and trying to act strong for everyone?' Maree looked directly at me. I nodded. 'And then I felt a tap on my shoulder and a woman stood there telling me everything would be OK. Alayne hugged me, offered me a lift home, offered me a place here and I've never looked back. Haven't touched a drop since, well that's a lie, I drink when we have a night out and we arrange plenty of them.' All the women laughed together. It came out more like a cackle. 'I mean, I would never dream of drinking during the day or in secret anymore and I'll tell you something else, I don't miss it one bit either.' She shrugged. Jean rubbed her arm. Maree placed her own hand over Jean's. 'I see now I was just lonely. The people here, Alayne and these girls have shown me it's OK to carry on without Joe. He would have wanted that.'

Maree wiped at her eye. 'And now we're in danger of losing it.'

'I don't understand?'

'They've lost their funding. The centre has to come up with the money to run the place themselves. Alayne has gone to the bank to see if they will help her out, but she's not holding her breath. She acts like everything is fine, Alayne does that a lot, she doesn't like to burden people with problems. She's fighting a losing battle with the bank, though. Rumour has it that a building firm wants this place. Prime spot for apartments overlooking the sea. They were safe until now, but the tenancy agreement runs out at the end of the year and the landlord has upped the price to double what they were paying.'

'How can they do that?'

'Landlords can do whatever they want.'

'But, if this place is helping all these people, couldn't you contact the council or something and get them to step in? What about the papers or the radio?'

'Oh, don't worry, we won't give up this place without a fight. Alayne asked us to stall doing anything until she met with the bank manager.'

'So, are you in? Are you going to try the place out?' Mo asked.

I already knew if I stayed, if I came to this place, it would force me to be more assertive. Being here had already made me step out of my comfort zone. I also knew there was no actual decision to be made. From the moment I walked back in, I'd known.

'I'll try,' I said and meant it.

Samira

Despite a hunched back and a hobbled walk, I tried to ease in to the room. The art class was packed. It didn't matter if I'd tap danced in, the students, too engrossed in their own conversations to notice, didn't even glance at me. For a moment I considered turning around, slipping out and leaving the centre. It would take too much effort to infiltrate the groups and my back was aching. Alayne appeared beside me.

'Glad you came,' she said. I wasn't sure if it was a question or a statement.

'Are you here for the class?' I asked.

'As a student. Samira is an unbelievable artist. We're lucky to have her here.'

'Is she one of your pass it on people?'

Alayne beamed. 'You could say that. Samira was one of the first students I told you about.'

'An initiate you helped?'

'An initiate, yes, although I think they helped me more.'

Then the girl who could only be Samira, walked in. It was the girl from the first visit, the girl who had looked at me as she hung up the pictures. The girl with the lightest blue eyes I'd ever seen. She was breathtakingly, disgustingly, make you feel like shit about yourself, beautiful. Talented and beautiful. I felt a pang. Here I was, overweight, unhealthy and in pain, and this younger girl was more together than I could ever be. A low beckoned.

Laden with supplies, Samira waved at the class with difficulty. Alayne rushed up and gathered some of the load; an assortment of flowers and fruit. A red apple escaped from the bundle and rolled off the table. It landed with a splat on the floor.

'Don't anyone eat that one,' Samira said, laughing. Once picked up, Alayne walked back to where I stood and Samira saw. I squirmed as she approached.

'It's Dawn, right? Did you go to Knockfarraig Secondary?'

'I did. I used to bus it from Crookstown.'

'Oh, I love those painted houses all in a row over there.'

'That's one of ours. We're the bright yellow.'

Samira's hands went to her cheeks. 'That's my favourite one.'

'Mine too,' I said, blushing. *Dammit, the girl was beautiful, talented and bloody nice.*

'I better get on. Speak later, yeah?'

'Sure.'

Samira returned to the top of the room. A hush came over the rowdy class. Some sat, some stayed standing, but they all waited for Samira to speak.

'Hey everyone, as you probably noticed, I've brought some new props. You don't need to use them, they're just for inspiration. You know the score, use any medium, use any method, paint, sketch, collage, whatever takes your fancy. Before you get stuck in though, I just want to show you something on using white that we've been doing in college.'

Alayne rubbed her hands together and whispered in my ear. 'Watch this.'

Samira selected a white piece of paper and clipped it to an easel. Using a pastel crayon, within seconds she drew and shaded an oval face in yellow. Selecting a red, she coloured with light strokes over the yellow until the oval resembled the colour of skin, then with a heavier hand, shaded the mouth, making lips. She added grooves for cheeks, curved lines for a nose, leaving two unshaded orbs for eyes. Within seconds, Samira took a brown and added an iris and eyelashes, stroked lines that became hair, circles that became nostrils. With a black pastel, she coloured the pupil. My mouth dropped open. In less than two minutes, Samira had drawn a child's face better than any I could do in my lifetime. Not only that, the girl made it look easy, like anyone could do it or the image just dropped on the page.

'Sorry, I'm getting to the bit now,' Samira said, as if it was a chore to watch her. I closed my still open mouth. 'This is a basic face shape, I'd need to add shading and shadows to complete it but for this class I wanted to show you how you can add white to make it more three dimensional. This is the magic ingredient.' She held what looked like a white correction pen.

Samira got to work adding two dots of white to the brown iris and black pupil in the eye. She added it to the bow of the mouth. Once satisfied, she stood back.

The child looked alive on the page. Despite Samira's protestations that the piece needed more work, the child had transformed, real, full of personality, mischief and wonder.

'Do you see what it does? The white tricks your eye into seeing a three-dimensional figure. If you look into someone's eye, light always reflects somewhere. Adding it to the picture makes it more realistic, makes the image pop from the page. Experiment with this. Whatever you draw or paint, see how the use of white can bring the piece to life. Here's another example if you are drawing a flower.'

Samira blackened out a page and then, with the white pastel, drew a large circle. Inside the circle, she drew a series of shapes: first a square, then a straight line, followed by a rectangle. That was all she drew.

The circle transformed into a drop of water, a rounded, ready to drop from the page circle. I felt a rush of excitement, something I hadn't felt in a long time. I was going to enjoy this class.

'The white adds realism to every piece. Waves, hair, nails, glasses. Any object that light reflects on. So, let's get started and if you need help, just shout.'

Alayne looked as excited as I felt. We grabbed pages and drew fast, trying everything Samira showed us. It wasn't till much later while in bed that I wondered if in that moment the pain had left, or the distraction made me dull it out. Either way, when I thought about drawing, I couldn't remember being in pain.

In between sketches, I had watched Samira, working the room, helping people when they needed it, but going back to that child on the easel. Shading and correcting. When the class was over, she signed the page and held it out to Alayne as a gift.

'You should use that for your portfolio. It's too good to give it away.'

'I'll make a print. You know my rule, anything I make in here I want you to use.'

'Samira wants me to use them to drum up interest in the centre,' Alayne said. 'But I've told her it's too much.'

Were these people for real?

Stupid

Alayne was sitting straight-backed with her eyes closed when I walked in.

'You're here. Good. Join me on the other seat.'

I left my bag and coat by the door as there was nowhere else to put them in the bare room. I sat in the chair opposite. Alayne's eyes stayed closed. Her chest expanded as she breathed. The silence went on for long enough to get awkward. I shifted in the chair and Alayne opened her eyes as if she had just woke up.

'The art of sitting.'

I laughed, not sure what to say.

'I know it's funny, right?' Alayne said, wiggling her bum to wake it. 'It's silly because it seems simple. Easy even, yet it's the easy things people find impossible to get a handle on. Especially now when everyone is used to constant stimulation. We always, me included, have to have something in our hands, whether it's a phone or a remote control or a pen or a book or a drink or food or cigarette. Most people don't know how to sit without turning a TV on in front of them. So, for now, we are going to enjoy the art of sitting.'

'What do I do?'

'You just sit. You just be. That's all you have to do. I know you have been feeling the pressure to talk around me, so I think we need to do something different. Let's just take in the day. At first, it's going to feel dead awkward. Each sentence or worry that races up to you, just go with it or bat it away. Focus on the sounds of the room. The sound of your lungs filling. Focus on the sound of traffic outside. Or birdsong. Anything that makes you feel lighter. OK? Ready?'

'I guess,' I shifted.

'It's going to feel strange, but that's a good thing. All change is strange.'

'How long will we stay like this?'

'However long it takes.'

'What takes?'

'You'll see.'

Alayne closed her eyes and settled back in the chair. Why was I afraid? I closed my eyes. Alayne was right, straight away, the thoughts came. *This is stupid.*

I took a deep breath. *Focus on the breath.*

There was no reason to get upset or feel uncomfortable, but sitting did, I wanted to run away.

It's going to feel strange, but that's a good thing.

I took another breath. Listened to the in of it, listened as I exhaled. I heard voices then, outside the window, far enough away that I couldn't decipher what they were saying, only hear the melody of it. There was comfort in those voices giving a vocal runway to land and focus my revolving mind on. My shoulders relaxed a little. The pressure of getting it right lifted. The hums carried me. When I concentrated on them alone, thought subsided. The minute I let the hums in, I felt like I flowed along with the rhythm, becoming lighter, body less, drifting like sleep yet awake. I moved with the hums. In what could only be brief seconds of my mind wandering, I felt a calm that I never in all my life had experienced.

I snapped open my eyes. Alayne was looking at me.

'You felt it?'

I nodded. I couldn't speak.

'Well done, Dawn. Nobody feels it the first time.' Alayne looked genuinely impressed.

'What was that?'

'You let your silence in. You listened to the noise around instead of the constant voice inside. If you do that each day, you reset the brain. The silence lets the malfunctioning mind know that you are once again taking over. That it needs to stand down and allow you to connect with all you are. How did it make you feel?'

'Well, I wouldn't say I connected with all that, but it felt peaceful.'

'You know what I'm going to say, don't you?'

'That's my homework for the week?'

'See? You're an absolute genius. You could take over.'

Alayne stood. I followed suit.

'Speaking about taking over. Have you thought about what you could do to help out here?'

'What, already?' I asked, the good feeling already leaving.

'It doesn't have to be straight away, but soon. I'd like for you to try something in the next few weeks?'

'Few weeks?'

'It doesn't have to change the world or anything. There are talents that you have that could be put to good use here. Look around you while you walk. Think of ways you could improve this place. You knew you would have to do this when you started.'

'Yeah, but I thought you'd wait until I'd finished being helped. You're still teaching me.'

'The best way to learn is to teach.'

'I don't understand.'

'If you truly want to learn about something, learn how to teach it. There are reasons we make people do this Dawn. Believe me, it's tried and tested. It has to be something you love, though. Let me know next week what you think that could be.'

'Fine,' I said.

'You're lucky you have this information at your fingertips. Within seconds you can have a thousand solutions. Do you know how I had to gather information and figure out what I wanted to do when I was younger?'

Alayne wasn't wanting an answer.

'I had to go to the library and search and read book after book. Knowledge took time. Now it's so available it becomes almost dispensable and throwaway because there's no work in it, it's irrelevant. Tell me this Dawn, have you looked up solutions for your injury?'

My mouth gaped open. I closed it before answering. 'Course I did. I found out more about my injury than my doctor.'

'That's not the same. That's diving into the problem. What I asked is did you look for a solution?'

There was no malice in her voice. Alayne looked on with interest. I stayed silent. Course I'd looked for a solution. But why was nothing coming to me? I *had* focused on the problem. When I met Alayne's eyes, I saw someone different.

'I'm listening.'

'Look up gentle stretches for low back injury and see what shows up. Type the exact words: disc herniation solutions. There will be millions of articles. Use common sense, logic will tell you which of them are a sell. Follow the one's that resonate, the ones that make sense. If I were you, the first thing I would do when I got up is stretch. Get your body agile first before everything else, like jobs and classes. Then take a walk for at least ten minutes. Not too fast, don't push yourself. Use the time to list all the things you're grateful for. Or daydream about getting better or plan what you will do this time next year when you have recovered. Or use that time to let the silence in like we just did. Whatever it takes to get you feeling good by the time you finish that walk.'

The List

Despite going to the centre, the pain hadn't lessened. It was chronic and unending. Each hour could be different, with altering symptoms. There could be numbness or tingles or burning or shivers. There could be poker stabs or criss-crossing machete slashes of an attack that made me blind with their intensity.

At the same time, I wanted to believe Alayne. Believe that there was a way to get better. That if I could find a way, someday I would feel healthy again. For the moment the pain wasn't going anywhere, so instead of wallowing and sitting in my room suffering like I had done since the injury, I grabbed the sheet of stretches Alayne had given me. Why hadn't I thought of extra stretches? Why hadn't I looked for a solution?

No attacks, just solutions.

I eyed the discarded card for the chiropractor next to the sheet. Manipulation brought images of bending bones to where they shouldn't bend. Of pushing someone where they didn't or couldn't go.

I am not going to a quack.

The first one looked simple enough. The child's pose, I remembered trying it years ago in a yoga class. Facing the floor, I knelt, then put my hands out in front. Lowering, I sank back until my bum touched my heels, keeping my hands flat on the floor. Ignoring my ball of a belly that prevented the stretch's potential, I focused on where I felt the stretch most. In the lower back. In my butt. Once settled, I slid my hands out further in front so I felt the stretch in my arms. I stayed there for a few seconds and felt the pull on my shoulders and took a few deep breaths. As I changed to sitting, my hips clicked.

The next one required to lie down on my back. I did as instructed, slowly and carefully, I followed the diagram, locking my fingers in place at the back of my thigh and dragged my leg towards my chest. My stomach had to go; my thigh couldn't reach the stretch because it blocked the way. The stretch burned in my hip and my lower back made another clicking noise when I lowered my leg. The ache in my back was there, but it wasn't a warning that I shouldn't go further, or that it was about to lock in place; it was just the never ending ache that had become my normal. I moved on to the next one, which looked more complicated. Still lying, I pulled my right leg up to my chest again, but this time moved my foot to my left hip. The instructions said to hold it for one to three minutes, but there was no way I was getting to the end of that one, the burn blazing along the outside and back of my thigh, only counting to five before I dropped the leg. I batted away the disappointment.

Something is better than nothing.

The left leg was even worse. I forced myself to five, but it was a struggle. The next required sitting, so I rolled onto the floor and with my knees pushed into first a kneeling position, then sat. I laid my legs out flat and, following the picture, straightened my right leg and bent my left leg and crossed it over the right, putting my foot flat on the floor. Tilting my upper body away from the crossed leg, I kept one hand on the ground for balance and moved my other hand to the other side. My ankle, my outer hip of the crossed leg and my lower back just above my bum were sizzling. I counted to ten, saying the numbers fast. The other side was worse. As I tried to count, my leg shook, and I only managed to five before quitting. The nerves in my back performed a full tap dance now. How wrong I'd been when I had first looked at the paper and dismissed the stretches as too simple. My inflexibility, my rigidness, my pain shamed me and all I wanted to do was give up but there were only three more left.

The next required lying again, and I welcomed the cold floor. For this one, I bent my legs, cupping my hands behind my neck and raised my hips from the ground. This brought an extra dimension of ache, bringing my neck and shoulders into the pain mix from the weight shifting to those areas. The burning in my outer thighs and lower back and butt turned from a sizzle to an inferno. Holding my hips in the air for the count of five and then, up and down for eight single ones, I could only continue by lying my legs out flat in between.

Only two more Dawn.

The next one, the cat stretch, was another I had done before. Getting on all fours, I spaced my wrists out and pushed my back up and lowered my head so my body formed a sideways C. Then, once happy I stretched for long enough, I raised my head and dipped my back, pushing my stomach out. This one felt more like it, still painful, still a stretch, but more than anything, like it was helping. I felt that one in my neck and lower belly and butt. It elongated me, stretched areas that felt it needed to.

Last one Dawn.

I lay face down on the floor. With my arms staying at my side, I pushed my head up and raised my upper body. It wouldn't go far, but at least my face lifted from the ground. Stomach, lower back and butt felt that one. After ten counts I gave up. Lying there, I just breathed, and let the sweat bead on my forehead. I was done.

After I grappled back to standing, instead of going to bed to rest, I opened the journal and sat at my table, wincing as I did. It took a moment to focus on what I had even sat for.

'Right, this time I'm going to start with little steps.'

I sat, drummed my pen on the empty blank page. Nothing came.

'Come on, you've done this before. You started a sewing class last year.'

I didn't answer that I hated the class. It was one thing to be mad enough to talk to myself, but it was quite another to argue back.

I wrote a header:

What I can do to get a life.

I underlined it three times. Not so much for emphasis, but to give time to think. What could I do? I closed my eyes and thought about what the consultant said. OK, he had been horrible, but maybe he had a point about putting pressure on my spine. From purely a health perspective, getting in shape would be a good idea, but how?

I wrote:

Go to the library and find books on how to get better from an injury.

Get fit. Find a goal that I can complete in a year. Like a marathon or something.

Start a course? Commit to one subject at the centre, at least.

Start cooking again.

As I wrote the words, a static sensation ran up my arms. I had loved cooking before my injury. Chopping hurt my neck or standing in the kitchen for any amount of time was asking for trouble, never mind pain taking away my appetite. But maybe I could adapt how I cooked? Maybe I could learn to cook healthy foods? That might be an idea. I wrote another line.

Learn about healthy foods/baking.

For the first time since the assault, or even a long time before that, I felt some satisfaction. It felt good to try. As I sat back in my chair, the motion caused a twinge which turned into a spasm. I tried to get up, but I was stuck. I laughed due to the irony of the situation, and because if I didn't, I would cry.

'Fuck my life,' I said out loud, smiling as I said it and reaching for a painkiller. This time I wouldn't dwell, or wallow, I would wait for the medication to kick in and go about my day in pain because if I wanted a life I had to pursue it.

As I waited for my next class in the canteen, the woman with the pink hair I'd saw the first day blowing on a trumpet sat next to me. 'So, you're the new girl everyone is taking about.'

She nudged me playfully on the shoulder and I tried not to wince. 'Here, I smuggled in supplies. Don't tell the granny brigade, though. They'll jump on me so fast I won't be able to breathe.'

She handed me a toffee. 'I shouldn't. I'm trying to stay off sugar.'

Pink lady appraised me. 'Eat the toffee, woman. Life is too short to be hard on yourself.'

She unwrapped her own and popped it into her mouth. 'I'm Rita, by the way.

'I'm Dawn.'

'You settling in, OK?'

'I guess. I'm trying to. You like it here?'

'Oh, I do, pretty girl.' She winked at me and tapped her nose. 'I make it my business to know things around here. You got some kind of injury, I take it?'

'Yeah, I hurt my back.'

'Are you seeing anyone?'

'I went to Mr Nevin.'

'Up in the city?'

'Yeah,'

Rita rolled her eyes. 'That fool. What did he say to you?'

'To lose weight.'

'That would be him alright. That's his go to. Blame the patient and let me guess, inject you with an epidural?'

I grinned.

Rita didn't so much speak, but boomed. Everything about her was loud: the hair, the voice, the attitude. The opposite of me.

'It's a money revolver. Charge people to inject them with a painkiller. As soon as it wears off, you'll have to go to him again. There's no fix there. He has it pretty sown up, if you ask me.'

'You've been to him?'

She popped another toffee in her mouth and spoke through chews. 'Tried and tested and thrown out the window. Are you able to move? Exercise, like?'

Pink lady or Rita, didn't make the usual reactions people made when talking about my injury: there was no sucking in of breath, or shaking of the head, or saying you're so young to have back trouble as if it was my fault my body failed. I knew it was my fault, but still hated the implication from anyone else. A kindred spirit to back injuries, Rita knew what I was talking about.

'Some days I can manage stretches and, if I'm lucky, a walk. Other days, it's a win if I can pull myself from the bed. I shouldn't moan. There are people out there in worse pain.'

Rita sat back in her chair. 'Don't you ever feel bad. It's painful for you and it's what you're going through. That pain is yours alone and nobody else's and if you need to talk and get it out, you get it out. Otherwise, it goes off, goes rotten inside you.' She wagged her finger. 'Nobody but you can understand what it feels like to go through that. Don't feel ashamed, you've earned the right to complain.'

I like you Rita.

Rita held her hand up in the air in a signal to wait as she chewed on a tough piece of toffee that required some help. Removing the top tier of false teeth, she scraped the culprit out of the back tooth with her finger and popped the toffee in her mouth. She didn't put the teeth back in until after she smacked her gummy lips together, showing off how the top of her mouth fell in. Rita didn't seem to care what she looked like. 'I know what you need. Come down to the pool with us on a Monday morning. They do a water aerobics class for us oldies, but it would be good for someone crocked as well.'

I smirked; the woman had a way with words.

'It takes away the pressure on the clapped-out joints.'

'Really?'

'Really. Come and try it with us.'

'I'll have to check it with Alayne. I might have a session with her.'

'Leave Alayne to me. It's time you have a lesson with Rita instead.'

Wading

Here's the thing thin people will never know and a heavier person will never admit to; it hurts to exercise when you're curvier. It is more than effort. Even getting up from the couch is exhausting. The thought of it is tiring. People confuse being larger with laziness, but try carrying around an extra couple of kilos with you every single day. Being heavier destroys energy. It depletes you. It destroys self-worth, too.

I would start off small. If I pushed too much, it would send me over and my body wasn't ready for it. I clicked on a yoga video. The instructor was shiny and skinny and as soon as she started, got herself in a ridiculous position. Not for me. I escaped out of it. Typed in yoga for people with back injuries.

The first video showed a group of elderly women sitting around a circle.

This is more like it.

The video started with sitting exercises.

Leg straightening. One at a time. Right foot. Straighten and put back on the floor. Ten times. On the third, I could feel it. I stopped at eight.

That's OK, small steps and build up.

Then it was the left foot. The bad one. I only reached six.

It's only a benchmark. It's where I've started.

Next it was marching both legs while sitting. I had to lift my thighs to help them up. The old people on the video didn't even break a sweat.

It was horrifying how unfit I had become. How did I let myself get like this? I stopped the video. My back was hopping in pain. I felt ashamed. I sipped some water.

Alayne's voice sounded in my ear as if she was standing next to me. *Speak to yourself as if you're a friend.*

So, I tried.

You are trying your best. You had a bad thing happen to you and you couldn't move. Which meant you gained some pounds. It wasn't your fault. You coped with it the only way you knew. Every day, you are learning new things. Even if you don't complete the video today, each day you try, you get stronger. Until one day you will do it. One day, it will be too easy. Then you will move on to another video. And another. Until you are so fit, you could post your own videos. You can do it. So what if you can't today? Your arms still work. Do something with them.

So, I did.

* * *

The swimming pool was cold. I shivered as I made the long walk to the pool. The chill of ventilated air and the thought of exposure made me rush with my arms hugging my body. The water was an inviting hug after the shame of walking in a swimsuit. There were twenty other women in the pool and if they weren't wearing swimming caps, I would put money on each woman being grey underneath. There wasn't a person there under seventy. Except me.

It was hard not to recognise Rita, with her pink wisps of hair sticking out from the swimming cap. Conversing with three other women, I wouldn't approach, my plan was to stay near the side and try to blend in. Rita turned and when she saw me, waved, her loose skin on her arms making more ripples than the water.

'Come on chick, don't be shy. The girls are all dying to meet you.'

I waded through the water. Although I could still feel a pull on my lower back, Rita was right, it was easier than walking on land. A lot of hairless, capped women smiled and enfolded around me.

'This is Dawn, lads, don't be too hard on her now if she doesn't keep up the pace, her back is crocked.'

'Oh, that's horrible. How did a young one like you do that?' One lady asked.

I froze. I didn't want to speak about it. I didn't want to lie either.

'I... It was...'

Rita placed a hand on mine under the water.

'Agnes, you know the score, a lady never tells. Just because we were never ladies and spilled our guts to anyone that will listen, don't mean anyone else has to.'

The group of women broke into laughter. Rita leaned into me. 'Don't mind Agnes, her nose is always getting her in trouble. Don't explain yourself to no one if you don't feel the need to.'

I nodded, relieved. Behind the wrinkles and cataracts, steely eyes looked back at me. There was a reason for that steel with Rita. She had earned her confidence the hard way.

A petite, fit, healthy, pony-tailed girl stepped out to the edge above. One of those pretty, perky, life is good types, that never had a bad day or gained an extra pound.

'Are ye all up for a bit of exercise?'

'Yes!' the gaggle of women shouted back. I resisted the urge to roll my eyes.

Try Dawn, try.

As if knowing, Rita nudged me. 'Have fun. That's half the battle.'

I waited. The woman turned on some music, a generic, upbeat song. Rita and the old posse clapped to the beat. I didn't.

'Right, let's march on the spot.'

The gang of women did as asked.

'Remember, swing those arms as well. We want to get maximum use of those joints.'

My arms swished in the water. To my surprise, I could lift my legs and complete the moves. The water gave a bounce to the body, gave a flow, and lifted up my weightless limbs much easier. It still hurt, but it was a pull rather than an ache; a sore stretch instead of a stab. Doable. After a few seconds, I could feel my face getting slick. I pushed away the thought of the last time my heart rate had pumped through exercise, my eyes closing at the image of the alley.

'Make sure you have enough space around you to stand tall and make circles with your arms.'

As I did the kicks and the bends and the poses, my relief grew. I wouldn't have to be carried out of the pool on a stretcher. Being there could help make me better. I was reclaiming my body. I would master my pain. It may take another year. I may have a million more setbacks, but for the very first time since the assault, I could see a me without the injury. That alone was worth all the effort. The goal didn't seem unachievable anymore. It seemed reachable. Attainable.

I glanced over at Rita, but she was too wrapped up in the moves to notice me. What I could see were pink lines running down the woman's neck and forming a bright pink pool around the water. I moved closer to tell her, then thought better. It would only bring attention, and what would she do once she knew? She'd have to leave the pool and ruin her fun. I checked the women behind and to the other side of Rita, and they all seemed oblivious. I carried on and pretended I saw nothing.

By the end of the session, no amount of water could cool the red skin on my face.

'Same time next week girls,' Lila, the instructor, said.

The women filed to the pool stairs. Each woman's legs bore the scars of a lived life. Varicose veins, age spots, the splayed blue legs of spider veins, bulges of sagged skin once higher up. It was meant to be like that, reminders of the life the person lived. My own bulges were too young for the body I owned. Each woman didn't seem hung up on their appearance like I was. Each one of them were smiling, enjoying their time, with not a bit of shame between them. How much would I enjoy it if I just dropped the guilt? Who was I trying to impress here, anyway?

I caught up with them quickly and in the changing room, I opened my locker and pulled Rita to one side, and offered her a towel, hoping to stop her before anyone else saw the pink leakage running all the way down from her head to her legs. Rita waved it away.

'No need, I've my own. You'll only ruin yours.' Rita winked at my confusion. 'There's a difference between not caring and not seeing Dawn.'

Rita walked past humming, the pink dripping onto the floor, while I still held the towel in midair. As I looked back through the small square window in the door out to the pool, I watched Lila section off the pool, pulling plastic cut off lines across the surface with another staff member. Another person was using something to clean the water. Could I bottle even a little of Rita's courage? A woman like that was just what I needed in my life.

Muffins

The next day, I couldn't raise my leg. Searing pain stabbed me in the thigh. Unfamiliar from the locked in, stifled, unmoving kind I felt in my lower back. This was unending, unstopping, throbbing and relentless. It was vomit inducing and mood changing and depressing.

I was a fool. Being in the water, I felt like I was doing something worthwhile, like my body would thank me for it and yet here I was, the next day, suffering. All the different exercises had pushed my body too much.

It didn't take as long to get out of the bed as it would if my back was caught. Rather, a nagging sensation. A stay-with-you-forever-as-you-were-never-getting-better pain. A reminder that I shouldn't try because it was never giving up ache. I felt the black hole open and the vapour of depression move along and coil around my waist, inviting me back to the dark. In the past, I went without resistance, but today, I couldn't succumb. Today I had obligations. I couldn't believe a tub of toffee muffins would be the drive I needed to not give up.

In the kitchen Mum baulked when she saw me.

'Are you in pain?'

Of course I am, you stupid woman.

I resisted the urge to snap, even though it would be easy to lash out and blame someone, anyone, for what was happening.

'I feel like I've aged twenty years.'

'You look like you have. Sit down and I'll get you some painkillers and a cup of tea.'

Mum helped me into the seat. My eyes welled at her fussing. No matter what she took from me, the next time, all was forgiven.

'I'm sorry, Mum. I'm sorry for all the times I've been rotten to you.'

'Shh now, don't you worry about any of that. I'm your mother. I knew what I was signing up for.'

'Yeah, in the teenage years. My tantrums have lasted longer than that.'

Mum flicked on the kettle, then filled a glass of water and popped two tablets from the sleeve. She placed them in front of me.

'I have to wait to take them with food. They kill my stomach otherwise.'

'Want some toast?'

'Anything, thanks Mum.'

As I bit into the toast, Mum sat across with two steaming mugs.

'They were never big enough to be tantrums,' she said. 'I always saw it as you needing an outlet. With everyone else, you always kept in your feelings. In a strange way, it was a compliment that you felt safe enough to lash out at me, knowing I wouldn't leave. Once I understood you needed that, it made it easier to take.'

I bit down on my lip instead of my toast. Was that what it was? I had always seen it as a reaction to her annoying ways but she had a point. She was the only woman, the only person, I answered back to. Well, apart from Ciaran, but with him I hadn't attacked, rather than spilled. Mum had taken the brunt. I covered my face with my hands and cried. 'Mum, I can't do this anymore.'

She knelt down on the floor and hugged me. 'I don't know how you've coped so far. You're an inspiration.'

I looked at her, surprised. 'An inspiration?'

'You've been so brave. I'm proud of you.'

'But I feel weak.' My voice caught.

'You're not, though, are you?' My mother's eyes challenged me to answer.

'I feel weak.'

'You're stronger than you know.'

'Everyone keeps telling me that.'

She rubbed my arm, and I knew that was the end of our heart to heart. 'Do you want me to ring the centre? I could explain you won't be able to make today.'

I groaned. 'No, I have to go in. I promised to give them the muffins and Samira wanted to go through my pieces. I could do with a lift, though.'

Mum looked at her watch and for the first time I didn't feel annoyance at the gesture. How did I know Mum didn't have plans? I always assumed she didn't have a life, but what did I know? When was the last time I found out anything about her?

'I can drop you in but can't hang around. I have to get back to bring your dad to golf.'

By the time Mum parked outside the centre, my mood was as dark as the pain.

'Will I wait for you? If you just want to pop in and then come home?'

'No, I'll try to stay.'

'Well, I'll just go home and drop your dad and then come straight back. I've a few messages to get, anyway. Just ring.'

I struggled to open the door. After helping me out of the car. We stood side by side, unmoving.

'I don't know if I can do this.'

'Then don't Dawn. Come home. I'll go in and tell them how bad you are. But we'll have to go to see someone about this. You can't go on this way. We'll put you in the recliner and I'll get you everything you need. I'll pick up some good books in the library and get you some treats and you can have a sleep and feel better.'

I wanted to. I wanted to bury myself under a duvet and forget the world. The door to the centre opened and a person I didn't know walked away. 'No. I promised. Can you get the muffins out of the boot?'

Mum left me and came back laden with muffins. 'Will I bring them in for you?'

I shook my head with force. It was wrong of me, but I didn't want her coming to the centre. I wanted it to be all mine, to not have to share it.

If Mum had suggested staying at home a few months ago, I would have reacted differently, gone straight to the accusation. *You just want me to stay at home and never get better. So that I'll stay with you forever. You want me to rot in the house beside you.*

But that was yesterday's Dawn. Here, I could see, Mum was only trying to help, she was as clueless as me about what the best move was, about what the next step to take should be. What mattered was she was trying. I took the big box of Tupperware from her.

'I'll manage. Thanks though. Now that I'm standing, I'll be able to walk.'

'Are you sure?'

I nodded. 'Even if I just go in and see Samira and give the muffins. If you don't mind, I might ring after that.'

'Anytime Dawn.'

I felt Mum's watchful stare as I moved, but I never looked back, I couldn't even if I wanted to. My walk was more like a waddle. A not so cute duck. Or a female hunchback with a big arse to boot. By the time I reached the door, I wanted to turn back. Why was I acting the martyr? Nobody would care if I didn't bring the muffins. A part of me wanted Alayne to see me, for her to witness what pain I was used to dealing with and that it wasn't all over, that the woman didn't cure me with a few chats and positive sayings. I wanted to show Alayne she had, in fact, failed.

There was no one in the halls. Activity sounded from everywhere. The noises coming from each room drowned out my grunts. By the time I reached the first door, which was only a few steps away, it was as if I'd just completed a full on twenty-six-mile marathon.

I didn't get the reaction I expected from Alayne. There was no rush, no gushing. Alayne just nodded from the desk, like she expected it. She said something to the class and walked towards me.

'Can you manage to my office?'

The office seemed a lifetime away, but I nodded, anyway. Alayne took the muffins and held out her arm, and I linked it and shuffled to the office.

'Do you want to go home?'

'Do you think I should?'

'It doesn't matter what I think, Dawn, you're an adult. You make your own boundaries and set your own limits and goals. What I think is irrelevant.'

'Not to me. What do you think?'

Alayne bit her lip. 'I think you did some exercise and your body is reacting to being pushed, using muscles you haven't used in a while. It won't feel that way to you, the pain will feel like a setback.'

'I thought I was out the other side, that everything I was doing here meant I could move on and get better.'

'The road isn't straight. Sometimes there are good days and other days aren't so great, but the bad days strengthen you.'

'What do you mean?'

'Getting through them proves to you how strong you are.'

I rolled my eyes. On purpose. Hoping, wanting Alayne to see me.

'Strength doesn't have to mean pushing yourself. Strength can also mean listening to your body and accepting the bad day. To say no to effort and instead recognise you just need to rest and reflect. Did you consider going to the chiropractor?'

I shook my head.

'For now, go home and rest and come in when you feel better.'

'I was full sure you were going to tell me to suck it up. Change my attitude or something.'

Alayne laughed. 'Do you think I'm a tyrant?'

I didn't answer.

'Attitude helps, but you can't change anything while you're deep inside pain. Shift it slowly. Let it settle. You've been doing a lot, Dawn. Your body just needs to recuperate. You'll know best when you're ready to come back to us.'

'Thanks. Will you hand out the muffins, make sure Rita shares them this time and tell Samira I can't stay?'

'Course. Fair play to you for bringing them. Do you need a lift?'

'No, Mum knew I'd probably call. I'll wait in the canteen for her until she comes back.'

'Dawn, one thing.'

'Yeah?'

'Promise me you *will* come back.'

I laughed, snorted more like.

'Often, when there's a setback, people give up. If you wait until the pain is completely gone, you'll never return. Or when you're at home and all you're thinking about is the pain, it intensifies. Remember to come when it's bearable.'

Alayne smiled a smile that told me she had seen it many times before.

In bed, my dreams goaded, bringing images that mocked me once I woke. I dreamt of running, of being with Ciaran, of a life without pain. When I opened my eyes, all I wanted was to close them again and forget my real life. I wanted unconsciousness again.

Combined with being in my childhood bed, felt like I'd taken a step backwards. All the years I'd lived in a different place as my own person, yet nothing had changed. I was still in my old bedroom, still lying on my old, single, lumpy mattress that I left behind all those years ago, thinking I would never lie on it again, staring at the same outdated posters and photographs on the wall.

That wall. I pulled back the duvet and took agonizing steps to the photos and stroked Ciaran's cheek. It didn't get easier. Missing him hurt as much as the back pain, but deeper, coming from inside of me, his absence in my life left a void I couldn't explain. I studied the other pictures now, pictures I had avoided since I was back and saw they were all of him. Whether he was in the background, or the main objection, I searched for him now. How had I played down how much I loved him? Wasn't he the one I had always wanted next to me in a photograph? Wasn't he the one I wanted next to me now? Ian's pictures didn't make the wall, all ripped up or cut out of.

Flashbacks of life came to me from those pictures. Of a dream that made me see Ciaran differently. Of putting on makeup and deciding that night would be the night I said something. Of him looking away when I approached and going over to the lads. Of Ian putting his arm around me after I saw Ciaran with someone else.

Other images of Ian came now. An arm red and burning from being twisted. Him calling all the time, knowing my parents, knowing no matter what way he acted, everyone accepted him; it didn't matter what he did when they didn't see. Somehow, they integrated in the blame, becoming part of it, turning into unknowing conspirators to my staying in the relationship.

Sand Dunes

June 2008

Before I left the house, I checked myself. In the last few weeks, I did that more before meeting Ciaran, or around him, aware of where he stood or how near he was or how he looked at me, or if he laughed when I told a joke or not. Whether it was just a guy thing or a specific Ciaran thing, I didn't know, but something had changed. Ever since the first night he walked me to the bridge, our conversations had deepened, and I'd found myself not wanting to leave him, not wanting to say goodnight. Even that gesture had to mean something because some of the other lads were from Crookstown, Ian, Seanie, Tessa and Rolls, but Ciaran and I always snuck off separately, finding some way to walk only together.

On our walks, there were never silences, yet the more we talked the more I found I wanted to know still, searching his eyes to see if I could work out what he wanted, looking at his lips and wondering what it would feel like to kiss him. I put it down to puberty - inevitable for two people our age from the opposite sex to become attracted to each other; two balls of hormones waiting to explode on someone else; I was, anyway, my emotions flitting from one extreme to the other, my attraction to guys becoming all-consuming, even what you could class as infatuation, fizzing out if the guy spoke or showed interest back. Sometimes I wondered if I was dying for the thought of any love, that

I would settle for anyone. Ciaran, or the interest in Ciaran, had crept up on me though, until it became normal to want him around, to want him near, to speak and see him. He just got me. The thing was, Ciaran seemed oblivious to my growing feelings. He treated me like any of his other friends, and except for walking me home, he'd shown no longing for me at all. His stance was playful, a gentle banter, never hurtful. He was everything I wasn't: brave, confident, talkative, easy to talk to. He dragged the words from me inventing a game where he would start a sentence and stop midway and it would be my turn to finish it. In his company, words loosened, and I didn't need to overthink. When I had news, he was the first one I looked for. On a night out, he was the one I wanted to talk to, the one I wanted to laugh with. He was the first on my recents on my phone.

And then I'd had the dream. I dreamt of us, alone, sitting on a cliff, our bodies close as we watched the sunset. I could feel the anticipation of what was going to happen next, hoping he would make a move, any move, and then, as the darkness of the night crept in, Ciaran took my face in his hands and kissed me. When I woke, I could still feel the tingle on my lips, could still feel his warm breath against mine, could still sense the shock and excitement running through me. Since then, I couldn't see him the same way. How could I see him as a friend when I had felt the softness of his lips? I had felt a tenderness between us that was real and couldn't go back from; even though it hadn't happened, once felt I didn't want to undo it. Ciaran acted as normal, as if nothing had changed, because to him I was the same girl, the same friend I'd always been. After that, I scrutinised everything he did, the linking of my arm, the tilt of his head when he said goodbye. Did it mean he was sorry to see me go? I wanted to tell him, needed to, but since the dream, I'd become nervous around him and my words dried up.

Geared up to tell him how I felt or at the very least to ask him could we go to the Debs together in September, I weaved through the crowd down the beach, the smoke from the BBQ forming a halo over everyone's head and tried to ignore the butterflies in my stomach. His was the only face I was looking for, nodding at each of the lads when they saw me, but I moved on quickly, not wanting to lose my nerve, or the words I had practiced.

I like you Ciaran.

And then the crowd made a gap and there he was, sitting on a log dragged from somewhere looking out to the sea. Sensing me, he turned in my direction and I smiled at him, a smile so broad it could crack my teeth and then I saw something, only a flicker of his eyelid, but it was enough to make the butterflies quieten and my stomach squirm. Whether he saw my desperation, or he got scared, or realised I was going to say something he didn't want me to say, he dropped his gaze and hopped from his seat, walking into the middle of the group of lads, draining his bottle of beer in one go. I changed course, stunned but hiding it, greeting the girls, hugging them and chatting as if nothing was wrong when really I was reeling inside, trying to process what had just happened. As I sat on the sand and pretended to have a good time, I watched him when I hoped no one watched me, as he drank bottle after bottle of beer, which wasn't like him. At first, I hoped it was him working up the nerve to talk to me, but after a while, when it became clear he was purposely ignoring me, I could only guess he was keeping his distance. Hurt floored me and I found it hard to move. I ran through our last interactions and wondered, had I messed up, had I become too flirty or clingy?

A fight broke out by the fire pit, two of the lads pushing and shoving and was over before it begun but when I looked back at Ciaran, he'd disappeared. The way he acted, confused me. For years whenever we saw each other, we went straight to the other, magnetised, the action unthought of, and now I hated I was even thinking of it, that the act of moving near to me had changed to unnatural. It took some time to work up the courage to confront him, but what forced me was my ultimate worry that something was wrong, that something had happened. I searched a long time, going from group to group with no sight and then walking the length of the beach. On the way back, I stood in the dark, not wanting to join the others just yet, the noise too loud for my overactive brain. Had he slipped home? Why hadn't he talked to me? I trudged the sand, disappointed. By the sand dunes, two white feet stuck out against the black. Girl's feet. Next, I saw shoes discarded on the sand. I heard a laugh. Ciaran's laugh. As my eyes adjusted, I made out two shapes, blended into one. A man on top of a girl. While I had worried about him, Ciaran had been behind the sand dunes, rolling around with Marissa Daly.

At the end of the other side of the beach away from Ciaran and the others, I sat on the sand, letting the wind batter my face. A person sat next to me. It was Ian.

'All right?' He asked.

I cleared my throat and nodded in answer.

'I see Ciaran's happy out back there. I always thought the two of ye were a bit of a thing, but sure, his loss is my gain.'

He put his arm around me and I didn't shake it away. I didn't correct him or tell him no. Even when he kissed me, I didn't object. Ciaran didn't care for me, so what mattered? At least someone did.

Rolling

The thoughts of my old life made me want to dive into the new one in front of me, starting with my room. It badly needed a clean. Scooping out my dirty clothes from the wash basket, the chiropractor's card fell out of my trousers. I left it on the floor, with the excuse I couldn't bend, but knowing the real reason was I couldn't face making that call.

I didn't stop until the room transformed. One by one, I took down the old pictures but didn't have the heart to take down the last one, the biggest. Again I stroked Ciaran's face, then moved on to cleaning windows, wiping down tabletops, making my bed. Mum, hearing the noise, popped in.

'You OK?'

'I'm trying to do a good thing.'

Mum looked around the room. 'You've done a great job. It's good to see you up.' She saw the card on the floor and picked it up. 'What's this?'

'Alayne recommended him.'

'Well, there's no time like the present to go. This can't go on.'

She handed me her phone and gave me a look that said; you know what to do.

'It's just a spasm. I've been getting better.'

'Looks to me like you're right back where you started.'

She was right. The pain was as bad as that very first day. Or worse, if that was possible. Everything was on fire and there was a gnawing in my bones, bringing out a need in me to bite down on something, anything, that might distract me for a moment. It clawed and scraped at me, a thousand needles in my skin and I couldn't take it any longer, I wanted out of the room. Or the strongest medication I could get. If there was alcohol in the house, I would have drank it straight.

I picked up the card Mum left on the bedside locker. What would be the harm in ringing? Apart from Alayne being smug about being right, I could just get some advice over the phone. Maybe if I heard his voice I could get a feel about whether he was trustworthy or if I threw a few questions, I could gather if he knew what he was talking about.

The phone dialled twice before a woman answered.

'Better days clinic, how can I help?' The woman asked in a melodic, chirpy voice.

'Hi, I don't know if you can help me. A friend, I mean, a teacher of mine, recommended the chiropractor there. Alayne thinks you, or your clinic, I mean, might help.'

'And you're not so sure?'

'I'm not.'

There, I had said it.

'Here's what I know. I've worked here five years and have seen people carried in, or walking with their heads down because they've been told what they have is incurable, yet a month or two on they are like different people. I have seen patients leave this treatment with no trace of pain in their bodies.'

'Are you a chiropractor?'

'Hell no.' She laughed. 'I enjoy seeing the change, not being the one to do it. Don't get me wrong, not everyone walks out dancing or cured and there *are* quacks out there, there are people that say they are healers when they don't have any credentials. Do your research before you go to *anyone*. We can't fix everyone. It depends on what is going on, what type of injury, or whether you help yourself, or how your body responds. Look, the only thing I can promise you is this: the doctor won't tell you he can help you if there's something else outside the clinic that will get you better faster. He will tell you the truth. He will point you in the right direction.'

The girl spoke a good game. A blast of pain reminded me to listen.

'Look, change is scary. If you're unsure, how about I get Dr Fischer to speak with you? He's in with a patient now but should be out any second.'

'Please.'

I closed my eyes and waited.

The man's voice was calm. 'Hello, Dawn?'

'Hi.'

'Dr Fischer here. I hear you're wondering if we can help. Do you want to describe what's going on?'

I kept my words to a minimum. 'I have a back injury. Herniated discs.'

'Lower or upper back?'

'Lower.'

'Have you had any Xrays?'

'An MRI. That's what diagnosed me. Before that, the doctor thought it was muscular. Can you help me?'

Way to go with your beliefs Dawn. One second you vow never to go to a chiropractor and the slightest bit of extra pain you're begging the man to save you.

'Until I examine you, I can't tell what is going on.'

'I'm so sick of chasing different things that don't work.'

'Come in, bring your MRI and I'll go through them. You have my word I won't adjust you unless you give me the go ahead.'

'Alayne said to trust you.'

'Alayne Adams?'

'That's the one.'

He chuckled. 'She's quite persuasive. You're the girl she said might ring? In that case, come in and I'll give you a free check. That way, at least you know.'

'Book me in.'

The chiropractic clinic was in a new glass front building overlooking the water in Knockfarraig. There had been money spent on the place. Its decor was plush: velvet suede high-back chairs you could lean your head on and keep your spine straight. There were expensive woods on the shelves and tables and thick carpet that felt soft under my feet. An impressive mural ran the full length of the main wall. Without introduction, the receptionist greeted me.

'Dawn, I'm Sandra, the girl you spoke with on the phone. Are you too sore to sit or is it better for you to?'

'I can sit.'

'Brilliant. The bathroom is through the white door there by the plant. I'm just going to give you some forms to fill out and once you're done, the Doctor will see you.'

Sandra handed me a clipboard with a four-page form on it. It was more detailed than any form I had filled out in any clinic I had gone to so far. On the first page, there were two outlines of a full body, one of the front and one of the back, and asked to draw on the diagram where the pain was. It didn't stop there. It requested specification: S for stabbing, B for burning, P for pain, N for numbness, T for tingling. The second page went into further detail. It listed a long line of ailments and asked to tick which ones I had experienced in the last six months. The first ten were associated with the back: Low back pain, neck pain, shoulder pain, tingling in the legs, numbness in the toes. Tick, tick, tick, tick, tick. There were other questions I hadn't expected: Did I have heartburn? Were there any issues with my menstrual cycle? Did I experience headaches? Or stomach issues? The last page had a long picture of the spine and lots of space for notes for the doctor.

I wanted to resist, but the place already impressed me.

The Doctor came into the room helping a person with a cane to the counter.

'Sandra, will you ring a taxi for Marie?' He placed a comforting arm on the woman's shoulder and looked her right in the eye. No avoidance like Mr Nevin. 'Marie, we'll see you soon OK?'

'Thanks Doctor,'

The man was dark, with black hair that rested under his ears. His eyes were brown and his skin was just as dark. Dressed in a navy lambswool jumper, white crisp shirt, and suit trousers, I guessed he was in his late forties.

He looked me in the eye when he said my name and shook my hand as if he was happy that I came. I almost cried at that. At how different it was from the way Mr Nevin spoke me to in the consultant's office.

'Dawn, come into the back with me and we can have a chat. You brought the MRI?'

'I did.'

'Great. We're already ahead of the game then.'

I sat down on a chair, trying not to look at the imposing leather bed in the middle of the room. The doctor read my form for a second.

'The injury happened about four months ago. Is that right?'

I nodded, knowing what was coming.

'Can you explain how you fell?'

His pen lingered about an inch from the page, ready to make his own notes about the injury. I took a breath. This man was a person who wanted all the details. Who needed them to piece together the puzzle like a jigsaw. I would have to explain it, as the angle I fell might be the precise fact he needed to make sense of.

'It wasn't a normal fall. A man pulled me back by my hair. He attacked me.'

He didn't write, just inched his face nearer, keeping his eyes on me. 'I'm sorry to hear that, Dawn.'

I nodded in answer. *Please don't ask me anymore about him.*

'How did you land?'

'On my back.'

'Was it hard ground?'

'Uneven. Cobbled. When I came to, my legs were at wrong angles. Kind of twisted like.'

The doctor scribbled some notes. 'Did you feel pain straight away?'

'Yes.'

'Where on your body did you feel the pain?'

'In my lower back. Down my legs. I found it hard to move. I could only get up by rolling onto my side and then my stomach. Then bringing my knees up and pulling myself to standing.'

'Did you have pain anywhere else?'

'Pain in my face and a headache, but that was,' I hesitated. He waited, his eyes encouraging me to continue. 'Because the guy punched me there.'

And there it was. He was going to make me speak about it. He lay his pen on the paper.

'That must have been traumatic. How have you dealt with that?'

'Lots of tears. I get nightmares. Alayne's helping me.'

Although I still can't speak about the attack with her.

He nodded. 'You're in good hands there.'

I didn't answer.

He pulled the image of my damaged spine from the envelope and attached it to a white box, flicking a switch on the side and lighting it up.

He sucked in his breath. 'You must have been in a lot of pain the day you got the MRI.'

How do you know that?

'See how straight your spine is?' He ran a finger down the straight line of the image, then leant down the side of his table and picked up a life size model of a spine. 'See how curved it should be? You must have been in spasm.'

I nodded.

'Do you know what each part is?'

'Kind of, I've looked up my injury.'

'Well, these white blocks are your discs. The clear pieces in between each one are almost jelly like in substance to make movement possible.' He flicked at a spiky piece that came out of the side of the model. They were yellow. 'This is a nerve. Do you understand what they do in the body?'

'Aren't they like the messaging system? They tell the body what to do.'

'Spot on.' He placed the spine back on the floor and turned to the light box again. With a ruler, he made some lines on the film.

'I can see disc herniations in three places. See here.'

He pointed to one disc. To where the jelly substance ballooned out the side.

He gave me a sheet with the same image of the spine that was on the back of the form, but this time it had the vertebrae numbered and a line out of each one with a list of symptoms.

'As you can see, each vertebra is associated with a specific area of the body. So, for example, if the C1 is misaligned, it may not come out as pain, but you may experience dizziness or headaches. The C2 could exacerbate eye problems. If the T6 is subluxated,' he pointed to the middle of the spinal image. 'You may not have pain, but you may have digestive issues.' He ran his hand down to the lower end, stopping about three discs away from the end of the spine. 'At the L3, you could experience irregular periods or menstrual problems. Does that make sense?'

It did.

'It reminds me of reflexology. How each part of the foot is supposed to represent a part of the body.'

'That's right. Each nerve runs to a specific destination. If something disrupts the nerve's path, it effects how that nerve works and, over time, can cause problems. It's my job to work out where the problems are and put them back into alignment. I don't heal anyone. All I do is correct. It's your body that takes over and heals you.'

'Why can't it do it by itself?'

'It can. It tries. But it depends on the type of injury and the severity. It also depends on how long you have the injury, whether it is genetic, how much damage has been done, how much secondary injuries have occurred. It depends on the type of nourishment you give it or if the body is being bombarded with toxins or stress. The body will do as much as it can, but sometimes it has to work overtime. If the person is doing everything possible to help themselves, the body, tissues, and cells will renew and heal. Life can get in the way, though. I'm here to make sure the body is working at its peak potential. Like I said, it's the person's body that takes over and heals.'

'Do you think you can heal me?'

'Let's get you on the bed and see.'

I lay down with my head on the rest. He placed a hand on my shoulder. 'I know you're nervous. All I'm going to do now is palpate you. The MRI helps me understand what's going on inside. The form you fill out helps me understand what you've experienced, but my fingers and hands give me the full picture. Like a blind person reading from braille, I can tell more by doing that than anything else. Using my hands, all these methods give me a full understanding for the report of findings. Are you OK if I proceed?'

'I am.'

'Let me know if anywhere I touch is sore.'

I sucked in a breath and nodded. He made a scribble on his form. He started from my neck. His touch was gentle but thorough, using a sliding or kneading motion rather than poking. It surprised me how tender I still was, after all that time. There were places other than my back that made me flinch. My neck, on the right, on the edge of the bone, hurt. My shoulder blade felt tender to the touch. An area to the side of my hip made me want to pass out when he tipped it. Once he had worked his hands over every part of my back, he pulled his seat over.

'Can I get you to roll onto your back Dawn?'

Holding out his hand, I used it as a hoist to turn on my side, then roll. He slid his wheeled chair along the floor until it rested by my head, so when I looked up, he was upside down. He cupped his hands around the base of my skull and tapped his fingers along one after the other, in a way that reminded me of the nursery rhyme for itsy, bitsy spider. Then his fingers moved down until they reached my shoulders.

'You can sit up now Dawn.'

He stood and held his hands out for me again, letting me hold and lift to a sitting position. I noticed he didn't pull, and that gave me more faith in him; experience had taught him that would bring more pain.

'The type of injury you have is very familiar to me, something I work with every day. I have had many, many patients with low back pain that have made a full recovery. It all depends how your body responds to treatment, but I'm confident it's something I can help you with. What I would suggest is focusing on getting the curvature back in your spine. Then we will have to work on your muscles. Some of them have gone into protection mode and are tight. It won't be a quick fix. There will be days when after working on your body it may feel worse. The nerves will need to do their thing to heal. You may experience extreme tiredness, you may become very emotional after an adjustment, that's all completely normal, good, even. Any change will mean it is working.

Listen to your body. When it wants rest, it's telling you it wants to heal.'

For once I wanted to trust a man and for him to prove I was right to. I wanted to be fixed. With a smile, I said goodbye and walked out onto the street, straight into Ciaran.

Blast

Ciaran. His smile was broad and his eyes lit up on seeing me. Without second guessing or questioning, I hugged him, regretting it as he squeezed. I let go. Ciaran didn't, only loosening his grip.

'I forgot to go easy. Did I hurt you?'

'Yeah, but it was worth it.'

He let go and only then did I remember all that went on in between our last meeting. I looked at the floor. 'How come you're around these parts?'

He looked at his shoes. 'Long story.'

A long story you don't want to tell me.

'I mean, for talking about here. I don't have to be anywhere for a while. Want to grab a coffee?'

'Mum is around somewhere waiting. I guess I could ask if she can hang around.'

'I was speaking to her. It was how I found this place. She said she had to go home for a while so I can give you a lift home after?'

'You have a car?'

'I do.'

'So you're both conspiring against me?'

'It was the only way I could get to see you. Want to go to Mac's?'

Mac's was all the way down at the end of the street. 'If you don't mind going slow.'

'Sorry, you're sore. Is there somewhere closer? It's been a long time since I had a coffee in Knockfarraig.'

'Mac's will be grand. They still do your milkshake.'

He offered me an arm to link, and I took it. 'Ah come on now Dawn, I'm a grown man. I can't be ordering milkshakes anymore.'

'You're so ordering it.'

He grinned. 'I am yeah. Screw adulthood.'

A twinge made me halt and Ciaran stopped and held me straight, bringing us closer. It was like stepping back in time, to a stage where there was no pain or girlfriends and it was just him and me.

'I've missed you.' I couldn't help saying it.

Ciaran looked relieved. 'Same. I've been walking around like my right arm's chopped off.'

'Well, I've been walking around with a back injury, so I think I win on the misery stakes.'

Ciaran ordered us milkshakes, and I took too long to get into my seat. Once he was sitting, I raised an eyebrow at him.

'You're here. I keep wanting to touch you to make sure you're real.'

Ciaran rubbed his thighs and laughed. 'Same. I nearly walked past you, you looked so different.'

I felt the blush spread over my cheeks. 'I look a state.'

'What? No, I mean the hair. It's good. You look good.'

In his company, I felt myself softening and I laughed more in five minutes than I had in months. The milkshake tasted sweeter; the sun came out and shone, the lights glowed, even my pain didn't matter.

He scooped up some milkshake. 'So, I'm here to ask you a question.'

I sat back, braced myself. 'Go ahead.'

'I was wondering if you'd be my best friend again?'

I allowed myself to breathe. 'I never stopped.'

He played with his milkshake. 'Yes, you did. I want to be there for you, but you haven't let me. You've blocked my calls, stopped speaking to me, completely cut me off. That isn't what a best friend does.'

'Come on, Ciaran, life has been awful. I needed space. I couldn't deal with anything else but the pain.'

'I was something else to deal with?'

We looked at each other.

Tell me what you want, Ciaran.

'You and Kristin needed space, too.'

Ciaran reached for my hand across the table. I hesitated, knowing I wanted to, but afraid, so afraid to touch his skin, to feel his warmth and not melt, not react, not blurt out everything he didn't want me to say. His hand cupped mine.

'What I wanted was for you to be my friend again. Can I? Will you allow me to be your friend? Will you let me back in?'

Friend.

I wanted to take my hand away, instead I squeezed it. Doing nothing with Ciaran was still better than everything without him. 'I could do with a friend.'

Ciaran, throughout the years, flashed before me. In this café, sitting at the same booth, sharing a milkshake when we couldn't afford two. Feeding each other with the straw. Or sitting on the bridge, close enough to notice the hairs that had grown on his upper lip. Tracing each one with my eyes, burning them into my memory. Every change on his face, every new freckle formed, was exciting. Or Ciaran beside me on the beach, the night of the Deb's, his dark tux disappearing in the night so his face and white shirt were the only things visible. The sweet, brief taste of him that one time. Or how he lifted me from the bed after my injury, how he'd dropped everything to come around and help, how tenderly he'd washed me. And then I saw him and Kristin, him with his arm draped around her, how happy they looked, how oblivious to me.

'So?'

'So,' he said, smiling.

'Ah, come on Ciaran, spill. Why are you walking around Knockfarraig on a weekday?'

'I'm taking some time off from my job.'

'How come?'

'You don't have to be the only person to have a crisis about what they want to do, you know?'

'OK.'

'I just always imagined living a crazy life when I was younger. Travelling and seeing the world and it just hasn't happened. The furthest I've gone is Cork City.'

'Hold on, what about Australia?'

'That was a three-month trip one summer, not the same as living it up abroad.'

'It's more than what I did.'

'Well, I asked.'

'You know I couldn't get the time off. Greene promised me a raise if I stayed. Fat lot of good it did me.'

'You could come this time.'

He sucked on his milkshake.

'I'm sure you'd want someone with a back injury slowing you down.'

'We could wait until you're better. I'd need to save and make a plan, anyway.'

'How are you going to save if you've quit your job?'

'I've moved back home.'

'What?'

'Dad has a massive build on for a housing estate. The deposits are paid with a strict deadline of completion by next year, so he's offered me more money than I can refuse to help.'

'Construction? You'll be wrecked.'

'You've some cheek. I worked every summer for my dad until I left university, remember? If I keep my head down and save everything, I can have a plan in place by the time it's finished.'

'How's Kristin about all this?'

Ciaran looked pained. 'Not happy, but what can I do? I'm not going to be a freeloader and expect her to pay my way and it's going to be early morning starts on site, so it makes sense to not have the drive.'

'It's forty minutes from the city, max.'

He scowled. 'Like I said, I won't be a freeloader.'

I didn't challenge him. It would only look like I was trying to get more information about their relationship. By Ciaran's crossed arms and furrowed brow, it was conversation over about Kristin. I changed the subject.

'I've been going to a place to help me get better.'

'The place you came out from?'

Ciaran shifted, relieved to be talking about something else.

'Nah, that's a chiropractic clinic, today was my first appointment, so time will tell. The place I'm talking about has classes, like art, so I'm drawing again. I don't know if it's helping, but it gets me up in the morning and stops me from wallowing in the bed. The woman who runs the centre gives me sessions too.'

'Like counselling?'

I nodded. 'Yeah, like counselling.' It surprised me I didn't redden. 'I'm a brand new me. No drinking. Exercising. Talking to someone. Alayne thinks I need to find my voice, that I need to speak up for myself more.'

'I like her. Is it working?'

'I don't know. I guess.'

'Sounds like I could do with going to that place.'

I straightened, picturing Sam and Ciaran meeting.

Ciaran's face fell. 'Calm down, it was only a joke.'

'No, I think it would help you. I could check it out.'

Ciaran relaxed. 'Nah, sure I'm going to be up to my neck with the site. I'd like if we could hang out sometimes though, if you wanted?'

'I'd love it. There's nothing to do in Crookstown.'

'All it was good for was getting locked. And from the sound of it, that's out with you?'

'Yeah. Parent's rules. For once, I'm following it. Alayne suggested giving it a break.'

'I hated drunk Dawn.' He sped up when he saw my crestfallen face. 'Only because of the way it changed you around guys. Drink made you lower your standards. You were better than the dickheads you chose.'

I took a moment, letting what he said digest. He hadn't said it to hurt me.

It was the truth.

'I hated drunk Dawn too. Why are you here, Ciaran?'

'What do you mean? I just explained.'

'No, I mean here with me now. Did you come looking for me?'

'Course. As soon as I dumped some stuff, I called to the house and your dad said where you'd be in town. Look, I missed you. I wanted to see you.'

'Would Kristin be happy with you talking to me?'

He tsked.

'You rebel.'

'She doesn't get to tell me what to do anymore.'

I flashed him a quizzical expression. He played with his straw, scooping the last of the milkshake out and letting it drop.

'She made me choose.'

'Between what?'

'Between you and her.'

'Me? But there is no me.'

His eyes flicked to me, then back to his straw.

'There has always been you, Dawn. I knew it. Kristin knew it. She didn't believe me that either of us wouldn't act on it. When she saw our texts, she gave me the ultimatum. I'm trying to work it out because I do love her.'

'You love her?' I tried my best to keep my voice even.

Ciaran winced. 'I do. I really do. But I don't know if I can be with someone who doesn't trust me. Or think they can tell me who I can be friends with for no reason than being insecure. I don't even blame her, I dropped everything when you text. I looked forward to them. Reading them was like getting to know the Dawn I loved in school again.'

'Loved? In school?'

He covered his face through splayed fingers. 'Oh yeah, I had a huge crush on you.'

'Why didn't you ever say?' He shrugged. Raked his fingers through his hair.

'I need to work out what to do next. At least if I'm honest, I'm not messing anyone around. So, I moved back home like you to figure things out.'

'Ciaran, if you can work it out with the girl you love, try to.'

He looked away, stared out the window for the longest time. Then he nodded, his mind made up. 'You're right, I love Kristin. I just have to show her she can trust me and there's nothing between us.'

Nothing between us. Had I just convinced the love of my life to pursue another woman?

'Look, I'm not expecting anything. You've built your own life here and I don't want to disrupt that, but I'm just hoping to hang out sometime as friends.'

'I would love that,' I said, plastering on a smile.

Deb's

Ian was the opposite of Ciaran. He was quiet, like me, so we could spend hours in silence unbothered. Back then, being Ciaran's opposite was a good thing, for it meant I couldn't compare the two and instead, left me wanting to know more about Ian. Speaking little, I found it hard to read him and that was exciting.

There were warning signs from the start. Whenever I did talk in company, he would cut across me and finish what I wanted to say, which at first felt like he was helping me; appealing for a girl who struggled with giving her opinion, because it allowed me to step back from conversation. Ciaran's constant push to talk had forced me to step out and let people see me, to search and find the right words no matter how uncomfortable it could be but then he coupled with Marissa and his presence disappeared overnight, and the loss of him, of his friendship, was so sudden it left me barren and I clawed at ways to cope without him, convincing myself it was refreshing to have someone accept me as I was, happy I stay the same. With Ian, there was no need to move forward.

I didn't pursue a relationship or look for an alternative for Ciaran. Ian just kept knocking at my door. There was no asking if I wanted him to call or even become his girlfriend and, like all things in my life, I didn't offer an opinion, just doing what other people wanted me to do. Living in Crookstown, he knew where I lived and every afternoon he knocked at my door to go meet the lads, and with that action, being seen walking to Knockfarraig together also somehow stamped me as Ian's, putting an immediate end to my walk home with Ciaran. Not that he even wanted to. Glued to his new girlfriend, he didn't even look in my direction anymore.

Ian had no fear introducing himself to my parents, as they had known his family for decades. They welcomed him into the house. As a boyfriend, Ian was persistent and intense, wanting to spend all our free time together and, after seeing Ciaran too many times with Marissa, when it was clear he didn't want me even as a friend anymore, I gave in and stopped hanging out in Knockfarraig as much and instead stayed at home with Ian, flinging full force into the relationship until the feelings I pretended to have became real.

It was the first time someone had shown a blatant interest. Unlike Ciaran, I didn't have to second guess whether Ian liked me, and as the weeks rolled by, I found love crept up on me for this quiet guy. So it came as a surprise when the words he chose were hurtful, when he dropped comments with deliberate intent to twist a wound.

Words like, 'Why would you do that for, that's stupid?' or, 'How would you know?' jutted in when I told him about my day. Comments that jarred me and made me go inwards, avoiding conflict, avoiding an argument. After I retreated, Ian would continue on with the conversation as if nothing had changed and I would stay locked in time and place, relaying the words, wondering what I'd done to irritate him, how I could learn not to repeat it. Until he would get annoyed and announce I was sulking and he was going home because he was sick of my moods and my head would reel from the confusion, from the twisting and even though I would understand that he was the one who had started it, who'd dropped the comment and changed the course of the conversation I wasn't able to explain it, I wasn't able to put in words what happened so I tried to rectify and placate and calm and make up.

Only about a month in to our relationship, one afternoon when we were walking to Knockfarraig. Ian bumped my shoulder. 'Heard Ciaran had a free gaff last night, but instead of having a party, the sneaky fecker brought Marissa home. Lennie saw her this morning sneaking out.' I watched a seagull soar up above me in the sky, trying to keep my reaction under control. Ian stood in front of me, forcing me to stop. 'Ciaran told him they never slept. Didn't go into more details, but Lennie said he didn't have to, the grin on his face said he got some. What was it Lennie said Ciaran told him?' Ian trailed off, tilting his head as if thinking, but when he looked at me, the way he looked at me, I knew he was going to say something that would disrupt the course of my life and that he wanted it to. He rearranged the features on his face, acting uninterested, but the sides of his mouth turned upward at what he was going to say next.

'Ciaran told him he's never felt this way about any girl before.'

It took everything I had not to react, even though my stomach felt like it dropped to the ground and my breathing caught in my chest, and I wanted to run home and hide and not speak to anyone ever. Ian studied me and I knew, I couldn't give him what he wanted. If I showed him he would go in worse, he would turn.

Ian smiled at me, and said almost in a whisper, as if it was only for us. 'It's a good thing you met me. Looks like you never had a chance with him.'

I should have walked away from him then. I should have seen it as a glimpse into the real Ian, a snapshot of what way our relationship would go, but I didn't, I stood in front of him, heartbroken. And ashamed for ever thinking Ciaran would want me. And if I'm telling the truth, a thrill also ran through me because even though Ciaran didn't care, here was Ian caring enough to want to provoke me, that he was laying it out that he was insecure, showing me he loved me enough to feel jealous. That had to be love, right?

Now I see what he did as abuse, but back then there wasn't the information or clear lines there is now. Then it was confusing because he was never physical and back then, society only classed bruises or a man getting physical as abuse. What he did was more subtle, more sneaky that I'd question whether it was even wrong. It was putting his arm around me and running his finger along the roll on my back, saying, 'You've put on a couple of pounds.' Then, stroking my bright red horrified face. 'Hey, don't worry, it just means there's more of you for me.' It was whispers drip feeding the reasons I was stupid or fat or just plain wrong. If I disagreed, if I spoke back, it was raising his voice, finding a voice to raise, while he put his face close to mine in warning if I did anything he disliked.

Looking back, since working with Alayne, I could see his behaviour was wrong, but at the time, his words burrowed down until what he said gained value. The person being controlled never sees what is going on from the outside of the situation. It's like standing in front of an object looking down. Even when you're not allowed to touch or pick it up, you can see the top. You can see at least two sides are square and from outside, it is obvious it's a box. But being inside is different. You can't see the sides, the lid, the way out. All you see is darkness.

On days when his words hurt me, afterwards, as I cried alone somewhere, I vowed to break it off, practicing inoffensive words meant not to trigger him over and over until I could say them without thinking.

I'm making you miserable. You deserve better than me.

By then, he was so integrated into my life I didn't know how to remove him from it. My parents loved him. Ian played GAA for the senior team my dad coached, and every Sunday he would come around for dinner without an invitation. Mum even laid out the fancy dinnerware. And then I would see Ciaran and Marissa, and my heart would break a little more and anyone, even Ian, was better than being alone. I think in that lay the real problem. Ian knew how I felt about Ciaran and hated me for it.

Why did Ian want me when he knew I loved someone else? Why had I let someone treat me like that? It had started a precedent, becoming the benchmark of how all my relationships went after, staying unrequited like with Ciaran or bordering on abusive like Ian. When Kristin announced on my birthday that Ciaran loved me for years, it had been more than a surprise; it was a complete landslide, because if he had given me one sign, if I had thought for one moment he had seen me as anything other than a friend, I would have made sure my life turned out differently.

Come on Dawn. Is that true?

I thought of the Debs. It had been the talk of the whole Summer. Held in September, by then we had officially left school. The Leaving Cert was done. The teachers were no longer our bosses. We were free. Getting ready, I imagined it was Ciaran's house I was going to and not Ian's. Since getting with Marissa, we had not been alone with each other at all.

Ian, in his tux, both nervous and handsome. Seeing him, the blonde hair against the dark suit, made my stomach flip. Yet there was a part of me that didn't want to go with him, didn't want to pretend. Still, I did, acting like I knew I should react. Playing along, feigning excitement when I walked down the stairs, coy when he gave me the corsage, demure as I smiled for the photographs, but inside I wanted to go already; I wanted to see Ciaran, and couldn't wait for Ciaran to see me.

Seeing him made everything worse. It hurt to not be the girl walking beside him. It hurt to see him in a three-piece dark navy suit, making the lads wearing tuxedos look juvenile in comparison. How handsome he looked, how happy he seemed, Marissa and him looking like the model couple. All I wanted to do was run to him. There was a slight widening of his eyes when he saw me, just a half an inch of a difference and I took that and kept it close to my heart, that one glimpse he may find me attractive and then he was gone, whisked away with Marissa and the table she sat at.

Ian was on the shots and had been going hard at it since before we sat in the limo. At the table, the night I had looked forward to for months took on a sourness. The air wilted, and the energy and effort waned. The food was bland and chewy. Ian was less talkative than ever and if anyone spoke, he responded with a loud disapproving grunt that resulted in the table going from excited chatter to stunted awkward chit chat. I couldn't help but take glances over at Ciaran, having the opposite time, laughing and messing like we all should. Only one time did Ciaran look over and meet my glance. I blended away from the table, only seeing him, his face, his questioning expression, turning to a softening, then to a sadness, a look that said he was sorry for the awkwardness between us but he still cared, he was still my friend. All of that with a softening of the eye, but with Ciaran, there never needed to be any words. Ian leant over, his voice coming out like a growl.

'Stop it.' Giving me a warning look that said he saw, that he knew what I was thinking and he was right. I wanted to sit next to Ciaran, I wanted to be at his table.

By dessert, Ian had knocked his second glass of wine over. Cleaning it up with napkins, I asked him to go easy. He shouted at me to fuck off loud enough for half the room to hear. No one defended me. No one came to my rescue. In fact, everyone at the table laughed. I dropped the napkin on my plate and dragged my feet to the bathroom. I looked at my reflection in the mirror. There I was all done up, in the most beautiful dress I would probably ever wear, and the guy I was with had just told me to fuck off. And the thing was, I knew I would say nothing when I went back to the table. Talking back with Ian got me in trouble.

Sticking up for myself got me shouted at. I would pay for asking him to go easy for the rest of the night. And the thing was, in a room full of students, no one would say anything. Our friends found it funny, sniggering when he called me a fool or pointed out what I had done wrong.

Wasn't I overreacting? It was only one sentence, and he was drunk. He didn't mean it. Couldn't help it. Hadn't I provoked the reaction by staring at Ciaran? How would I feel if Ian was staring at another girl for the night? Like Ian said many times before, I was oversensitive, always wanting to make a scene. Yet, despite my reasoning, I couldn't leave the bathroom and go back out there. I closed the door of the cubicle and putting my feet on the closed lid; I listened as excited girls came and went, reapplying makeup, catching up on gossip, and in between their chat I cried, and after a while the tears stopped and I calmed, enough to redo my makeup and leave the bathroom.

When I returned, the table was empty and the dance floor full. The music pumped. Ian was nowhere in sight. I joined the circle of people around the dance floor, crowded around a couple, who were putting on a show in the middle of the room. A few people dipped their heads when they saw me, embarrassed, which I thought was over the scene at the table. It took a second to process it was Ian slow dancing with a girl. Not dancing, more fumbling. As Ian dance shuffled, he moved the girl, Janice Dunlea, around, and their profiles came into sight. Their bodies, their foreheads, their mouths all joined. I saw a flash of tongue, his, and he leant over her until she was almost horizontal. Her hands disappeared under his tux. They were going for it.

Before stopping myself, before talking myself out of it, I broke through the crowd and made the lonely walk. I tapped him on the back.

Ian broke away. He shrugged, puckered his lips and nodded as if expecting me, then came close to my face, looking me up and down.

'With you, I'd have to graft, and it won't even be worth the hassle.' He nodded at Janice. 'This is guaranteed.' He scrunched his face. 'Piss off. I'll find you later.'

Right then, I saw who Ian would be if we stayed together and what I would have to become if I wanted him to stay. He was laying it out. He was testing how far he could go. If I put up with that, all I could expect was a lifetime of being hurt.

I backed away and saw a hundred faces watching me. Some looked away embarrassed, some were almost gleeful with the drama of the night. Whatever the reaction, the entire ballroom all knew Ian had just cheated on me and I couldn't find one caring face in the crowd.

I weaved through the dressed up young adults in the foyer until I left the hotel. Outside, the cool air hit me. Not wanting to stop and afraid Ian would follow, I continued out of the car park. My destination was only a few streets away, to the beach, but hoped the five-minute walk would be far enough for Ian not to think of it and try to find me. It was too early to go home. Only hours before, my parents had stood for photos. I couldn't ruin it for them. It was too late to hop on the bus to Crookstown. Checking my watch, my plan was to sit an hour on the beach and once enough time had passed to give a plausible excuse, I would walk to the taxi depot in the middle of town.

Cold September sea air cut through my coatless, sleeveless arms, and made me shiver. I wouldn't be able to stay the full hour with the drop in temperature. The shivers intensified, and I wondered if it wasn't from the cold at all but the shock of what I'd seen.

On the beach, the sea spread out in front of me like black tar. I sat on the sand and didn't care if it dampened my dress. The sound helped. The crashing and withdrawing of water from sand whooshed in my ears, giving me something else to focus on. Until there were footsteps and, seeing a dark male figure rush toward me, fear gripped around my throat. Ian had followed me. From my position on the sand, and the tightness of my long dress, I wouldn't even be able to get up quick enough. I thought about screaming, but just before I did, I heard a voice.

'How's my girl?'

'Ciaran?'

'That's me. You OK? I hear Ian made quite the scene.' He sat down beside me. 'Come back up Dawn, fuck him.'

'I can't Ciaran. I don't want to. If I go back up, he'll want to continue. He's drunk, and he's not nice when he's like that.'

'Christ, why are you with him?'

I turned to see his blacked out, shadowed face. 'I was just asking myself the same question. It's slim pickings in this town. All the good ones are gone.'

I heard an intake of breath, felt him shift closer too. The dark helped, bringing down the fear, taking away my embarrassment.

'Do you love Marissa?'

Ciaran didn't answer.

'I'm sorry. It's none of my business.'

'Why do you take that from Ian?'

'You left me Ciaran, and I don't understand what I did for you to drop me like that. You stopped talking to me and I've missed you so much it's hurt.'

In the dark, he found me. A kiss soft enough to wonder at first if I was dreaming or if it was the wind. Until it deepened and I understood all the sensations that had never been there with Ian. The electricity, the static, the buzzing in my head. Every nerve ending felt alive.

Noises sounded in the distance. Marissa's voice shrilled out from the road. Ciaran broke away, wiped at his mouth. My heart sank when he stood up. 'I'm sorry I shouldn't have done that. I have to sort this OK?'

As he walked over to Marissa and joined her by the wall, their embrace was lit up from the streetlight. He didn't pull Marissa for a chat, or let her down, but spoke to her like a boyfriend, like a man in love. Smoothing her hair, stroking her jaw. I got up from the sand and trudged towards them. On closer inspection, I knew I was right. Ciaran was nowhere near breaking up with Marissa. He'd wrapped his arm around her waist and was talking to her in a way I could only wish for.

'You've a good guy there, Marissa. Look after him.'

Marissa looked like she was sucking on something sour. 'Were you with her?'

Ciaran scowled at me.

'Don't know if you saw Ian up there, Marissa, but Ciaran was just checking how I was, that's all. I'm getting a taxi now.'

I walked past them, feeling the fool. He loved Marissa. It wasn't right to get between them.

'Dawn,' Ciaran called.

I turned around and waited for the words, any words, that came from him.

'Come back to the school. Finish the night.'

Marissa's lit up frown was obvious.

'Nah. I'm done with Knockfarraig,' I said, and walked to the taxi rank.

That night I learnt the words I wanted to say for years got me nowhere. Words changed nothing. Words didn't set me free or improve my life. In Ian's case, words got me shouted at, brought hostility, confrontation and arguments. In Ciaran's case, it didn't change who he loved. Staying silent kept me safe. Not talking kept judgement away.

The next day, I accepted the full-time role in Greene's. College wouldn't be an option anymore as I had enrolled in the same place as Ciaran and couldn't do it. What I needed was money for an apartment and a life and a fresh start from Knockfarraig and Crookstown. Unaware that Ciaran would ring me up two months later, living in college digs and still going out with Marissa. There was no hostility or heart to hearts. We both acted like nothing happened, that the kiss didn't exist. Until that birthday dinner.

Sam

Before Kristin there had been a Marissa, and after her, a Terese and a Fiona. Back then, I accepted the kiss was a mistake on Ciaran's part, an error in judgment caused by pity for what Ian did to me, caught up in the moment of being on the beach that night. Ciaran over the years, gave me no reason to question it as anything else. Now, knowing he had felt something as well, I had to accept timing had never been our friend. Even if he had loved me for years, it didn't matter; he was with Kristin now and I had lost my chance.

I didn't wallow in depression. Or let the sadness come. Giving up on ever being with Ciaran had the opposite effect. I began getting up earlier and taking time over my appearance. Each morning, I noticed the changes from the stretches and walking. The rounded face sunk in a little. My cheekbones naturally dipped again. My back was nowhere near cured, but as the days wore on, I asked Mum to drop me further away from the centre, and this extra movement, coupled with not staying in bed all day, helped shift some pounds and take some pressure from my back.

Each morning, I walked the long way around the building, just to have the excuse to pass the gardens. Some days I saw him, others I didn't. Not that I wanted to forget Ciaran, or replace him, with Ian it had proven that didn't work. What I needed was to move on and seeing Sam brightened my day, so what was the harm? I discovered if

I went early, I wouldn't see him, yet if I delayed until after nine, there was a chance. Most days he didn't look up when I passed, too busy concentrating on digging or moving something or examining yet there was something about the intensity of his concentration that gave me a thrill. Too focused and oblivious, it made me wonder if the moment I looked away, he looked at me. Maybe it was my imagination, but the possibility pleased me and I would take anything I could get.

Until one day. As I touched the petals of a purple flower, I heard a voice behind me.

'So when am I going to get to show you what I do?'

I stepped back, unsure of what to say. It was the first time he'd spoken to me. There was no asking of names or pretending. Bright blue eyes and highlighted blonde hair. The time spent working on myself didn't work, the words still didn't come. All I could do was stare.

It hadn't been easier to talk to guys, it had been too much alcohol.

Sam grinned as if he'd expected that reaction. He raised an eyebrow. 'Alayne said you were interested in learning about flowers?'

Having a subject shook me out of it.

'I might be a lost cause. Could you show me what to do without killing them? The longest any plant has lasted with me is four days.'

He knelt beside me, and a waft of sea and sweat floated towards me, not off-putting but intriguing. Here was a man unafraid of hard work, or getting his hands calloused and digging into dirt and not running away when the soil showed worms and bugs. Sam stroked the petal of the purple flower. 'It's easy. Treat them like you'd treat a boyfriend. Give lots of attention, listen to it, act on what it wants.'

I was unsure if he was still talking about gardening. The way he grinned at me made a thrill run up my body. Nobody had looked at me like that since my back injury. I willed my face not to burn.

'Pop by sometime and I'll show you. I take my lunch at two, so I'm always free then.'

'That wouldn't be fair to take up your free time.'

'It wouldn't be the worst way to spend my lunch.'

A bit of my old confidence with guys came back. 'Are you a charmer, Sam?'

He bit his lip, his tooth ground down on soft, bulbous, pink flesh. 'Only when I see potential.'

'Is that what I am? Potential?'

'I'll make a master gardener out of you yet.'

This time I blushed.

Stupid, pale Irish skin. Had he been talking about gardening the whole time and I'd taken it up wrong?

'You'll have your work cut out for you, but I'm up for trying. How's Thursday? I usually finish around that time.'

'It's a date,' Sam said.

I walked away, confused.

Alayne stood at the entrance, waiting.

'I see you're getting on with Sam.'

'You set it up.'

'Be careful.'

'We're just talking.'

'Flirting, you mean.'

'So? It's the first time I've smiled in months. I thought this place is about happiness. Am I not meant to have fun?'

'No, not at all. I just don't know if fun is what you'd get. You're doing so much self-work at the moment, it would be a shame if you switched your attention to a guy.'

'Do you want me to stay single until I'm better?'

'It's not my place to tell you what to do.'

'Yet you are.'

'I'm not.' Alayne sat on the pebbled wall that lined the garden and sighed. 'OK. I am trying to, I'm sorry. It's none of my business. For what it's worth though, Dawn, I don't think it will work.'

I scowled. Alayne reminded me of my mother. Making judgment without knowing all the facts and getting her point across as passive aggressive. I had thought she was different; I had thought she knew me. If she had, if Alayne had known me at all, she would know that statement was like noticing a moth and lighting a flame. All I had learnt wouldn't matter. Patterns were just that, in a world where I was doing everything differently, when challenged, I would fall into what I always done. By warning me off, it had the opposite effect and lighted a new or extra interest in Sam. Even though I trusted Alayne, even though I could see Sam might be trouble, for that very reason meant I would have to pursue it.

'Do you want to continue the session out here or go inside?'

'Here's fine.'

'People don't get what they want Dawn, people get what they believe they deserve. What do you think you deserve?'

'To be healthy again. Love. Respect. A job.'

She pulled at a weed and shredded it in her fingers. 'Do you though? Anyone can say what they want, they can list off necessities like it's their weekly shopping, but what do they seek? What do they reject? What do they draw a line through? Do you think it's love you would pursue with Sam?'

'Come on Alayne, haven't you ever been lonely?'

'But that's the thing Dawn, with some guys you just end up lonelier.'

A feeling only reserved for my mother rose in me. 'You don't know everything.' I looked over at the other end of the garden and saw Sam still there. I kept my voice low. 'We could be perfect for each other.'

'You can be in love with the idea of love and not look at the traits of the person. Before you go there with him, watch. It's important to not just listen to the words someone tells you but see their follow through, watch their actions. I can see I've annoyed you.'

'You know, I've taken your lessons. I've listened and never answered back, but this time I'm going to tell you, you're wrong. It's not your place to tell me who or who not to sleep with.'

'I thought we were talking about love.'

My cheeks flushed. 'Who are you to act so self-righteous? Just because you have everything sown up, you think that makes you qualified to tell people what to do? Where's your counselling qualification? Isn't this centre one big ego trip for you? Come here and Saint Alayne will cure you. All it requires is sitting and listening to her drivel for an hour a week and we'll throw in an art class here and there. Well, I'm sorry if I'm not the perfect fix.'

Alayne smirked, which incensed me more. 'Who are you to tell me what I want? I don't even know what I want. You think you have it all sussed, but you're going to lose this place and then what will you have? Nothing. Like the rest of us. You're a failure like me. A failed teacher and soon you'll be a failed centre owner or whatever you call yourself.'

I stormed past her as much as a person with a back injury could storm. It was more like a shuffle, but the sentiment was still there. Through the centre and out the door, the adrenalin only got so far before the pain took over. Settling on a bench overlooking the water a few buildings down, I waited for my breath to calm. I was chest heaving, ready to punch something, or scream at someone, livid. I tried to remember the last time I had been as angry with anyone. Even with my mother, as much as she annoyed me, I couldn't recall ever raising my voice to her. Snippy comments, yeah, and sighs, but even my mother hadn't been on the receiving end like that. Once the breathing regulated, the guilt came. That reaction wasn't right. The person in the garden wasn't who I wanted to be. The right thing to do was to go back and apologise, but I didn't want to.

Instead, I closed my eyes and imagined I was cooking. What would I make? Something sweet. Strawberries came to mind. Chocolate came straight after.

Images came in quick spurts: Pecans blitzed in a processor until they resembled breadcrumbs. Drizzled with walnut oil. Pressed into a cupcake case. Then popped in the fridge to set. Cream cheese in a bowl, mixed with some sieved icing sugar until smooth. Whipped double cream folded in. Chopped strawberries sprinkled into the creamy mix. Layering the cheesecake mixture in the chilled, pressed pecan base. Leaving to chill again.

Melted dark chocolate in a Bain Marie, mixed with a little cream to form a ganache. Poured over the chilled cheesecake forming a silky, shiny coating. Added thin slices of strawberry on top. Admired. Ate.

I licked my lips. It was almost possible to taste it. To smell it. All I had to do now was make it.

Digging

It took an entire night to decide to go back to the centre and an early morning to work up the courage to do so. When I entered Alayne's room, I cringed as I saw her tiding the desk, anticipating the awkwardness of the oncoming conversation.

Alayne startled, more at the approach by anyone, rather than me, then broke out a huge smile. 'Dawn, you're back. How are you?'

I knew I couldn't ignore what happened. I had to say something to move on.

'I'm sorry for what I said.'

'Why?' Her eyes stayed on mine but she walked towards me, her drop earring swaying as she did. 'I'll let you in on a little secret. That's the reaction I wanted from you.'

She hugged me gentle enough to not hurt.

'I don't get it.'

She looked at me. 'Passion Dawn, I wanted to push you. I don't care what you do with Sam. Like you said, it's your choice. I just used the fact it would be a walking disaster to get the very thing you need out.'

'I don't understand.'

'I needed you to lose it and see the world didn't end. That you will survive if you tell people your truth. That it's still alright if you give your opinion and the other person doesn't agree.'

I looked at Alayne like she was a stranger. 'Well, that's sly.'

Alayne laughed, full and hearty. 'I will do anything to get through to you.' She led me to the seats and sat so we faced each other.

'Why don't the words come?'

'I don't know.'

'What made you stop standing up for yourself?'

'I can't remember.'

'What made you think your opinion didn't matter?'

I shook my head, not ready to be pushed. Her words prodded at my subconscious, bringing up images I didn't want to see, didn't want to think about.

Alayne sat back in the chair. 'I think it's time you gave a class.'

I straightened, then regretted it, bringing a shooting pain down my leg. 'No way.'

'Why? Talk now Dawn. Explain out loud why. Come on. Why?'

'I don't know.'

'You can. It's right there. Just say.'

'I don't know.'

'Tell me why you can't talk, Dawn.'

Leave me alone.

She raised her voice, making me jump. 'Say it! Don't be afraid.'

I can't.

'Nothing bad is going to happen to you here. Just say the first words that come.'

Stop.

'Why are you so afraid?'

'Because I'll embarrass myself!' I roared over Alayne and once I broke my silence, I found I couldn't stop talking. 'Because I'm scared I'll go up there and the words won't come, and everyone will stare and think I'm stupid. Or I will find the words and they will be stupid because I'm stupid and have nothing good to say. If I stay quiet, no one will know what's in my mind, and they can't judge me. And I'm scared.

I'm scared of everything. Heights. The dark. Failure. Saying the wrong thing. Making the wrong decision. Dogs looking at me. Dark alleys. Crowded places. Speaking in public. Confrontation. It doesn't matter if what I have to say is right. It doesn't matter if the other person is wrong and I need to set them straight. The thought of facing them and saying it to them. I squirm. I do more than squirm. It feels like I might die. And the words that I have practiced a million times at home just whoosh away and leave me and I'm left there dry tongued and close lipped, feeling like a failure. I don't know how to combat that. You can't help me there. Because it doesn't matter how many times I practice, I'm left with a blank space when I try to retrieve it.'

My chest heaved, my hands shook and I gasped for breath.

'There we go,' Alayne said.

She waited for my breathing to calm and only spoke when I nodded I was ready.

'Where does it stem from?'

'I don't know.'

'When is the first time you can recall something happening?'

We sat in silence while I thought.

'I would have been young. In school, we'd take turns around the class to do things. If I had to stand up and speak, or read, a panic would set in. I would repeat my lines over and over in my head, trying to concentrate so I wouldn't lose where we were on the page but it didn't matter, after a while the words made no sense. The sound coming from whoever was reading sounded like warbles. Slowed down and jumbled up. It wasn't dyslexia. I could see and understand the words if I was on my own. It was just pure panic.'

'Looking back now, what do you think the panic was? What were you afraid of?'

'Of saying the wrong word. Of pronouncing it wrong and everyone laughing.'

Alayne nodded, as if it all made perfect sense. 'What would you think now as an adult if you met a child with a good reading ability and they told you they were afraid to speak out in class?'

'That they could do it. I would tell them to take a deep breath and don't worry about anyone else. That it doesn't matter if they get it wrong.'

'Really?' Alayne said, not convinced.

'Yeah.'

'Isn't that what you think you should say? Rather than what you believe?'

I pictured a small child sitting behind a desk with a book in her hands. The fear I felt came back as clear as if I sat in the chair now: Mrs Johnson's roar when she got angry, the fear of being shouted at, or hearing the sniggers from the others. My face burning to the point there was no white skin left, that even my scalp turned red. Breathing didn't help, my chest closed up, so I had to take little gulps to compensate. All the while, using my finger to follow the words the person next to me read, but the letters blurred and became scribbles on the page. Until it was my turn and sweaty palmed and ramrod straight, I would use every bit of concentration. If I couldn't find my way, couldn't find my start, Mrs Johnson would roar the first line and it would work like a jockey whipping his horse, or a runner hearing the gun. I would get hyper aware. The words popping more off the page. I took my time. Pronouncing each word with preciseness, way too slow. I heard the other kids mocking me, I heard Mrs Johnson huff in frustration. Even when I found the courage to speak, it made it worse. It was better to stay silent. By keeping quiet, no one could judge you. People couldn't size you up and assume about you. That's what the little me had believed and followed through with.

'What you listed a while ago, are they all your fears?' Alayne asked.

'God, no, I've way more than that. I'm afraid of everything. My whole life is taken over by fear. I'm afraid of picking the wrong person to love. Telling someone how I feel and them rejecting me. I'm scared that I will never get better, that I'm going to live with this pain for the rest of my life. I'm scared of being attacked again, of the court case and seeing that guy. Most of all, I'm scared that I will try to do my best and my best won't ever be good enough.'

The last line broke me. Speaking was overrated and exhausting. Alayne folded me into her arms, and feeling the warm hug, I let out the tears I hadn't known I'd held onto. For the attack. For the pain. For trying to carry on.

'Good girl.' Alayne whispered. 'You've needed to say all that. There's nothing set in stone. It's from our mistakes we learn. You are supposed to make mistakes. Own them, learn from them and move on to the next one.'

'But there are mistakes you can't undo.'

Alayne pulled away. 'Like what?'

I shrugged. *Sleeping with the wrong guys. Telling people you thought kissing them was like incest.*

'I'll let you into a secret. Every day I'm scared too, but I've learnt if I push through the little fears, it helps me get stronger until I can face the bigger ones. I've learnt to jump. Anyway, people don't care Dawn.'

'What do you mean?'

'You're worried about people you don't care about, judging you for what you say or do, about what they think of your injury or you as a person, when they aren't thinking about you at all. They're too busy worried about their own problems. Or worrying about what you think about them.'

It was like Alayne had written those words on a screen in front of me and highlighted it in neon yellow.

Nobody cared. Nobody outside the people that loved me cared about my pain. Who would take the time to judge me for that? Even if they did judge, that just showed what type of person they were. All those times, in a roomful of strangers, I'd cringed, convinced all eyes were on me, I hadn't once considered they might struggle too. When I exhaled, my breath felt condensed, heavier than the air around, full of a tension that I'd held onto.

'Conversation is the same. Most of the time, the person only half listens to what you're saying. They're too busy thinking about what they're going to say next. Or what they need to do after meeting with you, or listing what they will have for dinner. Replaying the argument they just had with their boyfriend. Or these days, checking their feed on their phone.'

'Is that what you do? Half listen.'

'Well. I'm the exception.' Alayne grinned, then turned serious. 'I can do it too. It's how I've recognised it. A few years ago, when I was younger than you, I was always stuck in my head. When I'm with someone now, it is my job to listen. I've also found if you focus on a conversation, a total focus, a giving yourself over to listen and observe body language, it becomes easier to read a person and discover the signals they don't talk about. To get to the heart of what they are feeling.'

'People lie. They lie all the time.'

'It isn't bad to trust people, it's a trait. I trust everyone until they show me not to. It's one reason I'm fascinated by body language. Now though, with the internet, people know a lot more about the unconscious signs, so they go out of their way to not show them to the outside. They've learnt how to not react. They can be trickier for sure. I go by the eyes. You can train your body to lie, but the eyes tell you everything. How has your back really been?'

'Awful.'

'Try distraction. If you focus on what's happening, on the pain, it intensifies, gets worse. You can't get to the solution by concentrating on how bad it is. Look for the solution. Picture living differently. If I were you, I would picture myself doing something active, something that at that moment would be impossible, like a mountain hike, or a swimming race or crossing the line of a marathon. Make it vivid. Picture the clothes you would wear while doing it. Imagine the actions you would need to take to get there. Most of all, feel how you would feel. How proud you would be when you reached the top or crossed that line. How ecstatic. No matter how much pain you are experiencing in your reality.'

'OK,'

'It sounds stupid, but try it for a week. Something inside switches. It gives hope. It gives a goal. When you feel good, you spread good feeling. When you're feeling good, ideas come to you. If you're in a positive state of mind, you're more inclined to help people and to want to help. Emotions can be infectious. Just watch the energy change in the room when an angry person comes in, watch the gloom and fear and dread move from one person to the next. Same when a positive energy enters a room, it can lift the whole place. If you feel bad, see it as a sign. It's just a heads up, from you inside, to let you know you are turning away from what it believes. That's why it feels so bad. You are cutting yourself off from your own love.'

'How do I stop the pain?'

'Pain has momentum. Like any emotion, it won't just go away. Before the pain comes in the morning, find something you like doing. Look for pleasure, look for enjoyment. If the pain sneaks up on you or comes on suddenly, try your best to distract yourself. It might seem impossible, but still try. If you can't move, daydream about something you love. Something you can immerse yourself in. It doesn't matter what it is as long as it distracts you.'

I closed my eyes. What did I love? My first thought was chocolate. That wouldn't work when I was getting fit and trying to lose weight. But

Alayne had said anything. It made me think of baking, of cooking and the buzz I always got from it. How I loved to take whatever ingredients were in my fridge and concoct something. What was in the fridge now? What could I prepare or cook? There was chicken and bacon and butter and crème fraiche. There were mushrooms and garlic. There was pasta or there was enough flour to make a pie. I could surprise my parents and make dinner. My mind drifted to dessert. There was chocolate and cream and hazelnuts, enough to make brownies. It would be easy to prepare a caramel sauce and drizzle it over. My mouth salivated.

'I love cooking. And baking. Anything with food.'

'There we go. Focus on that.'

'It's worked in the past. When I've been in pain or upset, I'll play out a new recipe and it helps. But if I carry on cooking, I'll put on more weight.'

'Do you think your weight gain was down to what you ate?'

I thought about that. The pain had caused me to not want to eat. Being confined to the bed meant I couldn't raid the fridge, yet I continued to pile on the pounds.

'It has more to do with what you believe or how you feel about the food you eat. Wasn't there a part of you that believed because you weren't moving, you would get bigger? How guilty do you feel when you eat something for enjoyment?'

The woman was right. It annoyed me how right she was.

'Once you have a few recipes, there's your class.'

'What, teach it?'

'It's a class we don't have here.'

'How do you do it all? Everyone runs to you with their problems and you just work it out. I know the centre's in trouble.'

'Dawn, if you are serious about finding happiness, you are going to need to accept your struggles. Life isn't smooth sailing. It's not meant to be. Striving for better brings challenges. What you can control is how you feel about them. I see them as waves. Immense waves that once I get over, I feel empowered because I did it. Instead of letting the waves upturn me or make me swim back to the shore in panic, I dive under. When I resurface, when I break through, the wave is gone. Issues never go away, there's always something, but that's life. Why is it hard for you to stand up for yourself, do you think?'

'I don't know.'

'Was there a trigger? Something you can pinpoint? A time in your life that you can remember it starting from, like when you were a kid?'

I shrugged, thought a while. 'Blaming my family would be the simple answer, but no. I grew up with parents who showed me they loved me every day. Too much even. I grew up with them telling me I could be anything I wanted, that there was nothing I couldn't do.'

'That's a lot to live up to.'

I hesitated; I didn't expect that reaction. 'It wasn't like that. They don't care what I do as long as I'm happy.'

'That can still bring pressure. It would be normal if you grew up feeling loved, to want to show them you fulfilled your potential. Feeling like you're mediocre, feeling you should do more with your life, is pressure. What do you think will happen if you say no to people?'

'I don't even think about it. It just makes me uncomfortable.'

'It comes from somewhere, though. What is your initial thought when you want to say no?'

'That I can't.'

'Why?'

'I don't know.'

'You do. Come on, spit it out.'

'I have no clue. I get this feeling in my stomach, a sickly feeling in the pit, and I tighten up.'

'Because?'

'Because if I say no, I might upset them.'

'And?'

'And that might offend them.'

'And?'

'And they might not like me anymore.'

'Ah.'

'Ah,' I said.

'How does that sound out loud?'

'Like it's stupid.'

'Do you think it's fair to you if you never put yourself first?'

'I just wanted to be a good person. A good friend.'

'But does that make you a good friend? You set boundaries with people when you first meet them. By always saying yes, you only show them one side of you. You send them a message that you don't trust them enough to show them all of you.'

Her phone rang at the same time there was a knock at the door. Bex popped her head around. The phone stayed ringing.

'Sorry to interrupt, but the estate agent is here.'

'I'm sorry Dawn, I have to go see him. Why don't you have a coffee in the canteen and I'll catch up with you in a little while.'

'Are you selling?'

Alayne shrugged. 'We ran out of funding. Apparently, the government can't afford to contribute anymore. I'm looking at other options, like loans or sponsors or different fundraisers and once I have all the information, I can work out what to do.'

'Will you have to raise a lot?'

'A place this size isn't cheap. The major problem is someone else wants the property and have plenty money behind them. That's why I have to have this meeting, to find out the price and see if it's achievable. If I could match it, I could buy it outright. Anyway, don't you worry, if this place goes, I'll find another.'

'It's perfect, though.'

'I know. That's why it's sought after. Can you imagine the people who would snap up an apartment overlooking the beach? Worrying doesn't help, it's more about getting our thinking cap on. There's always a solution, if you let it come.'

Alayne tapped me gently on the arm and left, her calm words in direct opposition to her straight-backed stance, clearly ready for a fight.

Slicing

I left the centre with a million things on my mind: what I would teach a class, what could help Alayne, what I wanted from my life. There were so many resources they could use. They already sold the vegetables and fruit, but if they were relying on that to save the building, they would be out the door in a month. It would have to be bigger. And more profitable. Thinking of produce, of whether I was right about seeing lavender in the garden, instead of stepping onto the street, I followed the path around to the back. Rita was having a smoke on the low wall.

As I waved hi, a text beeped on my phone.

Kristin's giving me another chance. Thanks for the talk. You always help me.

My heart sank. The lavender forgotten about and Alayne's words evaporated as if she'd never said them when I caught sight of Sam. He was bent over, shirtless, and I felt a stirring I hadn't felt for some time.

'You know Sam, right?'

Rita smirked. 'He brightens up the view. Shitty boyfriend, though.'

'What makes you say that?'

'He's worked through plenty girls in the town since he arrived.' Rita appraised me, then nodded. 'Although, maybe that's what you want from him, still, it's better to know these things before you jump in, so you're clear about what you're getting.'

'Maybe he's just waiting for the right girl.'

'Maybe.' She took a drag, screwing her eyes at me as she inhaled. 'Doubt it though.'

She was the second person to warn me about Sam in an hour. It only interested me more.

I crossed the path and meandered around the different boxes of plants until I was right behind him, then waited until he stopped digging.

'So, I was thinking about that date you mentioned.'

'Oh yeah,' he said, straightening up and wiping the sweat from his brow. I kept my eyes on his, but when he threw his shovel down, I took a sneaky look at his shirtless torso.

Oh my.

'If you wanted, we could ditch the gardening lesson and just get a drink?'

'You read my mind,' he grinned. 'How's tonight for you?'

'You read my mind,' I grinned back.

'How about Flynn's? At eight?'

'See you then,' I said, walking away.

I winked at an open-mouthed Rita as she passed. 'You're not the only one who can be wild.'

At home, I examined the cupboards and pulled out ingredients. The pain was there, and it was going to be there, anyway; I might as well try the distraction thing. Even in that second of a daydream, it had felt good. Standing would be an issue. If I brought all the ingredients to the kitchen table, I could manage by sitting and taking it slow. If it got too unbearable, I could always abandon mission. At least I would try.

I lost myself in the slicing and dicing of the chicken. In the peeling and mincing of the garlic. In the frying of the bacon. As I folded the hazelnuts into the mixture for the brownie, I stopped, holding the spatula in mid air. There was still pain, it hadn't reduced enough to forget it, but it had faded almost to background instead of it being the concern. I was under no illusion; the pain would come back with a vengeance when I tried to stand. I hummed, enjoying it. I got back to my work, which wasn't really work at all.

How had it turned out I had two guys I wanted to be with? I didn't want to hurt anyone. I let my mind run. My heart was with Ciaran, but he loved someone else. Even if I acted on it, there would be no going back, and what if we didn't work out? His friendship was worth more than the risk.

Sam was the typical type I kept going for. How had that worked for me in the past? I was meant to be living differently. Finding ways to overcome an injury, finding genuine friends, and searching for something I was good at and loved doing. I was changing, I could feel the change. Was it possible to find a different love as well?

Back

The drinks with Sam turned into one drink and a quick drive to his apartment. It was kisses at the door while he tried to get the key in the lock. It was half undressing each other in the hall. In the bar, I couldn't think of anything else I wanted from him and as soon as I saw him, I didn't want to speak. Up close, away from the centre, all I wanted was his calloused hands to touch me. It had been way too long. For once the pain stayed away, mostly because of my preparation of gentle stretches and a pre-meeting anti-inflammatory coupled with a glass of wine for courage, I was free to concentrate on him alone. I cringed once when he touched my thigh, imagining the lumps his fingers were running over.

He's here, isn't he? Stop stressing and go with it.

His hair smelt of sea and his tan went further than I thought it would. The only lumps on Sam's body were supposed to be there. I wanted to stand back and just take him in, admire the perfection of this man. If it had been a few months ago, I might have walked away, believing Sam was too beautiful for my wreck of a body. This time I allowed beautiful. Invited beautiful.

The next morning, it took a minute to remember where I was. His bedroom was tidy, which differed from the hall, where we had to step over shoes and even used a pile of coats and a bike to lean on while we steadied ourselves. It hit me that he had expected me to visit his bedroom.

He lay on his side with his back to me so far away he almost dangled over the side of the bed. It reminded me of the nights I spent with Jed. It all felt unreal, like I would wake up from a dream. I pulled at the sheet to cover myself, feeling exposed. The fun of the night before dissipated, and it left me with a vacuous space, a gaping I had tried to close. Nothing had changed. All those months working on me and here I was lying next to a stranger. What did I know about him? Only what he had told me. I hadn't even waited to get to know him. If I was going to be truthful, I had gone out of my way not to. And I knew why. Avoiding finding out who he was kept Sam the way I wanted – as my version of what I preferred rather than spoiling my ideal with what he was like. I recalled now how he kept on cutting across me while I spoke in the bar. How he scanned the room as I spoke. Or as I fell asleep, he mumbled something. At the time it hadn't registered, his words had bounced off. I had snuggled into him and for the first time in a long time, enjoyed holding a warm body. That was what I had wanted from him. Not sex, not a relationship, but intimacy, to smell a man, to hear another breath beside mine. It came back now, the words he had said.

Will I ring you a taxi?

I turned on my back, biting my lip at the pain of moving too quickly. Hadn't I got what I expected? I went for the same type over and over. A guy more interested in his pleasure than mine. A guy who lost interest as soon as he had me. A guy who, even before he got me, kept his options open. Who never committed, who was only half interested.

It wasn't even the men's fault. I never told them what I liked. As quiet in the bedroom and the relationship as in all other areas of my life. I did as told. It was about their likes and wants and all my effort went on looking like I liked it, too. It didn't even cross my mind to say if I didn't. I had always been too afraid to show how I was feeling, whether I liked them. How could a guy read my signals? That would change today.

First, I moved over and curled into Sam. He didn't flinch, which I took for a good sign. It felt good to have a body lined up against me. I glided my fingers and smoothed the strands of blond hair down as delicately as if it was a child's. It lit something. Its softness woke up the nerves in my fingers. I nuzzled into his neck, knowing it could go either way, but this time I would see, I would test him. My time was more valuable now; it mattered if I was wasting it.

Sam woke, stretching his arms above his head and straightened his legs as far as they would go. He glanced at me while doing it and I wondered if there was a flicker, a second, where he was trying to figure out who I was. He moved away a fraction, less than an inch, but it was enough for me to pick up. I removed my hand and lay on my back again, slower this time to prevent any locking.

He was just the wrong guy.

This time I would get out of the bed without begging. This time I wouldn't sleep with a man again to change his mind because I needed another living being inside of me.

Alayne's words came to me.

Continual mistakes are just bad habits.

I laughed too loud. I hadn't cared about him just as much as he hadn't cared about me. He opened one eye and studied me, and I knew he was wondering if he brought a nutcase home.

I patted his arm. 'Thanks for last night. It's been enlightening.'

This made Sam grin. He was so obvious—turned off if you showed any affection, but the minute you displayed disinterest he awakened.

'Stay a while.'

I leant into him and kissed him on the nose before whipping the sheet off my naked body and doing my usual procedure to stand. For the first time in my whole life, I didn't worry about cellulite or if I looked heavy or if my makeup had smudged. I stood with my hands on my hips and let him take me in as I surveyed the ground for my clothes. Thankfully, I'd had the hindsight to throw them over a chair so I didn't have to bend now and ruin my whole, empowered display.

How many guys hadn't cared about my few extra pounds? What they had picked up on was the way I held my arms around my breasts when they looked at them. How I turned the lights off. How I hesitated before undressing. There had been some that had used it, making a subtle point of keeping their eyes downcast, looking too long at my thighs as I walked to the bathroom. A silent insult that still told me what they thought. One guy, Trey, held up my skirt and made an exaggerated point of running his hand along the waistband, emphasising how long it took. It worked. I ate nothing but soup for a month until he'd dumped me anyway for a bigger girl. When he left, I gorged on every food imaginable and ended up bigger than what I'd started.

I laughed again, not at Sam, away in another time, thinking of another relationship. I had been a size ten when Ian first made comments. Instead of looking in the mirror and seeing I was beautiful as I was, I had taken his words and carried them for years. Believing a guy who mistreated me, more than what I believed about myself. Or another guy, Dean, who, when the relationship waned, gathered all the confided information and threw my insecurity at me just to get the last dig when I asked him to leave.

'Fat bitch. Look at the rolls of fat. You're a disgrace. If I were you, I wouldn't leave the house. You're an embarrassment.'

And what had I done? When he left, I climbed straight into bed and cried, staying there for the weekend and not moving. I had cried for him. Not just for the spiteful things he'd said, because that I would have understood, but I cried for losing him. Why would I want a guy like that?

Now I understood. Now it ran down through the centre of my being, down to what Alayne taught me, down to me getting up every day despite the pain and getting on with finding a life. It was down to committing to feeling good. Without realising what I was doing beforehand, without knowledge, I had raised my standards and people like Sam, as beautiful as he was, were in my past.

'Stay,' he repeated.

I looked down at him in the bed and smiled. 'I'd love to Sam, but you are a habit I've just broken.'

'I don't get you,' Sam said, laughing.

'And you don't need to.'

I gave him a broad, as unpsychotic as I could smile, then dressed with my back to him and left the room. I was done with guys that wanted a girl to stay silent in order for them to feel good, or wanted a one sided relationship or needed to put someone down to feel good about themselves. From that day on, I was going to find my voice.

Alignment

I lifted my arms until they joined above my head, and bending one knee, I moved to a tree pose. While holding position, I breathed in and thought about alignment. About straight lines meeting together, lining up with my body and mind. I exhaled as I let go of the pose. Then, doing the same with the other leg, I inhaled again.

The chiropractor spoke about alignment all the time. About achieving the natural curve and going back to the body's innate state. When Alayne spoke of alignment, she talked about combining mind, body, and soul, explaining if there was a disconnect something inside felt wrong.

Alignment, for me, was about lining up with what you wanted. Surrounding yourself with the right people, following routines that enriched your life. Finding what made you want to get out of bed in the morning. Wanting to live. Real alignment was about listening to your body and your mind and instead of ignoring it like I always had, I listened and gave it what it needed and my body was responding.

Each day I stretched. Even when I was sore, I did it. Even when my back locked in place and I had to lie there until it eased out. Attempting it again the next day and the next and the day after that until I did it without even thinking about it. When it became automatic to drop on the floor and do them before I even made breakfast. Until it became part of me. I incorporated more from my own searches: hamstring stretches, hip circles, neck rolls and calf lifts. There were other benefits to the extra's apart from managing the pain; my stomach shrank and didn't get in the way so much.

The adjustments, as Dr Fischer called them, weren't so much painful but awkward. He would position me in certain ways and then do a swift move he seemed pleased with. The getting up and lying down was an issue. There were times my legs wouldn't do as I asked, or my back stuck in the position, but I trusted him and in that trust I could relax, knowing he might one day fix me. Even though the adjustments weren't painful, the muscle work could be. When he worked on a tight muscle, I wanted to pass out. The actual pain came after, when my nerve endings fired and every part of my body screamed out in annoyance at what I had just forced them to go through.

The beauty of health is lost on the young. All the times I never even contemplated my health, it was just there and always would be. In the darkest of times, the pain reminded me of how much my life, the healthy life I'd lived, meant. I wished I hadn't taken it for granted. I wished I had treated my body better. Only once I was suffering, once my body failed, did I see its beauty. Only then did I notice the hard work it must have needed to put in, in order to continue to survive. Late nights. Partying. The constant bombardment of toxins from alcohol to hungover energy drinks and greasy, no good for you, next day takeaways. And that was just to my body. I hadn't fed my soul. Or added to the goodness bank of Dawn. I had just kept taking deposits out until there was nothing left inside. No wonder it gave up.

One task Alayne set was listing positives each morning and after this, I would reason how worse it could be. What if my body had given up altogether? What if I'd dropped dead with no warning? Or if it came to the surface as some incurable sickness? Since doing this, something shifted. Instead of running through a checklist of what parts of the body niggled on waking, a little hope had slipped in that what I suffered from wasn't permanent. I allowed the possibility that one day, whenever that may be, I would not suffer. On the good days, the days when the pain didn't meet me on waking, it was easy to daydream of a life without it. The bad days were tougher.

I pictured getting up and getting dressed. Pulling on leggings and a t-shirt. Closing the front door and, despite the rain, setting off. I started with a jog, but once warmed up, moved to a trot. It was the sprint that was the aim. Oh, to do that! A simple want, yet still far away. It was an art, the motion of one foot in front of the other at speed. Yet, it was something I would do. On that subject Alayne convinced me.

I stretched every day. I added extra steps to my walk or picked up speed. But it was still only a walk. Some days, despite all the positivity, I would have to abandon the mission or slow down or take a break. There was a lesson in that too. For once, I was listening to my body; I was caring about myself. For too long, I ignored my wants, ignored the voice inside that spoke about what I liked, about my wishes, until the voice didn't speak anymore. Now that I was listening, the voice inside wouldn't shut up. *Try this, Dawn. What about seeing how this goes?* It was like a constant mini Alayne inside my brain.

After the night with Sam, something had changed in me, as if that one mistake had placed a magnifying glass on all my previous errors. Following Alayne's advice, I got up early each morning to make something new, spending hours the night before pouring through cookbooks or just daydreaming about what I would like to cook next. As I dreamt, I found it was like I was floating away. I would let my imagination go wild; dreaming up cake recipes or ideal lists for dinner parties and found while doing it, pain and time would dissolve to a gentle hum, still there but not overtaking, and glad of the reprieve, the fun of it was thrilling. As I mixed or tasted, shivers of pleasure would run up my arms. Once baked or cooked or finished, I always left three portions for my parents and Ciaran, then brought the rest of my concoctions into the center to unleash on the growing amount of willing volunteers.

Most of all, I enjoyed watching people close their eyes as they ate. Compliments came because friends meant well, but with that first bite, I found Alayne was right, the eyes didn't lie. In those moments, I believed I could do something with food. As the times stacked up, with each muffin or cupcake or brownie, with each curry or broth, I gained more confidence, until it stopped being a hobby and became a dream.

Never in my life had I imagined working with food. It hadn't been an option. Work was grafting, separate from loving a profession. There had been times I enjoyed work; like when I made a customer smile, when I solved an unsolvable problem, when I finished an impossible task, but it had still been work. Food was different, there was no slog. There was no hard work. Could I make money doing something that made me daydream? As Alayne suggested it, little ripples of electricity danced up my arms, as if those words were important.

Placing some treats on Alayne's desk, I waited for her attention. She stopped what she was doing straight away.

'I think I know what I want to do.'

'Tell all,' Alayne said, opening the Tupperware and selecting a large piece of nut bread from the pile.

'I'd love to open a café. One with all the usual but also healthy options for people that can't eat certain foods, labelled keto or nut or gluten-free. Or treats that still taste good but have no refined sugar.'

'Cos they're sweet enough,' Alayne nodded.

'Sweet enough. That's would be a good name for a place.'

'Develop that in your mind. Where would you want it? What would you serve? Imagine, imagine, imagine. Come back to me when you have a solid idea.'

She laughed at my disappointment.

'You think I'm giving you the blow off now, don't you? I swear I'm not. This dream is new, so if I come along and fire questions, without meaning to, I could overwhelm and turn you off. Don't talk to anyone else about it yet. Let it grow. Plant the seed and nurture it and when it becomes so big in your mind, when it becomes a real standalone thing that once spoken about, no matter what question's thrown at you, it won't matter, because it won't be able to get destroyed. Nurture your dream until it becomes so solid, it becomes part of your life. Then when you're ready, come to me and I promise you, I will help you as much as I can.'

I grinned. 'OK, then.' The grin fell. 'Do you think I could, though? I've failed at everything.'

'It isn't failing unless you've finished. It sounds to me like you just had a problem finishing too early. The hard part is finding something you like to do, which you've done. Set a goal and promise yourself you'll see it out to the end, regardless of what the outcome is. It doesn't have to change your life and you don't have to have all the answers right now. Just see it through. When you love something, you will finish it.'

'Like what? Where do I even start with this?'

'That's for you to decide.'

'I don't know if I can.'

Alayne thought for a minute, twisting her teardrop earring.

'When I was about your age, I felt stuck, too. I was on maternity leave with my oldest child and I just felt like I had to find something just for me. Having my baby awakened a need to prove I meant something to the world, so that when she grew up, she would see I achieved something worthwhile. My thing, my love, was art, so I set myself the goal that I would somehow organise an exhibition. I gave myself enough time to make it realistic for me. I vowed that a year later, I would have twenty pieces completed. You understand?'

'Did you manage it?'

Alayne beamed.

'I did. A local paper got involved, and we had sections for lots of new artists. We made a ton of money for the charity and some artists received scholarships because of it. It was one of the proudest moments of my life. Walking around that room, seeing all the pieces, reminded me of who I was the year before. It reminded me of a tired, bordering on depressed mother who was unsure of her capabilities, unsure of herself. On that night, dressed up, in more of a groove with how to raise a baby without feeling like a total failure, I took every bit of that night in. To see what little old me had accomplished, I can't even describe.'

'Sounds good.'

'I can't lie and say everything was perfect in my life after that. Life has difficulties, but it changed me. The next time something went wrong, I had an achievement to fall back on. A, look what I could do when I didn't give up. Does that make sense?'

'It does.'

'Good.' As I left, Alayne called to me. 'Don't focus on the can't because they will come.'

'What do you mean?'

'You'll try to talk yourself out of it. Each time the can'ts come, and they will come, dismiss them. It's just your brain trying to protect you from getting hurt. When the doubts come, when things like, ''how could I do this?'', hit you, just answer, ''I don't know, but I'm having fun thinking about it.'' OK?'

'OK.' I tapped the door frame before turning around.

'Thanks, Alayne. For everything.'

Alayne beamed. 'Just doing my job.'

'Yeah, but it's more than that, isn't it?'

'All good jobs are,' Alayne said, winking, popping the last piece of nut bread into her mouth, then pointing as she chewed. 'Work with this Dawn. You're gifted.'

During art class, I sketched some pencil drawings. A shop window full of baked goods. Another of a table full of cakes and breads and stews and little bites. The drawings came alive on the page. I didn't know if it was because for the first time I was drawing something that had meaning, but they were the best I sketched. Once done, I slipped them into my folder, careful to keep them secret for another while.

I walked home that day. I wanted to walk through the town, eyeing up empty spaces or potential sites. What Alayne said earlier planted a nugget of wonder. A niggle that wouldn't leave, an excitement that bubbled under the surface of my skin, daring me to do as the woman asked and dream about it. All I wanted to do in the centre was leave because I couldn't wait to get home and be alone.

At home, I stuck the cafe drawings in the middle of the wall, above the picture of Ciaran, so I would see them the moment I woke up. All that space on the wall cried out to be filled. Inspired, I sat on my bed and researched different recipes with more than just the usual interest, this time as a plan. Over the next few days, or weeks or months, if I saw something that stood out, I would print or sketch or take a photo after I cooked it. I would research steps needed to open a business, the funding needed, pictures of rental sites. And I wouldn't stop until they covered the wall.

Narrow Beams

Ciaran walked along the top of the scaffolding without a care, carrying a hollowed block that was almost the same height as him. He was two floors high, balancing on a sheet of wood. If he dropped, or tripped, if he forgot his footing, he would fall over the side and die. Yet there he was, wearing no hard hat with only a high-visibility jacket to save him, as if the danger was someone not seeing him.

He hadn't seen me and I was glad, I didn't want him to have any distractions as the part he now walked on didn't have horizontal bars at the edges like the other sections. When he reached the end, he stacked the blocks on top, placing them next to the bare peaks of what would soon form the roof. He grabbed the rim of the half formed wall above and hoisted himself up and over until he disappeared over the other side, into a windowless, roofless room.

I stayed still and waited, not wanting to risk calling out in case his attention shifted when he was that high up. Heights were not something to be messed with, but Ciaran never minded them at all. Ciaran used fear as a mount, stepping on and using it to propel him further instead of stopping dead in the tracks.

Even though I'd met him there many times over the last few months, going for slow walks together or grabbing a lift after the centre so we could hang out, I'd never got used to the sight of him on the scaffolding or shaken away the feeling of danger. Really, I'd never got used to the sight of him anywhere. Seventeen years I'd known him, more than half my life, yet I still wanted to gasp every time, my stomach flipping at how handsome he was.

Not wanting to worry anymore than I was already, I sat on the wall and waited with my back to the site and contemplated leaving. Whatever complaints I had about my injury, it gave me the perfect excuse to hide behind when I didn't want to face a night out.

It was stupid. Here I was, all dressed up at a building site, waiting for Ciaran. But I had promised I'd meet him, that I'd finally brave going out.

When he appeared before me, I tried to stop my cheeks from reddening. For years I knew his features, knew every freckle, every concave of bone, every stray hair, yet the years had blended it into memories. It was times like this, in an unfamiliar scenario, he looked different, so it was as if seeing him for the first time. His ruffled hair, the smudge of dirt on his hands, his big brown eyes fixed on mine, took my breath from me. 'Ready? Looking good Dawnie.'

I steadied. 'I want to look good on my last day alive. They are going to rip me to shreds.'

Ciaran rubbed my arm. 'They won't. I've Kristin warned. She's softened, you know? The space has done us good, made us miss each other.'

I ignored the stabbing ache in my back. 'Missing each other does that.'

'It's been too long since we went out, my friend.' He shoved his hands in the pocket of his jeans and looked at me with filmy eyes.

'Don't start Ciaran. I'm only just holding it together. You start getting all sentimental and I'll lose it.'

'Right so. No speeches. Just fun. I'm filthy, otherwise I'd put an arm around you. Let's get moving. First stop my house, I'll have a quick shower and shave and then we'll drive to town.'

'If you insist,' I said.

The bar was as trendy as it always would be when Peter had any say. They all greeted me as if they missed me, with genuine smiles and hugs that made me wince. Even Kristin embraced me and whispered in my ear, 'I'm glad you came.'

Maybe this will be good for me.

In the packed bar with no seat in sight, I regretted wearing heels, wishing I'd chosen comfort instead of trying to impress. My back pulsed along to the too loud music. Kristin smiled my way but stood close to Ciaran, her body tilted towards him, closing him off from everyone else, staying private, staying intimate, and who could blame her? The last time we met her boyfriend's love for me had been the main point of conversation.

Too acidic at first, the wine coated my tongue and made me want to gag, turning sweeter on the swallow, more from leaving my mouth rather than it being a pleasant sensation. Would it look wrong if I left it and didn't drink? With my back complaint, if I wasn't drinking they would label me a killjoy for sure. I sipped on.

Peter played with my hair. 'It's just so... natural now.' He filled me in on the events of the last few months. Different jobs and boyfriends and messy night details that I laughed along with, but with each sentence made me feel further away from them all because I hadn't been there. When I tried to tell him about me, about the pain I'd been through, his eyes glazed over. The word pain has that effect on a conversation. People don't want the truth. Not really. What they wanted was for you to lie. To contribute to a game about who they are. About who you are. People want you to fit in with what they believe about you.

So, I kept quiet and listened and after a while, Peter made an excuse to go to the bar and I found myself alone.

Without conversation, I drank too fast. It was crazy how so much time had passed, how much I'd changed, yet old habits came back to me without want. I put down my second glass and vowed to go slower. The alcohol was already making me sway.

Ber caught my hand and tried to get me to dance. No one else was dancing, and not up to Ber's level of inebriation, I was afraid if I even moved, my back would lock. 'Sorry Ber. I'm kind of sore.'

'Ah, you're no fun,' she said, letting go of my hand. She carried on dancing beside me.

When was the last time I could let go of my inhibitions like Ber? The guilt came for refusing her, for not being on top form for everyone, bringing them down. I looked at the throbbing crowd, listened to the pumping music, and wished I could leave.

Every part of me felt uncomfortable. The heels threw my already fragile posture out. The waistline of the new jeans I bought rested on the precise trigger point. It hummed in the background, gaining strength. The bar was too hot, too crowded, too noisy. Or maybe I had been away from the scene too long. Or become too old. Until that night I had become proud of how far I'd come, getting healthy and fit but here I was a buffalo amongst gazelles. Underdressed, my layer of makeup wasn't enough compared to the bright, sparkly faces of the contoured women around me.

They knew they were meeting me tonight, yet this was where they suggested, I would have loved to sit in a snug of a bar with them, catching up, hearing the actual conversation without having to shout over the music but they hadn't even considered my needs, I was just expected to fit in. If I didn't turn up, would they have noticed? Peter was chatting up a guy at the bar and, from the look of it, getting somewhere. Kristin and Ciaran were in full on conversation, some part of her in constant contact with him, and if it wasn't for the glances my way every few seconds, I wouldn't have questioned whether it was for my benefit.

As if noticing my discomfort, Ciaran left Kristin and nudged me. 'See,

I told you everything was going to be grand. How you doing?'

The concern was there, the desperate hope that I was OK, that I could slot back in to our old life. I wanted to give Ciaran that. 'Great.' I beamed.

After what felt like five seconds, Kristin joined us, standing on the other side next to Ciaran. 'Having a good night?' she asked.

'It's great to be out. First time in ages.'

'I heard. Sorry about your back. Must have been a rough dose.'

'It was.'

'But sure, Ciaran has been telling me you're out the other side of it now.'

'I'm still in pain, but I've learned to cope with it better. I'm getting out of bed at least.'

For the briefest of moments, I thought I saw a flicker of an eye roll from Kristin, but if she was going to, she stopped herself. I changed the subject.

'How you getting on in Greene's?'

Kristin flashed a smile. 'You'll never believe what Jill did.' She moved closer. 'There's been stock going missing from the ladies aisle for months, not small amounts either, like there were these leather jackets, priced over three hundred euros each and the next day after arriving, one of every size went missing. This got Greene's nose right up, as you can imagine. You know what he is like for watching us, so for something that expensive to go missing while he was sitting in his office in front of those cameras nearly sent him over the edge. What pissed him off more was he told Jill where to put them, but she ignored him and put them facing the counter. Anyway, he was fuming because when he went to the security camera, it was in a blank spot. Fast forward a week and there's a knock on Sheila's door. You remember Sheila right, from the kitchen?'

'Course I do. Sheila's like family to Greene, been there all her life.

She still live up the north side?'

'That's right. Well, Sheila's daughter shouts to her mother, says there's someone outside selling clothes. Sheila looks out and there's Jill herself standing there, going door to door, ready to give the hard sell with a box of clothes and one of those leather jackets in her hand. If it came from anyone else, Greene wouldn't have believed his golden girl did it, but Sheila, well, he couldn't ignore her. Jill was out and guess who got her position?'

'You.'

'Me.'

Kristin tilted her chin. There was challenge in the tilt, and pride, but also mixed in with it a tinge of sadness for me. We had known each other for years, lived together, known what the other ate late at night after a drink, what clothes we slobbed out in when no one watched us, what we listened to when we were alone, what our private worries were and for a flash, we were back there, before she got with Ciaran and things got awkward, when we were friends.

'Good for you Kristin.'

The firing didn't come as a surprise. Jill walked a tightrope of pushing what she could get away with from the day she started. The expected glee I'd imagined didn't come, no happy spark ignited on hearing it. My stomach clenched tight. If I'd stayed, it would have been me that was promoted.

You may have had more money in your pocket, but you would have been even more miserable.

'I'm sorry,' she said. Whether she meant for the job or for the argument wasn't clear.

'I'm sorry too.'

We hugged.

Ciaran grinned, his relief apparent. 'I'm just going to the jacks,' he said. Kristin let go of me and watched him disappear. She took a sip of her drink and for a minute I thought that was conversation over, that she was going to follow him, but she turned to me again.

'How's Crookstown?'

'Strange at first. But better now, I think. It helped to have a friendly face around. Ciaran helped me to have something to look forward to, there were nights I wouldn't have got through unless he was there. Must have been hard for ye, though, being away from each other.'

Kristin straightened, flicked away her hair. I cringed, not meaning to upset her, remembering how fragile conversation could be, how quick her mood could turn.

'Ye've been meeting up? When?'

Shit.

'All I mean is I get it, Kristin. You don't need to worry. I'm not trying to get with Ciaran.'

Kristin's finger ran along her bottom lip, back and forth. Not a good sign. The finger stopped. 'You think you're getting in my way?'

'No, not at all. That's not what I'm saying. I was just trying to reassure you after the last time we spoke.'

'You had to bring it up, didn't you? I said it to Ciaran that you would, that you wouldn't leave it go. You think I need your reassurance? Is this girl for real?' Her voice was louder now than the music.

'I'm sorry.'

This is why I stay quiet. When I talk, the words get twisted.

Peter, sensing drama, stood beside Kristin and folded his arms. 'What's this now?'

Kristin turned to him. 'Dawn's just apologised for making out she could steal my boyfriend.'

Peter snorted. Whether it was from the pain or Kristin's attitude or the months that had gone on between us without a word, or from the sessions with Alayne, or from learning some gumption from Rita or from the years of holding my tongue or from seeing the guy I loved all my life happy with someone else or just because I was drunk, something snapped.

'What's so funny, Peter?'

'You. You're funny.' He straightened, glared at me. He'd wanted this to happen all along. 'You're a joke. A pity more like.'

'If I'm a pity, how can you laugh?'

Peter scowled. 'Ah, go away with the drama.'

That word went off like a trigger firing on a gun, there was nothing left to lose from talking.

'Me with the drama? I'm here five minutes and already you've filled me in on a year's worth of daily problems. Every week I listened. Not once did you check on me to see how I was. You make out you're this great friend but when I hung out with you on our own, all you ever did was bitch about everyone behind their back, but when we were all together, the person you'd bitched about would be the very person you'd arse lick. I could always tell when you'd bitched about me because the first thing you'd do was compliment me. You don't care about anyone but yourself. Everything has to be on your terms, where we drink or hang out, who we are friends with even. I'd say ye had a great laugh about me not being around anymore.'

Peter's mouth dropped open. Ber, with one eye half closed, slapped her thigh, thinking it was hilarious. Once I opened my mouth, I found I couldn't stop. If I was going to end this, end their friendships, I would tell them the truth.

'Ber, how can you let yourself get into this state all the time?'

'Piss off,' Ber said, the smile gone.

'Has anyone ever told you what you do isn't funny anymore? You are putting yourself at serious risk and I don't just mean alcohol poisoning. What if you fall? What if you vomit in your sleep? What if no one's there to go in a taxi with you?'

'Who are you, Saint Dawn? You think you're better than me now, do ya? I'll tear you in seconds.' Ber tried to run at me, but Ciaran, appearing behind her, held her back. Kristen held on to her other side and whispered in her ear until she calmed. Peter, recovered enough to think of something to say, crossed his arms and geared up for a fight.

'You're right we did laugh at you when you weren't around. We could just imagine the walking misery you were and laughed at how lucky we were not to be listening to it. And as for lecturing us on morality, we wondered if it was chlamydia that gave you your back pain. You've had more guys than I've had nights out.'

I recoiled.

'They were the same three guys.'

'Says you.'

'At least I've changed. What have you changed Peter? You're only a friend to someone if the person does exactly what you want. I've never met anybody as false as you.'

They stood in a line facing me, making a clear divide. Scorn faced me, even Ciaran looked shocked. Nobody spoke. I caught my breath allowing enough time to gather my thoughts.

'I'm sorry, I shouldn't have come. I hoped by meeting we could remember the good times, but it's only reminded me how depressing my life was before. So, I'm done. From the sounds of it, you're all done as well.'

'Good riddance,' Kristin screamed over Ciaran's shushes.

That does it.

'Why did you lie that night, Kristin?'

She straightened, slid her eyes to Ciaran. 'Shut up, you fool.'

'That's all I did around you. That's all you wanted me to do. To shut up. Well, no more. You lied Kristin, and you know it. You told everyone that I said I hated kissing Ciaran.'

'No, I didn't.'

'Yeah, you did. You said it was like incest.' Peter said.

Kristin screwed up her eyes at him. 'Stay out of it.'

'There you go. No loyalty from any of ye.'

Kristin left Ber and grabbed Ciaran's arm, tugging on his sleeve. 'I meant I didn't lie.'

'Kristin, you made out I laughed behind his back, but you know that was never the case. You knew how I felt about him, how I'd loved him. I told you over and over. How many drunken nights did I pour my heart out to you, telling you my secret, telling you how he was my ideal guy and I was afraid to say anything in case I messed it up? How many times did I try to work up a way to tell him how I felt and you would tell me to wait, making out it was never the right time? And what did you do next? You took my words and twisted them. You used them. No wonder you moved out of my apartment. Staying would have meant facing me, admitting you went behind my back and got with the only man you knew I loved. You are a sneaky, two faced cow who couldn't be content just to step on my feelings but you tried to ruin our friendship as well.'

Peter's mouth dropped. Ber drained her drink. Kristin was trying to say something to Ciaran, who looked disgusted. With me.

Twice now I walked away without wanting to glance behind. This time would be the last. I welcomed the blast of cold air as I stepped outside. I only stood for a minute, then headed for the taxi rank up the street.

'How could you attack them like that?'

Ciaran stood behind me, his hands splayed out wide.

'What do you mean, attack? For once, I spoke back. Hasn't that been what you've been telling me to do for years? I thought you'd be proud of me for sticking up for myself.'

He ran his hands through his hair, a look of pain on his face.

'You said you did Ciaran, but you're just the same as them. You say you want the best for me when what you really want is for me to fit in with what *you* want, into a nice little box labelled best friend. What have we been doing, Ciaran?'

He scowled at my question, looking behind in case Kristin was in earshot.

'Why didn't you tell her we were meeting?'

'Dawn. I was just trying to find a way.'

'Do you know what your problem is? You want the best of both worlds. To meet up with the girl who's in love with you on the sly for advice and still be with the girl you love on the weekends. Works well.'

He came closer. 'In love with me?'

I backed away.

'Look, thanks for bringing me to meet them, but it hasn't helped. We are all different now and I'm not the Dawn they want anymore. And do you know what? I don't want them either. All we were to each other was social friends, there for the good time. When I had something important on, they forgot to ring me. They liked me for my agreement, they weren't interested in my interests and deep down, I always knew that, so I kept my mouth zipped. No one wanted me to speak up. The look of shock on their faces tonight was a picture. But it didn't feel good, Ciaran. It only proved they didn't care.'

'Yeah, they're in shock, but it's not true about them not caring. They kept asking me how you were over these last few months.'

'If that's the case, why didn't one of them pick up the phone?'

'They were scared of your reaction.'

'Yeah, cos I'm known for being scary. Sounds to me they were more interested to find out if you had gossip. You know how hard those first few months were for me Ciaran, I could have done with some friends. You do a lot of soul searching on sleepless nights, spending hours dissecting my relationships, coming to a lot of conclusions. One night I tried to recall the last time one of them called me for anything other than a problem or an offer of a night out. I can't even remember Ber's surname. And that's all right. I expected bitchiness from Kristin and Peter tonight. I expected Ber to get pissed. Every time you suggested meeting up with them, I saw the train wreck coming but you were so excited, I didn't want to leave you down. I met them for you Ciaran. The only thing I hoped for, the only thing that reassured me, was that you would have my back and you don't.'

He shook his head. 'You've changed Dawn. I'm glad you're sticking up for yourself, I wanted that for you forever, but the way you were in there, the way you're speaking now, all judgmental and thinking you're better than everyone, I never thought that was you.'

My stomach flipped.

'You forget how you pushed me away at the start. They might not have been there for you but they're all dealing with their own crap, in the only way they know how. Did you ever consider it was hard for them to show up here? They could have refused. You say I don't have your back but I'm standing here with you, aren't I? Instead of being inside with my girlfriend. Don't you know the hassle I'll have for the rest of the night?'

'Go back in then,' I roared, making us both jump. 'I didn't ask you to follow me out. I love how I've become the villain here, Ciaran. Very convenient for you.'

He grabbed my arm.

'What do you mean by that?'

I went up close to him.

'You knew me Ciaran. Better than anyone. You knew my favourite colour, my favourite song, what I liked to drink, what my dreams and hopes were. Most of all, you knew how hard it was for me to say things. You knew I could never tell you how I felt. Let's be honest here, you knew. You knew I was in love with you. Every time I delayed on that bridge, you knew. You knew that night on the beach when you got up from the log and got with Marissa. You knew the night of the

Debs. Knowing me, you knew it had to come from you if you wanted something to happen. If you wanted it, you had to be the one to say the words. And you didn't. So, it's easy for it to be thrown around that it was a common fact that you loved me, but you never said it. You never told me.'

Ciaran's body shrunk, and he gulped.

'I was scared.'

I laughed. 'Coming from the guy who isn't scared of anything.'

'You've always scared me.'

'Well, I always thought you were too good for me. And if you're honest, I think you did too. You dropped me Ciaran, when Marissa came along you didn't speak to me or even look in my direction. The night of our Debs, I was so grateful for that kiss, for you even looking at me that night. It's funny, back then I didn't even consider you could want me. How could we work like that? You would always have been the teacher. You would always have to push me, challenge me and I would be the one who fought against it, afraid. I don't want to be afraid anymore in a relationship. I want to be equal.'

'All I've ever wanted is for you to see that.'

'You think? I think to you I'll always be second best.'

'That's not true.'

I put my hand up to stop him from saying more. 'It is. And Ciaran it's OK. You're allowed to be in love. You're allowed to want me only as a friend. I'll always be there for you. Over time, maybe we can go back to being friends but I need space to get on with my life and you do too and if we keep hanging out together, I'm dragged back and I'm not ready for that, as you've seen tonight. And now I've said what I should have said years ago, I'm going home.'

He turned to the club. 'Hold on and I'll drive you back. Let me tell the others and I'll give you a lift.'

'Go back to your girlfriend, Ciaran. Stop worrying about me, stop trying to look after me, I don't need a babysitter. If I've learnt anything through this nightmare, it's that I'm strong enough to get home by myself.'

And with that, I left him and the old life I lived before behind.

Heroes

When the alarm beeped, I stayed in bed, knowing what the day entailed. As I turned to switch it off, my back spasmed and kept me in the position. It was going to be one of those days.

With all I was doing, nothing cured me. It was still there, hanging over, reminding to not get too cocky. I couldn't bear the thought of going to a class. Or more so Alayne's session, as it was going to be a big one.

After the night at the bar, leaving Ciaran, everything since felt like effort, like having to lug a heavy load when I didn't have any strength.

Watching the people in the centre didn't help. Seeing Samira passionate about teaching art, Alayne fired up helping anybody and everybody, even Rita holding a class on self-esteem didn't inspire, it had the opposite effect. I covered my head with the sheet and closed my eyes.

Stop the pity party.

I heard the words as if someone else said them.

I'm entitled to feel sorry for myself.

Oh yeah? Says who? You think just because you have pain that entitles you to act this way? How many people have no one? How many people are trying to help you and you can't be bothered to get out of bed?

I'm in pain.

You were in pain the other day and you still went. Take some painkillers and get out of bed. Start living Dawn.

But I can't! It's too much.

Chicken.

I rolled over. In an argument with myself, I still lost. I had a point. Pottery was on first, which was a no go now as my back wouldn't handle bending over. Next was the session with Alayne. Was that it? Was I avoiding that?

OK smartie pants, since you know everything, how am I going to manage this?

You're going to do some stretches.

I don't think I can. I've locked in place.

Then ring your mum downstairs. Ask her for painkillers and some ice. Text Alayne and tell her the story. If you're still sore, book the chiropractor. Stop being a martyr, Dawn.

I took a deep breath. Stared at the spot on the ceiling that still had a microscopic line of pink paint from when I was ten. My father had loved me enough to paint the ceiling pink when I asked. I owed them this.

When I entered the centre, I was straighter. I had done the exercises, and loosened out. The pain was still there, but it had turned down in volume, in the background, aching enough to not forget, but calmed enough that I could walk. In the room, as I sat, I understood my hesitation. Alayne got right to it.

'Last session.'

'Last session,' I repeated.

'You know what this one is going to be, don't you? We need to talk about the attack.'

I closed my eyes. There it was. My back had known somehow and tried to help me avoid it. Too late now. 'What's there to say? I was lucky.'

'Is that what you think?'

'I don't think about it.'

'How's pushing it down working for you?'

'It's better than being haunted by it.'

'True. I don't believe in going over trauma repeatedly. But I'm also an advocate for letting the pain go. Have you let the pain go?'

I stared at the picture above, instead of looking at her. A painted Alayne urged me on. 'I think about that man every day.'

'What is it you remember?'

'His eyes mostly.'

'Can you describe what you see?'

'They were an unusual green with a black spot on the iris. I remember looking at those eyes in a haze from being pulled down onto the floor by my hair and thinking he seemed desperate, like he would do anything, like he could do anything to get what he wanted. He could have raped me and I didn't move. Didn't even try. I didn't get up. Didn't run or ask him to stop or plead with him to leave me alone. All I did was lie there and let him, like I've done all my life with everyone around me. When I think of him, when I get scared at night, when the nightmares come, it's about what he could've done. It's his eyes I see. Before that day, I couldn't imagine anything that beautiful being harmful. Until he punched me in the face. It was those eyes that caught him, that were his downfall. It is those eyes turning that I see at night. One minute I am thinking how beautiful they are and then they are half closed and the edges have turned to hate. What if he raped me? What if he kept hitting me? Or if he had a knife? I'm angry at putting myself in that situation. For ignoring my surroundings, ignoring my gut feeling. I knew that alley was trouble, but I went down there anyway. I caused it.'

'You didn't. He attacked you, Dawn. It can never be your fault.'

'I never fought back. I froze.'

'He attacked you from behind. No one could expect that, nobody could fight back from that.'

'But before he punched me, when he put his face up to mine, I didn't move. He could have done anything to me and I did nothing.'

'Believe it or not, that was your survival instincts. People that fight back can get more hurt, especially if the attacker is desperate. He would have done anything to not get caught. He wanted to get in and get out of there as quick as possible. When they arrested him, he had a knife, yes?'

I nodded. 'How did you know that?'

'Your mum had a word when she booked you in.'

I nodded again. This time it didn't bother me that Mum had talked to someone.

'You're right, he could have done much worse to you Dawn. Your instincts told you not to fight. That was going to be the best option to get him away the quickest. You can't beat yourself about what you did in that situation. What that man done to you was wrong. So wrong. And what did you do after he was gone?'

'I got depressed and hid in bed.'

'No, you didn't. Right after you got attacked, what did you do? When you were down with your back on the ground, unable to move, what did you do?'

'I got up.'

'You didn't just get up. You rolled into the dirt. On your hands and knees, despite having three ruptured discs, you found the strength and the resilience and the control to get your legs moving and find help and go home. How about what you did with the guards?'

'What do you mean?'

'Because of you, they found the guy. That man, an addict, has gone into a treatment centre. From what I hear, he is responding well and is determined to do things differently.'

'How do you know that?'

'Bex works with a homeless centre and made some enquiries. I'm only telling you because I want you to have closure, not to forgive him or anything, but so you know he isn't this evil guy who is going to one day be hiding in wait around another corner. Dawn, because of you, that man may change his ways. He might not, but you've given him a different choice. You removed him from a situation he didn't remove himself from and, as his desperation with his addiction increased, he could have done much worse to someone. How many lives did you save there, Dawn? How many people did you stop getting assaulted by your bravery? Desperate people can make desperate, disastrous choices. By going to the guards, you changed the path of his life and the path of your own.'

I scrunched up my face in confusion. 'How did it change mine?'

'You don't think it did?'

'No.'

'By going to the guards, you made a subconscious and conscious action. That action announced you wouldn't allow people to hurt you anymore. Like you said yourself only a few minutes ago, you lay there and let him hurt you like everyone else. I would reckon there was a pattern of that for a while, Dawn. Would I be wrong?'

I met Alayne's eyes then. There was no pity, only encouragement.

'You're not wrong.'

'It was just the story you told yourself. By reporting what happened to the guards, you did more than make a statement. You set a new intention. An action that said, "no more." Action is a powerful indicator of what you believe. Way more than even what you say.'

'Right,' I said.

'What did you do when the doctor told you what was wrong was muscular?'

'What do you mean?'

'You didn't accept his opinion. You trusted yourself enough that you knew your body more than him and that something more was going on. Or what about when that locum told you your spine was crumbling? Did you vow never to move again and just accept that was your lot?'

'No.'

'No Dawn. Outside of what he suggested, you researched. You looked for other opinions and became knowledgeable, became your own doctor. Even though not bowing down meant further investigations, with prodding and poking and an MRI and epidural and horrible consultants and therapies that didn't work. Yet you kept going when most would give in.'

'In fairness, that was more Mum than me.'

'Is that so?' Alayne straightened in her chair. 'Do you see what you do?'

'I don't get you. My mother pushed me to get out of the bed. To come here.'

'I've noticed you do this. You belittle yourself. If you'd given in, if you'd given up, it wouldn't have mattered what your mother wanted, she wouldn't have been capable of getting you out of bed. She wouldn't have been able to force you to move. Sure, your mother and father's support has pushed you on, but be under no illusion it was you that lay down on that MRI. It was you that stayed in these classes. You opened your mouth and spoke to the guards. It was your body that found the strength to get up from that floor. Even when the pain was bad, you showed up every morning. You're the person who's shown up. Give yourself credit.'

Alayne's stare bore into me.

'Make a list of things you've done, any achievements or things you endured. Whenever you doubt yourself, I want you to run through your list and use it as proof that if you carry on, no matter how hard, you will achieve it. By not giving in, you will conquer the pain. The solution will come when you keep searching. It has to come. Hindsight is just a way of joining the dots. You can use it to punish yourself or just learn what not to do the next time. Tell me this, if you had never had your injury, would you have come back to Knockfarraig?'

I shook my head in answer.

'Would you have stayed with your parents?'

'No way.'

'So, your mother wouldn't have suggested going to this place?'

'She might have tried, but I wouldn't have listened.'

Alayne stayed silent. I thought.

'Which would have meant I wouldn't have met you all. I wouldn't have started the course. I wouldn't have lost my job. My friends though, that happened before, on my birthday.'

'You can't lose true friends. The thing is, your change started that night, on your birthday. You refused to stay unhappy then. It set a chain in motion.'

'So, I caused it?'

'You did, but not in the way you want to blame. You're responsible for where you are now. Look at what you have already accomplished. Change can bring great pain, but you pushed through it. You've looked at your life and evaluated it. You've cut loose what wasn't beneficial. That takes great courage.'

I blushed.

'You're my hero.'

As I left the centre, heroes were on my mind. Who would I consider as mine? Growing up, it was Ciaran and my father, in the last few months Alayne and Rita. I thought about Mum sitting in her car waiting to drive me home. All the things she had done for me as a child, all the things she still did well into my adulthood. The times she listened, or just let me rant. All the times I took out my pain on her. All the times she hovered in the background waiting in case I needed her. Her love and attention and care struck me all at once and an overwhelming need to show the woman how much she meant took over. I checked my bank balance. Then I made a phone call.

My hands were full when I opened the boot. I shoved the bags inside, making sure she didn't catch sight of them yet. As I sat in the car, I placed a hand on Mum's arm, wanting to connect, to have her feel the warmth of me, yet the gesture left me lacking, unsatisfactory in its sentiment, so I leant over and kissed her on the cheek. Mum's hand went straight to the spot, holding it there as if wanting to keep it in place.

'What's that for?'

'It's long overdue.'

She patted her hair and, once composed, started up the car.

'I'm going to make it up to you starting from today.'

'You don't need to make up anything to me, I...'

'Stop. I have tonight and tomorrow planned. No is not an option. I've bought us face masks and foot oils and nail varnish so we are going to have a home spa day and then tomorrow I have a whole thing arranged, but I'm keeping that as a surprise. Dad helped.'

Mum kept her eyes on the road, but they glistened. 'That sounds perfect.'

At home, I waggled the nail varnishes at her. 'Hot pink or racy red?'

'Oh Dawn, how could I ever?' she said, giggling.

'Just wait, Mum. You might surprise yourself.'

She tapped the colour.

'Hot pink, good choice.'

I got to work massaging her hands. Mum closed her eyes, sat deeper in her chair.

'I wanted to do something to show my thanks. These last few months, I couldn't have got through all of this without you and I need to explain I never hated you, Mum. I just couldn't face you. You expected things from me and I wasn't stepping up and doing them. I avoided you because I didn't want you seeing how much of a failure I was.'

Mum smiled, keeping her eyes closed. 'All I want is for you to be happy. I loved that you were living it up. It was brave. I was never like that, I always let everyone decide for me. Even when your dad asked me to marry him, I never considered there could be a no.' She squeezed my hand. 'Don't get me wrong, I love your dad.'

The nail varnish brush dangled in the air. When was the last time we had such an honest conversation? When was the last time I thought of my mum as her own person with wishes and dreams and choices? Had I ever?

'It hadn't felt like I was living it up.' I replaced the brush in its pot before it dripped. 'But that's in the past. I didn't know you felt that way, Mum, that you didn't make any choices. Well, we are going to change that starting tomorrow. You ready for what's coming?'

'Bring it on,' Mum said, eyeing the untouched prosecco bottle.

'Do you know why I stopped drinking?'

'No, you've never said.'

'Before you were born, I went through something similar and I couldn't talk to anyone about it. Your Dad tried everything to help and at the end of his tether suggested I go to the church at quiet times, as a way of getting me to at least talk at least say the words out loud. I couldn't talk to the priest but I used to sit there when it was empty and speak when I was sure no one else would hear. There, I asked for the chance to carry a child full term. I begged for a child who would live. A child I could nurture and lavish with love and watch grow up. Desperate, I bargained and made promises. The child would get everything. I would give up my life to look after him or her. Every week I would go to mass without fail. I would give up all vanities about my appearance. The last promise I made was to give up alcohol. A few weeks later, I found out I was pregnant and it was easy to give up all those things. After, even as you grew into an adult, I was afraid to drink, in case it was going back on my promise. I just couldn't jinx anything happening to you.'

'Oh Mum. You know you can't stop bad happening to me. Anyway, the worst has already happened and I'm still here.'

'That you are.'

I poured a glass of prosecco and held it out to her.

'Just one. As a toast to us.'

Taking a sip of prosecco, Mum splashed her feet in the warm water and taking the cucumber from the plate, arranged them on her eyes. 'I could get used to this.'

'We should make it a thing. A girl's night once a month or something.'

'I'd love that,' she said and with manicured fingers, held my hand.

Strokes

Mum walked in to the smell of a fry.

'Morning. You're to get this down you and then we'll need to hit the road.'

'Can someone tell me where my Dawn is and when she'll be coming back, please?'

I grinned and put the plate in front of her. 'Sorry, that Dawn is gone for good. You'll have to make do with this one.'

Mum picked up a fork and spoke in a voice barely heard, 'Thank you, my love.'

We looked at each other for a long time but the words were too big, with too much emotion for one morning. 'Come on. It'll get cold. I'll call Dad for his.'

Mum groaned. 'I've a bit of a head on me from the prosecco.'

I giggled. 'You had one glass.'

'I know, but I'm not used to it. I haven't touched a drop in years. I liked it though.'

We took the bus to town.

'First stop is your hair.'

She protested, but I put a hand up to stop her. 'I know Terry always does yours, but Antoinette is usually booked out for months, and she's doing me a favour. Don't worry. She won't do anything you aren't comfortable with.'

'But Terry will think I went behind her back.'

'Mum, do you like what Terry does with your hair?' I arched my brow.

Her hand went to her head. She met my eyes. 'No.'

'Well then. I'll deal with Terry. Be braver Mum.'

She took a deep breath. 'OK, so.'

After introducing Antoinette to Mum, I chose the comfiest seat by the window and settled down with some magazines. Every so often, I took a quick peek and watched the way Antoinette reassured my mother. She coloured and snipped and blow-dried until her magic was over. The tight perm was gone. The harsh brown disappeared. Now straight, Mum's hair was longer, tucking behind her ears in a bob. Antoinette angled a soft fringe that sloped down mum's forehead and ended behind her ear, making her features soften, drawing the focus towards her eyes. Beautiful eyes.

'Is that me?' Mum whispered, touching her face on seeing her reflection.

Two hours after we entered, the woman that emerged from The Cut hairdressers was twenty years younger than the woman who walked in.

Outside, I took my mother's hand.

'We've only just begun. No more catalogue for you.'

I led her into the biggest shop in Cork City. The door of the department store swung open by a doorman. The shop floor hummed with activity from a hundred makeup aisles. I gestured for her to go up the escalator and only stopped when we got to the information desk.

'Hi, I have Mrs Moloney here for her consultation.'

Mum gasped and turned to me. 'We can't.'

I waved Dad's credit card at her. 'We can. Dad said you are to buy everything you like.'

A girl appeared dressed in a silk blouse and tapered trousers. 'Mrs

Moloney, we are going to have such fun.'

The girl showed Mum what clothes suited her body shape. What colours were most flattering to her skin tone, her eyes and hair colour. She piled on tops and trousers and dresses and boots. Then it was down to the makeup hall for a lesson. I stood back through it all and just watched. With each passing minute, Mum grew more animated. It was funny, but until that day, I hadn't thought she'd ever like anything like that. I'd reduced and limited her existence to being only a mother, my mother. Never seeing her as a woman, not a living, wanting, growing person who had their own wishes and preferences, whose life shouldn't just amount to looking after her child.

On the bus home, an idea came to me.

'Why don't you come to the centre with me on Monday? There's lots of people your age and there's a real group spirit and they have a better social life than when I lived in town. I think you'd like it.'

'I couldn't. I wouldn't even know how to talk to new people. And I'd only get in your way.'

'You wouldn't get in my way at all and they're very welcoming. Do you remember how you pushed me to go, even when I didn't want to?'

'Yes.'

'Well, now it's my turn to push you. The time there has taught me if you want something to change, change something. Anything.'

Mum looked out the bus window, then nodded. She stroked the handle of the bag of clothes.

'OK then.'

Run

It was a fine day for a walk. With plenty of time to get to the centre, I chose to walk from Crookstown along the water to glimpse the view. I waved at Mrs Callaghan as she hung out her washing. The woman's arm jiggled as she gave a massive wave back. Mrs Corry stood in her rollers and smiled. It was one of those days when you were reminded how beautiful life was. The breeze lightly tipped against my face, warm and welcoming. The sea was calm and gave me that same feeling. It was funny how you could look at the same things you always saw, yet they looked different.

I stopped walking. Done a quick body scan.

There was no pain.

No sciatica. No throbs. No stiffness or duck walk. No neck pain or headaches or tiredness or tweaks. No numbness or nerves on fire or achy muscles. What I felt was alive. What I felt was tingles of energy running through my veins.

When was the last time I felt pain? Days at least, weeks even. Its leaving was so gradual I had forgotten what it was like. I laughed. A full laugh, not caring if anyone on the street thought I was crazy. I *was* crazy. Delirious, even. What I wanted to do right then was run up to each car and each passerby and embrace them and tell them that no matter how they were feeling, if life sucked right then or if they were feeling down, if there was something they wanted and it wasn't coming to just keep going because one day it would happen. I looked to the sky and tears filmed in my eyes.

'Thank you,' I whispered.

I thought of all the times this day seemed impossible. When the belief consumed me that I was destined to exist in pain for the rest of my miserable life. I placed a hand on the wall I had been walking beside, the very same wall that I climbed up and stood on and contemplated jumping from. How different was that girl from who I was now? I had dragged myself from the lowest depths of me and for a long time I hadn't believed I would ever improve. Yet here I was, getting better. There would still be setbacks, the pain could come back tomorrow, but I took how I was today. Lighter, yet stronger. I jogged at first. My steps were soft as I landed on the footpath, as if I bounced, as if I was in line with the world and we worked together. Before I knew it, I was running to the centre.

I Am

Alayne picked up a note on her desk, read it, and stuck it on top of her notepad. 'Have you heard of I Am?'

I shook my head.

'In the time of Moses, at the burning bush, Moses asked what he should say to the Israelites who sent him and the reply was: ''I am what I am. Say this to the people of Israel, I am has sent me to you.'''

I couldn't help my eyes from rolling. Alayne's laugh surprised me.

'I know we are done with our sessions and I don't want to talk to you about religion. I was just thinking of the importance of any sentence with "I am." They are more than statement sentences. A power hides behind them, a magnetic force. When you use "I am" negatively with sentences like, "I am always late." Or, "I am a failure." Or, "I am broke." It sends out powerful negative signals which have implications. Jesus is quoted in the bible using "I am"statements. "*I am the light of the world. I am the good shepherd. I am the way, the truth and the life.*" He was sending us an important message. How we speak about ourselves is very important. Try this and see how the statements can change your whole well being. Notice when you use "I am." If it is going down a negative route change it to a positive.'

On the way home, I ran through the usual words I used that started with "I am." In the past, it swayed more towards the negative rather than towards the positive. Even as a kid, I could recall many times I put myself down.

I am uncool. I am big. I am always saying the wrong thing. I am a loser.

I thought about the things it evolved to as an adult, remembering what I said on the wall in Crookstown.

I know what I am, what everyone sees me as. I am expendable. I'm weak and a coward. I am insignificant. I am miserable.

Or, when I'd first used the journal.

My life is a complete train wreck. I don't like who I am. I am unhealthy. I am failing in life. My body doesn't work. I am miserable and if I had a choice, I wouldn't be around me either. I am an embarrassment. I am useless. I am broken.

The rest of the way home, I tried to pull out words I could say that still felt true.

I am honest. I am loyal. I am kind. I am strong.

That last one stopped me. The other ones felt right leaving my tongue but that one didn't. Hadn't I started to feel strong, though? I changed it to a truer sentence.

I am getting stronger every day.

That I could believe.

I am getting healthier every day. I am doing everything I can to improve myself.

That would do. I repeated them.

I am honest. I am loyal, I am kind. I am getting stronger every day. I am getting healthier. I am doing everything in my power to improve myself.

Once finished, I repeated it again and again. As the words left me, I walked faster; the words pushing my legs along until I was almost bouncing along the path. I laughed at the shock of how good it felt.

Alignment. That was what I was reaching for. Fluidity. Balance. One line flowing through each other. Dr Fischer checked what was out of alignment, then corrected. Now I was focusing on correction as well. Which meant early starts and yoga. Long walks instead of Mum driving so I could feel the air in my lungs and clear my mind, ensuring I was ready for the day. It was art class with Samira. Clothes feeling looser, and more flexibility in my body. It was looking up at the sky instead of studying the ground. Looking forward instead of backwards. It was smiling again.

***

I laid out the different boxes of cakes on the counter in the canteen in front of Alayne and Samira. Banoffee cupcakes. Apple strudel. Strawberry cheesecake bites.

Months after I stuck the first bit of information on my wall, apart from one picture in the middle of Ciaran and I, that despite our fight I still couldn't take down, the rest was covered with sketches and proposals until there was no available space left. Instead of staying as a plastered, smooth piece of concrete, it had evolved into a business plan.

My palms were sweaty. 'I've been thinking of what I want to do. The idea hasn't left me. I want to run a café.'

'Where? You said before, you hated it here. Would you open it in the city?'

I blushed. 'Back then, I said a lot of things I didn't mean. No, Crookstown and Knockfarraig are my home now. There's nothing in the city for me anymore. Besides, if I was to make it work, I couldn't afford to rent a place to live as well. I've looked into loans and thought about going mobile for a while and building up some business working from home, but I can't see people's reactions to the food. When I imagine it, I see people chilling and chatting.'

Samira stood beside me and took a bite of banoffee, a drizzle of caramel staying on her lip. 'You know, there was a place in town that used to sell cakes like these.'

I shook my head, not remembering.

'It had loads of seating. It's been closed for donkeys. Can't remember it opening again.'

Alayne grabbed her jacket. 'Come on, let's have a look.'

We strolled through the town. Samira stopped by windows that were whitewashed in huge swirls. There was a tiny gap between one swirl. I peered in. On the left was a counter with a glass display coated in dust, big enough to hold ten full size cakes and still have room for lasagne and pies and a salad section. The dark meant I couldn't see how far back the building spread, but it seemed long. On the right, I counted three tables that backed along the wall before it disappeared to black.

'There's an upstairs too,' Samira said, her nose smudged up to the glass.

In the bottom corner of the door was a business sticker with one name displayed: DM Property.

Alayne saw it, too. 'Do you want it, Dawn?'

My eyes watered. I could only manage a nod. I didn't say out loud my fears. That a place like that would cost too much. That I wouldn't know where I would get the money.

'Then leave the negotiating to me. I'm going to enjoy this,' Alayne said.

Bench

The gang of youths looked up from the bench as I approached. I ran my finger down the edge of one envelope, more out of nerves and having something to occupy my fidgety hands than for anything else. The standing teens turned around when I neared. One not yet man eyed me up and down, ready for a confrontation.

'Hi lads. Sorry to bother ye. I'm looking for a girl who was here about a year ago. I think you were there with her.'

The guy shifted from side to side and curled his lip, waiting for what was coming. I resisted the want to run away, to give in to the intimidation, but I needed to do this.

'Ye might not remember me. I looked quite different.'

One girl stepped closer and stood beside the boy.

'I know you. You're the woman whose face was all bashed up.'

I smiled. 'That's me. I'm trying to find the girl that helped me. I didn't get her name.'

The girl addressed the half man. 'That was Lisa.'

He put his hand to his mouth. 'You were the one that was battered. Why do you want her?'

I resisted the urge to smile. Lisa was lucky to have friends that looked out for her.

'I wanted to say thanks. To you too, Wilkie, isn't it?'

He nodded. I handed him an envelope, which he ripped open

immediately. 'No way,' he said, pulling out the notes.

'No amount of money can thank you for what ye done, but I just wanted to let ye both know I'll never forget it.'

Wilkie didn't look up, he just stared at the money.

'Lisa's at the shop.' The girl pointed behind. 'You can wait.'

'I'll come back. There's somewhere I have to visit.'

As I walked towards the alley that changed my life, I realised how important it was to confront it. It hadn't been my intention to step foot on that street again, but now that I was in the city, I needed to see it; to walk it, to show it no fear.

That alley had been in my nightmares. Its smells. Its details more vivid than any other street I could recall. As I walked on the cobbles, I saw it for what it was. Just an alley. Nothing more. I stood in the exact spot he hit me, the place I fell down and squatted on the floor. I placed my hand on the damp concrete, not caring if it was wet from the urine that invaded my nostrils.

'Thank you,' I whispered. I looked up at the sky, and it was as if the clouds broke apart. Even on a dark day, the blue was there.

Voices

The class was full. One pink haired old woman, stood out in a sea of greys and browns and blondes. All eyes were on me and for once, I wasn't scared because this wasn't talking about me or my feelings. This was different. I was talking about something I loved.

The entire class had traipsed over from the centre and now stood in front of tables in the café. My café. I would never tire of saying that. After wiping away cobwebs, and painting the walls mocha and creams, Ash, Samira's boyfriend, even though I'd never met him, carved a wooden counter top that looked like the wood knotted and interweaved. It made the place. Suggested by my father, a wall of edible herbs, a living, growing greenery lined behind, framing the counter.

Dotted around the room were paintings of Knockfarraig landmarks from Samira and other students from the art class. It was my idea to place a price underneath that someone could buy if interested and raise money for the centre. Upstairs, a painted garden ran along the longest wall. It was so realistic, I considered placing a sign next to it as a warning in case anyone tried to walk through.

Everyone helped. Mum made cushions in different shades and textures of green to be placed on the many couches and chairs. It was a perfect mixture of trend and comfort. I hadn't opened yet. These were the first people in, and what better way to introduce people to the café by holding a class and giving back, fulfilling the promise I made to pass it on?

I took a deep breath. 'For a start, I just wanted to thank you for turning up today. We worked hard to get the place up to scratch and I hope you all like it.'

There were a few whoops from various tables and a lot of nods.

'I also wanted to thank everyone for helping. As you all know, the centre asks for a pay it forward gesture. If you learn, you then teach. For a long time, I didn't know what I was good at and didn't have a clue what I could show as a talent.'

A few people laughed at that. 'The centre helped me get clear about, well, everything. About what I was good at. About who I am. And I'm very grateful to say I've made so many friends too. I just wanted to say a massive thanks to Alayne for all the work she does. Thank you for being a pain in the butt.'

The crowd laughed. Alayne beamed.

'I mean it. What you do there is amazing. You never give up Alayne and from me I just want to say thank you for not giving up on me, or on all of us.'

The crowd got to their feet and clapped. Alayne hid her face in her hands and turned to the wall, giving her cheeks a quick wipe. When she turned back, the claps continued, so she blew kisses around the room. When the claps subsided and everyone sat again, I placed my hands on my brand-new counter.

'So you can try all the full calorie treats later, but who wants to learn to make chocolate mousse that won't expand your hips or make you feel awful afterwards?'

I took out some ingredients from my scrubbed display fridge and held one up in the air for everyone to see.

'We make the magic from these beauties.' I held up an avocado.

'Yuck,' Rita said, making a gagging gesture.

'I know, I know. Many of you may have tasted these before and only remember a blackened, sludgy mess. Just hear me out though and don't judge yet. Avocado is a super food. It contains almost twenty vitamins and minerals and is full of good fats, the omega threes, which are great for your skin and hair and have anti-inflammatory properties, and who doesn't need that, eh? Good fats help your body. It also tastes creamy, so is perfect for a dessert.'

I picked up a bar of chocolate. 'Now these are high end cocoa, unlike the normal chocolate bars you get at the shop counter. These are as dark as they come. Dark chocolate with a low sugar quantity is good for you.'

I broke up the bar into tiny pieces and walked to the tables, encouraging them to take a piece.

'Let it melt on your tongue for a moment. The first sensation is bitterness, but wait for the creamy hit.'

'Sorry Dawn, but that's rank,' Rita said, spitting it into a tissue.

I laughed. 'Don't worry, it gets better. Remember, you're used to the milky sugar hit. Your brain needs to get used to the sensation. Dark chocolate contains anti-oxidants which are linked with cancer prevention. It's also linked with helping brain function. The higher percentage of cocoa, the better.'

As the class continued, I lost myself in the actions. Enjoying it, I delighted in the expressions as people tried and liked the recipes. In the pride in the faces of Mum and Dad, Rita and Alayne. The sound of chomping and crunching followed by moans of pleasure were music to my ears. As the class tucked into their creations, Alayne sidled up and leant beside me on the counter.

'Well done,' she said. 'You've found your calling.'

'I'm going to make it a regular thing. Maybe in the evenings hold different cookery classes? Curry nights. Cake decorating.'

'Sign me up.'

'Never in my lifetime did I think it would be possible for me to feel comfortable talking in front of people. I meant what I said, Alayne. Thank you.'

'I know you did.' Alayne dropped the smile. 'On the subject of classes, maybe I could rent out the top floor from you at night?'

'For the centre?'

Alayne didn't speak, just nodded.

'Did you lose it?'

She nodded again.

'Oh Alayne, I'm sorry.'

She bit down on her lip, gave a slight shake to her head. 'Don't tell anyone yet. I'm looking at different places, and I've tried everything legally I can, but it looks like our time there is ending.'

'I'm sorry.'

Alayne twisted her teardrop earring. 'Don't worry. I'll work something out.'

'I don't doubt you for a second. Like you said, there must be something better on the way.'

'That's the spirit.' A hush had fallen as the crowd settled. 'I better let you get on. You've only wet the group's appetite. They're looking for more.'

Alayne side stepped to her table, with her head bowed and I felt a stab of regret. Why hadn't I noticed the difference in her before? Too wrapped up in the café, I'd ignored the change in her, but now I saw the retreat, the holding back, the brow furrowed in deep thought.

'OK, now I've shown you a healthy recipe. Who wants to make pecan pie?'

The crowd whooped. Alayne smiled.

I had to find the words. For thirty years, I chose silence over confrontation, staying quiet when I should speak. This time I couldn't.

'Before we do, though, there's something important to discuss. Alayne, I'm sorry, I usually do as you say but I can't carry on the class without doing something. Can you come back up here and tell everybody?'

Alayne shook her head furiously.

'Allow them to help. You don't have to do everything alone. This time we'll work it out together.'

'I can't,' Alayne said.

'You can. If anyone taught me talking helps, it's you.'

Alayne laughed, then wiped at her eyes. 'True. I just don't want to ruin everyone's mood.'

'It's their centre too.'

Before the end of the day, the crowd had made phone calls to every politician, newspaper, radio and television station they could think of. One news channel came down to the centre and, spreading the word through a social media campaign, every past student helped by the centre turned up. The clip shown on the six o'clock national news gave a panoramic view of everyone in the garden lined up, and there were so many, there was no more available green to stand on and they had to spill out to the front of the building.

There were live discussions on television about further education buildings being protected and heated debates on air about the rich always getting what they wanted through any means necessary. The stories of change from some of the more colourful students were green-lighted for a documentary. Politicians trying to win votes promised the centre would not close and was there to stay.

I didn't care what anyone's agenda was for highlighting the issue. What I cared about was keeping the centre open. Even if we failed, what mattered was knowing I'd played a part in trying to save it and by saying what was on my mind, by using my voice, a million other doors opened with opportunity. What I cared about most of all though, what filled my heart with more warmth than I could ever imagine, was when Alayne smiled the next time, her smile was real.

Sunrise

The bell above the door of the café pinged as Mum opened it.

'Ready for your first shift?' I asked.

'Sure haven't I been cooking all my life? I brought the beetroot.'

'Great. I was thinking of putting your porridge bread on the menu if you'll allow it?'

'Only if you name it after me.'

I grinned at her. Dressed in a velvet green suit jacket with a green satin camisole and jeans, the woman was a million fashion miles away from the brown wool wearing, perm haired lady she once was. 'That's a deal.'

'So where do you want me?'

'Well, the food's all prepped. I'm just waiting for some muffins to beep. We've already run out of cottage pie. There's enough satay to last us through the lunch rush. So, for the moment it's just floor service like collecting the plates, checking if anyone needs anything like top ups for coffee and tea. You remember how to use the till like I showed you?'

The door pinged again. Facing me, Mum didn't see the customer who had just walked in. 'I think so. It seems pretty straightforward.'

'Hi,' the customer said, putting his hands in his pockets and rocking on his heels. He surveyed the room. 'Wow,' he said.

Seeing my gaping mouth, Mum stepped in. 'Ciaran, how are you doing? How's your mam? I haven't seen her for ages.'

'She's good, Mrs Moloney. She's up in Galway at the moment. My sister Sarah had twins there a month ago, so mam went up to help her on maternity.'

'Ah, that's lovely to hear. Your mother was a bit lost when ye all left.'

'It hit her pretty hard.' Ciaran spoke to Mum, but didn't take his eyes from me. 'I was wondering if I could have a word Dawn.'

'I'm kinda busy,' I said, pointing to the full tables.

'I can come back. Whenever suits.'

'Sure why don't you have a coffee and a catch up together upstairs? I'll shout if I need you.'

'Mum, it's too busy.'

'Would you go on? You'd swear I was some young one that didn't have a clue.' She pointed to the list on the inside wall. 'The prices are all here. I can see what's available. I'll keep an eye on the satay and make sure the bottom of the pot doesn't burn and I'll listen out for the timer on the muffins. I can manage and if I can't, I'll call you. Go on now.'

Mum made a shooing gesture as I opened the fridge, making me laugh. 'I was just going to pour a coffee.'

'What would you like, Ciaran?'

'What would you suggest?' He asked me.

'Depends on what you want,' I said.

He scanned the glass counter tops and then looked right at me. 'I want it all,' he said.

I pulled out a tray, scooped out two ladles of satay into bowls. I placed an assortment of brownies, flapjacks, and carrot cake on a plate and swept up some cutlery. Pouring coffee into a pot and lifting the tray, I said. 'Come on, then.'

Neither of us spoke until we settled.

'I love what you've done to the place. Mam and Dad used to bring me here when it was the cake shop. It was the best place in town.'

'I hope mine live up to the memory.'

'If they're anything like what you used to bake, they will.'

He took a taste of the satay. 'That's good.' He shovelled another mouthful in. 'It's so good.'

I let him eat. It was pointless trying to talk with his head that close to the bowl. I sipped my coffee instead. Once finished, he sat back in the chair and smiled.

'I've missed you,' he said. I didn't answer. 'You know it was the first Christmas we were apart since we met?'

I nodded.

'Did you not get my messages?'

I shrugged.

'I did but I didn't listen to them. What was the point? We'd only go back to the way we were. If I turned up at yours at Christmas, it would only ruin the day. Kristin, seeing me, would have turned the festive mood.'

He shook his head, prodded his food. 'She wasn't there.'

'Oh, I just assumed ye both went to Knockfarraig. Sorry.'

'You're OK. She should have been there. It was just that she didn't want to. We didn't want to. I'm not with her anymore.'

'I'm sorry.'

'Don't be. It was never going to work.'

I picked at my satay, not wanting to make eye contact. The space between us felt dense, weighed down by too many unanswered questions.

'So, change of subject. What's it like being a cafe owner?'

I smiled, relaxing, *that* I could talk about.

'All the things I loved about work, the busy days, the flow, the helping people, I have it now, but it's different because I only have to answer to myself. Mistakes are mine, but if it works, it's all mine, too.'

'It suits you. I don't think I mentioned how much brown hair suits you better.'

'Now you tell me you didn't like the blonde.'

'Why would I say anything when you liked it? I always thought the blonde made you blend in. It just didn't seem like it was really you. The brown brings out your features. Makes you Dawn again.'

I looked straight at him.

'I'm not though Ciaran, I'm not the same Dawn. I'm not the old Crookstown Dawn and I'm not the Cork City Dawn either. I've changed.'

'I can see that.' Ciaran shifted in his seat. He ran his finger along the rim of his bowl. 'I've thought about what you said that last time we saw each other outside the bar. You were right.' This time he didn't look away. He gave a small nod. 'I knew. I pretended I didn't even to myself, tried to ignore it, but I knew you loved me back. Every time we got close, I got with someone else because I was afraid. I pushed you away. Why did I waste those years, Dawn?'

'I don't know.'

'After Christmas, after you wouldn't answer my calls and texts, once the contract finished with my dad, I took that trip I'd planned for years. Funny, I had to go away to find what I was searching for.'

'What did you find?'

'Not what. Who.'

My stomach lurched. Ciaran was here to tell me all about some new love. I straightened, bracing for his next words.

'You. I sat on a beach in Dubai, with everything I could possibly want around me, yet all I could think was how it couldn't even compare to being on Knockfarraig beach with you. On the trip of a lifetime, the holiday I dreamt about for ten years, I realised I didn't want to be there without you. All the time I pictured it, you had been by my side.'

He broke off a piece of carrot cake and nibbled. 'I didn't go home

straight away. Taking some time off was good for me, I think. I've
spent years rushing, years running to the next relationship. Being on
my own made me think hard. The girlfriends I went with were all a
certain type, all mouthy and confident and fiery, the opposite of what
I wanted and when I understood that, it hit me. Me and Kristin could
never work. None of my relationships could work.'

'Why?'

'They weren't you.'

He outstretched his hand and this time when he placed it on mine, I
didn't move it away. Instead of changing the subject, or batting away
the opportunity, I took it.

'I was hoping you'd say that.'

Our first date was in the water, the day before my birthday, on the
hottest day of the year. We met in Knockfarraig, in the meeting spot
of the bandstand. I brought a bag with swimming gear as instructed,
with no idea of what he had planned.

We ran into the warm water as clear as thick glass, making everything
visible below. Even six feet out, the water was still only up to my waist.
There were no waves for once, except from some slight rolls along the
surface every so often, the water was flat as far as the eye could see.

'We've seen every type of wave there is here, haven't we?' I asked.

Ciaran came closer. 'Yet no day is the same.'

'How could I have hated this place?'

'It changed. Or we have, I guess.'

'If you told me a year ago, that I'd be here with you, able to swim,
living back in Crookstown and loving it, I would never have believed
it. It seemed like there was no way out. Back then, I wouldn't have
believed I'd ever be happy again.'

'Yet here you are.'

'Yet here *we* are.'

We bobbed together, unsure of what move to make. He dived under and resurfaced a few feet away. He wiped the water from his face and then stood watching me, unmoving. I knew if I swam towards him, I would end up in his arms and our friendship would cross over and move to something more. There would be no going back.

I stayed where I was.

As we lay together on towels, letting the sun dry our wet bodies, I dozed and let out a contented sigh. I awoke to Ciaran nudging me. He propped himself up and lay on his side, watching.

'You're creeping me out,' I said, laughing.

'So, I've been thinking about tonight.'

'Oh yeah?'

'Have you ever watched the sunrise?'

'Like sat and waited for it?' He nodded. 'No, not that I remember. I've been up when we've pulled all-nighters, but I never went out and watched it.'

He tsked. 'You've never seen your namesake?'

I nudged him. 'Course I've seen the dawn. You asked me if I waited up all night for it, that I didn't do.'

'Why don't we? Start your birthday with a bang. We could go home, grab some stuff and come back and stay here for the night. We could make a fire and drink warm wine and watch the stars and, in the morning, when the sun breaks through, we could welcome the day together.'

I scooped a handful of sand and let the grains escape through my fingers.

* * *

As the last of the day lingered, before the sun set and the night came, Ciaran turned to me as we sat looking down at the water on Loophead cliff. 'So, what are your plans for your birthday this year?'

'To be braver. To push what I have been doing even more.'

'No gloom?' He raised an eyebrow.

I chuckled. 'Funny that. I don't think the gloom will appear this time. I know now why it used to come. It was me feeling like another year had passed and I was so far away from what I wanted. A year ago I broke. That birthday dinner changed how I saw my life. When Greene didn't give me the promotion, when he failed to see my worth, when our friends proved they didn't care and a man in an alley hurt me so bad I had to learn how to live a different life. It's crazy to say, but I'm glad my back got hurt.'

'How's that now?'

'Pain forced me to become selfish. It made me put myself first. My world reduced to my survival, to my bodily functions and aches, to my feelings, my body, and the pain. Because of that reduction, all the bullshit, the false friends, working in a job I'd grown out of but would never leave, the loneliness of that apartment left in an instant. I see now it had to be drastic, as I would never have made a move. I was too loyal, too afraid, too unsure. Wanting a different life wasn't enough, fear kept me stuck. And then I went to the centre and met Alayne. Getting out of bed became easier. My head settled in the right place. Until the day came when I looked forward to what lay ahead. My pain became a gift. I would never have come back here yet because of that, you came back to me.'

'I came back *for* you.'

I smiled at him. 'I know you did.'

'Before it turns dark,' he said, standing. 'I'm going to jump in. You coming?'

He held out his hand for me to stand. I took it.

Looking over the edge, I could see it was a long drop, but we knew the spot was safe for jumpers, deep enough with no hidden rocks below. Every summer of my teens, I had sat in that spot and witnessed many do it, but never tried. When it came to jumping, the sheer drop made me back away each time. The wind was silent for once, even though we were at a height.

'You want to be braver? All the years we used to come up here, you always backed away from the jump. Try it, Dawn. Let's do it together.'

'OK.'

'Trust me.'

'OK.'

He led me nearer to the edge. I wanted to go, needed to, but I couldn't. The fear of heights was still there, still strong. I let go of Ciaran's hand. My own shook.

'Ciaran I can't.'

He smiled.

'Trust me.'

He ran to the edge, and without any glance back or hesitation, he jumped.

Ciaran flew in the air, perfectly suspended, giving himself to gravity. I watched his leap of freedom. It reminded me of how stuck I was to the ground, how glued I was to the earth, how scared I was still of life. His body descended in slow motion, his voice roared, the sound of it echoing up, and then he disappeared into the water. I gasped and waited; afraid he wouldn't rise. Within seconds, he burst through the surface. As he treaded water, he grinned and waved, then shouted.

'Choose who you are Dawn.'

'Who do I choose? This is not who I am,' I whispered. 'This is not who I want to be. I don't want to be quiet anymore. Or afraid. I don't want to hold back.'

As I stood looking down, the leaving sun gave him an afterglow. I fast forwarded the night, playing out what I believed would happen. If I stayed and spent the night with Ciaran, two friends would get the kiss we waited fifteen years for and we would leave a couple. If I stayed up all night, I would have to face the dark. The time that scared me the most, the darkest time as Ciaran had once said. There was a reason I had never watched the sunrise; I was terrified of that time of night, with its silence, and the ghosts that came out to haunt you. It was the time of waking up from nightmares, of realising through the silence that you were alone in the world.

Ciaran flipped in the water, his shorts disappearing underneath, only for his head to arise and breakthrough again and give me the thumbs up.

This time he would be there with me and we could face the long night together. I had already faced my worst darkness alone and survived. After that, after overcoming that, the thought of getting through any night didn't seem as scary. Because wasn't that what I'd learnt? To take the frightening things and turn them. In facing them, in conquering them, my life had transformed. Behind the things that had terrified me the most, I had found the centre, found the café, found a way to understand Mum. I had found that lost thing I had begged for as I sat on that wall halfway between Crookstown and Knockfarraig when I had called out to the sea for help, desperate to find what was missing from my life yet not even understanding what it was I longed for. I knew now what I had needed. It was more than happiness; it was looking at my life and feeling I was doing something worthwhile, going to sleep exhausted but satisfied. It was jumping out of bed and looking forward to the day ahead or staying awake, bombarded with new ideas and inspiration. It was laughter and fun and hope. It was finding my voice. And true friends. It was discovering I was stronger than I ever thought I could be.

Looking down at Ciaran, I tried to make a decision about whether I should be with him. It might prove to be my biggest mistake, to take a chance on a friend and turn it into something more. There might be too much history between us, might be too many preconceptions. Or the opposite, I might give myself completely and he might turn out just as bad as all the others. He might hurt me. He might not be the one.

Or, he might turn out to be the exact person I'd always known I was looking for.

I closed my eyes and took a deep breath and then spoke to the waves, to the impending sunset, to the cliffs and Ciaran too: 'I will not let scary things stop me anymore.'

I thought about the 'I am' game Alayne taught me. My next words carried with the wind.

'I am unstoppable. I am never giving up. I am strong and getting stronger.'

I edged closer to the cliff edge. The waves crashed against the rocks. I wrapped my arms around my body in an attempt to calm my shivers. It was a long way down. If I jumped too near, I would hit the jagged edges. Ciaran said nothing, but looked up, his arms made circles under the water. That was what I would have to expect if I coupled with him; he would be there, gently pushing, daring me to do more.

I whispered. 'I know who I am. I am invincible. I am unbreakable. I am unwavering.'

As my foot tiptoed the edge, I let out a roar. 'I am Dawn.'

And then I jumped.

A Message From The Author

Even though The Breaking of Dawn is a work of fiction, some of the events are loosely based on my own life. I, like Dawn, injured my back when I was in my mid-twenties. It took years for me to heal and more time to get over the trauma and even when I did, more years had to pass before I could write about what happened. For me, writing is about taking any pain and extracting the lesson and then conveying it so it resonates with the reader. I hope I have done that here.

This book does not suggest that if you have a back injury, the only option is to go to a chiropractor. The body is an amazing force and will always try to heal itself. For some, medication is the only step needed to get over the inflammation. For others, epidural injections work. Others find physiotherapy, tens devices, stretches or rest do the trick. For me though, it was what worked, and I believed in it so much, I ended up working as a chiropractic clinic manager for ten years. In that time, I saw many instances of what I could only call miracles, but that, dear reader, is a whole other story I may tell another day.

If you are struggling with any type of injury or depression, the first thing you can do is talk. Please share what you are feeling with someone you love, a doctor, or a support group in your community.

If The Breaking of Dawn moved you, please consider leaving a review on the channel you bought it from.

Honest reviews help bring books to the attention of other readers. I would really appreciate if you could spend a few minutes leaving your feedback. Reviews help the buyer understand the 'feel' of the book so your review could be the difference in whether someone picks it up.

My deepest thanks,
   Natasha Karis.

Want more?

If you would like to read more about Alayne Adams subscribe to the Natasha Karis newsletter and you will get:

The Happiness Initiative - the interactive book Alayne wrote based on her teachings in The Initiates.

The Initiation of Alayne Adams - an uplifting coming of age novella about Alayne's own awakening.

The Summer Before - an exclusive novella you cannot buy anywhere else, giving the story that led Calista (One of The Initiates) to the detention room.

Induction - an exclusive short story you won't find anywhere else.

The Initiates - first chapter

You will also be the first to receive exclusive cover reveals and behind-the-scenes details and giveaways.

Get it today at: https://subscribepage.com/breakingofdawn

About the Author

Natasha Karis lives in Cork, Ireland, and spends her days navigating between writing and raising her three children. She has been known to write with a child on her knee. She writes contemporary, emotional, uplifting stories. Natasha carries a book with her everywhere she goes. Even though she has always been a voracious reader, she wasn't always a writer and has worked as a chiropractic clinic manager, a shoe store manager, and a Dunnes Stores girl.

She is the author of The Breaking of Dawn, The Truth Between Us, The Initiates, The Initiation of Alayne Adams and The Happiness Initiative.

Also by Natasha Karis

The Initiates

A suicide note. Five lost students. One teacher who will stop at nothing to help them.

When the Principal of Knockfarraig school suggests a series of detentions for some wayward sixth year students, teacher Alayne Adams volunteers. But the discovery of a note reveals one student intends to end their life.

Taking inspiration from a book based on ancient teachings, Alayne embarks on a series of life lessons that encourages each of them to discover ways to heal their pain.**The Kybalion states, when the student is ready, the teacher will appear** but there are many obstacles in their way. Can she steer them onto a path that will change all their lives?

With characters that will have you rooting and crying for them, this contemporary, emotional novel set in Ireland, will leave you inspired.

Includes a link to the eBooks The Happiness Initiative, a practical exercise book based on the teachings and The Initiation of Alayne Adams, a prequel novella that follows Alayne and shows what made her the teacher she became.

The Truth Between Us

A make or break holiday. A love that should last a lifetime. A truth that threatens to rip them apart.

When Adaline decides to book a trip away to contemplate her failing marriage, her husband Andrew suggests he join her. As they embark on a last chance holiday to Cyprus, Adaline looks back over her life in the hope to fix what went wrong. But the past contains much pain, and a secret threatens to ruin everything. Can they confront the truth and still salvage the relationship?

The Truth Between Us is an emotional and uplifting tale about love, loss and hope.

The Initiation of Alayne Adams

What breaks you, can also make you.

Torn between partying with her friends and doing the right thing, Alayne's life lacks any direction. Until an incident leaves her spiralling. Left with nowhere to turn, Alayne struggles to find her way. But an encounter in a library opens up new possibilities and a chance to learn. Can Alayne change or will old habits prove too hard to resist?